PRAISE FOR ALLIE THERIN

"In the spellbinding second Sugar & Vice fantasy romance . . . the worldbuilding is laudably intricate and fascinating and returning readers should get back up to speed quickly. The result is an exciting, action-packed sequel that entirely lives up to the promise of the original."

—*Publishers Weekly*

"With the second vividly imagined installment in her Sugar & Vice series, Therin picks things up right where she left them in *Liar City* (2023), immersing readers in an intriguing, paranormal-shaded version of the U.S. while, at the same time, significantly heating things up between Evan and Reece as they move from being flirting friends to having sizzling sexual contact."

—*Booklist*

"Will satisfy those looking for more momentum in the series' central romance as well as fans compelled by the investigation. Second-act revelations will have readers clamoring for the next installment."

—*Library Journal*

"A twisty, dark, action-packed tale filled with shocking discoveries, devastating betrayals and emotional gut-punches . . . It's a masterclass in how to create and develop sexual tension."

—*All About Romance*

ALSO BY ALLIE THERIN

Sugar & Vice

Liar City
Twisted Shadows
Edge of Mercy

Magic in Manhattan

Spellbound
Starcrossed
Wonderstruck

Roaring Twenties Magic

Proper Scoundrels
Once a Rogue
Viscounts & Villainy

EDGE OF MERCY

ALLIE THERIN

ISBN-13: 978-1-335-62197-9

Edge of Mercy

For questions and comments about the quality of this book, please contact us at CustomerService@Harlequin.com.

Carina Press
22 Adelaide St. West, 41st Floor
Toronto, Ontario M5H 4E3,
Canada
www.Harlequin.com

HarperCollins Publishers
Macken House, 39/40 Mayor
Street Upper,
Dublin 1, D01 C9W8, Ireland
www.HarperCollins.com

Printed in U.S.A.
1 2 3 4 5 6 7 8 9 10 HDC 29 28 27 26

For the ravens of 3rd Avenue

CHAPTER ONE

. . . Nowhere is the danger of empathy more greatly illustrated than by the recent events in British Columbia: the sabotage and jailbreak at our Polaris Empathic Research Institute; the violent deaths of so many of Dr. Nichols's valuable scientists; the Vancouver ambush on Empath Initiative director Holt Traynor, who remains missing; and the subsequent raid on one of Stone Solutions' Canadian offices.

There are those who would claim these actions illustrate only the danger of corrupted *empathy; who would protest the three empaths who carried out these actions were previously pacifists incapable of harm. But we must remember that* every *pacifist empath is a ticking bomb with the potential to transform into a superhuman sadist, like the three corrupted empaths we now must catch.*

The events in British Columbia will not go unmet. We cannot tell the public the entire truth about empaths, but we will secure its unwavering support for our institution nonetheless. The empaths have their paranormal abilities, but we have opposed them since the emergence and are stronger and far more dangerous than they will ever anticipate.

They will find themselves cornered, captured and contained.

To that end, I'm coming out of retirement to handle this personally.

—Excerpt from a confidential internal memo at Stone Solutions

If Evan Grayson had been asked if it'd be hard to catch three corrupted empaths who'd raised hell in BC, he would've said *no.* Didn't matter that one of the empaths was his little brother, or that another had been a sunshiny therapist, or that the third looked real cute in an oversized hoodie. Grayson was the Dead Man: an elite anti-empathy defense without emotion or attachment; a perfectly engineered empath hunter, backed by the world's most powerful anti-empathy institutions and uniquely capable of finding and neutralizing any empath.

Or at least, he was supposed to be. But maybe that third empath had scrambled Grayson's good sense in the back seat of a truck and left his dick running the show, because here he was, days later, fully unable to stop shit.

"Are you kidding me?" Briony St. James's voice came through Grayson's Bluetooth earpiece as he tore down the Bellevue street, pushing the rental Prius to its limits. "How did they get past the new security?"

"I don't know yet." Grayson swerved past a Hyundai, which honked angrily at him. "But they set off alarms on thirteen of the twenty-two floors. They got in and they're not hiding."

The Prius's tires screeched as he made a sharp right turn into the parking lot and blew past the familiar sign.

STONE SOLUTIONS
DEFENDING AMERICAN MINDS

"Of all possible targets, they went for the flagship empathy defense facility. *Again.* Why? What is still here that could possibly be worth the risk?" There was a honk in St. James's background now. "Though I suppose it won't do us much good to catch them when your brother took out the Polaris empath prison."

"Oh, I'll find somewhere new to stash them," Grayson promised as he sliced through the parking lot and pulled the car right up to the building's front curb. "And I'm not playing nice this time. I'm gonna find a dungeon and throw away the key."

"*Hey,*" St. James said in his ear. "That is Reece you're talking about."

"And he's getting chained him up right next to Ms. Falcon and Alex." Grayson cut the engine. "You gonna catch your homicidal baby brother or mine?"

"We'll draw straws. Winner also gets to nab the killer therapist."

The line dropped. As he stepped from the car, St. James was already turning into the parking lot, in her boyfriend's borrowed Corolla from the looks of it, though in fairness, it wasn't like the past few weeks had left her any time to replace the Charger she'd driven as a detective on the Seattle police force. A moment later, she'd pulled behind the rental and leaped out to join him.

They drew their weapons in unison. Stone Solutions' sliding glass front doors parted for them—unlocked already, not a great sign at this hour—and they stepped together into the cavernous lobby. The white leather furniture seemed particularly bright at night, flanked by glass coffee and end tables all topped with an array of magazines. The three flat-screen televisions on the wall were currently dark, the lobby's lights reflecting off the glass frame of the large poster that read *We Support S.B. 1437: Protect American Minds.*

"Didn't you used to have a tracker on your truck?" St. James had automatically taken point, putting herself in the most exposed and dangerous position. "Why haven't we used that to find them?"

"This is your brother the car wizard we're talking about." Grayson tried to subtly shift in front of her and make himself the bigger target. "My tracker didn't make it fifteen minutes before he found it—"

"Evan, get the hell behind me and stay there," St. James snapped. "Maybe all the normal girls and boys swoon for that overprotective tough guy act, but save it for people who can't kick your ass."

"Yes, ma'am," Grayson muttered, falling back a step to cover her six.

They crossed the Stone Solutions lobby on near-silent feet. Grayson kept his senses on high alert to catch any movement, noises, or out-of-place scents, especially blood. But all was quiet.

Too quiet.

St. James suddenly nudged him. "The elevators."

Grayson glanced over to the elevator bank and the five sets of silver doors. Above each door, the illuminated sign was stuck on 20, and none of the elevators were moving. "Floor twenty is Research and Development."

"Oh, perfect," St. James said grimly. "Exactly where we want a bunch of corrupted empaths loose."

Suddenly, all five elevators began to descend.

St. James swore as she and Grayson stumbled back, both cocking their guns and raising them.

The lobby was silent save for the hum of the moving elevators. Grayson watched the floors tick down as the elevators passed 10, then 5, then 2. Then the elevator doors were opening all at once.

"Get down!"

But St. James hadn't needed to say it; Grayson was already at her side, both of them diving behind the receptionist's desk as security guards poured out of the elevator with bellowing roars.

"I think we found the extra security. Some of them, at least." St. James was on hands and knees, crawling around the side of their desk shelter to peer around the corner. "Jesus Christ. Are all of them thralled?"

Grayson chanced a look around the desk's other side. Eight security guards were rampaging through the lobby like a uniform-clad wrecking ball. One guard yanked the *Protect American Minds* poster right off the wall and swung it like a hammer into the nearest television, shattering the screen. Another guard sent a white leather chair smashing into the wall, while two more guards picked up the glass coffee table together, swung it back, and then launched it straight into the floor-to-ceiling glass windows.

Grayson and St. James both ducked back behind the desk as the window shattered. "They're going to find us." St. James had her gun out in front of her. "Do we dive in?"

Grayson readied his own weapon. "On your mark."

St. James nodded once. "Now."

They burst out together from behind the desk. Eight heads turned in their direction, but Grayson and St. James had the advantage of surprise and clear minds. Two guards rushed straight for Grayson, but he was faster, blocking one with an elbow and landing a right cross punch to the other that sent him into the wall.

On his left, St. James had squared off with a man twice her weight, ducking an oncoming blow and following it up with a kick that put him on the ground hard enough Grayson heard his skull hit the tiles. *"Evan."*

Grayson levered an oncoming guard over his shoulder and into the white leather chair behind him, then turned in her direction.

St. James had planted her foot on the guard's chest. "Look at him."

Grayson's gaze went to the guard. Then he paused. Under the raging fury, there was a spark of clarity in the man's eyes.

"Is he not actually thralled?" St. James was staring into the guard's face. "Just pissed off?"

"Projection?" But over the din, Grayson heard more engines pulling into the parking lot.

St. James must have heard it too, her gaze going to the shattered windows. "The cavalry's here."

"It'll be a SWAT team. Or three," Grayson said.

"Come on then." She was already running, leaving the guard on the floor. "We've got to find the empaths first."

A different guard lunged after her. Grayson sent him staggering across the lobby and caught up to her.

But as they approached the elevator bank, he heard a sound from down the hall. "This way." He sprinted in the direction of the noise, past the conference rooms, and burst through the door of the first-floor security room.

"Don't shoot!"

Grayson drew up short, so suddenly that St. James bumped into him from behind.

A familiar-looking security guard was cowering under the desk, knees drawn to his chest. "Don't shoot," the guard said again, rocking back and forth. "Don't shoot, don't shoot, don't shoot. Please. Please. I'm so scared. I'm so scared."

It took Grayson a moment, but then he placed him: Wayne Smith, the head of security who'd once caught Reece in the director's office in Research and Development, back when Reece had still been a violence-averse pacifist incapable of self-defense. He'd been rough with Reece, leaving him bruised and bleeding before shoving him in a storage closest.

Grayson had had some opinions about that. And while the pacifist empaths couldn't hit back, the Dead Man sure could.

St. James moved past Grayson into the room. She crouched down, glancing at the lanyard around Smith's neck. "Mr. Smith." She gripped his shoulder. "Mr. Smith, what's going on?"

Smith didn't seem to hear her. "I'm so scared," he whimpered. "So scared."

Grayson joined her on the floor next to Smith. "This is the guard that roughed your brother up before."

St. James frowned. "And he's still employed here?"

"He wasn't supposed to be," Grayson said. "But Stone Solutions and I haven't been seeing eye to eye for a while." He leaned in and touched Smith's face.

Smith startled and turned toward him. His pale blue eyes were wide and his skin blanched and clammy. He seemed overwhelmed with fear, but he was looking right at them now.

Grayson drew his hand back sharply. "He's not thralled either."

"Mr. Smith," St. James addressed the man urgently. "Can you talk to me?"

Smith swallowed. His shoulders were heaving, but he'd stopped muttering. Grayson quickly moved out of his eyeline; if Smith regained coherence, he'd recognize the Dead Man, and that sure as hell wasn't gonna help that fear.

"Mr. Smith," St. James said again.

Smith's eyebrows drew together. "Who are you?"

"My name is Briony St. James," she said. "I'm here to help. Can you tell me what happened?"

Smith was breathing hard. He drew his legs in tighter. "There was a break-in."

"Did you see who?" St. James pressed.

"I don't—I don't know," Smith said. "One moment things were fine. Then everyone started losing their minds. And then—then I thought I recognized—" He was tensing up again, fear clear on his face. "That empath," he said in barely a whisper.

St. James stiffened. "Which empath?"

"The one who broke in here before," Smith whispered. "But I don't know—I don't know what I saw. Jesus, I'm so scared—" He started rocking again.

"Is this projection too?" St. James asked Grayson, keeping her voice quiet.

"That's my guess," Grayson said, matching her volume. "One of the empaths made him feel fear, and it's still got him."

One of the empaths. Reece, obviously, based on what Smith thought he saw.

"But it will wear off?" St. James pressed. "Same with the guards in the lobby? Temporary projection, not permanent thralling?"

"Seems like it." Back in the lobby, Grayson could hear the newly arrived SWAT team dealing with the guards in the lobby, doing crowd control and breaking out handcuffs.

"Do you know what the burglars were after?" St. James asked Smith.

Smith pointed to the open door and the hall beyond with a shaky finger. "They went to the delivery room. I don't know what they wanted. There's nothing in there anymore."

"Anymore?" she repeated.

But Smith only shook his head uselessly. Whatever the empaths had come for, they seemed to be long gone now—maybe had been gone before Grayson and St. James even arrived, leaving a stage set behind them, perfectly planned to distract any would-be pursuers while the empaths themselves got away.

St. James sat back on her heels. "It's interesting, isn't it?" she said, still under her breath.

"In what way?"

"This guy is head of security. Knowledgeable about all of Stone Solutions' protections *and* can identify Reece. Would have been a lot smarter to thrall him." Her gaze was on Smith. "But Reece didn't."

"You're not suggesting mercy," Grayson said.

"It could happen," she said with a hint of challenge.

No. It couldn't. Corruption was permanent; the pacifists were gone, and the empaths were no longer capable of mercy.

But Grayson kept his mouth shut. When his empath brother Alex had destroyed his emotions, it had ensured Grayson would never feel hope again. But if hope for her own brother kept St. James going, he'd leave her to it.

He got to his feet, careful to keep out of Smith's view in case it sent fresh fear through him. They likely had only moments before the SWAT team joined them; anything St. James could learn before then might help. Grayson slipped out of the security room, but as he leaned against the wall to keep watch, his gaze stole down the hall to a closed door to a storage closet, the very same one Smith had locked the pacifist version of Reece in back on that November night those weeks ago. At the time, Grayson had been there to free Reece from Stone Solutions' clutches, but now his goal was to deliver Reece back to them, along with his own brother, and Cora Falcon too.

Grayson pulled out his phone—or, more accurately, *Reece's* phone, the phone he was stuck using after Reece had pulled a little switch in Vancouver. He'd discovered texts between Reece and Alex and tried texting the number himself, but his brother had already been corrupted for more than two years and was too even-keeled to take the bait. His texts sat on read with no response; he could perfectly picture Alex's eye-roll that Grayson had even tried.

Reece, though. Reece was still running around with *Grayson's* phone, and he'd always been easy to rattle. Grayson sent a pair of texts to his own phone number, then pocketed Reece's phone, gaze going back to Smith and St. James.

Reece could still be rattled, and that was Grayson's only motivation for texting a corrupted empath. Obviously. Grayson didn't have any emotions or feelings to override his judgment. Bad decisions were Reece's domain.

He just had to get Reece to make another.

CHAPTER TWO

This whole article is bullshit. I was still working on a brief in my office and I saw what actually happened in downtown Vancouver that night. There were at least ten giant assholes in fatigues raging on the street, tearing up cars and threatening pedestrians. Since when do the unhoused dress in tactical gear?

The worst of it was just outside Stone Solutions Canada's building. Who knows what kind of secrets they have up there? Is this just a cover-up for someone stealing anti-empathy tech?

I can't believe this story isn't bigger news. It's almost like they don't WANT us to know what's really happening.

—Comment left on an *Emerald City Tribune* article, "Vancouver police respond to altercation related to drugs, homelessness"

Reece took the truck west over the East Channel Bridge. The sky and water were a shimmering black, like the truck itself, like the corrupted lightning that had changed his empathy. It was sparking in him now, after their heist, reveling in the aftermath of the chaos and violence they'd caused.

"There's nothing of note in here." Cora was in the front passenger seat, going through one of the accordion folders they had taken from the security office at the back of the building. "Coffee deliveries. Office supplies. New chairs."

"Maybe Mr. Eton and Mr. Pelham here can point you to the right place."

At Alex's voice, Reece glanced into the review mirror, seeing a flash of glasses on the silhouette in the center of the back seat. Eton and Pelham—Alex's newly thralled Stone Solutions security guards—sat on either side of him like chessboard knights flanking the king.

"What do you want to know?" one of the guards said eagerly, adoration in his voice.

In the mirror, Alex's blond-brown hair caught the edge of a passing streetlight. *Same as Evan's,* a little voice in Reece's head noticed.

Reece rolled his eyes, annoyed with himself. So what if it was? Alex and Evan were brothers, and sometimes siblings had the same hair color. He should think of Evan only as the Dead Man, their most dangerous enemy. Alex was the only Grayson Reece could trust now.

Cora glanced over her shoulder. "We're looking for deliveries of materials, especially anything related to textiles."

"Oh," said the other guard. "Those were all shredded."

"Shredded?" Reece repeated sharply.

"Is that standard procedure?" Cora asked.

"No. Destruction happened early," said the guard. "We got the order two days ago."

"From who?" said Alex.

"Smith," the other guard said. "Dunno who told him to do it."

Reece only just managed to smother his groan. Of course it was Smith. Of course Reece had fucked up again.

If Cora and Alex had the same thought, or noticed his moment of self-loathing, they were apparently tactful enough not to comment on it. "Delivery records destroyed before we can get them," was what Cora said, lowering the accordion folder to her lap. "Isn't that interesting timing."

The flat sarcasm was layered with unsurprising frustration and bitterness. Stone Solutions had changed Cora from a kind-hearted therapist to a ruthless killer in an attempt to secure themselves millions in funding from a senate bill rider. They'd tortured her fiancé to death to make it happen, and now Cora had both corruption's enhanced empathic abilities and a personal desire to see Stone Solutions pay.

"A temporary setback," Alex said. "We have the flash drive Reece stole from Stone Solutions Canada to go through still. And our new friends here can write down what they remember, can't you?"

"Yes, sir," the guards chorused happily.

Reece took the exit onto Mercer Island, slowing to a stop as he approached a red traffic light. Behind him, he felt Alex lean forward to rest his folded arms on the front seats. "You just committed your second felonious B & E at Stone Solutions," he said wryly. "You can run a red light."

"Nope," Reece said firmly. "I heard too many stories from Jamey about criminals caught because of a busted taillight or other minor traffic violation. I will be driving safe and legal, thank you very much."

"Suit yourself." Alex's amused drawl was less pronounced than Grayson's, his voice more of a tenor to his brother's bass, but still familiar enough to make more memories threaten to rise.

Hey, Care Bear—

Reece shook himself. Hard. *Get it together,* he snapped internally. *You don't have enough control over your emotional projection to think about Evan.*

It was galling but true. Before corruption, Reece's empathy had already felt like a bear on a fraying leash. Now trying to control his empathy was like trying to tame a whole damn sleuth of bears hell-bent on a rampage. Reece was blaming it on the newness of corruption, but Alex and Cora were starting to give each other knowing looks anytime Reece's emotions rose. The absolute last thing Reece should do in an enclosed truck with the two of them was let his thoughts stray to a few stolen moments hidden in the trees off a Vancouver highway.

You want Alex to catch on? he berated himself. *To realize that his accent is enough to remind you of his brother—the one you jerked off in the back seat of this very truck? How well is* that *going to go over?*

That sobering thought was finally enough to clear Reece's head. He let Alex and Cora's conversation become background noise as he followed residential streets south, eventually pulling into the drive of the mansion formerly belonging to Dr. Jason Owens, the now-dead director of R & D at Stone Solutions who had been partially responsible for the murder of Cora's fiancé. It was an oversized house on an oversized lot at the end of its street, facing the water, with only the four-car garage and driveway visible from the road. It had privacy, plenty of space, and most of all, the three empaths had concluded it was the last place anyone would look for them.

As Reece idled for a moment, waiting on the slow rise of one of the garage doors, Alex said, "So what happened back there with Mr. Smith? I thought you were gonna add him to our collection with Misters Eton and Pelham. You said he'd be useful."

His tone was curious, innocent even, and not at all accusing. Reece felt his defenses go up anyway.

"I was. But I choked." There was no point in pretending. Alex and Cora could hear lies as well as he could.

"He might've recognized you," Alex said, still mild. "Might tell folks he thinks you were there."

"I know," Reece said, through gritted teeth. "But I can't get the damn projections under control."

Cora made a sympathetic noise, one that almost could have belonged back in her therapist's office. "Your empathy is just strong," she said. "You're working on it."

"But when will I get there?" Reece muttered as he inched the truck into the garage.

He put the truck in Park, and the others jumped out. Reece stared for a moment at the back of the garage, his mind returning to Stone Solutions and his encounter with Smith.

They'd been in the hall on the first floor. Reece had lit the place up with rage—so easy when the corruption meant anger always simmering on the surface—then recognized Smith lurking in the security room. *We should take this one*, Reece had said to Alex and Cora. *He's head of security. He could be really useful.*

But as Reece had started to step into the security room, his gaze had darted down the hall, back to the storage closet Smith had once stuffed him in. And suddenly he was remembering the fear the guards had had of him, the shame that he'd made them afraid, the guilt that he'd gotten Jamey sacked from her job.

And remembering Evan: how he'd come to Reece's rescue, pulled him out of the clutches of Stone Solutions, bundled him into the safety of the truck, given him the hoodie.

Reece had stood there, lost in memories—

And run out of time.

Now he tightened his jaw. He *would* have thralled Smith if they hadn't had to flee. He'd just been distracted by memories. Wouldn't happen again.

He was certain of that. The altered empathy vibrating in his blood wanted more violence, more chaos, to see blood on Reece's own hands. Corruption wasn't satisfied being a bystander to Alex and Cora committing murders and enslaving thralls any more than famine could be satiated by a simple snack.

Next time, Reece would be ready.

As he jumped down from the truck, there was a chime from his phone—or, more accurately, the phone he had stolen from Evan Grayson. He pulled it out.

Grayson: Y'all might've gotten away tonight, but you can't hide from me forever.

Grayson: And if you're using my truck as a getaway vehicle, you better be planning to buff every scratch out of my hood.

Reece stared at the screen, his irritation with himself happily seizing on a new target. Who the fuck did Grayson think he was?

Reece was texting back before he'd even thought it through.

Reece: What kind of amateur do you take me for? You think I'd scratch MY truck?

He started to shove the phone back into his pocket, but it chimed again.

Grayson: That truck title is still in MY name.

Grayson: And why would I trust you with MY truck when you were happy enough to leave Mr. Smith wrecked?

So they *had* found Smith. Probably questioned him, maybe even learned a few things thanks to Reece leaving him un-thralled.

That knowledge only stoked the anger in Reece's chest as his fingers flew over the tiny phone keyboard.

Reece: Is that supposed to make me FEEL something? Guilt? Regret? Make me run crying back to you for help?

Reece: Don't get me confused with the empath you thought you knew. Everything's changed for me.

Reece: But YOU are exactly the same. You think you're so untouchable, so unknowable, and your arrogance is your biggest weakness. I will run circles around you while you keep believing you're too special to fail.

Reece's phone went off again immediately.

Grayson: None of this is about me. I made you a promise: that there was nothing you could do that I couldn't stop. And one thing hasn't changed: I'm gonna keep that promise.

Reece's eyes narrowed. Grayson and his promise could go straight to—

"Reece?" Alex had poked his head into the garage. "You still in here?"

Oh great. Reece could feel the telltale prickles of projection along his skin. Alex and Cora had probably felt his irritation with Grayson all the way in the house.

"Cora is having Eton and Pelham guard Traynor," Alex said. "I mean, he's not gonna wake up on that dose he's on. But she's nothing if not tactical," he added admiringly.

Holt Traynor, the director of the Empath Initiative, was

their "guest" at Owens's house, sedated from medication they'd stolen when Alex had broken Cora out of the Polaris empath prison. Traynor had signed off on who knew how many empath experiments—maybe even the ones that had been run on Alex and Evan Grayson—and had once plotted with a still-missing scientist, Victor Nichols, to murder Evan.

At that thought, another flare of rage went through Reece. He forced it down. He should have let Traynor kill Grayson. Then he wouldn't have to deal with the Dead Man now.

Like hell you should have, a voice in his head immediately said. *No one touches Evan. THAT hasn't fucking changed.*

Reece closed his eyes, forcing himself to get control of his emotions. "I don't know how you can stand letting Traynor live," he confessed. "After what he did to you and your brother."

Alex leaned on the door frame. "I don't intend to let him live," he said, no sound of a lie in his words. "But I think he's still going to be useful. After all, Traynor can't be the only one who signed off on what happened in that bunker. And he sure as hell didn't predict how it went down."

That was true. No one could have predicted that Alex would transform his brother into the perfect emotionless weapon against empaths.

"You've never explained how you made Evan the Dead Man."

Reece hadn't realized he was going to ask the question until it had left his lips.

The garage seemed to have gone extra quiet. Then Alex tilted his head. "No, I haven't," he acknowledged. "But surely it occurred to you that I haven't told y'all for a reason?"

Reece frowned, trying to connect the dots. "Victor Nichols was trying to duplicate him," he said slowly, in realization. "It's all in that manual on that flash drive we stole, everything except what you actually did, because no one knows."

"And it needs to stay secret," Alex said. "The last thing we want is more Dead Men."

Reece nodded slowly. "But can you *un*do it?" he asked, again before he'd meant to.

"No," Alex said simply, without any hint of a lie's discordance. "I can't undo it, and neither could you. For all intents and purposes, Evan's transformation is permanent."

It was the truth.

"Speaking of that flash drive," Alex said, "I think it's got that whole list of other empaths on it. We should take a look."

Reece cleared his throat. "Yeah," he made himself say. "Yeah, I'm coming."

Alex nodded and disappeared back into the house. Reece's fingers had gone very tight on the phone.

He forced himself to take a calming breath. It didn't matter. It didn't matter that Grayson was permanently the Dead Man, that he would never have another emotion again. It was good, even. He and Grayson were enemies now, and they would stay that way.

He smashed out words on his keyboard, one last pair of texts.

Reece: You made that promise to the weak little empath who couldn't bear to say murder. It doesn't mean shit anymore. Not to me.

Reece: Stop jerking off to your own hair and pay attention: I am not your Care Bear anymore. Don't you get it, Evan? I'm the bad guy now.

He stabbed the Send icon, then shoved the phone into his pocket, following Alex into Jason Owens's house.

CHAPTER THREE

Operations progress as anticipated. Four still-living thralls were recovered from Polaris and have been moved to join the others. All salvageable documents and materials have been delivered to the location directed. Dr. Nichols himself has been safely relocated to Victoria and will arrive in Seattle later today. He requested we remind you that the Dead Man is not our ally and has shown compromised judgment, particularly in matters involving his empath brother and Reece Davies.

We have found no trace of Director Traynor. Our search continues.

—Message to [REDACTED]
transmitted from [REDACTED]

Vivian Marist would admit that one of the top perks of being Stone Solutions Canada's president—and of course, the entire company's current interim CEO—was a perk the public didn't know about: the Orion Lodge.

Designed by Cedrick Stone for their most senior leadership to study strategy and emotional defense, Orion was a triumph of both luxury and anti-empathy engineering, a secret and guarded fortress set on more than one hundred acres in the British Columbia mountains, with two indoor pools, an on-call masseuse, a spa, meditation pods, and rooms with their own saunas and cold plunge tubs.

Orion, however, also had the top-of-the-line business facilities one might expect at a corporate lodge. And at 4:07 a.m., Marist was not, in fact, getting a massage. She'd just been woken by news of another break-in at Stone Solutions' flagship Bellevue campus and was hurrying down the hall to one of Orion's conference rooms.

As she stepped into the room, she frowned. The coffee service had been set in the middle of the table, but the lodge's IT director should have been there, ready to patch her in for her call—

"Vivian."

Marist glanced over her shoulder in surprise, to the doorway. For a moment, she had thought the voice belonged to Cedrick himself.

But it wasn't Cedrick Stone who had joined her. It was Charles.

She tried to keep the shock off her face as he stepped into the conference room. A tall and formidable-looking man in his late sixties, Charles Stone was a legend in his own way, someone who'd witnessed the empath emergence in real time and moved from military contracting into empathy defense. He'd been appointed the first director of the Empath Initiative, securing Cedrick the grants needed to start Stone Solutions before entrusting the EI directorship to Charles's own close friend, Holt Traynor.

On paper, Charles had retired from the empathy business. Clearly things had changed.

"What an unexpected pleasure," Marist said, smothering

her surprise as Charles stepped into the room. "I thought we'd be doing this virtually."

"Given the events of the past few weeks, I felt it necessary to come in person," Charles said. "My apologies for being late. I was due for a check on Cedrick."

"Of course," Marist said a little more softly.

Given the need for secrecy around empathy, Stone Solutions operated a medical facility—complete with private morgue—in Kirkland, not far from their Bellevue headquarters, where patients with empathy-related injuries could be treated. Cedrick Stone himself, however, was here at Orion, in the small medical wing, receiving round-the-clock care while he was still catatonic after his encounter with Reece Davies.

Naturally Charles had stopped in to see him; he was, after all, Cedrick's father.

They sat together in two of the oversized white leather chairs that surrounded the conference table. "Have you had any word from Holt since the Vancouver incident?" Charles asked Marist.

She shook her head. "He was supposed to meet us at the dock that night. I'm still not sure why he took his team to that warehouse instead."

"Given that several of his team were thralled and turned loose to rampage through downtown Vancouver not long after, I think we can assume he encountered the corrupted empaths." Like Cedrick and most of the Stone Solutions leadership, Charles kept his voice and expressions exceedingly neutral, even when discussing the possibly unpleasant fate of a longtime colleague. He'd likely helped develop some of the emotional control curriculums they'd all taken in this very lodge.

"Holt's body wasn't among the murdered," Marist pointed out.

"That might be worse," Charles said dryly. "If the empaths thralled him."

"But even so, Holt will still be dead by now," Marist said. "Empath thralls don't last more than a day or two before burning out unless we intervene with life support."

"Perhaps," Charles said enigmatically. "Nevertheless, I don't enjoy uncertainty. I'm taking precautions, such as having Victor Nichols moved to a safe place while circulating the claim that he's presumed dead."

"That's wise. He's likely in great danger." Marist cleared her throat. "I've heard a rumor or two about Victor's research methods—nothing I've ever taken seriously, you understand, because he's not an easy man to work with so I suspect people just like to gossip. But if they know he's alive, the empaths may feel they have reason to target him."

"Genius is always slandered," Charles said with a shake of his head. "Victor has given me invaluable input over the years. I've never cared about methods when they deliver results like his." He steepled his fingers. "Do we know what the empaths wanted tonight?"

"Head of security saw three empaths go into the delivery room," she said. "Though Mr. Smith also says the room was empty."

"At my order," Charles said. "Certain records should never available lest they be demanded in discovery by lawyers—or other unscrupulous parties."

Stone Solutions already had draconian document retention and destruction policies. But Charles was taking precautions, as he'd said, and it had served them tonight. "Smith recognized Reece Davies. It appears Davies is now corrupted and working with two others, suspected to be Alex Grayson and Cora Falcon."

"And of course, I also have Mr. Davies to thank for Cedrick's condition," Charles said in a particularly unreadable tone. "I read the Dead Man's report and other accounts of the rooftop incident in November."

Agent Grayson's report had also pointed out that Cedrick had engineered Cora Falcon's corruption and planned to use Davies's half sister to conduct corruption experiments on him. But then, many might feel that simply another attack on a genius. After all, Agent Grayson had questionable sympathies toward the empaths that had garnered him much resentment from others in the empathy defense sector.

Marist generally gave Grayson more grace. Even before he'd been changed into the Dead Man, Grayson been altered by his own empath sibling when he was just a child, and his protective streak toward empaths was very possibly a side-effect. That said, his judgment in lying about his brother's death and protecting Davies had tried even her good will.

"It's past time that Mr. Davies was brought in," she said. "Though as you're aware, given the events at Polaris, we'll need a holding facility."

"That will be handled," Charles said confidently. "In the meantime, I want the heat turned up on all empaths. We'll be tripling our advertising spend, effective immediately."

"I thought that was planned for Q2," Marist said, somewhat delicately. Next year's budget had been created in anticipation of the passage of the big anti-empathy bill in the Senate, S.B. 1437—and with it, the much-needed rider that would pump piles of funding into Stone Solutions. Even retired, Charles ought to have guessed their current budget was stretched.

"We can speed up that timeline, thanks to some good news. I can't share yet, but you can drop hints at tonight's board meeting." He tilted his head. "Though given the damage to Stone Solutions' headquarters, I suppose we're going to have to find somewhere else to hold the meeting." He picked up his coffee again. "Just one more thing I have to thank the empaths for."

His eyes had narrowed, just at the corners. Marist picked up her own coffee. The empaths had brought Charles Stone out of retirement and pissed him off to boot.

She almost pitied them.

★

Stop jerking off to your own hair and pay attention: I am not your Care Bear anymore. Don't you get it, Evan? I'm the bad guy now.

Grayson sat in the parking lot in his rental Prius, gaze on Reece's last text.

A memory rose, unbidden: twilight in the truck's back seat, Reece under him, flushed and glowing, pupils blown so wide with surging empathy that those big brown eyes had become onyx black, possibly the prettiest damn thing Grayson had ever seen. Reece's voice had been gravelly with desire as words had spilled into the no-man's-land between their lips.

I can't believe I ever thought it was hard to look at you. I can't get enough now, can't stop looking.

If we could touch, I'd fucking climb into you, lose my goddamn self, it'd be heaven.

I'd let you call me Care Bear forever.

Reece was right. He wasn't that empath anymore.

"Leave my hair out of this," Grayson finally muttered, as he tucked the phone away in his pocket and stepped from the car.

Breakfast pickings were slim at 5:09 a.m. on a weekday, but as a former detective who'd worked at all hours, St. James had known of a coffeehouse that would be open. She was already inside, the lone customer ordering at the counter as Grayson opened the door and slipped into the café's warmth to join her.

"And an extra shot in that mocha," she was saying to the barista. She glanced over her shoulder at Grayson. "On me."

He shook his head and held up his credit card. "On Stone Solutions."

St. James turned back to the barista. "Make it three extra shots. And a smoked salmon bagel. And a bear claw."

Grayson ordered most of the items on the breakfast menu and the biggest latte they had. He'd already drunk half of it by the time they'd carried everything over to a small table along the window and sat facing each other in rickety wooden chairs.

"Tonight was embarrassing," St. James said as he unwrapped a breakfast sandwich. "I don't know if I can handle empaths making me look like a fool. For fuck's sake, I taught Reece how to tie his shoes."

Grayson took another long sip of the latte, then bit into bacon, cheddar and egg. "Corruption lets the empaths access paranormal insight into others. Ms. Falcon was a veterans' therapist for years. She's drawing experience from her patients."

"Yeah, and in fairness, Cora is terrifying," St. James said. "But Reece can't even navigate our bank's website. How is he suddenly a criminal mastermind?"

The breakfast sandwich was already half gone. Grayson popped the rest of it into his mouth. "Probably because your little brother is gonna be accessing insight into *you*. And respectfully, ma'am, you're pretty terrifying too."

"Flatterer." St. James let out a long sigh, running her hands over her face. "I've chased a lot of bad guys over the years. I never thought Reece would be one of them." She looked up, her exhaustion suddenly apparent in the slump of her shoulders, the red tinge to her warm brown eyes. "I guess you're probably one of the only people on the planet who understands."

Grayson made a grunt of assent. "At least I know how it was done to Alex, even if I haven't found everyone responsible."

He picked up a mini-quiche. "But I've gone over that night in Vancouver so many times. I still don't know what caused corruption to fully steal Reece."

She eyed him for a long moment, then nodded at his pile of breakfast items. "Hungry?"

"Not like there's time for regular meals when we're on a case like this."

"That's true, but we do have food at our house, at least," she said. "I keep telling you that you're welcome to stay with me and Liam."

She did, and it was kind of her. Grayson had been pulling his rental Prius into the first random motel with a vacancy every night since he got back to Seattle. A couple of times, he'd slept in the Prius itself. "I guess I hadn't expected catching the empaths to take long," he admitted.

Your arrogance is your biggest weakness, Reece had said.

Grayson drained the rest of the latte and set the empty cup on the table. Reece's priorities were questionable these days, but his empathy was more accurate than ever. Someone else might've said something like that to get under Grayson's skin, but Reece knew that wasn't possible. He'd simply been speaking truth, and Grayson would be a fool to ignore that little tidbit about himself.

Because yeah, he might've been arrogant. After all, he and St. James shared their mutual advantage over almost any adversary: They'd been altered by their empath siblings to be stronger and faster than any normal human could ever be. But *almost any adversary* didn't include their little brothers: Reece and Alex knew these strengths inside out and would always be ready to counter them.

Might be time to accept he wasn't going to catch the empaths easy and find a place to stay for more than a few hours' Wi-Fi or sleep.

St. James reached for her bagel. "There is another place you could stay if you wanted to be downtown and not out in the sticks like me." When Grayson tilted his head, she said, "Liam still has a key to the studio apartment he sublet to Reece."

Grayson's eyebrows went up. "*Reece's* studio?"

"Why not?" she said. "I mean, what are the chances he'd be brave enough to show his face?"

"Oh, I'd *welcome* Reece showing up," Grayson said. "He could come right on over and straight into my—" *arms* "—handcuffs," he quickly finished. "Handcuffs. They're right here. Waiting. Anyway, wouldn't it be awful rude of me to use his place without permission?"

"I think we have bigger problems than manners right now," she said dryly.

Before he could answer, his watch vibrated. He glanced at it. "I think Ms. Marist finally got back to me."

Grayson pulled his phone back out of his pocket. The background was still set to a picture of Reece, beaming at the camera in a bear hat with Grayson fast asleep on the king bed behind him. Their night in Vancouver together, when Reece had been happy and Grayson had been—not happy, obviously, but comfortable. Safe. Having his last decent night's sleep.

He ignored the picture, pressing the email icon situated between Reece's bear ears. Marist's email was at the top of his inbox.

Subject: re: re: Break-in

The extent of the property damage is still being assessed. Security footage has been deleted. Head of security is the only person aware empaths were on premises; he saw three empaths going into the empty delivery room and has positively identified Reece Davies.

Grayson still didn't understand why had Reece left Smith un-thralled to reveal his presence and actions. Was it part of some twisted game?

He relayed what he'd read to St. James, then scanned the rest of the email. "Security guards were told there was a materials leak in Research and Development, a volatile steroid that was accidentally distributed through the vents," he said as he handed the phone to St. James so she could read it too. "It's being blamed for security's sudden rage."

St. James's eyes were on the email now. "And they're offering the guards a financial incentive in exchange for a litigation waiver and an NDA. Buying them all off so they keep the company's secrets. Gross." She frowned at the screen and read out loud. "'There's also the question of where we're going to keep three corrupted empaths now that your brother has destroyed Polaris. But Stone Solutions will, of course, handle that.' The hell they will."

"Not like we can build a facility ourselves," Grayson pointed out. St. James knew it as well as he did: It wasn't easy to find safe places for empaths, not when you knew the truth about their abilities. You needed somewhere the corrupted empaths couldn't break out, but also somewhere that the unscrupulous couldn't get in.

Polaris had turned out to be a giant failure in every respect. Its director, Dr. Victor Nichols, was now presumed dead. Grayson, obviously, didn't put much stock in presumptions of death.

"Maybe not. But I'm going to have some big opinions about where the empaths go." St. James's gaze had gone back to the phone, her fingers flicking over the screen. "It's not going to be your *dungeon*. And it has to be safe from ghouls like Nichols." She made another noise of disgust and read from the phone again. "'Finding the empaths is our highest priority, Evan.

We need to be working together.' As if. We're not working with Stone Solutions on this or anything else." She passed the phone back to him. "Has Marist said anything about Director Traynor?"

Unbidden, Grayson's memories once again went back to Reece and the truck, and their last few minutes at that dock north of Vancouver, before everything had gone up in flames. Grayson had just learned of Alex's break-in at Polaris and had been planning to send Reece to safety and then meet up with the team at one of the two rendezvous points he'd been given.

What do you mean, rendezvous with Stone Solutions or *the Empath Initiative?* Reece had asked.

Because I gotta pick one, Grayson had explained. *I got one location from Director Traynor of the Empath Initiative, and a different location from Vivian Marist of Stone Solutions Canada.*

Reece had frowned. *They sent you different locations? That's weird, isn't it?*

Grayson hadn't thought too much of it. Marist and Traynor were usually on the same page, but there'd been a lot going on.

Go to the location Vivian Marist sent you, Reece had said at the dock only minutes later.

Grayson had trusted him and gone to Marist. Then the empaths must've ambushed Director Traynor, and no one had seen him since.

Grayson shook his head. "I haven't heard anything more," he said. "You planning a check-in with Dr. Easterby or Mr. Lane?"

She nodded. "I'll call Aisha as soon as it's a reasonable hour of morning."

Back in November, Grayson had bought an isolated house on a stretch of Salt Spring Island shoreline in BC, thinking it could be a safe place for Reece. Now it was Dr. Aisha Easterby, a medical examiner with Stone Solutions, and Dominique "Diesel" Lane, a bouncer from Seattle's fake empath club, who were at the safe house recovering from their ordeal at Polaris, where they'd been drugged by Dr. Nichols but unharmed by Alex and Cora.

Why the two empaths had left them alone was as much a mystery as why Reece had left behind the un-thralled head of security, Wayne Smith.

Grayson got to his feet. "You want another mocha?"

St. James shook her head. "I'm going home to Liam." She pointed at his phone. "Can I get Stone Solutions emails too?"

I can't compromise my email. National security.

He paused, the words held on the tip of his tongue. The Dead Man was supposed to work alone. He wasn't even supposed to take pictures of himself; he sure as hell wasn't supposed to share his classified emails from Stone Solutions and the Empath Initiative.

But St. James had been one of the best detectives on the West Coast. And when she said, *I guess you're probably one of the only people on the planet who understands*, that went both ways. Maybe their partnership could only be temporary, until the empaths here were caught, but he was lucky to have her.

"Of course," he said instead. "I'll set that up."

After she'd left, Grayson got a second latte and sat back at their table. Alone, obviously, because he didn't have a Liam—or anyone else—to go home to. He never would. That was the difference between a detective and the Dead Man.

He pulled his phone back out of his pocket to set up email forwarding to St. James, his gaze catching Marist's name and his last conversation with Reece playing in his head again.

Marist? Surprised to hear you pick Stone Solutions over the Empath Initiative. I was thinking if I had to pick, I'd meet Director Traynor.

No. Go to Marist.

It'd be easy enough to assume Reece had sent Grayson to Marist because he was already corrupted and planned to ambush Traynor. But more of Reece's words from the truck echoed in

Grayson's memory, spoken as the two of them had leaned so close into each other that he had felt that empath body heat.

Look me in the eyes and say, "Reece, I promise I'll come back to you."

I need to know you're going to be safe. Promise me, Evan.

Those couldn't have been the words of a corrupted empath. So, what had happened? When had it happened, and how?

And maybe most puzzling of all—*why?*

He lit his phone screen, once again illuminating his background picture of Reece in the bear hat Grayson had bought him. Bright smile and even brighter eyes, the pacifist angel who'd made sure Grayson could get a decent night's sleep.

Without planning to, Grayson found himself opening his text messages, his fingers beginning to type.

What happened to you, Care Bear—

He hit Delete instead of Send, and the letters vanished from the screen.

CHAPTER FOUR

You won't see any updates on their socials. You won't hear about it on the news. But here at Eyes on Empaths, *we KNOW that something big must have happened at Stone Solutions last night.*

HOW do we know? Because the Stone Solutions Board of Directors ALWAYS meets at Stone Solutions headquarters in Bellevue—except TODAY, when they're borrowing a conference room at American Minds Intact.

Still not convinced? We heard DIRECTLY from a savvy Eyes on Empaths *reader who works at Stone Solutions. According to Anonymous, staff had to use the service elevators this morning because construction crews are replacing the front windows.*

Maybe they can fool the public, but WE know when something is suspicious—just like we know there's more going on with the empaths than we're being told.

—Gretel Macy, blogging for *Eyes on Empaths*

Reece woke late, with a headache and a crawling along his skin.

Evil is hungry. It was such a cliché. And yet he felt it, like his body was crackling with electricity, a lightning storm looking for a target. It wanted to strike and revel in the destruction it left behind.

Reece pushed the thought away. It would settle. He was just even less of a morning person now.

He reached for his phone out of habit, then yanked his hand away before he picked it up. He didn't need to see Grayson's texts again, definitely didn't need to see if Jamey had sent more messages. Even Liam and Diesel had tried texting. He should block them all.

But you won't, the little voice in his head said. *You need to know if someone tries to hurt them. Your sister, your friends, your—whatever you and Evan are.*

Reece huffed. He and Evan were enemies, obviously.

Say it out loud, if you're so sure it's true, the voice in his head needled him.

Reece threw back the covers and forced himself to his feet.

One of the changes corruption had brought was a heightened awareness of the emotions around him. He followed the sense to the kitchen and found the other two empaths sitting together at the breakfast table, Alex scrolling on his phone while Cora peered at the screen of a laptop. On the wall, a television was playing local news with the sound muted.

Reece squinted into the too-bright light pouring in the many windows. "Thralls?"

"Guarding Traynor," Alex said without looking up. "Y'all's friend Ms. Macy has already posted about last night."

To Reece's fuzzy and headache-addled brain, his accent sounded extra reminiscent of Grayson's. One more thought to carefully ignore.

Cora did look up, meeting Reece's eyes. "'Y'all's friend,' he says, as if he isn't a blogger himself and a genuine fanboy of *Eyes on Empaths*."

"It's not like I *agree* with her," Alex said. "But she knows what's going on better than the news. And she cares about the truth."

Reece side-eyed him. "Didn't Gretel tell everyone we can mind-control pumpkins?"

"If you had actually read October's featured story," Alex said long-sufferingly, "you'd know Ms. Macy was speculating that an empath could influence the emotions of the person carving the pumpkin." He gestured at the three of them. "And she's not *wrong*."

Reece rubbed his temple. *Eyes on Empaths* was not going to help the headache. "Are you still in touch with her?"

"She hasn't texted since our last exchange. And I'm not texting her, for the obvious reasons." Alex held out the phone. "Though she has dedicated tags for both of you."

"You'd have your very own tag too, if she knew what you were," Cora said to Alex, as Reece glanced at the phone.

On-screen was a picture of the auto show he'd gone to in Vancouver, he himself just visible on the picture's edge, wearing the hat with bear ears that Grayson had bought him. The photographer had obviously been focused on Grayson, though, centering the tall figure speaking into his phone. So annoyingly good-looking, obviously drawing the eye of several others in the photo.

Even if Photo Grayson's own eyes were on Reece.

Reece quickly averted his gaze. "She's also tagged this one for your brother."

"I know." Alex wrinkled his nose. "I do try not to see her whole readership lusting after the so-called *Dead Man*." He scoffed. "I can't believe Evan has a secret code name. He probably thinks he's Batman."

Cora snorted. "So the thralls wrote down what they could remember of Stone Solutions' recent textile deliveries. I'm searching for warehouses and shipping lines," she said, pointing to a piece of paper next to the laptop. "Then Alex pointed out that in the meantime, we could relieve Stone Solutions of some of their current materials."

Reece perked up. "Oh?"

"Don't get excited yet," Cora said ruefully. "Because according to our new friends Eton and Pelham, after delivery, materials for empath gloves are stored in locked vaults on the second sublevel. And for security reasons, the codes are known only to leadership—and the head of security, Wayne Smith."

This time, Reece did groan, his palm covering his face, the sensation of his own warm bare skin instead of cold gloves still unexpected. "And I let him go last night."

"But we can get him back." Alex held out the phone again. "There's a reason I'm on *Eyes on Empaths* this morning."

Reece took the phone. On-screen was an article dated that morning, titled in Gretel's signature exuberant style.

BOD Meeting Moved to AMI—What's Going On at Stone Solutions??

"So they had to move the board meeting to American Minds Intact because of our break-in?" Reece scanned the article. "But if the board is going to be at AMI—" his eyes closed, his corrupted empathy automatically leaping up to make connections for him "—then they're going to want all the security they can find, just in case we show up again. Which means Smith, because a different man might stay home today to recover, but Smith is so derisive of the whole concept of empathy, he won't even have it for himself. He'll be there."

He opened his eyes to see Alex and Cora nodding along. "He's going to be tougher to get to now, though," Cora said. "We'll need a plan."

The black lightning brought an answer. "Grand larceny,"

Reece said. "AMI's offices are in a high-rise, but there's an AMI storefront at street level. Instead of trying to infiltrate a conference room on the upper floor, I bring Eton and Pelham to rob the store. Security comes down. I pick off Smith."

"You said *I*, not *we*," Alex pointed out.

"Because this is my fuckup," Reece said more tightly. "I'm the one who left Smith un-thralled. I'm going to do it right this time."

Cora and Alex exchanged a glance. "Eton and Pelham won't do well away from Alex," Cora pointed out. "Thralls have limited lives anyway, but the farther they are from the empath they're devoted to, the faster they start deteriorating."

"True," Reece said lightly. "But maybe turning two deteriorating thralls loose in an AMI store sounds like a damn fine time."

"Well, now I don't want to miss it," Alex said wryly.

"Come on," Reece said, pleadingly. "You two keep looking for the warehouses and ships. I have a lot of practice fucking things up, but let me fix this."

Alex and Cora exchanged another look. "Okay," Cora said, sounding like it was against her better judgment. "But promise you'll call us if Stone Solutions brings in the— Ugh. Speak of the devil."

Reece followed her gaze up to the television. On-screen was an advertisement for Stone Solutions, children and puppies running in slow motion across a meadow with fake mountains generated in the background. Curved text scrolled over the screen: *Protect our minds. Protect our future.*

"This has got to be the fourth time this ad has played," Alex said, sounding bored. "At least Gretel would never believe we can emotionally control *dogs*."

Reece took a breath through his nose.

Alex glanced his way. "You're good, right?"

Reece blew the breath out, too hard. "Why wouldn't I be?"

"Uh-huh," Alex said skeptically, sounding far too much like his brother. "You do remember if you project anger, there are thralls here now, and they'll start fighting?"

"I *know*." It was fine. Reece was fine. He'd grown up having his shows interrupted by worse Stone Solutions commercials than that. And maybe it never really stopped stinging, but he wasn't that helpless pacifist anymore.

The on-screen text was still scrolling: *A bill in Congress would mean safety measures around empathy: Tell your representatives that you support S.B. 1437.*

Reece's jaw tightened. On second thought, maybe he and his hair-trigger temper shouldn't be watching this. Alex was going back to his phone and Cora's gaze had returned to the laptop, so Reece took the moment to slip out of the kitchen, back to his room.

As he closed the door behind him, his eyes went to the phone that still sat on the nightstand. Before he'd realized what he was doing, he'd picked it up, sitting on the edge of the bed and pulling up his last text message to Grayson.

Reece: Stop jerking off to your own hair and pay attention: I am not your Care Bear anymore. Don't you get it, Evan? I'm the bad guy now.

Grayson had responded early that morning.

Grayson: If I were someone else, that threat might be scary.

Grayson: But I'm still the Dead Man. So maybe you're the one who doesn't get it, sugar, because handling bad empaths? Handling YOU? Kinda my whole job.

Reece's fingers were already moving. You weren't complaining when I handled YOU in the back of the truck—

Fuck, no, DELETE. Jesus. Reece threw the phone across the bed like the bad decision enabler it was.

Whatever treasonous cell in his unhinged brain that had always gleefully ignored common sense in favor of panting after Grayson had unfortunately survived corruption intact. But it didn't matter, because Reece was going to ignore it. Going to put Stone Solutions and Grayson both firmly out of his mind and plan a robbery.

Except he'd already picked his phone back up.

Reece: No more Mr. Nice Dead Man, is that what you're trying to say? Please.

Reece: If you're so sure you can handle bad empaths, come and get me then.

He stared at the words he'd just texted Grayson.

In hindsight, maybe he could have written something that didn't sound so much like a damn invitation.

When Jamey had gotten home, she'd fallen into bed with Liam for a moment of sleep, waking when his alarm went off only a couple of hours later. He kissed her temple, then got up, disappearing into the shower as she rolled over to grab her phone and call Aisha.

"Hey, Detective," Aisha said fondly as she answered.

Jamey broke into a smile. "You sound better," she said, happiness warming her chest as she settled against her pillows with the phone. "How are you doing?"

"It takes three cups of coffee, but then I feel almost like a real person," Aisha said wryly. "How about you? What's the latest?"

Jamey sighed. "Evan and I are getting our asses kicked by our little brothers and a therapist."

Aisha snorted softly. "I can't speak to your brothers, but I wouldn't underestimate Cora."

As Liam's shower started, Jamey's gaze went to her bedroom window, speckled with soft raindrops. "You mentioned you talked to Cora at Polaris, before the break-in."

"She was drugged and strapped to a table when I found her. Who knows what she'd already been through?" Aisha said, a rare note of anger in her typically sunny voice. "Yes, she's dangerous and still responsible for a lot of death. But after what Stone Solutions did to her and her fiancé, I can't help but feel some sympathy."

"Yeah," Jamey reluctantly admitted. "But you're sure you're not extra sympathetic because she's pretty?"

"Obviously not," Aisha said just a hair too quickly.

"Obviously," Jamey said dryly.

"Just because I like girls doesn't mean I like bad girls." Aisha paused. "Cora did call me Harley Quinn, though. That was kind of cute."

Lord save them from bisexuals inclined to bad decisions. Jamey rubbed her temple. "How's Diesel?"

"Poor guy mentioned that he really, really wished he could make an appointment with his therapist to process everything. But since his therapist is—*was*—Cora . . . well."

Jamey winced. "Yeah."

"But he's getting better," Aisha said, voice lighter again. "He told his club that he caught a bad flu in Vancouver and won't be back to bounce for a few days. They responded that he should take all the time he needs. McFeely's might be a fake empath club but apparently it has very real benefits," she said. "Stone Solutions, on the other hand, isn't somewhere I can keep working, even as a clandestine medical examiner, and I'd rather work with Evan and his undercover support network, the Vanguards, anyway."

In the shower, Liam had started humming, the tuneful resonance welcome when everything else in Jamey's life felt dissonant and harsh. "You're not working, though, right? You're resting?"

"Well, I've been thinking about what might be on the flash drive the empaths stole from Vivian Marist's office at Stone Solutions Canada," Aisha said. "What if it had the names of other empaths? Evan had theorized empaths might be drawn to seek each other out. If that's true, then the corrupted empaths might realize they can target the pacifist empaths."

"That's a good point," Jamey mused. "Maybe we can do something to protect them."

"I'm reaching out to all of them," Aisha said. "If I find any who don't have a safe place to lay low for a few days, we'll come up with a plan."

"A few days," Jamey repeated.

"Because that's all it's going to take to find your brother and get him back," Aisha said with a firm kindness that had Jamey's throat tightening with gratitude.

"Thanks," she said, swallowing. "Nice to hear that from someone. It's obvious Evan doesn't believe we can save the empaths."

"No, he doesn't." Aisha sighed. "For what it's worth, I know Evan can't have actual feelings about what happened with your brother. But I think, in his own way, he's taking it very hard."

"What do you mean?"

"They were getting close, wouldn't you say? Driving up to Canada together? Sharing hotel rooms? You even got a picture when Evan's not allowed to take pictures of himself."

"Not *allowed*?"

"He's supposed to be a classified weapon," Aisha said more quietly. "Stone Solutions, the Empath Initiative—that's all they see in him, and they want to control the Dead Man as much as they control the empaths."

Jamey frowned. "*We* don't see Evan that way. And Reece especially would never see him like that."

"No, Reece would have had empathy for even the Dead Man," Aisha agreed. "But now, very suddenly—he's corrupted. And none of us know why. Even without feelings, I don't think Evan is taking it well. He tried so hard to protect him."

I've gone through the events in Canada so many times, Grayson had said to her over their predawn coffees. *I still don't know what caused corruption to fully steal Reece that night.*

"*Steal* Reece" was the phrase he had used, like Reece had been pulled away from him. But then, Grayson had originally bought the safe house where Aisha and Diesel were recovering to keep Reece safe.

He'd taken a literal bullet to try to save Reece.

Jamey sighed. "You know, if Reece had sent me that Canadian selfie with anyone else, I'd assume they were hooking up," she admitted. "But those two can't even touch."

"To be fair," Aisha said, sounding thoughtful, "an empath is plenty creative to get around that hurdle."

"Oh my God," Jamey said. "That is my *brother*."

"In fact, if you're curious—"

"I'm not."

"—you can check *Eyes on Empaths*—"

"I won't."

"—and read the fan fiction someone posted about them," Aisha finished. "It's pretty inventive. There's this part where Reece—"

Jamey quickly hung up.

The Stone Solutions' jet had taken off from a small private airport on Vancouver Island, and now landed at another private airport near Seattle. Dr. Victor Nichols opened his umbrella as he descended the airstairs. A black Maybach waited alone on the tarmac, the driver, Mr. Huang, standing motionless next to the back seat door.

Nichols strode briskly over to the car. "Dr. Nichols," Huang said as he got the door.

Instead of the typical bench, the back of the Maybach held twin executive seats flanking a console. Charles was already seated in the far recliner, the tray table unfolded and a laptop in front of him. He looked up as the door opened. "Ah, Victor! I trust you had a good flight?"

"Tolerable." Nichols slid into the recliner behind the driver's seat as Huang shut the door. "I didn't expect you to come yourself."

"I'm skipping out on a board of directors meeting, it's true, but I wanted to see you in person. You're a particularly valuable member of my team. I'm grateful you were canny enough to escape Polaris."

In front of Nichols, Huang had taken his seat behind the wheel. The custom-designed divider between the front and back was already shut, enclosing them in a soundproof bubble where even the wheels against the tarmac were barely audible as they got underway. "The pilot who flew me to Vancouver Island had some opinions about our abrupt departure. Are we in danger of her sharing her knowledge about me with others?"

"She's been handled," Charles said dismissively. He gestured to the small screen embedded in the seat in front of him. "You're just in time for kickoff. Cedrick loves football, you know. Our box at Lumen Field was his purchase."

Nichols did not give one solitary fuck about football, and Cedrick was a juvenile idiot whose luxurious upbringing had made him believe he was invincible. But he was hardly going to say any of that to Charles. "How is Cedrick?"

"Unchanged." Charles's tone was extra flat. "Truth be told, I find it galling that the empath who put him in that state is currently free."

"You can thank the Dead Man for that," Nichols said just as flatly. "Both for Davies's freedom and for the destruction of Polaris by the brother Grayson told us was dead."

For years, Nichols had run the Polaris prison for corrupted empaths. Stone Solutions was the public face of empathy defense, manufacturers of the anti-empathy gloves the pacifist empaths wore, but the public were naive and stupid fools without any clue of the far greater danger corrupted empaths posed beyond the endlessly debated privacy concerns.

That was where Nichols had come in.

"Evan can be a challenge, it's true," Charles said. "But unique as he is, he has his uses. He's certainly trying to stop the empaths now. We simply need to be certain he sees the logic of continuing to work against the empaths. It's not as if he can be swayed by emotion."

Nichols suppressed a noise of frustration. It had taken ages to get Director Holt Traynor of the Empath Initiative to agree that Evan Grayson was too dangerous to live, that they needed to focus on creating emotionless soldiers without Grayson's lingering protective instinct toward empaths. But now Traynor was missing, and others simply didn't understand. "I don't believe Grayson is *unique*," Nichols said. "He's an experiment. His immunity can be duplicated in someone without his complicated loyalties."

Charles glanced at him out of the corner of his eye. "You still think so?"

He said it simply, curiously. Not a challenge; a genuine question.

"Yes, I do," Nichols said. "I was close, at Polaris. The irony that it was Evan Grayson's brother who destroyed our facility is not lost on me."

Charles picked up one of the Maybach's custom flutes from the console. "I have always appreciated your work with Polaris," he said. "Most people wouldn't have the stomach for what needs to be done to truly understand the corrupted empaths. Even a man like Holt doesn't want the details."

Nichols let his gaze rest disinterestedly on the back of Huang's head on the other side of the divider. That was true. Traynor of the Empath Initiative understood the danger normal humans faced from corrupted empaths—understood the vital role Polaris had played in the empath ecosystem. But when it came to Nichols's experiments, Traynor had always chosen plausible deniability.

Don't tell me how the sausage is made, Traynor would say. *Just tell me how much money you need and show me where to sign.*

"It's unacceptable to have Polaris inoperative," Charles went on. "Knowing minds like yours are solving our biggest empathy problems brings me quite a bit of peace." He reached into the laptop bag at his feet and withdrew a large padded manila envelope, which he held out to Nichols. "Here."

"What's this?" Nichols said, taking the envelope. He could feel the outline of two small vials inside, along with something larger that gave beneath his fingers with the softness of fabric.

"The envelope contains a potentially useful item," Charles said, "along with a sample of the laboratory materials that were saved from Polaris."

Nichols's fingers tightened on the envelope. Some of his research had survived. Charles wouldn't give this back to him freely, though. "I take it you have a request of me."

"I have been fighting empaths longer than the three children who broke into Stone Solutions last night have been alive." Charles steepled his fingers. "They were after delivery records; I protected those, but it seems plausible to think they may be after the contents of said deliveries, most likely the materials for the gloves that keep the rest of us safe. Those materials are also well-protected, but it seems prudent to take some extra steps to protect the access codes and prevent the empaths from interfering."

Nichols tilted his head, waiting.

"I have a favor that needs to be entrusted to the right partner," Charles said. "And as you know, I always repay my favors."

CHAPTER FIVE

To: [REDACTED]
From: vivian.marist@stonesolutionscorp.com
Subject: BOD meeting

An impactful strategy meeting for the Stone Solutions Board of Directors is planned for this evening. An event of this caliber clearly cannot be held at Stone Solutions until security is strengthened and the lobby windows are replaced, but AMI has graciously agreed to host the meeting at their downtown headquarters.

Obviously AMI is not responsible for empathy defense, and so of course is not quite as secure as Stone Solutions itself.

I'm sure you remember which empaths are responsible for Stone Solutions' current state.

And who is responsible for those empaths currently being free.

Stone Solutions would appreciate the Dead Man's presence at the meeting.

"'Stone Solutions would appreciate the Dead Man's presence,'" Grayson repeated, reading over Vivian Marist's email.

Surely looking for the empaths was a better use of his time? But while they could split hairs over whether Cora Falcon's current freedom was Grayson's fault, his horse wasn't very high when it was his own brother who'd sprung her from Polaris. And Reece being corrupted and free was, of course, entirely Grayson's fault, so he settled for sending Marist a polite *yes, ma'am* in response before getting back on the road.

American Minds Intact's headquarters was in a nondescript downtown high-rise, halfway up a hill and not far from the water. Soon enough, Grayson was pulling his rental Prius along a stretch of yellow-painted curb on the busy street, just past the overpriced AMI shop that took up half of the building's first floor. Clothes with the AMI logo were displayed in the window: a tote bag that read *Our Minds, Our Business*; stainless steel travel mugs with the AMI logo; a mannequin wearing a hooded sweatshirt in the neon yellow of a safety vest with *Empathy Is Danger-y* spelled out in big letters. They sure were scraping the bottom of the barrel when it came to slogans.

He was early for the meeting but climbed out of the car anyway, ignoring the AMI store in favor of the coffeehouse next door. He got a latte and stepped back out to the sidewalk, standing under the coffeehouse's awning and out of the flow of relentless foot traffic as he pulled out his phone. He'd gotten more emails, but his thumb went, unbidden, to the texts from Reece.

Reece: No more Mr. Nice Dead Man, is that what you're trying to say? Please.

Reece: If you're so sure you can handle bad empaths, come and get me then.

"'No more Mr. Nice Dead Man'?" Grayson repeated out loud as he sipped his coffee. "When have I ever been *nice*?"

Maybe when you pinned Reece down on your truck's back seat and made him come with his own gloves, said a little voice in his head.

Grayson twitched. He carefully ignored any rising memories as he sent a text back. Because he *would* take that invitation and come and get Reece.

In a completely platonic, law-and-order sense of the phrase.

Grayson: Pretty cocky coming from an empath who's gonna wind up back in my handcuffs.

As he tucked his phone away, his sensitive ears caught a familiar distant chime, the same message alert he'd once used on the phone Reece had stolen.

Grayson looked up automatically, glancing up and down the street. Pedestrians were flowing both ways, huddled into their coats. There was a small bottleneck blocking the sliding doors of the AMI store, where a couple had apparently decided to make out right in the doorway. Other than the couple, though, almost everyone he could see had their eyes on their own phone; could've been any of them using his old model.

As he turned toward the building, a flash of movement in the sky caught his eye. He looked up to see a bird high overhead, strikingly jet-black against the gray clouds. Countless crows called Seattle home, but this bird was bigger, with a wedge-shaped tail; a rare and remarkable sight in the city.

Grayson's gaze tracked the raven as it glided through the air, then flapped its wings and disappeared past a cluster of evergreens toward the water. The trees' many shades of green were vivid and bright with life against the silvery day and the mirrored gray of the sky and sound. Above his head, the lightest of rains had started up again, nothing like a Texas downpour, but a soft mist that he could barely hear against the awning.

Grayson was very still for a moment.

Once upon a time, he'd loved the Texas Hill Country: the rolling and wooded green hills that went on for endless miles, the hidden lakes and rivers that stretched out blue as the sky above. Where a hundred-degree day might be followed by a sunset you couldn't take your eyes from and then a warm night bursting with countless stars overhead.

Awe, Alex had explained back when they were sixteen and thirteen, and Grayson had just gotten his license and seized any excuse to take their dad's truck for a drive through the hills or to stargaze from the bed. *That feeling that steals your words, that's bigger than you, like your heart and breath don't fit in your body anymore. It's awe.*

But that, of course, had been the Before Days. Now there wasn't a single sentiment in Grayson able to experience awe or appreciate the beauty of nature anymore, whether it was a hawk in the blue skies over green hills in Texas or black ravens against shimmering mist and mountains in the Pacific Northwest. He was letting old habits distract him again, and now more than ever, he couldn't afford to let memories dictate any of his actions.

He drained the coffee cup and tossed it in the recycling, then went into the building to find the elevators and the board of directors meeting.

"Where's Alex?" Eton asked for the third time.

Reece took a breath through his nose. They'd been staking out the AMI store for about twenty minutes. It was not going great. "Alex wants you to be here," he said, also for the third time. "Remember?"

Eton's expression turned dreamy. "Okay. Whatever Alex wants."

Reece took another breath. Alex had been right; the thralls did not do well away from him, and Reece was in an AMI store where the slogans were painfully terrible and his temper was strained as hell. It wasn't a great combination.

Across the street, a Prius had pulled up at a stretch of yellow curb, illegally parking in front of the neighboring coffeehouse. Reece quickly turned away, before a flare of anger could escape and influence any hapless shopper caught in his orbit. Jesus, people were irritating. Could he thrall the city into following the goddamn traffic laws?

"The man," said Pelham as Reece flipped through AMI-branded flannels with more force than necessary.

"What man?" Reece said with an edge.

"The *man*," Eton said insistently.

Reece glanced out onto the sidewalk. A stream of pedestrians was passing by like a ceaseless river. "Who?"

Pelham shoved Eton out of the way. *"Coffee."*

Eton bared his teeth in response.

Alex hadn't been kidding; both thralls were far more agitated and less communicative with Reece alone, away from the empath they were devoted to. Reece needed thralls who were actually helpful.

His gaze went to the nearest shopper, a woman in her late thirties who was stiffly browsing the clearance rack with a pinched, resentful face. He could thrall her and give her an outlet for that bitterness.

Or maybe she's unhappy because it's difficult to get by in an expensive city, said that little part of him that just would not shut the fuck up. *She's looking at smaller sizes than she would wear herself; maybe she's trying to find something she can afford for a kid. Even if she does hate empaths, are you really going to thrall someone's mom?*

Reece clenched his jaw.

"The man," Eton said, and shoved Pelham.

Not again. "Would you stop?" Reece snapped.

"But The Man," Pelham said insistently, speaking the words as if they were a title. "Texting."

Reece's phone chimed. He pulled it out of his pocket.

Grayson: Pretty cocky coming from an empath who's gonna wind up back in my handcuffs.

Reece's lips pinched together. That arrogant dick—

Eton shouldered Pelham so hard he stumbled, just as the thirtysomething shopper started flipping clothes so aggressively they flew off the rack.

Keep it together, Reece snapped at himself, jamming the phone back in his pocket. He straightened up and turned toward the door. And as he did, his gaze went through the store windows, to the tall figure in jeans and a tan coat outside the coffeehouse on the sidewalk. The man was staring down the street, turned at an angle that hid his face, but there was absolutely no mistaking the all-too-familiar silhouette that Reece had once had under him and over him in the F-150's back seat.

"Shit."

Reece dove behind another rack, this one of neon-yellow hoodies, eyes wide and heart pounding.

"See?" Eton said. "The Man."

"Next time say *the Dead Man.*" Reece was already pulling out his phone. Of *course* Grayson was here at the board of directors meeting. Stone Solutions and AMI had an incestuous relationship, and the Dead Man was right in the middle of things. And of *course* Reece had fucking missed it, because corrupted empathy could figure out where Wayne Smith was likely to be, but a stolen moment in a truck hadn't changed Grayson's immunity to empathy.

And now he was *right fucking there*, those same broad shoulders that had filled the cozy truck cab, the same strong body that had been less than an inch from Reece, all his to touch until even empath gloves and that Dead Man armor couldn't hold back Evan's physical desires—

Pelham abruptly pointed at the doorway. "Love!"

"What?" Reece followed Pelham's gesture, and his eyes landed on a couple suddenly making out in the store's doorway. He winced; no question which emotion he was projecting *now*. "Son of a bitch."

He pushed through the circular rack of hoodies and out the other side, not stopping until he was disappearing through a curtain at the back of the store. He ducked into a dressing room and slammed the wooden door, taking deep breaths as he smashed out a text message to Alex and Cora. This was fine; everything was *fine*. He could handle this—

The dressing room door suddenly opened, revealing Eton. "The Man left."

"Oh," Reece said a little weakly. "Good—"

Eton suddenly made a snarling noise and turned away. A moment later there was a loud clattering, maybe the rack of clothes at the dressing rooms' entrance, followed by several shouts.

Shit. The thralls were not doing well at all. And Grayson was literally overhead, at the board of directors meeting in the AMI offices on the sixteenth floor. If things in here got out of hand, he'd be part of the responding team.

His phone chimed again, two messages simultaneously.

Cora: Don't take on the Dead Man alone.

Alex: Get out of there. Leave the thralls.

There was another shout, this time a woman, and the sound of shattering glass, like the thralls had broken the three-way mirror. Reece quickly darted out of the dressing room. Eton and Pelham were at the end of the hall of dressing room stalls, grappling with each other. Reece could run now, leave them here to cause chaos.

And murder, the little voice in his head said. *Because they're not going to stop at chaos. There will be murder.*

A woman screamed, running out of her dressing room in an AMI T-shirt as Eton and Pelham crashed into it.

Reece didn't care who died in here. He didn't care—

But he was already moving. He slammed the dressing room door shut on Eton and Pelham, grabbing a chair meant for a waiting patron and jamming it up under the handle to keep them in there. At the same time, he reached through the tumult of emotions inside him for the fear he'd felt the first time he'd realized Evan Grayson was the Dead Man.

And as he strode through the curtained archway back into the store, he let it go on purpose.

Around him, the AMI erupted into chaos. People began to scream and stampede for the door, knocking down shelves and racks, leaving AMI merchandise shattered and trampled underfoot.

Reece grabbed a hoodie and an AMI-branded selfie stick off the floor as he joined the crowd, cutting through the cash wrap and out on the street. How long did he have until word of the chaos reached the AMI offices upstairs and they sent the response? Probably four, maybe five minutes, and then Grayson would be heading straight for Eton and Pelham.

Unless Reece could redirect him.

He darted around the illegally parked Prius and crouched in front of the hood. "I should have guessed this was you," he said aloud as he jabbed the tip of the selfie stick through the grill. A moment later, his press-and-push maneuver was rewarded with a quiet *click*.

Reece tried the unlocked hood, and it lifted easily. He reached for one of the ignition coil bolts, and it loosened under his grip.

"As I said," Reece muttered as he unscrewed the bolt. "Come and get me."

"—as we align on this deeper dive, just here, you can see S.B. 1437 will be a true game changer, leading to a predicted share price increase of more than six percent—"

Grayson watched Vivian Marist make emphatic circles on a projected slide with a laser pointer as heads around the conference table considered the figures. The board of directors meeting had been going all of five minutes, and they were already discussing profit. He recognized a few of the folks around the table, including Beau Macy, the AMI president, listening attentively to the promise of even more money.

Grayson didn't own Stone Solutions' stock.

His gaze drifted out the floor-to-ceiling windows, which framed a view of the sound and Bainbridge Island. The interior wall was likewise floor-to-ceiling glass, so that the view could be enjoyed by anyone walking past the conference room. The Stone Solutions' board of directors sat around the solid mahogany conference table in oversized leather chairs every bit as nice as the ones at Stone Solutions itself. AMI liked to claim they were underdogs in the fight against empaths, but they sure weren't hurting for funds.

"—and if we circle back," Marist continued, "we see that

leveraging the synergy of S.B. 1437 and our disruptive new media campaign *together* could move the needle nearly seven percent—"

Three people passed the conference room's interior windows on their hall patrol again, including head of security, Wayne Smith, and two members of the undercover response team. Grayson edged his way a little deeper into the conference room before he was seen.

"Vivian," one of the directors said, a white man with prominent eyebrows. "Will you be addressing the recent SEC filing?"

"Well, the specifics around Cedrick's illness are still sealed," Marist said apologetically, "so nothing new will be added to our public disclosures—"

"Not *that*," said the director. "The 8-K Cedrick filed in October."

"Oh." Marist frowned. "Well—"

The conference door was abruptly flung open. "Ms. Marist! Mr. Macy! There's a panic happening in the AMI store—they're destroying property—"

Beau Macy was getting to his feet, but Grayson wasn't waiting to hear the rest. Panic meant fear, and a crowd suddenly set off by an emotion likely meant they'd let the empaths play them again. They'd targeted the first-floor store while all of security and response were up here guarding the BOD on sixteen.

He pushed off the wall and darted out of the room, dodging the guards as he skipped the elevator and went for the fire stairs. He could hear the screaming by the ninth floor, and the crowd noise was nearly deafening as he burst out the ground-floor door onto the sidewalk. He twisted his way through the thick, panicking crowd and pushed into the AMI store.

Then he paused. The store floor was covered in destroyed stock but empty of people. Had everyone already run out?

As he stood there, ears pricked for sounds, his watch buzzed. He pulled out his phone.

On-screen was a picture of his F-150, parked along a stretch of curb under a bare-branched tree, and two texts.

Reece: You want to use those handcuffs? I'll be at the Space Needle for the next 10 minutes.

Reece: Better hurry. All these tourists might make me twitchy.

Grayson shoved the phone into his pocket, sprinting back to the front of the store. Several others were shouldering their way in through the sliding doors, not the security guards from upstairs but at least eight of the high-level responders from the Stone Solutions operations team.

"You armed?" Grayson checked.

"Yes, sir," one of them replied.

Grayson hesitated, but they'd be trained and ready for whatever might be in the store.

They were not ready for Reece.

He slipped out around them and ran for his car, dropping into the driver's seat and starting the engine. He pulled away from the curb and into the thick of traffic, cutting to the middle lane so he could turn and head for the Space Needle.

And that was when the engine started sputtering.

"What the hell," he said out loud, pumping the gas. But the car had slowed to a crawl, and then it came to a stop, right in the middle of the downtown street.

As Grayson pumped the gas again, jamming the Start button, his watch buzzed. He yanked out his phone.

It was a new selfie of Reece, perched on the back of the F-150's open tailgate. He was wearing one of the highlighter-yellow AMI hoodies with *Empathy Is Danger-y* emblazoned across the front and holding some short metal rods up for the camera.

Reece: Though I guess it might be hard to hurry without these.

Around Grayson's stalled Prius, traffic was backing up, honks filling the air. Pedestrian traffic was at a complete standstill, some people still screaming, others just staring.

Two more texts came in.

Reece: These are your ignition coil packs, btw.

Reece: Just in case you don't know enough about cars to recognize them. :)

The chaos continued around Grayson as he stared at the picture of Reece. "All right. If that's the way you want it," he finally said. "No more Mr. Nice Dead Man."

CHAPTER SIX

So excited to find more of my fellow Captain Feelings fans! They canceled this graphic novel series way too soon. Does anyone have a digital scan of Volume Three? It's the one where our intrepid empath captain faces off with his nemesis, Dr. Stoic, when a corporation tries to build a high-rise over a community garden. It's a classic!

—Internet forum post

"I understand, Dad," Gretel Macy said into her phone, for the third time. "*Yes*, I will write about AMI store, but *no*, I won't make AMI look bad, and *yes*, I'll—sure, all right, of course you have to go."

Gretel hung up and set her phone to the side. She ran both her hands through her hair, then looked back up at her computer screen.

There had been sudden, inexplicable panic at the AMI store, resulting in property damage and the entire staff and all the patrons fleeing the premises. Her dad was demanding *Eyes on Empaths* help with damage control; her readers were begging her for more details. She needed to be writing.

And instead she was staring at the giant mind map that stretched across both of her oversized monitors, a collection of clipped images, links to blog posts and news articles, and note after note speculating about connections and links.

Empath Initiative > oversees empaths but funded by military. WHY???

Stone Solutions > receives millions from Empath Initiative for empathy defenses

Cedrick Stone > father was first director of the Empath Initiative, family fortune made from military contracting. Still hospitalized: location secret.

And below all those notes, the inexplicable picture Alex had texted her, of Seattle Police Department Officer Stensby and a large blond man in military camouflage standing outside Cedrick Stone's office in Stone Solutions, sent after Stone Solutions had experienced yet another break-in and fire.

I did promise you a story, Alex had texted.

It was a story all right, but one Gretel didn't know how to read yet. And Alex himself was a mystery too, who'd seemed to vanish as abruptly as he'd appeared. Good-looking, smart, and one of the best listeners she'd ever met, and she didn't even have his last name, just the memories of their brunch and their stop by her dad's AMI event.

Gretel frowned and reached for her coffee. The cool liquid touched her lips, and she grimaced. How long had she been hyper-focusing on all this and ignoring the story she was supposed to be writing?

Long enough her coffee had gone cold. Again. She made herself get to her feet and stretched.

She hadn't shared the picture Alex had sent with anyone else. Alex hadn't told her to keep it secret, but it didn't make any fucking sense. Why were a cop and his buddy involved in a break-in and a fire at Stone Solutions? How had Alex gotten the picture—had he somehow been there? But then didn't that implicate him in the fire?

She'd finally been able to identify Stensby's companion, at least. She'd seen him at a couple of AMI events, and someone had been asking her dad for lists of AMI members who were cops and active or former military. She'd gone down that list, running names on the internet until *Keith Waller* turned up pictures of the same big blond man on an airsoft course's social media page. Stensby had been in a couple of the pictures as well.

She'd called the airsoft course already, but had only been told that Mr. Waller apparently no longer worked there. The woman she'd talked to didn't know where he'd gone. He'd been the manager; seemed like an abrupt departure.

Gretel frowned at her monitors again. She had articles to write, other things to research, but she had that itch in her brain that just wouldn't let this go.

In the days following Senator Hathaway's murder, Cedrick Stone had been implicated. Stone Solutions had, of course, denied the accusations. But Stone hadn't been seen or heard from again since that night.

And yet Alex had a picture of the outside of his office. He'd claimed he was going to write a story about Stone Solutions' security for his own empathy blog.

Tell me about your blog, she'd said to Alex. *What's it called?*

I haven't been bold enough to name it, he'd said in that warm Texas drawl. *It's just a place for my thoughts right now, really.*

She had his first name and a topic. Was that enough to find his blog?

Gretel set her still-cold coffee on the desk and got back in the chair.

★

Grayson's first call outside the AMI high-rise was to Diesel at the Salt Spring Island safe house, where he was recovering with Dr. Easterby.

"Hey, Blondie." Diesel sounded a little rough when he answered the phone, but then, spending days as a mad scientist's prisoner did a number on you. Grayson would know. "What can I do for you?"

On a night not long ago, but somehow a million years gone by, Grayson had hopped an emergency flight from Burlington, Vermont, back to Seattle and found Reece fleeing the fake empath club, McFeely's, and brakeless on I-5 thanks to an act of sabotage. When they'd finally gotten Reece's Smart car safely stopped, Grayson had sent it to Diesel's cousin's auto body shop for repairs. But since Reece was driving around in Grayson's stolen truck, his car was still waiting at the shop.

"You think your cousin might be open to some extra work on Mr. Davies's Smart car this afternoon?" Grayson asked. "It'd be hell of a rush job, but I'd pay like it."

"I bet he would. Andre loves a challenge," Diesel said. "What did you have in mind?"

St. James arrived on-scene just as Grayson was hanging up with Diesel. They stood together on the sidewalk, watching the chaos still surrounding the AMI store as an unmarked Stone Solutions ambulance that looked like a plain delivery van pulled up outside the building.

Grayson nodded at the ambulance. "That's for the thralls they found in the dressing room. They'll be taken to Stone Solutions' private hospital in Kirkland—heavily sedated and on life support, obviously."

"And no question this time that they were thralls." St. James frowned. "Who do you think barricaded them in a dressing room? They probably saved a lot of lives."

"One of the store patrons, maybe," Grayson said. "Could've been one smart, brave soul in the crowd."

"Hmm." St. James didn't look convinced. "We don't know which empath made the thralls."

Grayson tried to keep his voice on the nicer side of flat. "Considering my texts, I think Reece is the obvious answer."

"Not necessarily," she countered. "Mr. Eton and Mr. Pelham are Stone Solutions security who didn't report to work today. They could have been thralled last night by any of the three empaths."

It was a stretch, but Grayson let it go. He had something else he wanted to ask for from her.

He told her his idea, and she agreed and left to make it happen. He then spent the next few hours cleaning up the mess Reece had left behind at the AMI store, to the unenviable soundtrack of Vivian Marist, Beau Macy, and the entire Stone Solutions board of directors ranting about public image. Beau had, of course, immediately brought up the possibility of an empath conspiracy, and even if he fortunately still had no idea what kind of empaths were actually behind this particular event, there were still gonna be some messy media clips that weren't gonna help the public view of empaths.

Finally, though, he'd had the Prius towed and called a ride to Andre Lane's auto body shop to pick up the Smart car. Now he drove—carefully—through downtown, finding the entrance to the parking garage for Liam's building off one of the less-trafficked streets. In the garage, he followed memory up the ramp to the spot Reece had once directed him to park in, back when they'd arrived together in the truck, that night in Seattle a few days and a million years away.

He inched the Smart car into the spot assigned to the studio. The upgrades Andre had put in were exactly what Grayson had asked for—and not quiet. By the time he'd parked, four people were watching him, their eyebrows up as he unfolded himself from the driver's seat and awkwardly got out of the tiny vehicle. Admittedly, even alone, at his size he probably still looked like an entire circus exiting a clown car.

As he stood, he could see over the edge of the parking garage and down to the street below. The coffee shop where Keith Waller had once stalked Reece was closed for the night, but Grayson could hear a bar nearby, voices spilling out into the night. The other tenants had already disappeared through the glass doors into the elevator bay as he came around to the back of the car and popped the hatch. He held up his phone, making sure a full view of the engine was visible in the frame. He didn't want Reece to miss it.

"We're gonna see how you like someone helping themselves to *your* wheels," he muttered as he snapped a picture.

He locked the car and, instead of following in the others' footsteps, found the fire escape and stairs to the lobby's office, where St. James had left Liam's key with the office manager. He took the elevator from the lobby up to the fourth floor. As it rose, he caught his reflection, the dark circles beneath bloodshot eyes, the three days of stubble on his jaw, the grease in his limp hair. The past few days sure hadn't done him any favors.

He found the apartment number, unlocked the door and stepped inside, gaze darting around the studio. They'd gotten ahold of the building's security footage from the garage and elevator cameras, but there hadn't been any leads that way, and in the chaos of the last few days, St. James had only had time to peek in the apartment itself and confirm Reece wasn't staying there.

Grayson moved through the small space, taking the time now to do a deeper search. *Someone* had obviously been through the apartment at some point. The furniture had been left behind, including the television on the wall and the screen that partitioned off the bed, but the drawers and closet had all been emptied. The dishes remained in the cabinet, the top shelves still empty like he'd ribbed Reece about, and the pantry held a handful of staples like dried noodles, sugary vegan cereal and shelf-stable plant milk.

But Grayson had spent a night here too. And when he and Reece had left together for the airsoft course the next morning, his duffel bag had still been on the coffee table, the comforter and pillow folded on the couch he'd slept on and his toiletries in the bathroom. Now the comforter and pillow were on the floor, his bag was gone, and the bathroom had been emptied of everything, even his products—a crying shame when Grayson's hair was in desperate need of deep conditioning.

He almost could've imagined his night here with Reece—until he searched the messy unmade bed and found something familiar wedged into the crack between the mattress and the wall: the University of Texas hoodie he'd given Reece.

He tugged it loose and held up the wrinkled garment, the memories rising with it. Reece had slept in the hoodie the night they'd spent here together. Had Reece somehow snuck past the cameras and cleaned everything out, leaving the hoodie on purpose? Or had the empaths sent thralls, who probably wouldn't even have seen the hoodie tangled in the sheets?

Grayson set the sweatshirt to the side. Didn't matter. Either way, nothing surprising about finding the sweatshirt left behind; probably more surprising he hadn't found it in the dumpster. Looking for any sign of the old Reece in this new Reece was for St. James and Dr. Easterby. For people still capable of feeling hope.

Not the Dead Man.

Grayson sat on the edge of the bed. Someone with a typical sense of smell wouldn't have caught it, but a familiar scent still lingered on pillowcases.

In the airsoft course's parking lot, their bare hands touch, Reece's skin warm against his own. But Grayson is the Dead Man, and so he has to scramble to catch the suddenly unconscious empath before Reece tumbles off the truck's tailgate and crashes to the gravel. He gets Reece in his arms just in time and holds him upright against his chest, the same subtle scent of his hair directly under Grayson's nose—

Grayson ignored the memory and pulled out his phone; he was here for a reason, after all. He opened the picture he'd just taken in the parking garage and texted it to Reece. With any luck, it'd piss Reece right the fuck off; that empath deserved a taste of the receiving end of grand theft auto.

He set the phone to the side and lay back on the bed. He could almost hear their voices from that night here together, like the ghosts of Past Reece and Past Evan still haunted the studio.

But not only does no one give you credit, you know full well everyone is underestimating you, Grayson had said. *And you let them.*

I don't know what you—

Drive like an empath?

It doesn't matter how people interpret that, Reece had protested, even while he was dodging Grayson's gaze. *All that matters is they drive safer.*

But you know they think it means drive like a cute little pacifist carefully following all the rules. Not drive like a professional joyriding my truck like he stole it—because he did.

Grayson stared up at the crown molding, remembering more of his words to Reece.

That's right. I'm on to you now. Because I promised you that there's nothing you can do that I can't stop, and I'd be pretty bad at that if I hadn't learned my lesson about underestimating you.

Reece was right; he *was* arrogant. And he hadn't learned his lesson about underestimating Reece at all.

But he'd made Reece a promise, and he was going to do everything in his power to keep that promise—and stop him.

It was fully dark outside now, raindrops pattering against the black glass framing a view of city lights, even the weather reminding him of his night here with Reece. Normally, Grayson could just ignore memories and they disappeared, but tonight, the voices of the ghosts kept echoing around him, so that even the Dead Man couldn't forget he was in Reece's bed.

How can you be so smart and intuitive and yet not realize I need to be the one between you and the door? Grayson had said, as he'd prepared to sleep on the couch instead of the bed, despite Reece's protests. *Oh, that's right: because when it comes to danger, your common sense pulls a vanishing act.*

Reece had blinked in surprise. *Did you just call me smart?*

And once again, when I'm talking about your safety, I might as well be talking to a rock.

You did call me smart. Reece had lingered at the end of the couch, his gaze on Grayson. *And somewhere back around your circus analogy, I think you said I was cute.*

Grayson breathed in the familiar scent beneath him.

Yeah. He had said that. And that hadn't changed, even if Reece had.

From downtown, Reece had gone back to Owens's mansion. Cora had met him there, and Alex had joined not long later with a new thrall in tow that Reece recognized from the Seattle police force.

"Officer Kosler." Alex added in an aside, "He pulled me over for speeding. It didn't go how he expected."

Reece stared at Kosler, a storm of emotions in him. For fuck's sake. Kosler hadn't even liked him; why should Reece care if he was Alex's thrall now? "I didn't get to thrall Wayne Smith today," he said, trying not to look closer at the emotions. "We still don't have the fucking codes for all the glove materials."

"Because Evan was at AMI today," Alex pointed out. "We'll find Smith tomorrow."

I should be able to handle Evan, Reece started to say. *Just like I should have been able to thrall Smith, or thrall that woman at the store today, or maybe just not fuck up absolutely everything I do.*

But before he could get the words out, Cora said, more urgently, "Come look at this."

Reece and Alex moved closer to the built-in table in the kitchen. By unspoken agreement, this space had become their war room. Probably an odd choice when Owens's mansion also had a study and a formal dining room, both with bigger tables, but maybe even corrupted empaths were automatically drawn to the social spaces of a house, where people would be most likely to congregate.

The list Eton and Pelham had written of textile deliveries was off to one side. Cora had Grayson's laptop open, the flash drive sticking out the side. She was staring at a spreadsheet, her expression very dark.

Alex gestured down the hall. "Go find the man in the bedroom and guard him," he said to Kosler, who eagerly disappeared down the hall. He then slid into the booth seat across from Cora. "What is it?"

Cora gestured to the flash drive. "I found a glove materials supplier list to cross-reference with the delivery list, then wanted to pinpoint all cities with empaths. Except I found *this*." She turned the laptop around and pushed it across the table, in front of Alex. "Nothing we do will ever come close to the sick and twisted minds of these fuckers."

Reece leaned down too, peering at the spreadsheet. "I've seen this," he said in immediate recognition. "In the R & D director's office, that night I broke into Stone Solutions for the first time. This is the list of American empaths and who Stone Solutions thinks our trigger points are for corruption. There's me, and Jamey next to my name." A flare of anger rose; he slammed down on it before it could escape his control.

Cora's voice had gone tighter. "This version has some extra columns."

Alex pushed his glasses up his nose, peering at the spreadsheet as he slid the bar along to show more data. Reece leaned closer. *Suggested Approach*, the next column was titled, and there was more writing in the box next to Jamey.

Leverage St. James's enhanced strength and healing to prolong the process, potentially inducing a more powerful corruption in Davies—

"Jesus Christ," Alex muttered. "Is this—"

"Suggestions for how to torment our loved ones to see how it would twist us?" Cora said. "Yes. And it goes into more detail in the next columns."

"You're fucking kidding." Reece could barely hear himself over the ringing in his ears, could only just sense Alex's and Cora's matching rage over the fiery burning of his own skin. "Stone Solutions came up with this?"

"Maybe, or maybe these columns were added by Victor Nichols from Polaris," Cora said in disgust. "Seems like his style."

"And here's my row." Alex tapped the screen. "Whoever came up with this shit, they must've been compiling these ideas for a while, because the scientists at the bunker actually tried a couple of these suggestions on Evan—"

Reece shoved away from the table. He heard his name but ignored it, hastily retreating from the kitchen before his anger could escape and set off the new thrall—or worse, the neighbors. He scrambled down the hall into his bedroom and slammed the door shut for good measure.

They didn't get their slimy hands on Jamey, he reminded himself as he leaned against the door, blood pressure so high he could barely think. *Stone Solutions, Polaris, those creeps who had Alex in Texas—they didn't hurt Jamey.*

That was true.

But they *had* hurt Evan.

Fresh fury was coursing through him, fists clenched so tight they hurt. Reece forced himself to take a breath. Held it. Let it out, more slowly. Did the cycle again. And a third time, until the rage threatening to boil over had finally receded to a simmer.

He slid down, all the way, so he was sitting on the floor, his back against the door, still breathing slow and deep like therapy had taught him ages ago for his panic attacks. He would get himself under control. He would. He *had* to.

Corruption had a way of amplifying rage until it was clawing at his skin to get free.

He leaned his head back, resting it against the door, and closed his eyes. He just needed to get enough control over his anger to be sure he didn't flip the neighborhood from HOA to MMA. Even he could handle that.

His phone chimed.

Don't look do NOT look whatever that is it's not going help you calm down—

Too late. Reece had already pulled out his phone.

"You have got to be *fucking kidding me.*"

The words burst from him out loud as he stared at the picture Grayson had just sent: a photo clearly taken in the parking garage where Reece had sublet Liam's studio apartment, of the studio's assigned parking spot. And parked in that spot was Reece's Smart car, the hatch up and the tailgate down so that the engine was clearly visible—the *new* engine, which took up a sizeable chunk of the back of the car and had the word *Hayabusa* clearly stamped across it.

A text accompanied the picture.

Grayson: Since my rental is out of commission I got a new ride. What do you think?

Reece ground his teeth together and smashed out his response onto the keyboard.

Reece: What the FUCK have you done?

Two minutes went by, Reece's blood pressure ticking up point by point as he stared at his car. Then another text popped up.

Grayson: Just a little upgrade.

Reece's fingers flew over the keys.

Reece: You put one of the world's fastest motorcycle engines in a SMART CAR. That is a mod people do because they CAN not because you SHOULD.

And I KNOW you didn't think to upgrade the stock brakes along with it. Meaning you turned my car into a 300+ horsepower DEATH TRAP.

His phone chimed again immediately.

Grayson: Remind me: whose fault is it I had to replace my rental?

Grayson: And she's MY car now.

Reece's fingers tightened on the phone. Grayson was baiting him. That's all this was. Reece had stolen his truck and incapacitated his rental, so he'd retaliated by stealing Reece's Smart car and putting an outrageous upgrade on it. He was trying to make Reece say or do something stupid, but Reece was smarter than that. Reece was in control. Reece was going to put the phone away and go back to the kitchen to plot large-scale revenge with Alex and Cora.

Except he was already typing back.

Reece: WHY do you have MY car at MY apartment?

A minute went by.

Then another picture lit Reece's screen, this time a selfie of just Grayson, lying on top of what was obviously Reece's rumpled comforter.

Grayson: Maybe you're too chicken to text me your location unless you've sabotaged my car, but I'm not scared of you.

Grayson: So come on over, sugar. You know where to find me now.

Son of a bitch.

Reece stared at the picture.

Grayson was in his apartment.

Grayson was *in his bed.*

In the photo, Grayson's head was tilted against Reece's pillow, his normally flawless hair now unwashed and messy. He was wearing some Washington tourist T-shirt that he must have grabbed on the road, too small for his broad shoulders and fitted too tight to his chest and biceps. His hazel eyes were bloodshot, and the stubble on his jaw was too thick to be stylish, bordering on a scraggly beard.

Gone was the perfectly groomed and photo-ready Dead Man. In his place was something much more raw: Evan the Unedited Hot Mess.

And Reece couldn't tear his eyes away. There was nothing posed or staged about the picture. It obviously hadn't been sent to turn anyone on. Nothing more than a quick photo captured with the sole intention of trying to piss Reece off.

And it had. Reece was furious.

But it wasn't fury alone coursing through Reece with the power of a freight train. Nothing could have possibly looked hotter to his empath brain than this unfiltered and starkly honest picture of Grayson sprawled out in Reece's bed.

And there was no way Reece was going to keep control of his emotional projections *now.*

"I have to get the fuck out of here."

Reece was already scrambling to his feet. He shoved his phone in his pocket and grabbed the truck keys.

Two minutes later, he was on the road, tearing up the street but still seeing the mirage of Grayson everywhere he looked.

Come on over, sugar.

Reece had to get control. He had to.

Maybe if he fed the corruption, the black lightning would get bright enough that he wouldn't see memories anymore.

He slammed on the gas, like he could somehow outpace the storm inside him, and headed for the highway, to drive anywhere that Grayson wasn't.

The building staff at Stone Solutions had their own break room on the ground floor, a windowless space with two round Formica tables, a few plastic chairs and an old refrigerator next to an even older kitchen counter. Nothing like the break rooms on the higher floors, with their sweeping views, comfortable furniture and daily fresh fruit delivery, but they had their own coffee maker on the ground floor, and Wayne Smith wasn't much of a fruit guy anyway.

He picked a plastic pod of coffee from the basket and fit it into the machine, the scent filling the small space as it brewed into his mug.

Warren poked his head around the door. "Doing a perimeter check with Hank."

Smith grunted in acknowledgment. New safety protocols: no one alone and frequent check-ins. Management had promised the containment issue in R & D had been handled and the negligent parties fired. None of the security team had been fired over the property damage; in fact, they'd all received an extra two weeks' pay—conditional upon signing an NDA agreeing not to talk to the press.

Smith had signed. They all had, because groceries didn't buy themselves. But it had been a weird night. And it felt weird to insist on safety protocols following a lab leak, and the sudden panic at the American Minds Intact store had been weird as hell.

Everything about empaths was fucking weird. Maybe it was time for Smith to find another job.

The coffee finished with a loud hiss. Just as Smith reached for it, he heard a sound beyond the door, like soft shoes on the linoleum of the hall.

Smith paused. "Warren?" he called. "Hank?"

There was no answer.

Smith reached for his mug again, more slowly. He was used to a plethora of odd noises at night, bulbs flickering, machines beeping, the building settling. Except he'd put in fifteen years as night shift security. That had sounded like footsteps.

But then, he was a little jumpy from the other night. Maybe it was just the pipes, or Hank and Warren heading out for their perimeter check.

He picked up his mug and strode down the hall to his security room. He settled in his big leather chair, gaze on his many monitors and the camera feeds around the building, and sipped from his mug.

The soft and measured patter came again, *tap-tap-tap* from the hall.

Smith whipped his head around. "Who's there?"

No response. Nothing but the low hum of computer equipment surrounding him.

He stared at the door he'd left open behind him for a long moment, then shook himself. "Fucking paranoia," he muttered to himself. And ugh, he'd sloshed his coffee when he jerked, droplets now speckling his khakis.

He set the coffee mug down on the desk and looked around for a napkin or paper towel.

"It's Smith, isn't it?"

Smith's head shot up, his eyes going straight to the doorway. A brown-haired white man he didn't recognize was standing in the frame, studying Smith with pale blue eyes behind glasses. He wore a white lab coat over his clothes, like a doctor, and was holding something in his hands, small and knit, by the looks of it, maybe a winter hat.

"No visitors," Smith snapped out, his pounding heart making him extra sharp.

The man only rolled his eyes. He gestured at something out of sight down the hall. Then three more men were coming into the room, two large and brawny, the third holding a syringe.

Smith was out of his chair instantly. "What's going on?" he said, pulse skyrocketing, his eyes widening.

"I'm afraid you're being asked to expand your services to the company," said the blue-eyed man in the lab coat as the other men approached. "Rather permanently."

CHAPTER SEVEN

As the days go by after the murder of Senator Hannah Hathaway, we look to the governor to see who will be appointed to fill Hathaway's seat and perhaps take up the mantle of her popular bill, S.B. 1437, which would introduce several safeguards around empaths and the use of empathy.

The bill has received vocal support from several institutions including American Minds Intact and Stone Solutions. "S.B. 1437 will codify much-needed protections for non-empaths," said a member of the Stone Solutions leadership team. "We'll bring our full support to see it pass."

—*Emerald Tribune*, "Empathy debates heat up again in state senate"

Somewhere in downtown Seattle, a car alarm was going off. Grayson rolled to his back, caught momentarily between sleep and waking.

The wall stretches out in every direction, too high and too wide to see around. There's no way over it, around it, or through it. Nothing to see but gray, and gray, and gray—

And the impression of wings, sleek feathers so black they glimmer with ripples of light, like stars against a night sky or snowflakes catching in dark hair—

Grayson's eyes popped open, everything disappearing in a burst of white: a smooth white ceiling, white crown molding, the white light of a winter morning pouring in through the windows.

He stared blankly into space for a long moment, hearing his own breaths fill the studio apartment he'd once slept in with Reece.

Had there just been—in the gray—

The ring of his phone filled the studio, and his thoughts slipped away like birds on the horizon. He reached for it, head still on the pillow as he hit Speakerphone. "Grayson."

"Evan, it's bad."

St. James's voice was tight, way too tight, on the verge of angry, heartbroken tears like he'd only heard from her the night she discovered Reece's corruption.

Grayson sat up in the bed. "What's going on?"

"I can't talk. Check your email." And St. James hung up.

Grayson blinked at his phone for a moment, like the picture of Reece could give him a clue. Then he clicked on his email icon.

The top message's subject line leaped out at him.

URGENT: Stone Solutions Head of Security dead—suspect Reece Davies

It was from Vivian Marist.

Grayson stared at the subject line.

Yes, it had only been a matter of time before they had solid proof of Reece committing murder. But they hadn't had that proof until now. No wonder St. James was a wreck.

Grayson read through the email. Stone Solutions' head of security, Wayne Smith, had been found dead in a storage closet during the security shift change. His blood work had been sent upstairs to Stone Solutions' own lab; preliminary tests had already come back with adrenaline levels far higher than normal.

There were pictures attached. Grayson flipped through them. The storage closet at the end of the hall was the same one Reece had once been locked in. There were red streaks smeared under Smith's eyes, and his face was contorted into shock.

The final picture made Grayson still. There was no mistaking what was next to Smith's body, because Grayson was still seeing it every time he opened his phone.

A familiar winter hat, complete with bear ears.

His phone began to ring, and it was St. James again. Grayson answered. "Hey." He tried not to sound like he was saying *I told you so.* Even he knew this wasn't the time. "I just saw—"

"This is bullshit," she said, cutting him off. "It wasn't Reece."

Well. Denial was one way to take the news. "Jamey," Grayson started.

"You're going to try to tell me he did this, because you believe it, just like everyone else," she said hotly. "But unless and until Reece looks me in the eye and tells me that he murdered someone, then I am going to keep hope and faith alive. And no one, not even the Dead Man, can change that."

Grayson's gaze fell on the windows, speckled with raindrops in the pale dawn. "That's your prerogative, Detective."

"Reece didn't kill this security guard."

"It's Wayne Smith again. The same guard who roughed Reece up in November, when he broke into Stone Solutions," Grayson pointed out. "This is what corrupted empaths do. What they *enjoy* doing."

"But I helped get Cora in custody in November," Jamey

said. "So tell me why, when Alex and Cora were burning down Polaris, they didn't come for revenge on me."

"You're a tough target. Ms. Falcon already knew she wouldn't win against you—"

"But they spared Aisha and Diesel too."

"I know you want to read hope into that," Grayson said. "But corrupted empaths are sadists; they crave their victims' pain and rage and fear. Dr. Easterby and Mr. Lane were drugged and tied to beds; not too much of a stretch to think the empaths were after prey with a little more fight."

"Or maybe Alex and Cora recognized that Aisha and Diesel were victims too. Maybe even corrupted empaths are still capable of mercy."

"I saw the photos of Mr. Smith," Grayson said. "I'm afraid your brother didn't show him any mercy last night."

"Reece didn't do this," she snapped. "Aisha and I are going to find a way to save him, and your brother, and Cora. This changes nothing for us."

"It changes nothing for me either," Grayson said more quietly. "I don't have a heart to break."

She hung up on him.

Grayson held the phone, gaze on the screen and the image of Reece beaming at the camera in the bear hat. That empath was gone. Why was Grayson even holding on to the picture?

He opened Settings, his thumb stretching for Delete.

But instead of hitting it, his thumb slipped to the bottom of his screen, and he opened his text messages instead.

> Grayson: Message received. Don't bother coming over. I'll find you.

He sent the text to Reece. He looked at the picture again for a moment, the dark hair visible as a fringe under the bear hat. He raised his gaze back to the window, and for a moment almost thought he saw a snowflake in the falling rain.

The twenty-second floor of Stone Solutions' headquarters in Bellevue had once been Cedrick Stone's personal CEO suite, with a large entertaining area, a corner office, a private staircase from the roof's helipad and enviable views of Mount Rainier. After Alex Grayson's break-in and arson, however, Vivian Marist had been forced to have an eighteenth-floor conference room converted into a temporary CEO's office. With any luck, the board of directors would see fit to make her position as interim CEO more permanent, and she could remodel Cedrick's office to her tastes.

So far they'd kept the head of security's death out of the papers. It had to stay that way. No one could know that in this very building the night before, Stone Solutions had yet again been breached by the very empaths they were supposed to be protecting the public from.

No secret lasted forever. It was inevitable that someday the truth about empaths would leak. But when it did, Stone Solutions had to appear to be an impenetrable force capable of defending the innocent. Otherwise the public would look for another champion. And that would be terrible for share prices.

She stepped off the elevator and to her door. But as she opened it, she stopped short. Charles Stone was already there, pouring coffee into a Stone Solutions mug from the carafe that had been left for her on the mini-fridge.

And he wasn't alone.

"Vivian!" A strikingly handsome man held out his hand to her, tall and broad-shouldered, with lovely deep brown eyes in a face that appeared sun-kissed but was likely the highest quality bronzer. He was in his early fifties, but if he was hiding gray in that thick, dark hair, it was expertly done.

What the hell was Lucien Braun doing here?

"Lucien." Marist expertly smothered her shock as she shook Braun's hand. "This is a surprise." Her gaze darted pointedly to Charles.

"I simply had to share the good news," Charles said as he handed the mug to Braun. "I realize we have some unexpected business to deal with this morning, but when does business ever go as expected?"

Marist did generally expect business to go without the murder of their head of security, but she forced a smile instead. "And what's that?"

"It will be formally announced this afternoon that the governor has picked a replacement to fill Hannah Hathaway's senate seat for the remainder of her term." Charles gestured at Braun. "And we could not have asked for a better man."

Marist froze.

"No one could ever replace Hannah," Braun said, hand on his heart. "I just hope to serve the people of Washington how she would have wanted—particularly on matters of empathy."

"He'll be backing Hannah's anti-empathy bill," Charles said. "And of course, Stone Solutions will be backing Lucien."

"I see," Marist said delicately, her gaze going to Charles again. "Well, of course allies are *very important*."

Charles twitched, what would have been a wince on a man with less emotional control.

A too-loud ringtone, bright and perky, suddenly cut through the room. "That's the governor now," Braun said, glancing at his phone without turning off the ringer. "My apologies, is there a place I can take this?"

Charles pointed to the door that led to the small adjoining room that held Marist's desk. Marist kept the irritation off her face as Braun disappeared into her temporary office. As soon as he'd shut the door, however, she snapped her gaze back to Charles and spoke in a heated whisper. "Tell me you're joking."

"Lucien is perfect for the job." Charles wasn't meeting her eyes. "Whip-smart, camera-ready and firmly on our team."

Had Charles lost his mind? "He isn't even a politician—"

"He's more than ready for politics. He's been our best lobbyist for a decade," Charles said. "His law firm has gone international now; it's one of the governor's biggest donors."

"But I bet American Minds Intact donates more," Marist said pointedly.

Charles twitched again. That blow had struck home. "I realize Lucien has something of a reputation," he said, clearing his throat. "And it's natural to be concerned about that following him into the senate. But everyone has their vices, and really, when you look at the greater scheme of things, a fondness for beautiful women is quite forgivable—"

"Not to Beau Macy, it isn't," Marist said. *Because Beau will never, ever forgive the man who had an affair with his wife*, she didn't have to add. Charles knew. They'd all been there at the raucous party where Stone Solutions' preeminent lobbyist, Lucien Braun, and Beau Macy's wife, Adele, had fucked the weekend away on Cedrick's yacht.

"We cannot lose American Minds Intact, Charles," Marist said. "And that means keeping the AMI president as an ally."

"But we must look to the silver lining," Charles said persuasively. "Hannah had many strengths, yes, but we all knew her political potential had a limit. Her vices were far less understandable."

That was unfair, in Marist's opinion. Hathaway's struggles with alcohol and opioids had been attempts to fill a painful void. "Her father's suicide hit her hard."

"I have a nation to protect. I'm afraid I'll leave empathy to the empaths," Charles said shortly. "Even before Hannah's death, I was grooming Braun to replace her in the senate. I've known him nearly thirty years, and I'm pleased the governor took my suggestion in his appointment."

Took his suggestion. As if Stone Solutions, and the Stones themselves, didn't donate more to the governor's campaign than everyone else put together. Of course the governor had done what Charles wanted.

"Think of the benefits, Vivian." Charles picked up another mug. "Lucien understands the importance of pushing S.B. 1437 through the senate immediately."

"I might have chosen waiting a few months for funding over angering American Minds Intact," Marist muttered.

Charles waved that away dismissively, pouring coffee from the carafe with his other hand. "The affair was years ago. Beau will come around. And you will too: When the bill passes, we'll be able to add a driving range to Orion. Won't it be a treat to practice your swing there?"

Marist pursed her lips.

"You have enough to worry about trying to keep another empath murder out of the public sphere," Charles said in a persuasive tone perfectly manufactured from years of his own emotional training. He held out the freshly poured cup to her. "Let me handle Beau. You get the Dead Man on the line and figure out how to catch Reece Davies."

Marist sighed but took the coffee.

CHAPTER EIGHT

Are you against sharing thoughts and feelings with others? Do you believe emotions should stay locked away? Do you want to be part of a community of like-minded Americans protecting their minds from the dangers of empathy?

*Don't wait! Join now and receive a discounted price on your first month of membership!**

**Terms and conditions apply.*

—Direct mail flyer for American Minds Intact

Reece woke late, and with a headache. It'd been almost dawn when he'd calmed down enough to come back to Jason Owens's house. He'd snuck in and fallen into bed and a twitchy, restless sleep.

Now it was full morning, the sun too bright and making him mutter a curse as he reached for his phone. He had one text from Grayson and several from Jamey.

Grayson's was short and curt: Message received. Don't bother coming over. I'll find you.

Reece squinted at it for a long moment, but the words still weren't making sense. He sent a pair of grouchy texts back.

Reece: It's too early for your cryptic Fear The Mysterious Dead Man bullshit.

Reece: What the fuck are you talking about?

He switched over to Jamey's texts instead.

Jamey: You better not have done this

Jamey: I can forgive you for robbery and B & Es but this is the LINE

Jamey: I know you're too chickenshit to respond to me but listen asshole: I will find out who really did this. I am telling everyone it wasn't you.

Jamey: And I better be right.

Reece stared at her messages in a mixture of confusion and rising irritation. She was being just as cryptic as Grayson, and she didn't get to boss him around. Not anymore.

She's worried, said the little voice in his head. *Obviously upset. And she's right: You're too big a coward to respond.*

Reece took a breath through his nose, shoving the voice away.

His phone chimed.

Grayson: Is that really how you're going to play this?

"Play *what*?" Reece ground out, like Grayson could hear him. "Why do you never explain yourself—"

"Hey."

Reece looked up at Cora's voice.

She was standing in his doorway, her long braid rumpled where it lay over one shoulder, like she'd slept on it, and her expression grim. "You better come see this."

She sounded uncharacteristically urgent. He shoved his phone in his pocket and threw back the covers, grabbing one of his old hoodies off the floor and pulling it over his T-shirt as he followed her out into the kitchen.

Alex was already there, at the table. They'd kept Eton's and Pelham's cell phones for information, and now he held one of them out to Reece, who stepped close and took it.

On-screen was an email chain involving several people with Stone Solutions email addresses. The subject line was short but shouty.

Smith dead??

Reece stared at the email, as uncomprehending as he'd been with Grayson's and Jamey's texts. "What the hell is this?"

"Stone Solutions' head of security, Wayne Smith, was found dead in a storage closet this morning." Alex's own anger was simmering under his voice. "The last time he was seen was around 2:00 a.m. Staff was told it was a heart attack, but one of the guards on the email chain is swearing he heard Smith had blood tracks under his eyes."

Cora took the seat next to Alex. "So either there's another corrupted empath out there that we somehow haven't met conveniently killing the head of security that we wanted to thrall . . ."

". . . or, more likely, someone wants it to *look* like this guard was a victim of a corrupted empath killing to people in the know," Alex finished for her. "The guard we wanted, who also conveniently has a history with you in particular, Reece. I bet the storage closet he was found in was the same one he once locked you in."

The understanding sank in. "I'm being *framed*?" Reece tore his gaze away from the phone. "At 2:00 a.m., I was buying doughnuts in Tacoma; they're right there on the counter. You can both hear I'm telling the truth. I didn't do this."

"No, you didn't," Alex said a little more dangerously. "And I want to know who did."

"He's taking this personally," Cora said to Reece. "Like a master vampire who's pissed that his coven was attacked."

"People could at least do us the courtesy of blaming us for the *right* deaths," Alex said. "After all, if they want us to murder our way through Stone Solutions, we can certainly oblige."

Reece blew out a long, hard breath. His stomach was roiling with every kind of anger and the deep desire for vengeance, to fucking well *oblige* anyone who wanted him to stack up bodies.

But deep, deep down, buried under the fury, he could sense another feeling he didn't want to have: the painful ache of loss for Smith.

It made him even angrier. Why the hell should he be sorry Smith was gone?

Alex was getting to his feet, turning to Cora. "Someone took out Smith before we could get those codes for the materials storage, but you've got the list from Eton and Pelham and some good leads on piers. I say we find a new way to send a message to Stone Solutions."

Reece viciously stomped down on the grief before Alex or Cora could sense it. "Let's go, then."

"You can't," Alex said sharply.

"Your sister was a detective," Cora added. "You know that even if the cops weren't told the reason, they've sure as hell been told to look for you."

The mention of Jamey threw Reece's morning texts into stark relief.

I know you're too chickenshit to respond to me but listen asshole: I will find who really did this. I am telling everyone it wasn't you. And I better be right.

Someone was trying to frame him, but Jamey hadn't fallen for it. His brilliant sister, so full of faith—Jamey knew the murderer wasn't him.

But Grayson, on the other hand.

Message received. Don't bother coming over. I'll find you.

Grayson believed he had.

Reece realized his hands had balled into fists. "So I'm, what? Grounded?" he spit out, with much more of an edge he'd meant.

"If that's how you want to see it." But then Alex put his hand on Reece's shoulder. "I've been hiding a long time, and I know a thing or two about it by now," he said more softly. "You go out now, you're gonna project that rage all over the place, and you're gonna get caught. Am I lying?"

Reece clenched his teeth. "No," he admitted. Alex believed that was true.

"Just lay low today," Cora urged. "We'll be back soon."

Reece watched as they walked out of the kitchen, leaving him alone. Jesus. Even corruption couldn't stop him from always fucking everything up.

Evan never thought you were a fuckup, the little voice in his head said.

Absolutely not. He could not think about Grayson right now.

Except he'd already pulled out his phone.

It doesn't matter if Evan believes you murdered Wayne Smith, Reece reminded himself, even as his fingers tightened on the phone. *Evan is an arrogant asshole who's not as smart as he thinks he is. This is proof. Proof that he's all looks, no brains.*

Proof that he doesn't know me and never has.

That thought did not help.

Reece tried breathing through his nose, gaze going to the room's large windows that framed the gray sky mirrored by the gray waters of Lake Washington. His blood pressure was too high, his skin prickly and hot. If he didn't calm down, he was going to lose control of the anger, project through the house, maybe to the neighbors beyond.

I don't care what Evan thinks.

I don't care if he thinks I've murdered half of Seattle.

I don't care if I DO murder half of Seattle.

I don't care.

He glanced back at his phone, Grayson's last text staring up at him: Is that really how you're going to play this?

And before he meant to, he was texting back.

Reece: We're not playing anymore.

★

Grayson had just gotten into the Smart car when Vivian Marist called his phone.

"Where are you?" she said, instead of hello.

He tossed his hat onto the passenger seat. "Heading to Kirkland to see Wayne Smith's body." They would have taken Smith to the private Stone Solutions hospital with its private morgue. Grayson could check on all the other empath victims who were being treated there while he was at it.

"Good," said Marist. "Come to Stone Solutions afterwards."

He turned the key, then twitched at the sudden volume. That

Hayabusa engine wasn't subtle. "To see the crime scene? I saw the pictures." And Grayson had already seen that exact storage closet the night he'd rescued Reece from Stone Solutions, believing he was still too innocent to end up at Polaris.

He touched his shoulder, where his clothes covered the small round scar from the bullet he'd taken that same night.

He really had thought Reece could be saved.

"We're preparing for the governor to announce Senator Hathaway's replacement," said Marist.

"Respectfully, ma'am, I need to find Mr. Davies, not waste time with politics," he said, as he headed for I-5.

"This is of relevance to the Dead Man," Marist said impatiently. "Senator Braun plans to take up Hannah's agenda, not just her office."

"Which one?" Grayson said dryly. "The anti-empathy agenda and S.B. 1437 that's gonna give Stone Solutions all that money? Or the one you and I both know was Senator Hathaway's *real* agenda at the end, withdrawing that bill of hers?"

Marist gave a short sigh. "I worked for Hannah for years, you know. I considered her my friend. Her death was a tragedy."

What a neat little dodge, to redirect to her friendship with Hathaway and not acknowledge the near-loss of that pile of money earmarked for Stone Solutions. "Yeah," said Grayson. "A tragedy engineered by two of your colleagues."

"Perhaps," Marist said more sharply. "But last night, our head of security was murdered by Davies—an empath you promised us was harmless. Telling us we don't need to worry about empaths that are, in fact, big giant problems has become something of a pattern with you, hasn't it?"

Grayson didn't have a response to that.

"If you're not coming to Stone Solutions, tell me where you're planning to search for Davies," Marist said. "I'll send a team to you."

He took the ramp up to I-5, eyes on the traffic as he pressed down on the gas. "The teams can respond to thralls, not the empaths themselves," he said as the Smart car accelerated with an ear-splitting whine. "We can't risk any innocents near Mr. Davies."

"Yes, but—Evan, what on earth is that racket in your background?"

"My car."

Marist clucked her tongue. "I thought you drove a truck."

Grayson hadn't told anyone yet that Reece had his truck. Just one more mistake he'd made when it came to Reece.

"My truck was stolen." He cut off an SUV and ignored its honk. "I have reason to believe Mr. Davies has it."

"Why didn't you say something?" she said. "Send us your new car's information; I'll get your record updated so you don't accidentally get towed from our building. And I'll have your truck reported stolen. We'll have an APB put out to every police officer and Stone Solutions agent. We will find Mr. Davies."

Grayson's gaze stayed on the interstate, the gray asphalt under the gray sky. He'd been protecting Reece, and an innocent man had paid the price. It ended now. "Yes, ma'am. We will."

The remains of Victor Nichols's room service lunch were cooling on the hotel suite's dining table next to him. The muted television played a local station in the background as he leaned forward to examine his laptop screen.

Charles had forwarded a series of pictures and surveyor maps showing hundreds of acres in the Olympic Mountains. In one of the pictures, a portion of a building could be seen, set into the side of the mountain with a suggestion of more below ground. Nichols's pulse picked up.

He'd need to see it in person, of course. But this was very promising.

On the dining table, Nichols's phone began to ring. He picked it up.

"Well done," Charles said in his ear.

"I *am* the preeminent expert on corrupted empaths," Nichols said dryly. "I know a thing or two about how they kill. Granted, the illusion of a corrupted empath kill and the chemical actuality of it are very different things. You've had the body disposed of as instructed?"

"Of course," Charles said. "Did you get my email?"

On the muted television, a commercial for Stone Solutions was playing. Nichols looked at his laptop instead, the photos and surveyor maps. "You have my full attention."

"We'll call it Olympia," Charles said. "And if our next steps go off without a hitch, it will be yours to run as you see fit."

"Funded and staffed as I see fit?"

"Indeed. And I will personally deliver the first guest straight to you."

"We do have to catch him first," Nichols pointed out.

"It's been set in motion."

Nichols's gaze lingered on his pictures. "When will we move forward on part two?"

"Soon," Charles promised. "In a way, I have the empaths to thank for helping select the next target. They need to understand exactly who they've gone to war with."

CHAPTER NINE

Why waste time asking "who signed what" or "who authorized what" for the experiments that took place on the Grayson brothers in that Texas bunker? I don't see why we need to investigate or drag any of that into the light.

We should instead consider the advantages of Evan Grayson's new state. Evan has been improved. He is stronger and faster than ever yet no longer has emotions or attachments to interfere with his work. He's as dead inside as a corpse now—and in the fight against empaths, that's exactly what we need.

—Comment by H.T. on a Stone Solutions manual, *Anatomy of a Dead Man*

Jamey sat at the kitchen table, coffee in front of her and her headphones in her ears. On the other end of the phone line was Aisha Easterby.

"So you think Reece is being framed?"

There was no skepticism in Aisha's voice, just the compassion of a doctor and the open-mindedness of a scientist. Jamey wrapped her hands around her coffee mug. "Grayson thinks

I'm being naive and emotional, even if he's too polite to say it in those words."

"Well, I think Grayson should remember you were already a detective when he was still partying in college," Aisha said a little more dryly, "and he should listen to you."

Jamey snorted. "I don't have proof either way," she confessed. "But I've seen a lot of crimes. And I don't think this was Reece." She watched the rain falling on the trees, trying to put a gut feeling into words. "There's a body and a neat pile of evidence implicating Reece. Too neat."

"Like a magician's sleight of hand? Someone wants your focus on their illusion so you don't pay attention to the real trick?"

"*Yes*," Jamey said. "Reece is a lot smarter and more competent than he lets people think. He wouldn't have left evidence like this."

"But what if he *wanted* you to know it was him?" Aisha said, careful and gentle.

"Then he would have done something more dramatic. Something Stone Solutions couldn't have quickly hushed up, like they've done here." Jamey bit her lip. "Look, I know it sounds like I'm grasping at straws, that I'm just refusing to believe that Reece is really corrupted and capable of murder—"

"Or maybe you've got killer detective instincts," Aisha said firmly, "and you also know Reece better than anyone else does. I agree with you. He didn't do this. Let's find proof and remind Evan that *innocent until proven guilty* still applies to corrupted empaths."

Jamey let out a quiet sigh of relief. "Thanks," she said gratefully. "How's it going with the pacifist empaths?"

"Diesel and I split the list. All of them are present and accounted for, and most have safe places to lay low for a few days," Aisha said. "But we've got ten that still need protection." She coughed. "Good thing Grayson has a whole safe house here."

"You're not serious," Jamey said, even as a grudging smile began to play on her lips.

"A house full of empathy and compassion? Why wouldn't I be serious?" Jamey could hear Aisha's smile in the words. "Diesel's into it too. And where are you going to get a safer place than a safe house with a former marine?"

Maybe not surprising that Aisha and Diesel were in sync now, considering everything they'd been through together. And maybe combining ten empaths and two kind but traumatized sweethearts in a safe house wasn't the worst idea.

"I don't hate this plan," Jamey admitted.

"Evan will back us, I know he will, and he'll handle all the costs," Aisha promised. "We'll get them in the air tomorrow. What's the best airport?"

"I'll check with Liam, but my first thought is Bellingham," Jamey said. "We can fly them in from all over the country without them coming into the lion's den of Seattle, and then Liam could fly them up to Salt Spring from there."

"That's perfect," Aisha said.

"We'll have to make sure they all find and leave their Stone Solutions trackers at home, though," Jamey added. "Last thing we want is those assholes finding out we're moving a whole group of empaths under their noses."

"You got it."

"And Liam and I will fly up tonight, check on you both and make sure the house is secure."

"Absolutely." Aisha sounded happier and more hopeful than she had since Jamey had pulled her out of Polaris. "We're going to make this happen, Jamey. Have hope."

Jamey held her phone for a moment after they hung up, looking at her texts, her unanswered messages to Reece.

She wasn't giving up. But Grayson couldn't feel hope. He didn't have any hope that he could save his own brother.

A memory played in her mind, a phone call from the SPD's Officer Stensby, but the voice on the other side a stranger with an accent like Evan Grayson's.

Apparently Officer Stensby punctured the brake fluid in Reece's car earlier today. It's likely all drained out by now.

I have a personal interest in Reece's safety, so if you could get in touch with some of the folks back in Seattle and see if anyone can find Reece before his brakes fail, I'd be real appreciative.

I imagine you don't want him to die either.

Jamey had seen Stensby two days later, with her own eyes, in a bloody fight with scientists at Polaris and almost certainly under thrall himself.

Alex Grayson's thrall.

She rolled the phone in her hand for a moment, then opened her text chain with Stensby and began to type.

Jamey: I think Alex Grayson has this phone now. And if I'm right, I have a message for you.

Jamey: I know Reece didn't kill that security guard. Someone is framing him and I'm going to find proof.

Jamey: You helped me save Reece once before. Help me again now.

Jamey: I am not your enemy.

She sent the texts and then leaned back against the kitchen chair, exhaling.

Alex Grayson was the reason Evan Grayson couldn't feel hope.

But Jamey could feel it for them.

Alex and Cora had gone, having the new thrall, Officer Kosler, drive them in his cruiser and leaving the F-150 in the garage. The house was quiet in their wake, no emotions emanating from the sedated Traynor in the bedroom, just the endless patter of partially frozen rain against the window. For the first time, Reece felt completely alone in the house, and the solitude seemed to amplify the prickling on his skin, like the black lightning in his veins was now on the outside too.

He tried to shake it off, heading back into the kitchen and sliding into one of the booth seats at the table. The sky outside the window was a silvery shade of white now, the clouds thick with the winter rain that speckled the surface of Lake Washington.

"All right, Reece," he said to himself out loud, reaching for Grayson's laptop where it lay on the table. "Time to be something other than useless."

As he pulled the laptop close, his phone chimed. He glanced down.

Grayson: Fine by me. Next time we meet, you're gonna get the real Dead Man. The one that doesn't play games.

That arrogance was not going to help Reece's temper.

Reece: I've met the real Dead Man already.

Reece: He's a dick.

The flash drive Reece had stolen from Stone Solutions Canada was also on the table. He picked it up and inserted it into the laptop, then opened the drive. He carefully avoided the spreadsheet. If he saw those extra columns again, the suggestions for how to make Jamey suffer in order to heighten Reece's own paranormal abilities, he would absolutely lose his already tenuous grasp on his anger. Instead, Reece opened another file, the one he had caught glimpses of in Vivian Marist's Vancouver office.

It's a broken instruction manual, more or less, Grayson had said that day. *How to make a Dead Man.*

Yesterday, the mere threat of Grayson's presence had meant Reece couldn't risk thralling Smith. And now Smith was dead, and they'd been forced to think of new ways to interfere with the glove manufacturing.

Reece was going to make damn sure Grayson didn't fuck up their plans again. Reece could fuck things up on his own just fine, thank you very much.

The file opened, filling his screen. Reece took a picture of the cover page and attached it to a text.

Reece: Remember when you didn't think your precious little Care Bear could handle what was in these big, scary files?

Reece: Can't stop me now.

Reece began to click through the manual. The first few pages were biographical information on both Alex and Evan Grayson: birth certificates, high school diplomas for both of them and a college diploma for Evan Grayson. Was Alex going to be thrilled that Reece was going through his past? Well, if Reece could find a weakness in the Dead Man, it would be worth it.

And he'd just try very hard not to look at the comments he remembered had littered the margins, from the likes of Victor

Nichols and Holt Traynor. No, he very definitely shouldn't look at those.

His phone chimed again.

Grayson: You want my past, you go right ahead and dig. You could learn everything in that manual and more from Alex himself anyway.

Grayson: It was still worth protecting your pacifist side from seeing what's in that file.

Reece's eyes narrowed.

Reece: It was pointless. Everything you did, everything you tried, from hiding these files to that bullet scar on your shoulder. POINTLESS.

Reece: You were never going to save me.

Shit. Reece hadn't meant to text that much. He dropped his phone on the table with more force than necessary and went back to the manual. He clicked on the next page.

And froze.

It was a picture of Alex, a little younger than he was now, a beaming ray of sunshine holding a box of canned goods in gloved hands. He was standing next to a cheerful hand-lettered sign that read *Food Drive!* and flanked by two others of middle age, a woman with tan skin and hazel eyes and a pale man with blond-brown hair, both of them waving at the camera with smiles of their own.

Alex and his parents, before they were murdered to corrupt him.

Distantly, Reece heard his phone go off again. He glanced down at the screen.

Grayson: I bought us time before corruption got you.

Grayson: So no. It wasn't POINTLESS. And I'd take that bullet again for the pacifist version of you.

Grayson: But you've made it real clear that's not who you are anymore.

Reece swallowed. His gaze lingered on Grayson's words.

He believes you're a murderer now, said the little voice in Reece's head. *Of course he doesn't think you're worth a bullet anymore.*

Reece shoved the phone to the side without responding. He forced his eyes back to the manual and the older picture of Alex with his parents in the days before corruption and the Dead Man.

Don't click to the next page. Don't do it.

Reece clicked down, too hard, even when he knew in his gut what he'd see.

And there it was: an old photo of Grayson, taken next to the same black F-150 Raptor that was now in Owens's garage. In the picture, the truck was parked in the dappled shade of a stately oak, the tailgate down and boxes of food donations stacked in the bed. Grayson was casually dressed in shorts and a college T-shirt, crouching down to play with the oversized retriever trying to lick his face.

And he was *happy.*

The sound of the rain had been lost to the pounding of Reece's heart in his ears. There was a golden summer hue to the picture, the sky a brilliant blue through the green-leaved tree branches stretching up above Grayson's head. His eyes were crinkled at the corners and his mouth was partially open, lips turned up like the photographer had captured him mid-laugh.

This was Evan before the Dead Man—the Evan in Texas who'd loved his parents, and his little brother, and apparently dogs.

And this picture was in a manual dedicated to his transformation, the upcoming pages a detailed recounting of exactly what horror he'd been put through in an underground bunker as twisted scientists following orders attempted to make the corruption in Alex even more powerful, and Alex had made him the Dead Man so they could escape.

I can't undo it, and neither could you, Alex had said. *For all intents and purposes, Evan's transformation is permanent.*

Reece yanked out the flash drive, the picture of Grayson disappearing from the laptop screen. He tossed the drive on the table, slammed the laptop shut and ran both hands roughly through his hair.

Fuck figuring out Grayson's weaknesses. He had a new plan: learn the names of every person responsible for what had been done to the Grayson brothers.

And find them all.

He could start with Traynor—

Reece abruptly stilled.

He hadn't realized he'd already gotten to his feet.

Distantly, he could hear voices outside, neighbors beginning to yell. He couldn't let this happen; couldn't deal with Traynor on his own before they could question him, couldn't let himself lose control and start a neighborhood brawl that could bring the police.

He took off for the garage at a sprint, snatching the keys off the hook on his way.

He could lay low in the truck again, somewhere far away from other people.

CHAPTER TEN

. . . and as if the infamous hypothesis that empath are modern-day "Incubus" wasn't enough, that team has sent in yet another request for an unspeakably large grant, this time for a new study entitled "My Brother's Keeper: The Spicy Secret Lives of Empath Siblings."

Can someone please explain to Ted that EI funds are for serious research, not clickbait?

—Internal memorandum at the Empath Initiative

Grayson had gone to Kirkland and the private Stone Solutions hospital, only to be stopped short by the morgue supervisor.

"I'm sorry, Agent Grayson," she said, "but there's no body for you to look at. Mr. Smith has already been cremated."

Grayson blinked. "Mr. Smith was a murder victim," he said. "Why would he have been cremated already?"

"National security," the supervisor said, like that should have been obvious. "The instructions I received were quite clear."

"Were they." Looked like Grayson would be stopping by Stone Solutions to have some words with Vivian Marist after all.

He checked on the patients before he left. Vanessa Whitman, the former research and development director, was in the nicest corner room, her catatonic state unchanged since she'd been thralled by Cora Falcon in November. There were half a dozen thralls in other rooms at the hospital now too, all heavily sedated: Officer Stensby and Keith Waller, along with two others rescued from Polaris, and the Stone Solutions security guards they'd found in the AMI dressing room, Eton and Pelham.

Far as Grayson knew, they'd never kept thralls in this state before. It was dangerous; if any of them ever woke, they'd be violent and deadly again, likely to die themselves within a few hours but with the added risk of taking more innocents down with them. Something else to ask Marist about.

Grayson arrived in Bellevue not long later, pulling the Smart car into his reserved parking spot as the volume of his engine drew stares from the three smokers huddled under a nearby awning.

But as he started to open the driver's door, the sliding glass doors of Stone Solutions opened, and Beau Macy, the American Minds Intact president, came storming out.

Vivian Marist was right behind him. "Beau, wait—"

"I will not be placated, Vivian! This is a travesty—a sheer mockery of the American political system! I will not be made a fool."

The three smokers were now watching Beau and Marist with great interest. Grayson hunched back into the car.

"Beau, please." Marist was having to take quick, mincing steps in her pencil skirt and very high heels. "I know Adele and Lucien have a—er, a *history*—but it was just the one weekend on Cedrick's yacht—perhaps a mere handful of other weekends—"

"Unacceptable!" Beau paused to point at her. "I will not stand for this. *AMI* will not stand for this. If Stone Solutions backs that piece of shit as our new senator, we're finished. *Finished.* AMI will find another company to support. You hear me?"

He turned around and stormed towards a Mercedes. Marist

threw up her hands. "Beau!" She chased after him. "Beau, be reasonable—"

Grayson eased his driver's door shut. On second thought, his conversation with Marist could wait.

Alex lingered in the back seat of Kosler's police cruiser, door open, gaze on the text messages from Detective St. James.

> You helped me save Reece once before. Help me again now.

> I am not your enemy.

"Aren't you clever," he finally said to the phone.

"Who are you talking to?"

Alex looked up. Cora was waiting for him to get out of the car. "Reece's sister got in touch," he said as he held up his phone.

Cora's eyes widened. "Alex, no," she said. "No, no, no. You do not want a piece of Briony St. James. No disrespect, but she is too dangerous, even for you."

Alex's eyebrow went up. "That wasn't a lie."

"Because I believe it," she said emphatically.

Alex slid out from the back seat, joining Cora on the pavement. Up ahead, the pier was bustling with activity as a ship made its way into port. Kosler was somewhere in the crowd, confirming this pier was receiving a very specific set of shipments.

Maybe they couldn't destroy stores of materials at Stone Solutions, but there were always other routes.

"St. James knew just what to say to make me want to respond," he said as they watched the small feeder ship making its way toward the dock. "I should have realized she and Reece weren't a one-way street: Reece picked up deductive skills from her, but she's clearly picked up a thing or two about human nature from him." He glanced at Cora. "St. James is the only one listed as a possible trigger point for Reece on that twisted spreadsheet of Stone Solutions. But he's corrupted. And she's still alive."

Their eyes met, a symphony of conversation passing between them in shifts of expression so subtle a non-empath would never have followed.

"You're right, it *is* interesting," Cora said, as if he'd spoken his thoughts out loud. "You lost your parents. I lost John. Yet Reece became corrupted without losing his sister."

"But Reece did call to ask us to meet at Director Traynor's location," Alex pointed out, "because he knew there was danger to Evan."

"Oh, come on," Cora said dryly. "We're not actually going to talk about Reece being hot for your brother, are we? I thought we were politely pretending we hadn't noticed."

"Are we gonna keep politely pretending right up until Reece has a breakdown and leads the wrath of Stone Solutions right to us?" Alex countered. "I don't want them to ever get their slimy hands on either of you again."

Cora nudged him with her shoulder companionably. "So Reece called us in to help take down Traynor," she said thoughtfully. "He used his own new corruption to protect the Dead Man."

Alex made a face. "I am never going to get used to that moniker. And that's not a lie." He picked up his phone again. "But Reece makes you wonder, doesn't he?"

Their eyes met, another silent symphony of meaning passing between them.

"You and me—we didn't have time to save anyone," Cora said. "We didn't even know what was happening to us until it was too late."

"But if Reece was able to evolve in time to save Evan,"

Alex said, "could other empaths do the same? Could they *choose* corruption, if they had the opportunity, and the knowledge—and a powerful enough motivation?"

"What an interesting theory," Cora mused.

Up ahead, Kosler was crossing the pavement, making his way back to them. "What are we going to do about Reece in the meantime?" Alex said to Cora. "What if he runs straight back to Evan? The *Dead Man* is not going to have mercy for Reece."

"You're the one who made your brother the world's most unique and dangerous empath hunter," Cora pointed out.

A memory rose in Alex's mind: Evan's voice, hoarse from screaming, with a surreal hollow edge from the echo off the bare concrete walls of their cell.

Do it. Whatever you need to do to make me stronger, do it. I will get us the fuck out of here, Alex, I swear it. Evan had swallowed, blood still streaking his face, his eyes haunted. *I don't want to feel anything anymore anyway.*

It hadn't been a lie.

Alex shoved the memory away. Fire had been too good a fate for that bunker. "Our lives would probably get easier if we just killed Evan," he muttered, typing into his phone.

Cora rolled her eyes. "We're obviously not killing the Dead Man."

"Why not?"

"Don't try to bullshit a fellow empath," she said, nudging him again. "I know why you torched that bunker in Texas. I would have done it too."

"Fair enough," Alex admitted as Kosler approached.

"Alex, sir." Kosler was almost bouncing on his toes. "It's not what you thought. None of the crates on the dock contain thread."

Cora frowned. "But Eton and Pelham specifically remembered seeing delivery paperwork for a company called Metallic Tailors that makes heavy metal threads for the empath gloves."

"Did they ever take those deliveries themselves?" Alex asked her.

Cora shook her head. "They just signed paperwork afterward. But according to their notes, it's one of the companies that delivers to Stone Solutions' Bellevue location from this pier."

"Metallic Tailors doesn't seem to ship here, but this *is* a delivery port used by Stone Solutions." Officer Kosler gestured at the ship coming into port. "And that vessel has a shipment of rare metals earmarked for Stone Solutions."

"Well, in *that* case." Cora glanced Alex's way. "I might have an idea for that shipment, then."

St. James's messages were still on Alex's phone screen. He tapped out a quick text and hit Send.

Alex: Find out where you can get vegan doughnuts in Tacoma at 2 a.m.

"Lead the way." He pocketed his phone. "Let's go have a word with those nice sailors."

Grayson figured that if Reece had been trying to send a message with the guard's murder in Stone Solutions, there was a chance he'd left more messages at other familiar places. He'd spent the afternoon looking, checking the airsoft course in Tacoma, the café where they'd shared a midnight meal, the shady bar in Renton, the sushi house downtown.

Nothing. No more crimes; no signs of Reece, or of Alex or Cora.

Finally, as the pale day gave way to a deep gray winter twilight, he gave up, and was driving on I-5 when his phone rang.

"Did you see the news?" St. James said when he answered.

Grayson accelerated, the Hayabusa engine screeching as he passed an eighteen-wheeler. "What news?"

"Stone Solutions apparently made a *donation* this afternoon."

He could practically taste the air quotes she'd used around the word. "Do I want to know what they donated?"

"A small fortune in heavy metals and rare earth elements," she said, "given to a renewable energy start-up for their windmills."

Grayson blinked.

"The ship transporting the materials docked in Seattle today, then immediately pulled back out of the pier and set sail for California," St. James added. "The ship's captain sent a press release to every shareholder and news station about the donation."

"That doesn't sound like the Stone Solutions I know."

"No it does not," St. James said. "Those materials were earmarked for empath gloves. The move is being wildly praised by environmental groups, but Stone Solutions is getting a lot of shit for not staying in its lane and keeping the materials for the gloves. Xenophobia trumps helping the climate."

Grayson was definitely going to hear about this from Marist. "We think the empaths are actually behind this?"

"What, you think they're capable of murder but not sabotage?" St. James said dryly. "Liam and I are flying up to check on the safe house tonight. I called to tell you to meet me for dinner first."

"I don't have time to eat."

"Make time," she shot back. "We need to talk."

He could guess what she wanted to talk about: She was gonna want to build a case for Reece's innocence. It wasn't worth it. Reece had finally crossed the line and become a murderer, just like Grayson had always known he would.

"You sure it's worth your time to talk to me?" he said honestly. "With respect, ma'am, you know I'm not gonna be swayed by emotion."

"Oh no," St. James said, deadpan. "And here I spent all my detective years building cases for the DA based on feelings. I don't know anything about hard evidence; we took criminals to court to learn the magic of friendship."

That cemented the suspicion that Reece had learned sarcasm from his big sister, even if Grayson had probably deserved it. But still, this was her brother they were talking about. "It's different when it's family."

"It is," she acknowledged. "But you're also being very stubborn about this."

Obviously the Dead Man wasn't being *stubborn.* But he bit those words back; he'd failed her when he let Reece become corrupted, just like he'd failed his parents and Alex before. Least he could do now was listen to whatever she wanted to say.

"Fine," he said instead. "Tell me where and when to meet you."

Gretel hadn't had much luck finding Alex's empathy blog the day before. In fact, searching the internet for *Alex* and *empaths* had been surprisingly devoid of results; surely there was at least one empath out there with that name?

But *Eyes on Empaths* was the number one empathy awareness blog in the Pacific Northwest because Gretel didn't quit. Sometimes people went by *Alex* in English when their heritage was something else—maybe Alex was actually Alejandro, or Alexandre, or Alessandro, or another version of the name. Maybe he wrote his blog under a different name altogether, or under his last name, and she just needed to find out what that was.

When they'd met, Alex had mentioned that he'd been at the AMI meeting that had been happening when Reece broke into Stone Solutions. Gretel didn't have a copy of the sign-in sheets, but her dad would. Beau Macy had a small army of AMI interns whose job it was to save everything and make sure it was neatly categorized. They would have scanned the sheets and reviewed the attendees, adding everyone to the mailing list and looking for potential new donors.

Gretel got to her parents' home in the early evening, absently drinking her mom's kombucha as she sat at her dad's desk in his home office and booted up his laptop.

"Charles, this an absolute outrage!" Beau was in his bedroom, but his voice was raised enough to echo through the house. "I can't believe you've come out of retirement to try to talk me into this. Not for one instant will I stand for it!"

Gretel set her drink down as she put in her dad's password. *Charles* was also a popular name, like *Alex*, but based on the context, she was pretty sure the Charles on the other side of the phone was Charles Stone—and he'd royally pissed off her dad.

She unlocked the laptop screen. Almost immediately, an advertisement for Stone Solutions popped up on the open browser. She irritably clicked it closed as Beau's voice came through the walls again. "Oh, you're bringing up *my* indiscretions now? So Lucien becomes a senator while *my* character is under assassination?"

Gretel winced. She was well aware neither of her parents was a model spouse, but she had no desire to be reminded of her dad's many affairs, just like she really didn't want to write a blog post about Washington's new senator when he'd had a public fling with her mom.

She tried to tune out her dad's call as she browsed his cloud drive. She opened the folder for November and scrolled through files from the night of the AMI meeting. "*Yes*," she said under her breath as she found a scan of the sign-in sheet for the press and opened it.

There'd been a decent amount of press at the meeting: a few reporters, a kid named Connor Kendrick from an unspecified high school, and some names she recognized from social media. And then, near the top, an entry in neat handwriting:

A.G., Untitled Blog

Beau shouted from the bedroom again. "You're lecturing *me* about share prices? When Stone Solutions pulled that little green stunt today and sent the stock careening? Stop changing the subject, Charles, and listen to me: AMI will *never* put its support behind Lucien Braun as senator, you hear me? Never."

Gretel pursed her lips, eyes on the letters A.G.

I haven't been bold enough to name it, Alex had said of his blog.

"And speaking of share prices," Beau said with an edge of real malice, "several of the other directors had questions about that October 8-K. Roger brought it up privately to me yesterday, actually used the word *suspicious.* But of course, *I* came to your and Cedrick's defense. I said, 'It's nothing to worry about. There's no one more trustworthy than the Stones.' But perhaps I should call Roger next and tell him I was wrong?"

Gretel stilled. Beau's conversation had just taken a very interesting turn.

There was a long moment of silence. Then her dad spoke again. "Well, I certainly am relieved to hear that." Beau sounded very smug. "I appreciate that you see things from my point of view now." He paused for a moment. "Why yes, Adele and I are free for dinner tonight. Generous of you to offer. And of course we can meet at AMI before; we'll get that pesky press release handled, and then we can all enjoy the evening and pretend this conversation never had to happen."

Beau's voice was growing quieter now, as he was apparently placated. Gretel mentally filed away the words she'd heard to look into later and focused on her screen. "All right, then, *A.G.,*" she muttered as she cracked her knuckles. "Let's find your blog."

A few clicks in a search engine later, Gretel was looking at an unassuming blog that seemed to be mostly articles and a handful of pictures: never of A.G., but of landscapes and cities in the western US. She followed the link for an entry the same day as the November AMI meeting.

> AMI likes to say that all monsters claim to be harmless and that's how they lure you under the bed. Of course, AMI members also think monsters only exist as foils to the heroes: that they are and have always been monsters, intrinsically evil, born not made.
> No one learned anything from *Frankenstein*.

Gretel leaned back in her chair. Her dad did say that when he was talking about empaths and their pacifism. And A.G. was also right that her dad saw himself as the hero fighting the empaths. Did Gretel see herself that way too? She'd seen Reece Davies bruised and bloody because he wasn't willing to fight back; counting herself among those who beat up on pacifists incapable of self-defense wasn't a particularly pleasant thought.

She scrolled back up to the top and the more recent entries, until she came to one that made her pause.

> Sugar and spice and everything vice; we keep telling you it's what empaths are made of.
> Maybe it's time for more folks to learn it for themselves.

It was dated the same day Alex had sent her the picture of Officer Stensby and Keith Waller outside of Cedrick Stone's office.

"And everything vice," Gretel repeated out loud, frowning. What the hell did that mean?

And who was *we*?

CHAPTER ELEVEN

To: Marist, Vivian <v.marist@stonesolutionscorp.com>

From: Whitman, Vanessa <v.whitman@stonesolutionscorp.com>
Subject: the yacht last weekend

Well THAT was one hell of a party. Lucien has certainly kept our funds coming in. I hadn't met him before but apparently he's known the Stones more than twenty-five years. I feel like he reminds me of someone, but I just can't think who.

(He's a lot better looking than I ever expected a lobbyist to be. Can't wait for our next brunch with Adele!)

Grayson drove to the Vietnamese café St. James had picked and was led to a two-person table along the windows. He took a seat, checking his phone as he waited.

It was only his own texts still on-screen.

Grayson: I bought us time before corruption got you.

Grayson: So no. It wasn't POINTLESS. And I'd take that bullet again for the pacifist version of you.

Grayson: But you've made it real clear that's not who you are anymore.

Reece hadn't responded yet. Maybe never would again. Reece had crossed a line for good last night.

Or maybe you implied he's no longer worth saving, a little voice in Grayson's head said, *and now he understandably doesn't want to talk to you.*

Grayson hesitated. But no, that was just one of the lingering quirks of growing up with an empath, that sometimes your inner voice was real focused on other folks' feelings. Reece didn't care what Grayson said or thought. Reece didn't even care if other people lived or died.

St James doesn't think Reece committed this murder, the little voice said.

Well, people didn't always make the right call when it came to their family. Grayson would know.

St. James was one of the best detectives on the West Coast.

Maybe. But Reece had fooled even the Dead Man into thinking he was innocent once.

Their conversation from weeks ago came back to him, when Grayson first found out Reece could hear lies and had been hiding that secret from everyone.

I've been trying all day to protect you from this fate, Grayson had said to him in the marina dry dock. *I just didn't know I was too late. Corruption's a one-way street. Once it starts, there's no coming back.*

Don't tell me that. Don't tell me I'm doomed.

Reece's eyes had been so big, so full of dread and hurt. But the truth was the truth, and Grayson had told him the worst truth a pacifist empath could hear.

Your powers will only get stronger, and you'll become willing to use them for pain and worse as the sadism sets in. You say you aren't a murderer yet, but you will be.

And now that day had come.

His gaze lingered on the messages again, on the last thing Reece had texted.

Reece: You were never going to save me.

Grayson's hand strayed to touch the bullet scar through his coat.

Maybe Reece had thrown it all back in his face, reminding him again that the pacifist empath Grayson had known was gone for good.

But retaliating by telling Reece he wasn't worth a bullet anymore sure as hell wasn't the *nicest* thing Grayson had ever texted someone else.

"Hey." St. James's voice cut through his thoughts. "Sorry I'm late. I promise it was worth it."

Grayson dropped his phone to the table, automatically rising to his feet and reaching to get her chair. "Not like I'm gonna get irritated—"

"Sit the hell down," she said, already taking her seat.

They both ordered pho and Vietnamese coffees. As the waiter left, St. James folded her arms on the table.

"I have a proposition," she said. "Innocent until proven guilty, right? So you give me every piece of evidence you have that Reece killed Smith, and I'll tell you why it's bullshit."

Grayson had expected something like this. "Fair enough."

The waiter set their phin filter–topped mugs on the table

and disappeared again. Grayson began to count off the evidence on his fingers. "Wayne Smith was killed by an empath. He has a history with Reece and was found in the same storage closet he once locked Reece in, with Reece's hat next to him."

"Is that it?" St. James said patiently.

"What do you mean, is that it?"

St. James leaned forward. "Try this: Wayne Smith was killed by an overdose, possibly of adrenaline, which could have been caused by an empath but could have been the result of a chemical injection intended to look like an empath thrall's death. Smith was chosen specifically because of his history with Reece—a history known to the real perpetrator, who also left a decoy hat at the scene."

Grayson paused. "You think Reece was *framed*," he said slowly.

"We're not dealing with run-of-the-mill crimes or run-of-the-mill criminals here," she said. "Why would Reece have killed Smith instead of thralling and taking him? He was head of Stone Solutions' security; he had to be more useful to the empaths alive. *And* Smith was cremated before you could get a look at his body, Evan. Tell me that's not suspicious as hell."

She was grasping at straws, desperate to find a way to exonerate Reece. "I bought that hat for Reece," Grayson said.

Her eyebrows went up. "*You* bought it for him."

"Yes."

"The bear hat."

Grayson casually turned his phone face down. "What of it?"

"Because you call him *Care Bear*?"

"*Called* him, past tense, and I don't think I have to explain my reasons." Grayson folded his arms. "My point is that the hat was from me, and no one else knew that, not even you. It's obviously a message from Reece."

"Is it, though?" She put her phone on the table between them, facing Grayson. On-screen was a familiar store's webpage.

"The bear hat is exhibit A. Available at a chain retailer in Canada with overnight shipping to Seattle."

She flipped to a new webpage. This time it was Gretel Macy's *Eyes on Empaths* blog, specifically the picture of Grayson taken at the Vancouver auto show and shared on the site. St. James pointed to the corner. "You can see Reece in the picture. He's wearing the hat. The real perp might not have known you bought it, but they knew it could be used to link the crime to him, with the bonus that the Dead Man would certainly recognize it."

Grayson took the phin filter off the mug and picked up a spoon. "What else?" he finally said as he stirred the strong coffee and sweetened condensed milk together.

"Exhibit B. Finding this was the reason I was late." She opened something else on the phone. "Recognize that truck?"

Grayson stared at the phone screen, watching a few seconds of grainy security video of what was unmistakably his F-150 Raptor pulling into a gas station.

And then Reece jumping down from the driver's seat.

"What's this?" he said.

"It's from last night," she said. "When Wayne Smith was in that security closet, Reece was buying vegan doughnuts in Tacoma."

Reece's movements were so familiar, the hands in the hoodie pockets, the messy hair. Grayson realized he was reaching for the phone, as if he could go straight into the video and somehow reach Reece.

He drew his hand back. "How did you find this?"

"Got a tip. From *your* brother."

Grayson looked up sharply. "Alex actually texted you? He just ignores me."

"Like Reece ignores me," she said ruefully. She touched the screen again, the video pausing with Reece mid-movement. "But yes, Alex texted me back. I don't think he wants Reece to take the fall for a murder he didn't commit either."

Grayson's gaze went back to the grainy image of Reece. "You can't trust Alex," he said. "And Reece could have thralled Wayne Smith earlier in the night and told him to lock himself in that same storage closet—"

"Exhibit C," St. James said firmly. "Wayne Smith only ever hurt Reece himself."

"What's that mean?"

"You're an empath specialist," St. James said. "*Think*, Evan. We're not talking about what regular people would do; we're talking about what an empath would do. Would Reece bother to seek revenge on someone who hurt only him? Or do empaths, even the corrupted ones, only go after people who hurt the people they care about?"

Grayson sat back in his seat. "I appreciate what you're trying to do," he said, raising his gaze to meet St. James's eyes. "I thought Alex could be saved once too. All it got me was strapped to a chair in an underground bunker. I don't want that fate for you."

Sympathy softened St. James's eyes. "But what did Alex do when you two got free?"

"He thralled them all and set fire to everything in that bunker," Grayson said. "Turned everyone and everything to ash in revenge."

"Yes, he did," she said. "But revenge for *who*?"

"I don't understand—"

"Was Alex getting revenge because he himself was hurt?" St. James said more quietly. "Or was Alex furious that his captors had dared to hurt his beloved older brother?"

Grayson opened his mouth, then closed it. They were quiet as the waiter returned, setting big bowls of pho in front of each of them and a plate of greens, jalapeños, lime wedges and sprouts in the center of the table.

"Why would someone murder Smith and frame Reece?" Grayson said as the waiter left.

St. James set her phone down. "*That* is the question we need to be asking."

"But even if Smith's murder somehow was a frame job, Reece did set thralls loose in the AMI store," Grayson pointed out. "A lot of folks could've died."

"Maybe," she said. "Or maybe Reece trapped the thralls in the dressing room and cleared out the store before anyone was hurt."

"Why would *Reece* have been the one who trapped the thralls—"

"Because everyone else in the store was stampeding out in *fear,*" St. James said. "And if you accept the theory that Reece was projecting that fear, then it follows that the crowd would have been too overcome and too busy fleeing to secure the thralls, making Reece himself the most likely option."

Grayson's gaze went, unbidden, back to the image of Reece on her phone.

"Reece's compassion has always been his greatest strength." St. James picked up her chopsticks. "Maybe he's on the edge of mercy, his pacifism hanging on to that cliff for dear life. But I don't think he's fallen off yet."

She pointed at him with the chopsticks. "So I'm going to solve the case of who's framing my brother. And maybe *you* should take some time to consider why, exactly, you're so determined to believe he's unsavable."

*

Charles: The timeline must be moved up.

Charles: We enact phase two tonight.

Nichols eyed the message from Charles Stone, then pocketed his phone. Fine by him. The sooner he got out of Seattle and into his new facility, the better.

A town car was waiting outside his hotel at 7:00 p.m. on the dot, just as Charles had promised. Nichols had been driven to Kirkland, and the three-story unmarked building that served as Stone Solutions' private hospital and morgue.

An unmarked van was waiting in the delivery bay, a pair of men in dark coats waiting at its door. The interior of the van would be indistinguishable from an ambulance, but the exterior was far more subtle and forgettable on Seattle's streets.

A few minutes later, Nichols was in one of the hospital's finest rooms, a large corner space dedicated to the care of one patient. And there, sedated and unconscious on the hospital bed, hooked up to an IV drip, was Vanessa Whitman.

Nichols eyed her dispassionately. He'd met Whitman a time or two, before her brief stint as Stone Solutions' director of research and development, which had ended when Cora Falcon had thralled her and left her catatonic. Whitman was an endocrinologist who had been involved in the experiments on Falcon and Reece Davies; perhaps she would have been pleased to be part of tonight's orchestrations.

Well. Perhaps not if she'd known she was going to be the test subject.

Nichols touched his pocket. The syringe was there, along with the second vial, the very last of the limited supply he had crafted in Polaris.

But Charles had promised there was more. And with any luck, the new Olympia facility would be everything Charles had promised, and Nichols would be able to resume his work.

He straightened, pulling his hand from his pocket. "Load her up," he snapped at the waiting orderly as he turned back to the door. "We're taking her downtown."

CHAPTER TWELVE

Emerson Blackthorne leaned against the floor-to-ceiling glass of his skyscraper corner office. His pretend fiancé, empath Riley Davids, had kept his promises, his ragtag little conservation start-up working hard to make their neighborhood greener—and Emerson's company's reputation sparkle by association.

Compassion had no quantifiable value. It only got in the way of more important life goals, like making money. Yet somehow planting trees in the new park with Riley felt more rewarding than watching stock prices rise.

Emerson's brooding gaze went to the traffic far below. It was supposed to have been a fake engagement to an empath. Surely it could never become something real?

—Excerpt from the controversial romance novel *Engaged to the Empath*

Reece had driven for hours, until the storm inside him was quiet enough that the prickles on his skin had subsided. Night had long since fallen when he finally found himself downtown, turning off one of the busier streets to a narrower one.

He pulled the truck into a passenger loading zone, uphill, with the water down behind him, and idled for a moment.

You can't stay here, he told himself. *This truck is not subtle. Grayson might have told Stone Solutions you have it or reported it to the police. AND we're only blocks away from your old apartment. Evan himself could find you.*

Reece put the truck in Park anyway. "Let Evan find me," he said out loud. "I'm not scared of him."

Lie.

Reece clenched his jaw. Great, he was going to get pissed off again if he wasn't careful. But why should that make him angry? So what if part of him was scared of Grayson? That was just smart. Grayson was the enemy.

Say that out loud, if you're so sure.

Reece sat up abruptly, looking into his own eyes in the rearview mirror. "The Dead Man is my enemy," he said, nice and slow, enunciating every word.

Not a lie.

Despite the cold winter night, there was plenty of traffic downtown still. Reece let the noise swim around him as he sat back against the seat. There it was. Irrefutable proof that he believed the Dead Man was the enemy.

But not Evan, said the voice.

"For fuck's sake," he said out loud.

A cheerful chime chirped in the truck's cab. He'd been gone for hours; it was probably Alex or Cora checking in. He pulled out his phone.

Grayson: Do you still have your bear hat?

Reece stared at the text. "What the fuck," he said into the quiet cab, as if Grayson could hear him. Why would he ask that question?

He should ignore Grayson. What business was it of his what hats Reece had?

Or actually, no.

He *would* answer.

Reece stretched across the truck and reached into the glove box. He yanked the bear hat out and pulled it onto his head.

Then he held his phone out in front of him and took a selfie, making sure to flip off the camera. He didn't bother with a text, just sent the picture straight to Grayson.

A couple of minutes ticked by.

Then his phone began to ring, Reece's old phone number on-screen.

Obviously he wasn't going to answer that. He wasn't going to answer, he absolutely was not—

He hit Accept. "What?"

Grayson's deep drawl rolled through the phone. "You just took that picture?"

"I had a photo shoot last week, actually, *Empaths in Animal Hats*. It's an upcoming gallery exhibit," Reece said bitingly. "Of course I just took the fucking picture. Why?"

There was a pause.

"I'm sorry, does me asking a question mean you have to ruminate on how mysterious to be?" Reece snapped. "What is the big deal about a hat?"

There was another pause. Then Grayson said, "Because an identical hat was found in a storage closet in Stone Solutions, next to Wayne Smith's murdered body."

"You've got to be fucking kidding," Reece said. "Why would I have left my hat at a crime scene?"

"So that I would have known it was you," Grayson said.

Reece paused. That should have pissed him off, Grayson once again being so arrogant and making everything about himself.

Except Grayson wasn't wrong. If Reece wanted him to know he was murdering his way through Seattle, the hat would have been a good calling card.

And irritatingly, instead of angry, some part of Reece felt a tiny bit better. It wasn't that Grayson didn't know him at all; he'd fallen for the framing because the real killer had manipulated him with something deeply personal, something that could trigger memories and cloud the judgment of even a man without emotions.

Not that it mattered. Obviously. "Well, Evan, you *are* my obsession," Reece said, infusing it with years of practiced sarcasm. "Practically my every thought is about you."

As the words left his tongue, he had to bite back a swear. They hadn't been a lie.

"You can give me a hard time if you like, but *someone* killed Wayne Smith." There was a new echoey quality to Grayson's voice, like he was in a stairwell. "And I want to know who."

"Gosh, if only you knew a great detective," Reece said dryly.

"Your sister doesn't think it was you. But you still haven't said one way or another."

"Why would I tell you anything?"

"'Cause I'm asking you, Reece."

Askin'. Some traitorous part of Reece had always liked that stupid accent, and apparently always would. "Fine," he bit out. "Sorry to disappoint, but this murder isn't mine."

"*This* murder. As in, *this murder isn't mine because I still know killing is wrong*, or *this particular murder isn't mine, but boy howdy, wait until you find the stack of bodies that are*?"

Reece rolled his eyes. "Pick the answer that helps everyone sleep at night."

"It wasn't that one," Grayson muttered.

"Why are you acting like you care?" Reece snapped before

he meant to. "What difference does it make to you if I murdered the guard last night or if I murder ten people tomorrow? You're certain it's going to happen. And hey, just for old time's sake, guess what? That wasn't a lie," he added with a sharper edge. "I am truly certain that's what you believe."

In Grayson's background, a car door slammed shut. "Yeah?" Grayson said, voice gone lower, low enough to raise goose bumps on Reece's skin. "Then how about you say for me, 'Don't worry, Evan, I'm never gonna kill anyone 'cause I still know murder's wrong.' Is *that* gonna be a lie?"

Reece hung up instead of answering. He'd already talked too long.

He held the phone in his hand for a moment. On-screen was still the selfie he'd just sent Grayson, his own face looking back at him.

It was like looking at a stranger.

And then his eyes widened. "Shit," he said out loud, tossing the phone to the passenger seat and frantically turning the key. "Shit, come on, girl, let's go."

Because in the picture, through the truck window behind his head, was the distant curve of the Seattle Great Wheel, lit up like a beacon against the night sky.

Clear evidence of Reece's downtown location that even Grayson wasn't going to miss.

The truck's engine opened up with a roar as he floored it up the hill, away from the water. There was still downtown traffic slowing him, even on a freezing late evening, but it was fine. This was *fine*. Yes, he'd accidentally sent Grayson unmistakable evidence that he was downtown, and yes, the high-rise with the studio wasn't far away, and *yes*, Reece had heard Grayson's car door slam, but it was all *fine*, he wasn't going to catch up in the fucking *Smart car*—

Reece heard it before he saw it—the unmistakable whine

of one of the world's fastest motorcycle engines. He looked to the right, just in time to catch the sight of his own Smart car barreling the wrong way down a one-way street and heading straight for him.

Reece swore again as he accelerated, blowing past a Do Not Enter sign as he cut across the intersection against the light and the wrong way up a one-way of his own. He took the first opening, another left turn onto a thankfully mostly empty street, and gunned it.

After a handful of blocks, he glanced in the rearview mirror.

Fuck. There was Grayson.

Then the sound of sirens up ahead had his gaze snapping forward.

Fuck fuck *fuck*. There were the cops.

Reece made another left, careening back downhill toward the water. Maybe he could lose them all in the traffic and narrow streets near Pike Place—

At the bottom of the hill in front of him, a delivery truck pulled forward even as the light changed, blocking the whole intersection.

A flurry of thoughts went through Reece's mind in the space of a heartbeat.

The F-150 is big and it's blocking the Smart car's view—

Grayson can't see the delivery truck and he's barreling downhill with a Hayabusa engine and stock brakes—

You can swerve at the last second but he won't be ready to match you—

He'll be fucked—and all you have to do is keep straight.

Reece tightened his hands on the steering wheel.

And then, in the second heartbeat, he yanked the steering wheel right.

The truck's tires screeched as he turned into a narrow alley, fishtailing dangerously but not flipping. Reece tore down the alley, a local shop's outside racks of clothes and tourist knick-knacks flying up around him as he knocked them down with the wide truck.

At the end of the alley, he shot across the street and into a parking garage entrance, taking off the red-and-white-striped barrier arm like a bowling ball cutting down pins. His tires screeched again as he sliced through the garage, then took out the second barrier arm as he popped out onto the street on the other side.

He turned right again and floored it. A moment later, he was up the ramp and on I-5, with the cops and Grayson and the Smart car nowhere to be seen.

One moment, Grayson was chasing the F-150 downhill.

The next, Reece had suddenly cut right, down an alley meant for pedestrians.

And as the F-150 disappeared, Grayson could see what was at the bottom of the hill: a delivery truck, blocking the intersection.

He slammed on the brakes. The Smart car squealed, and Grayson had just enough time to swerve to the opposite curb right before the base of the hill.

He screeched to a stop, eyes fixed on the delivery truck. He took a breath. Then another.

If he'd hit his brakes only a second or two later, he wouldn't have stopped in time. His tiny car would have gone straight into the side of the delivery truck.

And he never would've seen the truck in time if Reece hadn't pulled the F-150 out of the way.

Around him, people were honking, the delivery truck only just now inching its way out of the intersection. He could still hear the sirens of the police cars, maybe responding to the APB that had been put out on the F-150.

Grayson ran a hand over his face, his heart beating unusually fast.

"Reece," he said out loud, a little helplessly. "I don't understand."

In the console, his phone began to ring again, Vivian Marist's name on the caller ID. Grayson picked it up. "Grayson."

"Evan." Marist sounded like she'd had a terrible shock. "You have to get to AMI headquarters right away. It's Beau Macy and his wife, Adele. Reece Davies killed them."

CHAPTER THIRTEEN

Congratulations on your promotion to director, Emily! Stone Solutions leadership has been watching your career for a while now. Your dedication to our vision is appreciated.

—Three-year-old corporate e-card sent to Emily Lowe

With St. James and Liam flying back up to the safe house to check on Diesel and Dr. Easterby, Grayson had sent a message and made his way alone to the high-rise that housed American Minds Intact headquarters. The AMI store on the ground floor still had a Closed for Repairs sign on the door.

Stone Solutions response had already arrived, the unmarked cars forming a line along the downtown street. An unmarked Stone Solutions ambulance was also on scene, parked just to the side of the building's entrance. Rubberneckers were slowing, both on the sidewalk and in passing cars, all of them watching curiously.

A blank-faced woman with short hair and intelligent brown eyes was waiting for him in the lobby. She introduced herself as Director Lowe. "I was told to expect you," she said to Grayson. She didn't sound particularly enthusiastic, but then, she was director of response operations at Stone Solutions—

the team that responded to suspected empath crimes. Her past few weeks wouldn't've been good ones.

They entered the elevator, and Lowe pressed the button for floor sixteen. As they rode up, she handed Grayson a pair of medium-sized latex gloves that were gonna fit tight as sausage casings on his hands. Grayson awkwardly rolled them on as they stepped off the elevator into AMI's luxurious lobby. At least twelve others were already at the scene, some taking pictures, some dusting for fingerprints.

"Over here," Lowe said grimly.

Grayson could have followed the blood trail for himself. Beau and Adele Macy were on the floor, slumped against the reception desk. They were both dressed in winter coats and accessories.

"Office services found the bodies when they came in to clean and water the plants," Lowe said as Grayson crouched down next to the bodies. "We intercepted the 911 call. Obviously we're still waiting on the official report, but by the looks of it, they were both bludgeoned to death by someone strong enough to shatter bone."

"What's the suspected weapon?"

Lowe pointed just past the desk, where a bloody golf club was lying on the rug. "Beau Macy kept a set in his office."

That would explain the blood. And the amount of it. Grayson touched Adele Macy's hair with one gloved finger, pulling it slightly out of the way. "Diamonds," he observed. "And those are real nice heels for a slushy winter night."

"They're both dressed up," Lowe confirmed. "They must have been heading somewhere after this. They hadn't even been here long enough to take off their coats."

Grayson's gaze went to the bodies again. Beau in a thick black coat and a scarf, Adele in a long tan coat with a stole. "Has their daughter, Gretel, been told?"

"Officers have been dispatched to her apartment," Lowe said. "Of course, the daughter will not be getting details."

That was procedure. This was a suspected empath crime. Stone Solutions would pack the bodies away to their own lab and spin a story. Gretel would never be told the real cause of death.

Grayson looked up from the bodies. The blood trail continued on from Beau and Adele Macy, heading down the hall toward the offices. "Who tracked that blood?"

"The perp." Lowe's tone had gone even more grim. "And you need to see this."

Grayson straightened up and followed Lowe. The blood was still red against the white flooring, a partial outline of a footprint here and there—bare feet, not shoe prints.

The trail led into the third door. "Office supply room," Lowe said, standing to the side so Grayson could go in.

He stepped to the threshold. The office supply room had three large copy machines, boxes stacked like Legos, and shelving along the walls that held a selection of pens, highlighters, dry erase markers and notepads of all types and sizes.

And there, in the middle of it all, was the unmoving corpse of Vanessa Whitman, Stone Solutions' former director of research and development.

Grayson stared at Whitman's body. "Dr. Whitman killed the Macys?"

"Well," Lowe said dryly, "she was the weapon holding the weapon, at least."

Because an empath was suspected of thralling and controlling Whitman. *Reece* was suspected of it. "Dr. Whitman was being treated at the Kirkland hospital," Grayson pointed out. "I was there myself yesterday. How did she get here?"

"We have no idea," Lowe admitted.

Grayson stepped fully into the room, kneeling next to

Whitman's body. She was dressed in a hospital gown, her legs and feet bare and streaked with blood. In fact, the only part of her not splattered with blood appeared to be her hands, which were perfectly clean partway up her arms like something had covered them. "Was she wearing *gloves*?"

"She was, actually," Lowe said. "We took them into evidence."

If Whitman had been wearing gloves, that didn't mean anything good. "I need to see them."

A couple of minutes later, Grayson was holding a plastic bag that held a pair of black empath gloves, spotted all over with the rusty reddish-brown of dried blood.

"We took the serial number from the gloves," Lowe said. "It was sent to Vivian Marist."

All empath gloves were printed with a serial number, which Stone Solutions used to keep track of which empath had which gloves. The database with that information was limited to senior leadership. Marist had access. "I need to make a call," Grayson said.

Lowe nodded and gracefully stepped out of the room, giving him privacy. Grayson called Vivian Marist's cell phone.

She answered right away. "You're at the scene?"

"Yes, ma'am." Grayson's gaze darted to Whitman's body. "I'd like you to confirm how you know this was Reece Davies's crime."

"You were shown the empath gloves, yes?" Marist's voice was tight and high. She might have been holding back tears. "Obviously I ran them through the database. Those gloves were given to Reece Davies."

Grayson's eyes went back to the plastic bag and the bloody gloves. "When?"

"This year, on schedule."

Grayson nodded slowly. "And is there any other evidence that this crime was Davies?"

"What other evidence do you need?" Marist snapped. "He put his own gloves on Vanessa Whitman to send a message."

Maybe.

But Reece still had his bear hat, the same one that had supposedly been found next to Wayne Smith. When Smith had locked himself in a storage closet in Bellevue, Reece had been buying doughnuts in Tacoma. And when Vanessa Whitman had been turned loose on the Macys, Reece had been sending selfies to Grayson.

Grayson cleared his throat. "How did Mr. Davies get Dr. Whitman out of the Kirkland hospital?"

Marist huffed. "I'm sure we'll figure it out. I'm completely shaken that an empath somehow got in."

"Allegedly got in." Grayson looked at the bloody gloves again. "And you're completely sure Stone Solutions isn't missing any inventory?"

"What are you trying to imply?" Marist said sharply. "Jesus, Evan. Perhaps you don't have feelings, but these were my friends. Beau and I have worked on countless projects and events together. Adele and I have brunch when I'm in town. And Vanessa—" He heard her swallow. "Vanessa deserved so much better."

"She did," Grayson acknowledged. "And I know you're probably feeling a lot of horror and grief because this happened to your friends. But sometimes Stone Solutions forgets that this is how the pacifist empaths feel when violence is done to *anyone*, anywhere in the world."

Marist was silent for a long moment. Then she made an impatient noise. "Is there anything else?"

"No, ma'am," Grayson said.

He finished up at the scene and then took the elevator back down to the ground level. He slipped out of the building, calling St. James as he walked along the dark street back to the Smart car.

She'd just landed up at the Salt Spring safe house, and he filled her in as soon as she answered.

"What a fucking horror show." St. James sounded angry and shaky, even worse than Marist. "This is what I've been trying to tell you. The empaths have done their share of crime, but these murders are frame jobs, and I—"

"I think you're right," he said as he reached the Smart car.

St. James paused. "What?"

"You're right." Grayson opened the car door. "The American empaths get their new gloves every year, and they can turn in the old ones to be upcycled. Does Reece do that?"

"Always," St. James said. "There are rare metals in the gloves that have to be mined by human workers. Even with all the worker and wage protections that the empaths fought for, Reece wouldn't waste the materials."

"So he doesn't have any old gloves lying around?"

"Definitely not," she said. "It's not easy to get extra gloves. Between public scrutiny and their trade secret paranoia, Stone Solutions tracks every pair. And the pacifist empaths care so much about not scaring people that they willingly follow the rules: They don't share or lose their gloves, and turn them in for new ones on schedule. Why?"

Grayson dropped into the driver's seat. "The night in November, the first time Reece broke into Stone Solutions, he took off his gloves and stuck them in the glove box of his Smart car. They were still in there when his car was towed to Tacoma."

"That's right," St. James said. "One of the Vanguards sent some new gloves for Reece, a prototype to beta test. Reece liked them better; I don't think he wore the old ones again.

But the gloves they took off Whitman weren't the prototypes, were they?"

"Definitely not." Grayson said it with certainty; he was *very* familiar with the prototype, thanks to a certain incident in the back seat of a truck. "But Reece still would have saved his old Stone Solutions gloves to upcycle at some point, right?"

"Absolutely. And with the move from my house to Liam's studio, he would have been extra careful to keep his old gloves somewhere he could find them again. In fact, just to be safe, he probably left them in the—" She inhaled sharply. "Are you still driving the Smart car?"

"I sure am." Grayson opened the glove box and reached in, his hand closing around familiar material. "And guess what I just found in the glove box."

He pulled two empath gloves out of the glove box, holding them up to the streetlights. "So, yeah. It looks like someone used Ms. Falcon's thrall to frame your brother," he said, "and we've gotta find out who."

CHAPTER FOURTEEN

On hiatus.

—Blog home page, *Eyes on Empaths*

From the murder scene at AMI, Grayson had gone back to Reece's studio. He'd sat on Reece's bed again, turning the case over in his mind while the black glass of the windows turned lighter and lighter, until a quicksilver winter dawn stretched across downtown.

Finally, no closer to answers, he sent a text message to Reece, then set his phone on the nightstand and his head on the pillow.

The chime of his phone woke him a couple of hours later. Without sitting up, Grayson stretched an arm out for it and glanced at the screen.

Reece: The last time you texted "we need to talk" I ended up in your handcuffs.

TWICE.

Grayson yawned, rubbing his free hand over his face as he tapped out a reply.

Grayson: I got them right here if you miss them, sugar.

Reece's response came right back.

Reece: As if I plan to ever let you put them back on me

Grayson: As if I plan to ever give you much choice. That's what this whole "you're an empath, I'm the Dead Man" thing means

His phone chimed again.

Reece: You're not making me eager to talk

Grayson rolled onto his back, settling into the pillows as he hit Call.

Reece answered on the second ring. "What?" he snapped.

Grayson didn't mince words. "Beau Macy and his wife, Adele, were murdered last night at American Minds Intact headquarters—bludgeoned to death by Dr. Vanessa Whitman. Her body was also found at the scene. I'm sure you remember who she is."

The other side of the phone went deathly silent.

Grayson cleared his throat. "Whitman was wearing a pair of empath gloves. *Your* gloves, with your serial number."

Somehow the other side of the phone grew even more silent.

Grayson waited.

"Sounds like an open and shut case, then." Reece's tone was like ice. "Obviously I got my hands on Cora's thrall and killed them all."

"Would I be calling to tell you what happened if I thought you were behind this?"

"I don't know, Evan," Reece said bitingly. "Would you?"

Grayson's gaze went to the windows again. They'd been so close to each other last night. Where was Reece now? "At the time the murders took place, you and I were on the phone. Now, some folks might point out you could've been distracting me with selfies while your thrall was wrecking AMI."

"Some folks," Reece repeated with an edge. "Am I supposed to believe you think something different? Beau Macy hated empaths. Why wouldn't Cora and I have sicced Whitman on him?"

Grayson raised an eyebrow. "Did y'all even know where Vanessa Whitman was being treated?"

"Maybe I found out and put my old gloves on her as a calling card."

"Would've been pretty hard for you to pull off," Grayson said, "considering I found your old gloves still in my glove box."

"*My* glove box, asshole, and maybe it was an older pair."

"Says the empath still driving *my* truck, and you don't have any older pairs. You upcycled them all," Grayson said. "Who's framing you?"

"None of your business."

"Do you even know?"

"Also none of your business."

"Reece—"

"We will handle it ourselves."

"The hell I'm gonna let you," Grayson said. "You think I want you and Alex and Ms. Falcon *handling* anything? How many bodies is that gonna mean?"

"Sorry, *sugar*," Reece said with deep sarcasm, "but we don't need your permission."

"Reece, your sister and I don't know who's framing y'all or why," Grayson said. "Maybe they're trying to rattle you out of hiding. Maybe they're trying to start a war and Seattle's gonna get caught in the middle. Or maybe they just want to get their hands on all you empaths."

"Mmm, yes, and that's *so* different from what the Dead Man and his handcuffs want."

"Oh, I want to bring you in too," Grayson said honestly. "But I'm not gonna run who knows what kind of experiments. I just want to make sure innocent people are safe."

"Is that what you're doing? Not running experiments, just protecting the innocents by locking up the empaths?" Reece said darkly. "Remind me: How well did Polaris work out for the empaths you took there?"

"Reece—"

But Reece had hung up.

Grayson looked up at the ceiling. That had been a fair point. He had tried to take care of the corrupted empaths, only to unknowingly send them to a terrible fate.

He looked back at the phone. Their text chain was still open, with last night's picture of Reece in the bear hat, flipping Grayson off with the Great Wheel in the background.

Dangerous as hell now, it was true. But still so fucking cute.

And also an innocent victim, in his own way, just like Alex and Cora.

But just because someone had been innocent once upon a time didn't mean they stayed that way—and it didn't mean they could ever come back. Bad things happened to good people—*irreversible* bad things. It was one of those unfortunate truths that made life so unfair.

Except someone is framing Reece now, whispered a little voice in Grayson's head, *and maybe he does need your help.*

His eyes went to Reece's picture again, lingering.

Finally, he sent two more texts and then got up to make coffee.

Grayson: You can hang up on me all you want:
won't change that someone's framing you
and I'm gonna do something about that.

Grayson: And I don't need YOUR permission.

★

Grayson's safe house was in a small cove on Salt Spring Island, with a big back deck and a short backyard down to a wooden dock that jutted out over the waters of the channel. The morning was cold, the air crisp and damp with rain as Jamey stood on the deck in her coat and hat, the phone in her ear ringing uselessly until it finally went to voicemail.

"You've reached Gretel Macy of Eyes on Empaths*, the number one empathy awareness blog in the Pacific Northwest—"*

Jamey waited for the message to finish and the telltale beep. "Hey, it's Briony St. James. I think you know me from when I used to be a detective with the Seattle police. I got your number from Liam." She looked up at the cloudy sky and tried to find the words. "Gretel, I am so sorry about your parents. I know you might not want to talk, but if you could just text me, I'd appreciate it. I'm worried about your safety. I'm worried about you. I want to help. Just—get in touch. *Please.*"

She hung up. Jesus, this was awful. It had always been gut-wrenching to talk to the victims' families, and Jamey knew all too well what it was like to find yourself without parents too young. And with the secrecy around empaths, what had Gretel even been told about her parents' murder? Would she even be able to bury them?

Up at the house, the sliding door opened. Jamey tucked her phone away as Aisha and Diesel stepped outside to join her.

"Did Gretel pick up?" Aisha asked.

Jamey shook her head. Aisha and Diesel had twin expressions of grief that mirrored Jamey's heavy heart. It was true that Gretel was the brains and voice behind *Eyes on Empaths*, and none of them agreed with her views. But all three of them understood loss, and none of them had ever wished something like this on any of the Macys.

"She could be in danger too." Aisha was bundled in a puffy coat, her dark hair pulled back in a sleek ponytail and a stainless steel tumbler in her hand.

Jamey's eyes fell on Liam down on the dock, prepping the plane. "I was going to stay until the pacifist empaths arrived, but I think I have to go back to Seattle." She ran a hand over her own hair. She was so stressed her curls were getting fluffy. "Are the pacifist empaths safe at least?"

"I'm in touch with all of them," Aisha promised. "They're all en route to Bellingham today."

And Liam would pick them up in the morning and bring them to the safe house. Jamey blew out a breath. It would have to be enough.

Aisha and Diesel exchanged a look. Then Aisha cleared her throat. "There's something else."

Jamey raised an eyebrow.

"Victor Nichols was supposed be researching how to reverse corruption," Aisha said. "I want that research."

Both of Jamey's eyebrows went up. "You think he was actually doing it?" Jamey said skeptically. "Given—" She waved a hand helplessly, like it could sum up *given he was an evil mad scientist running a lab out of nightmare.*

"He was a sick person with sick methods, but he would have at least been faking it for Grayson. There might be something in there," Aisha said. "I'm looking for hope anywhere I can find it."

Fair enough. "Speaking of hope," Jamey said dryly, "do you think there's a chance Nichols did die in Polaris?"

Aisha was quiet a long moment. "I wish I thought there was," she finally said.

Jamey nodded. “Be safe,” she said, and hugged Aisha and Diesel goodbye.

After hanging up on Grayson, Reece tossed the phone on the bed and stormed off. Anger was crackling along his skin again; Alex and Cora would feel him coming before they saw him.

Sure enough, when he stepped into the kitchen, Alex and Cora were already looking his way. “You have to see the news,” Reece said, snatching up the remote for the wall-mounted TV.

A moment later, the headlines were flashing: *American Minds Intact president found dead—*

“Oh shit,” Cora breathed, as Alex’s eyebrows flew up.

“The part the news doesn’t know,” said Reece, “is the Macys were murdered by Vanessa Whitman. And she was wearing *my* gloves.”

Alex and Cora listened as Reece told them everything Grayson had told him. Alex’s expression grew darker and darker.

Cora ran a hand over her braid. “So they kept Whitman on life support all this time?”

“Apparently, but why did she kill the Macys?” Reece said. “Last I saw her, you’d put her in a state of gibbering fear, not homicidal rage.”

“There are drugs that could send a person into a rampage,” Cora said. “Some of them are on hospital shelves. But where has she been? And who did this?”

“I think it’s time to talk to Traynor.”

Cora and Reece both turned toward Alex. The three of them exchanged looks for a moment, a conversation of feelings, not words.

“Alex,” Cora finally said. “Are you sure?”

"Traynor's gonna know a lot of useful stuff," Alex said.

"But once he's thralled, we'll have limited time with him," Reece pointed out.

"And we'll make the most of it." Alex had gotten to his feet. "But someone out there thinks they can fuck around using your thralls and your gloves," he said, pointing at Cora, then Reece. "And they're going to find out that I'm not gonna stand for it."

CHAPTER FIFTEEN

...and we do, of course, appreciate the funding for this new line of experiments. Arrangements have been made and plans set into motion. I have no doubt Alex and Evan Grayson will provide us with many new datapoints on the boundaries of empathic abilities and their potential for both offensive and defensive military operations.

However, while I agree that we must learn the empaths' true abilities at any cost, it seems to me that all our research dances around the real issue: why did the empaths emerge in the first place?

That, to me, is the question we should be asking.

—Three-year-old email found on a recovered laptop in [REDACTED], Texas

Lumen Field was welcomely silent in the early hours of the morning without its typical crowds. Victor Nichols strode down the hall of the stadium's suite level, keeping himself on alert. He wasn't hiding per se, but he also had no interest in advertising his location to corrupted empaths until he had all the proper safeguards—and restraints—in place.

Finally, he came to Stone Solutions' luxury suite and opened the door. "Hello," he called, leaning in through the frame.

"Ah, Victor!" came Charles's voice from deeper in the suite. "Come in, come in."

Nichols stepped into the suite. The far wall was floor-to-ceiling glass, framing the bright green Astroturf of the field three stories below. In front of the glass were two rows of plush loungers with perfect views, and filling out the suite was a private restroom, private kitchen and stocked bar, and a living room–style seating area with a television.

Charles was seated at the bar, typing away on his phone. "I'll be right with you—"

Nichols cut him off. "I was not informed the Macys would be at American Minds Intact when Whitman was released."

Charles stilled. He set his phone on the bar counter, face down, and looked up, meeting Nichols's eyes. "Because I had no idea."

Nichols folded his arms.

"*No one* was supposed to be at AMI headquarters with Vanessa Whitman," Charles said emphatically. "Poor Vanessa's time was coming to an end; it seemed merciful to let her die, and if her death could serve the company she served in life—well, I feel certain that's what she would have wanted. But I certainly would never have sent my good friends Beau and Adele Macy to be torn apart by an empath's crazed thrall."

Perhaps. Charles Stone, however, had helped design the emotional control trainings conducted at the Orion Lodge for Stone Solutions' leadership. If he wanted to lie, it would be near-impossible to tell unless one happened to have a corrupted empath handy to hear it.

Charles shook his head slowly, the picture of sorrow. "This is a terrible tragedy."

"And yet stock prices are back up nearly five percent," Nichols said dryly.

"You own Stone Solutions stock, don't you?" Charles said just as dryly.

Nichols pursed his lips.

"People are looking for hope in the wake of this unthinkable tragedy, terrified to have lost a hero like Beau. Share prices reflect that Stone Solutions is that hope." Charles gestured at the suite around them. "We've engineered empathy defenses no one else has ever seen. Cedrick even ensured this very suite is reinforced with empathy-proof walls and glass."

Cedrick was so paranoid he wanted to be protected on the chance the empaths decided to storm a football game? What a pointless waste of resources.

Using Vanessa Whitman had been a pointless waste of resources as well. Nichols could have made a study of her; now her body would be disposed of, just like that guard, Wayne Smith. Would an empath's altered sibling, like Evan Grayson or Briony St. James, have been able to survive the rampages that killed Whitman and Smith, to be used again and again?

"Your frustration this morning is understandable. It's always difficult when experiments don't go as planned." Charles steepled his fingers. "Perhaps I have something that can cheer you up."

He picked up his phone again. "I do, after all, appreciate that you have done me two favors," Charles said as he typed something into the phone. "And as I mentioned, I always repay my favors."

A moment later, Nichols's own phone vibrated. He pulled it from his pocket.

"Staff and inventory for your new facility," Charles said as Nichols began to scroll through. "Just received this morning."

Nichols drew in a breath. This was even more resources than he'd had at Polaris. "When can I see it?"

"Today, if you like," Charles said. "I can have the helicopter take you."

Nichols gazed at a picture of the lab set into the mountain. His work could continue. That was what mattered, not the loss of a stuck-up doctor like Whitman or a pompous ass like Beau Macy.

He looked up. "And my guest?"

"I have a plan for that too," Charles promised.

Grayson was grabbing coffee from the shop across from the studio when his phone began to ring, St. James's number onscreen. He stepped over to the wall and answered. "Grayson."

An engine roared in her background. "We're in the air heading back to Seattle," she said. "I've only got a signal for a moment."

Grayson dropped his voice to a murmur only she'd hear. "Status of Mr. Lane and Dr. Easterby?"

"Better."

He watched the barista steaming milk for drinks. "And the pacifist empaths?"

"All en route to Bellingham today. Liam will pick them up in the morning," she said. "But listen: Aisha wants Victor Nichols's research on reversing corruption."

"You really think that man had a single piece of research worth saving?" Grayson said skeptically.

St. James cut out for a moment. "—don't know," she was saying as she came back on, sounding very honest. "But whatever might be in that research, I know that if someone is going to have their hands on it, I want it to be Aisha and not another ghoul like Nichols."

Grayson hadn't thought about it that way. "All right," he said, "I agree with you there."

Her response came in garbled and patchy. "—Aisha doesn't work there anymore—doesn't have access to their files—"

"The research wouldn't be that easy for your average Stone Solutions employee to get anyway," he pointed out. "Emergency protocols would have been initiated when Alex broke into Polaris. Deleting sensitive files would've happened automatically—"

The line died.

He palmed the phone for a moment. St. James had been right about all of it: The empaths were being framed—Reece in particular—and whoever was involved knew what they were doing.

And Nichols was still missing.

The barista called out his drink. Grayson stepped up to the counter and took it, still lost in his own thoughts.

There was, of course, the possibility that the missing Dr. Nichols was involved in the framing. If so, what was his motive? His endgame? What did he want with Reece?

Aisha and Diesel described Nichols's twisted experiments at Polaris, the little voice in his head pointed out. *Reece's liminal state wasn't supposed to be possible, and now no one knows how he became corrupted. He's a walking contradiction offering endless knowledge to be mined. Take three guesses what Nichols would want with him—*

The shock of hot coffee on skin jolted Grayson out of his thoughts. He glanced down at his hand. He'd squeezed the coffee so tightly the lid had popped off.

Grayson shook his hand, droplets splattering. He reached for the napkin dispenser on the counter. Wasn't like him to be careless like that.

But he'd been so focused on catching the empaths that he'd

let the search for Nichols slide. That ended now. If Jamey and Aisha wanted that research, Grayson would get it for them.

And if he could find Dr. Nichols in the process, he had some plans for that man too.

Vivian Marist stood by the windows in her temporary eighteenth-floor office, staring at nothing in particular. She had had plenty of rough days in her career, days she didn't want to show up or days she didn't want to face.

This was absolutely one of them.

And the empaths were yet again responsible.

Not all empaths were the enemy. She did fully acknowledge that fact. In fact, none of them were—not at first. But all of them had the potential to become terrifying killers posing the highest possible danger to non-empaths.

She hadn't known that when she worked for Hannah Hathaway. Back then, they'd been focused on privacy concerns—and Marist was cynical and realist enough to admit they were even more focused on Hannah's senate re-election. Anti-empathy legislation was an area ripe for political exploitation, to garner votes by leveraging fear that other people were a threat. Oldest trick in the book, and it had worked wonders for Hannah's career.

Whether it was actually good for America to foster fear instead of compassion, to set people against each other instead of working for the good of everyone, well. Those were questions for philosophers. She'd had a job to do.

There was a polite knock on the door. A moment later, it was cracked open, and Anthony Sayers, Stone Solutions' director of media relations, poked his head in. "Senator Braun is here. He'd like a quick word."

"Marvelous," she muttered.

"I had Felix interview Braun by the sign out front," he said.

"Great optics; I'll send the clips out with the release about the Macys' deaths."

Marist's lips tightened.

Anthony held the door wider, and Braun and his entourage walked in, at least six additional and likely unnecessary people. Marist reluctantly turned away from the window.

"Vivian." Braun stretched out to clasp her hand. "What a tragedy this is. A loss of a great American hero."

"Thank you," she said. "It's very shocking."

"I'm sure," Braun said sympathetically. "Of course, as Charles would say, we should look to the silver lining."

Marist could not have heard that right. "Excuse me?"

"Hannah's shoes will be impossible to fill," Braun said, "but now there are no more barriers to support for my campaign from Stone Solutions or American Minds Intact. I do appreciate having both such venerable institutions backing me. I've got three interviews already lined up for today; any chance you'd be available to join me?"

Marist stared at him.

He spread his hands. "Are you already booked?" he asked nicely.

She glanced at the others, then dropped her voice. "The bodies aren't even cold," she hissed through her teeth, too quietly for their assistants to overhear.

"Oh, I don't know about that." Braun leaned in close to her. "I fucked Adele, remember?" he added in an equally quiet undertone. "So I can tell you she was already frigid as hell."

As Marist's mouth opened in shock, he pulled back. "I think if you check your email this morning, you'll find the entire Stone Solutions' board of directors united in their support of me—well, all except for poor Beau, of course," he said, his voice loud enough to carry to the others again. "I look forward to having you on board as well. I hope I'm not imposing if we borrow a Stone Solutions conference room for the interviews?"

And Braun and his group left, leaving Marist staring after them.

Alex stood with Cora and Reece at the door to Traynor's room. "I think I should handle this," he said to them.

Reece frowned. "I can thrall him."

Cora put a hand on Reece's shoulder. "This one is Alex's."

Reece frowned, looking at Alex. They were the same height, making it easy to look into each other's eyes and read the emotion there. Reece's were like a choppy ocean, a tumult of emotions battering him around.

"You know I have unfinished business with Traynor," Alex said wryly. "I've been waiting for this for a long time."

Reece sighed but nodded. "All right," he said, grumpy but willing. He turned, heading down the hall with Cora.

Alex put his hand on the door handle, then hesitated.

The Macys had been murdered.

Gretel's parents.

Unbidden, it brought up the memories, walking into his home that night two years ago, the moments that had changed everything. A too-quiet ranch, the birds oddly silent. He should have known someone was there—

He took a breath through his nose. The memories would be useful fuel for what was coming.

He stepped into the room. Traynor was on the bed, Kosler at his side, ready to hold him down. As Traynor's eyes opened, Alex moved into his line of vision. "Hey, Director," he said winningly. "Welcome back."

It was obvious the instant Traynor recognized him, the way his eyes widened, the fear he couldn't hide.

"I see you remember me," Alex said, calm and casual, as

Traynor tried to sit up and Kosler forced him back down. "That's good. I remember you too."

He sat on edge of the mattress. "I'm sure you know where this is going, but I needed you to have a moment of full awareness of what's about to happen to you," he said patiently, like Traynor wasn't thrashing in the bed. "See, I can control your emotions, it's true, but it's never as much fun as seeing someone's independent emotions, you know?"

Fear and fury played together on Traynor's face. "You can't do this," he ground out.

Lie. Of course it was a lie; Traynor was well aware of what Alex could do. "You should be excited," he said, hearing his tone get darker. "Excited to see if those experiments in that Texas bunker were a success—if Evan's pain did make my abilities stronger."

Traynor recoiled as Alex leaned in. "I'm going to tell you in excruciating detail what Victor Nichols was doing to empaths and their siblings in Polaris," Alex said. "And then I'm going to tell you everything that happened to Evan. He *wanted* me to make him the Dead Man, do you understand? He was so broken after what happened to our parents, to me, to him in that bunker, that he never wanted to have another feeling again."

The fear won over the fury on Traynor's face.

"And when I think you finally understand what you and your cronies have done, I'm going to make you our sycophant the way you were for the Stones," Alex said. "You're going to tell us everything you know, and then, when you're no longer useful, you're going to die in the slowest and most painful way I can come up with. You have a lot to answer for, Director Traynor. I hope it was worth it."

CHAPTER SIXTEEN

A new senate bill would keep Americans safer from the dangers of empathy. Don't let others into your heart: say YES to S.B. 1437 and call your representatives today!

—Stone Solutions–sponsored ad

From the coffee shop, Grayson drove over to Stone Solutions in Bellevue. The receptionist directed him up to the eighteenth floor, where they'd apparently set up a temporary CEO suite. He found Vivian Marist tucked away in the office area, seated behind a large desk. She was on the phone, but looked up as he walked in.

"Taye, love, I've got company," she said in an undertone. Talking to her secret boyfriend, Assistant Director Jacobs of the FBI, then, and Grayson probably hadn't been supposed to hear that.

He waited politely, gaze going to the walls. He recognized the art as some of the Washington scenery that had hung in Vanessa Whitman's office, though Whitman hadn't had one of the telltale television-sized monitors mounted on the wall. He stepped forward, running fingers under the edge until he found the power source.

The screen lit up with the empath tracking map, blue dots spread across North America, three red dots clustered together to the side out in the ocean. Alex, Cora and Reece. Locations unknown.

Marist set the phone on the desk and looked up at Grayson. "I hope you're here to tell me Mr. Davies is in custody."

His gaze darted over the blue dots. Ten of the dots should have shown today as en route to Bellingham, Washington, but St. James and Dr. Easterby's plan had worked, and all of them were showing right at home. "I'm afraid things are a bit more complicated than I first realized."

"Aren't they always when it comes to you and the empaths," Marist said flatly.

Grayson ignored it. He was here for information, not to make friends. "You got an empath tracker map installed in here?"

Marist nodded at the screen. "That one was Cedrick's. It survived the—well, you know. The fire." *The one your brother set* hung in the air between them. Her face was impassive, but there was a hint of challenge in her eyes. *Whose side are you really on?* she might as well have said out loud.

Grayson ignored that too, turning off the screen and back to her. "I heard Dr. Nichols was presumed dead."

"And?" she said measuredly.

"Just wondering if you've heard any different."

"Your brother destroyed Polaris after *you* told us he was dead," she said more sharply. "And you're asking us to tell you about Victor?"

Grayson tilted his head. "How much did you know about Dr. Nichols's work at Polaris?"

Her jaw tightened, her hesitation short but unmistakable. "I never asked for details."

"But you might've heard a thing or two."

"I don't give credence to rumors," she said, but with less conviction. "Are you asking about Victor for a reason?"

"If you'll recall, one of my conditions for taking on the role of the Dead Man was that Dr. Nichols use Polaris's resources to research how to reverse the corruption in empaths," Grayson said. "I need a copy of that research."

"Everything was destroyed when Polaris went into lockdown," Marist said.

"I know," Grayson said, "but I don't believe for a moment that Dr. Nichols didn't have backups. Who did he work with most closely outside his little empire?"

"I'm sure I couldn't say."

"I'm sure you could try," Grayson said.

She pursed her lips. "Holt, perhaps," she finally said. "The three of us used to chat quite regularly, dinners and such. Victor and I have never been what you'd call *friends*, but he and Holt got on very well—as well as Victor ever got on with anyone, at least. He certainly never had any shame asking Holt for EI funding or backing."

"Would that funding or backing have led Dr. Nichols to send Director Traynor a copy of his research?"

"It's possible." Marist drummed her nails on the desk, her expression pensive. "Victor doesn't have much trust in the cloud. If he did make a copy of his research for Holt, he likely sent it on an external drive."

Like the one Grayson and Reece had found in her office, hidden behind one of her photographs.

But then she surprised him. "And you deserve to know: Nichols had an external drive with quite a lot on *you*. I have a copy in my office in Vancouver."

Not anymore, she didn't, not after Reece had stolen it. There was a hint of distaste on her face. She didn't seem to be Nichols's biggest fan; maybe she didn't look at the drive often and hadn't realized it was gone yet. "A number of folks have wanted to study the Dead Man," Grayson said. "And it's not like I've got feelings about that."

Marist's gaze flicked over him. "He was obsessed with the idea of trying to duplicate you."

"I'm a pretty good empathy defense," Grayson said. "I'd think all of Stone Solutions would want the same."

"Not all of us," she said more tightly. "I may not be one of your empaths, but I am capable of empathy. What happened to you should never be duplicated."

"I'd say thank you," he said, "but I know you don't just mean what happened in that bunker. You think Alex shouldn't've changed me. You think he's a parasite."

She met his eyes, her own cool and blue. "If he is and you're his victim, you're not exactly going to be able to see that yourself, are you?"

Grayson leaned against the window. "Alex has his issues these days," he admitted. "But growing up, he was the kindest kid brother anyone could ask for. So if you're looking for a monster, find out who had our parents murdered to change Alex into what he is now."

They held each other's gaze for a long moment.

"Would you like me to have someone check if Holt received a package from British Columbia at his DC office recently?" Marist finally said.

"Thank you, ma'am, but I'll start my search here," he said, "with EI's Seattle office."

Maybe Reece hadn't committed the murders he was being blamed for, but he was dangerously close to initiating a murder spree that started with Holt Traynor.

He leaned against the kitchen wall, narrow-eyed gaze on Traynor where he stood by the built-in dinette in the kitchen.

Alex and Cora sat at the table themselves, across from each other like adorable bookends, belying that they were dangerous murderers themselves. Cora had sent the thralled Officer Kosler out to the yard, ostensibly to patrol for danger but probably to keep some distance from Reece's hair-trigger projections. Reece couldn't blame her.

"Where has Vanessa Whitman been since November?" Alex asked Traynor.

"A private Stone Solutions hospital in Kirkland." Traynor was bouncing on the balls of his feet with his eagerness to answer Alex's questions. "That's where they take anyone injured in empathy-related incidents."

"So is Cedrick Stone at this hospital?" Reece barely recognized his own voice with its dark, gravelly edge.

Traynor looked at Alex. "You owe Reece and Cora too," Alex said coolly. "Do whatever they say and answer anything they ask."

Traynor turned to Reece, who had to tighten his jaw to squash the flare of anger. Last time he'd met Traynor's eyes, it had been at a warehouse in Vancouver, where Reece had been uncovering his involvement in plans for Evan Grayson's death. "Cedrick isn't in Kirkland," said Traynor. "He's being treated at Orion."

"What's that?" Cora asked.

"Stone Solutions' corporate lodge," Traynor said. "It's where leadership goes on retreats and for their anti-empathy training. It's *very* nice."

"You've been?" Reece said.

"Oh yes," said Traynor. "Stone Solutions spends a lot of money on me so that I'll keep *their* money flowing in."

Reece took a breath through his nose. Being reminded that the American government was in bed with corporate America wasn't going to help his temper.

"Where's this Orion Lodge?" Alex asked.

"British Columbia," Traynor said. "I don't know exactly where—they always took us by helicopter—but it has spectacular mountain views and was close enough for day trips to Whistler."

Cora propped her chin in her hand. "You were *skiing* while Cedrick Stone was having my fiancé tortured to death and Victor Nichols was experimenting on the empaths in Polaris." She looked at Alex. "Why is this asshole alive again?"

"I would like to know the same thing," Reece said tightly.

"Because he's going be useful." Alex's voice had an edge of anger to match theirs. "Aren't you, Holt?"

"Yes, sir," Traynor said eagerly. "I was careful never to get details about the Polaris experiments from Victor, you know. Plausible deniability is very important in our field."

"What about the details of the experiments on the Grayson brothers?" Reece asked, cold and quiet, before he could stop himself.

Alex glanced at him. There was no way the other two empaths hadn't guessed at Reece's complicated feelings where Evan Grayson was concerned, but Alex only looked back at Traynor expectantly.

"I signed off on those," Traynor said earnestly. "Charles said I needed to. But I was careful not to ask questions or get details there either."

Reece's blood pressure was high enough he swore he was seeing a red tint to his vision. "Charles?"

"Charles Stone," Traynor clarified. "He wanted to know if corruption was a fixed state or if a corrupted empath's powers could be increased through additional trauma." He leaned in and added, "It's tough to find something that could further traumatize an empath who's already corrupted, but Charles knew the Grayson family had been close to each other and thought using Alex's brother might work. And given Evan has his enhancements and is able to withstand significantly higher amounts of pain—"

Reece had to go or Traynor was going to wind up a bloody corpse on the floor.

He shoved off the wall and didn't stop, his feet taking him straight out the French doors and onto the deck, then down the stairs to the lawn that rolled down to the lake's edge. He crossed the lawn and stepped out onto the dock, shoulders heaving from the force of his breaths, gaze fixed on the green hills on the other side of the water and the houses dotted in among the green. People going about their lives, no idea Reece was here, drowning in fury, enough empathic power burning through him to ensnare anyone unlucky enough to be nearby—

Before he'd meant to, Reece had yanked his phone out of his pocket. His fingers moved on autopilot as he opened his text messages with Grayson, scrolling up and up, to the picture of him in Reece's bed. He stared at Grayson's face for a long moment.

And then he hit Call.

It rang several times, the toneless drone tinny and distant against the vastness of the lake and cloudy sky above. Then, finally, the familiar deep drawl floated up from the phone. "Grayson."

Voice alone wasn't going to be enough. "I want a video call," Reece snapped.

There was a pause. "What?"

"Alex gave you super hearing. I know you heard me." Reece's voice was still too low, too rough. Tension was vibrating under his skin, forcing him to pace as he spoke.

"Why?"

"*I got my reasons,*" he said, mimicking Grayson's drawl. "Isn't that the bullshit nonanswer you usually give? You keep bragging that you're not scared of me, so put your camera on and prove it." His voice broke as he said it, sharp as cut glass.

There was another pause, a longer one.

Then the line cut out in Reece's ear.

A few seconds went by. His fingers tightened on the phone, but then it began to ring again with an incoming video call.

Reece hit Accept, and Grayson's face filled his phone screen.

"This proof enough for you, sugar?"

Reece's fingers tightened on the phone for a very different reason. Grayson had cleaned up at some point, jaw shaved and hair styled, though his hazel eyes were still bloodshot and rimmed with dark circles underneath. He was obviously filming himself from the driver's seat of the Smart car, head nearly at the roof and broad shoulders blocking most of the view, but the background noise held the telltale sound of cars zipping ceaselessly past. "Are you on I-5? While using *video*? Evan Miguel Grayson—"

"You're the one who asked for this. And I pulled onto the shoulder before calling you back." Grayson was staring at him. "I wouldn't've expected that you knew my middle name."

Reece hadn't expected the old traffic lecture to fall from his lips. He shook himself irritably. "Yeah, well, just because you don't know me at all doesn't mean I have the same problem."

Grayson sat back in the seat. "Point taken," he said. "You didn't kill Smith, and I owe you an apology for believing that frame job."

"Oh, I wouldn't apologize yet," Reece said lightly, the dagger's edge still in his voice. "I don't think murder is off the table at all."

He stepped out onto the dock, feeling raw and exposed under the endless gray sky above. But his blood pressure had dropped a point or two the moment Grayson had come into his sight, whatever stupid brain cell that still cared about Evan Grayson calming the moment he saw the familiar face, whole and unharmed.

On the screen, Grayson tilted his head. "You planning to turn on your camera?"

"Maybe I'm *plannin'* on just watching Dead Man TV."

The dock's wooden planks were stained a deep reddish-brown that hid any evidence of the inevitable decay. Reece walked past the covered boat slip with its small skiff, heading farther out into the lake.

Grayson raised an eyebrow. "Or you're admitting you're scared of *me*."

"Don't you wish." Reece reached the end of the dock and sat down on the edge, letting his legs dangle so his sneakers were maybe a foot above the waters of the lake. He raised his phone and then turned on his camera.

There was no change in expression, of course, but Reece could tell the moment his image came on-screen by the way Grayson's hazel eyes flicked up, then down. He didn't speak, just took Reece in for a long moment. Maybe Reece was the empath, but he suddenly felt unbalanced and laid bare, like he was the book and Grayson was the reader.

He probably wasn't looking his best these days either.

"You okay?" Grayson finally said.

My skin is crawling and my blood is burning and all I want is to see people suffer but some wisp of conscience keeps holding me back and who knew pacifism could fight like hell? I was a mess before, and I'm still a mess now, and the only time I've ever been okay was those few days when I was with you.

"Never better," Reece said, in an unbothered tone, because Grayson wouldn't hear the lie twisting his words in the cold lake air.

"Uh-huh." Grayson didn't sound remotely convinced. "Someone piss you off?"

Reece huffed a dark kind of half laugh. "Yeah," he said truthfully. "Yeah. Someone did."

"The person who's framing you?"

"No," Reece said. "This person hurt—" *you* "—someone else."

There was a pause. "Of course they did," Grayson said, like that had held a deeper meaning for him. Then he straightened up. "Did something happen to Alex?"

"You mean besides having his parents murdered and his brother tortured because some sick fucks wanted to see what would happen to him?" Reece said with bite. "No. Why?"

"Because I talk to your sister more than you do now," Grayson said, and that flat voice didn't quite have an edge of its own, but it sure wasn't *soft*. "And far as I know, no one has hurt her lately except *you*."

"Why don't we leave our siblings out of this?" Reece said warningly. "What are you even getting at?"

"You're pissed at someone for hurting someone else," Grayson pointed out. "With St. James ruled out, I was trying to figure out whose pain could make you willing to call me."

Reece looked into his eyes, the warm shades of golds and browns in the familiar face. It took him back to that golden-hued picture of Grayson in Texas, the bright blue summer sky between the green leaves of an oak tree. Once upon a time, there had been smile lines next to Grayson's eyes, because he used to be happy, until Traynor and Stone and the others had taken that from him.

But while Grayson wasn't happy anymore, he also wasn't hurt right now. He probably needed more sleep, but he was safe in Reece's Smart car in Seattle, not a bunker in West Texas, and the sight of Grayson had settled the black lighting enough that Reece might be able to walk back into Jason Owens's house without murdering Traynor on the spot.

"Be careful with that engine," he said, and hung up.

CHAPTER SEVENTEEN

In this issue: Strength in Sensitivity; Countering (Uncaring) Culture; Soft Hearts in a Hard World.
Hearts Beat, *Vol. 9 (Seattle: 1992).*
—Digitized scan of an empath-run zine from Rainier University's archival collection

Grayson stared at his suddenly dark phone. "*Be careful with that engine*," he repeated. "The hell am I supposed to do with that? You didn't even tell me why you called."

Reece didn't seem to be calling back to explain himself either. "You always got to be a problem for me," Grayson said to the phone, and tossed it on the passenger seat.

He was gonna have to admit he'd missed another nuance to the corrupted empaths, though. Reece was being framed but was pissed over someone else's pain. St. James had suspected the corrupted empaths still cared for others more than themselves, and he'd have to tell her she might be right.

It wasn't something he'd considered before. He'd always assumed Alex's biggest moment of violence had been straightforward revenge for his own capture. Could St. James's speculations be right, that Alex had decimated that West Texas bunker because they'd hurt Grayson himself?

It was a theory, nothing more. But if there was a chance it was true, Lord help Seattle if anything happened to St. James. Cora Falcon had taken down more than dozen people after her fiancé was killed. Alex had done his own share of murders in that bunker and after the loss of their parents.

Grayson glanced over at the phone, sitting innocently on the passenger seat.

What was gonna be unleashed if a person Reece loved got hurt?

With no answers and no further calls, Grayson got back on I-5 and headed for downtown.

The Empath Initiative's Seattle office took up three floors of a nondescript government building near police HQ. The EI receptionist had been informed to expect Grayson and directed him to sign the visitor's log as she went to get the keys.

On the lobby wall, the television was playing, a panel discussion about what Beau Macy's death would mean for Seattle. Marist was there, her face set in a mask that gave nothing away. Grayson recognized Senator Braun next to her, and watched for a long moment. Good-looking guy, and not just by politician standards. He'd probably broken hearts once upon a time.

Or maybe Grayson was being reminded of another good-looking man with dark brown hair and eyes.

The receptionist returned and took him past a maze of cubicles, filing cabinets, stacked mailbox cubbies and combination printer-copiers to a long hall that ended in a closed door flanked by a modest plaque reading *Director.* "Mr. Traynor is based in DC, but he's here often enough he has his own office," she said as she fit the key in the doorknob. "I received instructions to keep it locked. No one has been in or out, not even the cleaning staff."

She unlocked the door and opened it to reveal an office that was almost shockingly neat—no family photos or other personal effects, just a single framed print of a battleship on the wall and a bulletin board that held a job safety poster and a printout of the federal holidays schedule. The desk was large, but its surface was nearly bare save for the keyboard, monitor, a mail tray and an empty laptop dock.

"Let me know when you're done and I'll lock back up." The receptionist disappeared, delicately closing the door behind her. Very savvy; she might not know he was the Dead Man, but she couldn't have missed that he'd just pulled enough strings to get permission to poke around in Traynor's sealed office. She wasn't gonna want to know what he was up to; plausible deniability was always useful, especially in government, where all the little things were supposed to be disclosed to taxpayers.

Grayson headed for the desk and started with the mail tray. He sorted through the stack—the inescapable paper coupons, an alumni magazine for Rainier University, political flyers, generic donation entreaties from American Minds Intact. The hutch above the desk likewise didn't turn up anything more exciting than office supplies. He crouched down behind the desk and glanced into the bins, which hadn't been emptied. The trash only held a couple of tissues, but in the recycling bin was a padded manila envelope.

Grayson fished it out. It had a hand-lettered return mailing address of a postal box in Prince Rupert. He slipped his hand inside, but the envelope was empty. He checked the mailing date: a couple of weeks prior, sometime after Cedrick Stone had been hospitalized but before Traynor had gone missing. He took a picture of the envelope and put it back in the bin.

Grayson took a seat in the desk chair—actually big enough to fit him comfortably, wasn't that a first—gaze going to the print of the battleship. Traynor had been army, not navy, but maybe he liked ships.

He began opening desk drawers. Most of them held more office supplies, but the bottom right drawer was lined with hanging file folders. Grayson pulled them out of the drawer and set them on the desk, methodically reviewing their contents: a selection of floor plans for EI offices around the country; a large yellow envelope labeled *Receipts*.

He gave the office floor plans a cursory glance, gaze lingering on the one from Port Angeles, which took up six pages all stapled together. Then he opened the envelope and began to sort through the most recent receipts. It was the typical spread you'd expect of a government employee on business travel: reasonable hotel rooms, moderately priced restaurants, transportation and gas stations. There weren't a whole lot of them, but then, Stone Solutions treated Traynor to every luxury they could get away with not documenting; he didn't have to foot many of his own bills.

It meant that the rental car receipt mixed in with the rest got Grayson's attention, particularly the mileage total racked up in a single day. It was dated the same day Grayson had gone to Vancouver with Reece, two days after the manila envelope with the overnight postage had been mailed from British Columbia. When had Traynor found time for a road trip? And where had he gone?

Grayson sorted through the rest of the receipts and found at least one of the answers: a receipt from a gas station in Port Angeles, dated the same day.

Grayson went back to his stack of office floor plans, pulling out the one for Port Angeles.

He took another picture and sent it to St. James. Then he called her.

"We just landed in Seattle," she said by way of answering, and he could hear an engine in the background. "What did you just send me?"

"Victor Nichols's research might be in Port Angeles."

Grayson explained Marist's comments about Nichols preferring external drives and what he'd found in Traynor's office.

"But there isn't an EI office in Port A," St. James said. "They started that huge one but never finished it."

It was true. EI had planned for a big research and development facility, bought up acres of land just outside of Port Angeles and started construction on offices and labs.

Then Stone Solutions stepped on-scene. And everyone decided it was easier to funnel taxpayer money into a private corporation and let them handle empathy defense—or at least, Charles Stone, who was head of EI back then, successfully lobbied to have the money given to his son Cedrick's new company instead.

"A half-built R & D campus that's been sitting abandoned for years seems like a pretty good place to hide something," Grayson pointed out.

St. James made a thoughtful noise. "I'll go look."

"I'll go. I've been before and know what's there," Grayson said. "You just got back, and at least one of us ought to be in Seattle at all times right now."

"Worst babysitting ever," she muttered. "You going now?"

Grayson glanced at the window. Night had already fallen, glossy and shimmery from the winter rain. "Morning, I think," he said.

She gave him an update on the pacifist empaths' travels toward Bellingham, and they hung up a few minutes later.

Grayson took the gas station receipt and the map, pocketing both before putting everything else back in the desk and then getting to his feet.

His gaze flicked to the window again, the flecks of white sleet against the dark glass. The empaths were dangerous, yes, but they were also being framed, and he'd be leaving town tomorrow. It was only for a day trip, but something about leaving even just for hours still had him pulling out his phone.

He palmed it for a second. No word from Reece since his inexplicable demand for a moment of video. If Reece was acting erratically, Grayson should wait, should let him make the next move, should see what he did, shouldn't text first.

He *definitely* shouldn't text Reece the words in his head: That would be a very bad decision.

Ironically, it might've been that thought that made his fingers move.

Jamey had just hung up with Grayson when a white BMW coupe she didn't recognize pulled into the driveway. She stepped out to her front porch as the Beamer's door opened and Gretel Macy climbed out of the car. Gone were the lipstick and tailored pencil skirts and pumps Jamey was used to seeing her in; instead, Gretel was in leggings and a giant sweatshirt, nose red and makeup smeared around her eyes, her gorgeous mane of hair artlessly tangled in a rat's nest bun on the top of her head.

"I got your voicemail," Gretel said awkwardly, and wiped at her eyes.

They had always been on opposite sides of everything empath, and hadn't even known each other beyond that, but Jamey was hurrying down the stairs anyway. "Aw, Gretel, I'm so sorry."

And then they were hugging. "Thanks, Jamey," Gretel said, muffled by Jamey's coat as she clung to the hug.

They stayed together for a long moment, Jamey's own losses stinging fresh. God, she missed Reece.

Finally, Gretel pulled back, fresh tears in her eyes. "Sorry to just turn up like this," she said thickly, wiping at her face. "I didn't know where else to go. I can't talk to the cops. And this probably doesn't come as a shock, but being a weird obsessive crackpot means I don't have a lot of friends."

"I'm glad you're here," Jamey said firmly, tugging her up the stairs to the deck. "Come inside."

Jamey put the electric kettle on, then settled Gretel at the kitchen table with a throw blanket draped over her shoulders. "You said you can't talk to the cops?" she gently prompted.

Gretel pulled the blanket tighter around her. "They won't even let me see my parents' bodies."

"I'm so sorry," Jamey said again as she put a few boxes of tea on the table, knowing how useless and insufficient the words were.

"And it's not just that. They won't *listen*." Gretel looked up at her. "My parents' murder was a fucking setup."

Jamey frowned. "What do you mean?"

"I was at my parents' house yesterday when my dad got a call." Gretel swallowed hard. "I heard part of the conversation. This person wanted to do dinner, but asked my dad to meet him at AMI first."

Jamey's eyebrows went up.

"Lieutenant Parson dismissed it," Gretel said, deeply bitter. "Told me it was a coincidence."

Jamey poured boiling water into two mugs. Parson had been her supervising officer when she'd been a detective on the force. Empathy-related investigations were a federal, not state affair, and shrouded in secrecy to boot; Parson very well might be under orders not to let the SPD follow any leads.

But Jamey wasn't on the force anymore. She could follow

any damn lead she wanted. "Do you know who called your dad?" she asked as she set a mug in front of Gretel and took the seat next to her with the other mug.

"I think I do." She wrapped her hands around the mug. "But no one is ever going to believe me."

Jamey leaned in. "I will believe you," she promised quietly. "You could tell me it was the president and I'd still believe you."

Gretel let out a shaky breath. There was a look of despair in her eyes that Jamey recognized all too well from other victims who believed justice was beyond their reach. "My dad mentioned coming out of retirement and called the person *Charles*. I assumed he was talking to Charles Stone."

Jamey's eyes widened. "Charles Stone as in Stone Solutions? Cedrick Stone's famous dad?"

Gretel nodded. "My parents are friends with all of them." She swallowed. "*Were* friends."

"Jesus," Jamey muttered. But the more she thought it over, the more it made a twisted kind of sense. Who else besides a Stone would have enough power and resources to pull something like this off? "Well, like I said, I believe you. Did you tell the SPD you suspect Charles Stone?"

"Absolutely not." Gretel reached for one of the herbal teas. "I don't see how I can even accuse a man like that. I don't know what to do. Except, well." She gestured around them. "Turn up unannounced at a former detective's house."

"Not a bad plan, actually," Jamey said. "Because I'm going to try to help."

"Really?" A watery smile played on Gretel's lips. "That's, you know." She sniffed. "Very *empathetic* of you."

"Hazards of growing up with an empath brother," Jamey said wryly.

"Guess so," Gretel said as she added a tea bag to her mug. "Is, um. Is Reece around?"

"Um, no," Jamey said awkwardly. "He's . . . out. Sorry."

"Probably busy mind-controlling pumpkins or whatever other crazy things bloggers are accusing him of these days." Gretel's tone was deeply self-deprecating. She sighed, resting her forehead in her hand, her nails ragged and bitten. "I've written so much shit about him and the others, and now here I am with my tragedy, wanting to see an empath and his sister." She wiped at another tear. "I'm just one more fucking hypocrite."

Jamey leaned in. "I told you, I'm glad you came," she said, quiet and truthful. "Will you stay here tonight?"

If Charles Stone had any inkling that Gretel suspected he was involved, her life would probably be in danger. And on a personal level, Jamey understood loss too well to want to let Gretel go home alone.

It was a relief when Gretel nodded. "Yeah. Yeah, that'd be great," she said with another shaky smile. "Thanks, Jamey."

CHAPTER EIGHTEEN

To: Marist, Vivian <v.marist@stonesolutionscorp.com>

From: Roger Spade <roger.spade@seattlemail.com>
Subject: October's 8-K

Cedrick is still in the hospital and I can't get anywhere with Charles. Vivian, we need to talk about this filing. Some of us on the Board of Directors have questions that still haven't been answered.

Reece stood under the triple spray of one of Jason Owens's giant and elaborate showers, glaring at the plastic bottles sitting on the shower shelf.

He'd held it together for the afternoon, but talking to Traynor had left him even more on edge, like an oily film had settled on his skin. First chance he'd gotten, he ducked into a cold shower to ice his feelings down.

But the shower made it so much worse.

After their break-in at Stone Solutions Canada, Reece had left Vancouver in Grayson's truck while Alex and Cora had gone ahead of him by yacht and arrived in Seattle first. Alex had immediately sent thralls to Reece's studio apartment to grab his personal things and bring them back to Jason Owens's house.

But the studio had also still been full of *Grayson's* things—clothes, toiletries, cologne.

The thralls had grabbed it all. And some of it now inhabited Reece's shower.

It's fucking shampoo, Reece snapped at himself, his freshly spiked temper refusing to cool even as he shivered under the cold spray. *Are you really so fragile you can't even handle Evan's stupid shower arsenal?*

No way he was going to be bested by Grayson's *hair*. He grabbed the closest bottle and poured some into his hand.

The scent hit like a gut-punch.

Evan, boxing him in on the truck's tailgate, their bodies distractingly close together as Reece tries to hide his missing glove—

Evan, passing him in the studio's kitchen, his T-shirt just sheer enough to show the muscles shifting underneath—

Evan, crouching in front of him in a Stone Solutions office, making himself a fortress between Reece and the box of torture books as he talks Reece down from a panic attack—

Reece slammed down on the memories, and forced himself through the coldest, fastest and possibly angriest hair wash of his life.

He *still* fucking smelled like Grayson as he went back to his room to dress, taking deep breaths as he tried to calm himself enough to handle a night in a house with an awake Traynor.

Evan wouldn't have smelled like fancy shampoo in that bunker Traynor sent him to. He'd have smelled like sweat and fear, like pain and maybe blood—

Reece shoved those thoughts down too, quickly pulling on jeans and a T-shirt, and then went to grab his other hoodie from the truck in the garage.

As he opened the passenger door and leaned in to grab the hoodie off the seat, his phone went off.

Grayson: I need to see you.

Grayson: Meet me tonight. On your terms, anywhere you like. You name the time and the place.

Grayson: And I will be there.

Reece stared at the words on his screen. "Are you fucking kidding?" he said out loud, as if Grayson could hear him.

Of course he wasn't going to *meet* Grayson. That was something old Reece did because he was too helpless and naive to make good decisions. He and Grayson were enemies now. It was bad enough they kept texting and talking, but enemies certainly didn't meet.

And sure, Reece could pick a public place where he'd have a distinct advantage: The more people around him, the more potential weapons he could turn against Grayson. He could turn their whole meeting into a trap for Grayson if he chose.

But Reece was wanted by the cops. He couldn't be seen in public places right now, and he wasn't stupid enough to meet the Dead Man in an isolated location where there would be nothing but the two of them and Grayson's knockout touch: He might as well put himself in a cell and hand Grayson the keys.

He needs to see you, the little voice in his head said. *Don't you want to know why?*

No. Reece did not.

Maybe he needs you.

Then that was too fucking bad for Agent Grayson.

What if he's in trouble?

Reece jammed his phone back in his pocket with a curse. Even if he was stupid enough to agree to meet—which obviously he *wasn't*—it was out of the question.

I need to see you.

Absolutely not.

As he grabbed his hoodie, the traitorous bear hat tumbled off the passenger seat and to the floor, like he'd needed yet another reminder of Grayson. Reece grabbed the hat, but as he opened the glove box to cram it back in, his gaze fell on another item stuffed inside.

A headband with black bunny ears, given to him by Ben Castillo, the McFeely's bartender, way back on that night Reece had stopped by the club and ended up in a high-speed brakeless chase on I-5.

All the empaths have them, Ben had said when he'd offered Reece the ears. *You should too.*

Reece reached into the glove box and pulled out the bunny ears, considering them.

On second thought, maybe he *would* meet Grayson.

Because there was one place in Seattle where Reece would blend in perfectly, wouldn't draw the slightest bit of extra attention—and could still have a crowd of hostages.

Sean Lennox had been head of Charles Stone's personal security for more than a decade and was accustomed to his habits. Despite the evening hour, Charles would be at his laptop in his home office. Lennox knocked on the closed door. "Mr. Stone, sir? Do you have a moment?"

"Come in."

Lennox walked into the expansive space and stood at attention. "I just wanted to be certain you saw the report from the West Coast monitoring team."

"I'm reading it now," Charles said. "It seems several empaths will be congregating in Bellingham. And coincidentally, this group appears to be our most isolated empaths, the ones with only small support networks or distant relatives. Isn't that interesting?" He leaned back in his chair, regarding Lennox. "How would you feel about a trip to Bellingham yourself?"

"I am always at your service, sir," Lennox said.

"Excellent." Charles leaned forward. "Let me tell you what I have in mind."

CHAPTER NINETEEN

Calling all Seattle fans of Dungeon-Free Dragons! This month's meet-up will be at the empath club. Get great food and join new friends for a peaceful RPG where we hatch baby dragons that safely grow into happy adult dragons.

—Post shared on social media

Reece: McFeely's. 11pm. Come alone.

Grayson kept the steering wheel steady with his knees as he glanced at his phone. "McFeely's?"

Behind him on I-5, someone honked. Grayson tossed the phone back to the passenger seat and grabbed the wheel again.

Of all the ways he'd expected Reece to respond to his request to meet, naming the fake empath club hadn't made the list. And tonight, with news of the AMI president's death still rocking Seattle, the club would likely be extra packed with people wanting to gossip.

In hindsight, letting Reece choose a place might've been a bad decision. Grayson was making an awful lot of those.

He drove back to the studio, where he stood at the kitchen island and ate two packs of Reece's vegan ramen out of a rainbow bowl as he read up on the old Empath Initiative facility out by Port Angeles on his phone.

Eyes on Empaths had done a feature story on the old facility two years ago. Gretel had gone in person and posted some of her own photos of the abandoned campus: an evergreen-edged parking lot with lots of potholes but no cars, a shell of an office building with several boarded windows, a pile of rusted construction debris with a raven perched on top. If Traynor had been there recently to hide a flash drive, Grayson would guess he'd picked the office building, where it'd be out of the elements, at least, and the floors were finished and safe to walk on.

You told Reece you needed to see him, a little voice in his head pointed out.

Grayson hesitated over his phone. But yeah. He had done that.

Why?

Because Grayson was leaving town tomorrow—leaving St. James alone to watch over a powder keg with potentially murderous corrupted empaths on one side and the folks framing them on the other.

But you're the Dead Man. You don't have needs.

And you most definitely don't need Reece.

Grayson put his phone down. It was time to go.

McFeely's had been put through a lot that one November night after Senator Hathaway had died. Between Cora Falcon's thralls, the panicking crowds and Reece smashing a historic window to escape, the club had needed to set up temporarily in a warehouse in Kent while the building underwent cleanup and repairs. McFeely's had just reopened that week in their previous location in Pioneer Square.

It wasn't much more than a mile from the studio, so Grayson opted to walk, leaving the Smart car in the building's garage instead of trying to find more downtown parking. It was a cold night, a light and partially frozen rain falling on his hat as he walked the sidewalk, trying to avoid any deeper puddles. The familiar smells of most urban downtowns were here, car exhaust and less pleasant human aromas, but at least layered over salty ocean air and rain. It was louder than expected, with pockets of people smoking on downtown corners, undeterred by the cold or the damp, and a steady flow of cars splashing through puddles.

He still couldn't explain why he'd told Reece he needed to see him. And he definitely couldn't explain why, as he'd been leaving the studio, he'd grabbed his own Texas hooded sweatshirt, the one he'd once given to Reece. He was wearing it now, zipped up under his coat, the hood pulled up over his hat to keep the rain off his neck. Reece wasn't gonna notice. Hell, maybe Reece wasn't even gonna show.

It was exactly 10:58 p.m. as he approached the historical building that hid McFeely's. More cars now lined the streets, though he didn't see his F-150 anywhere, and faint bass was floating out from the upstairs window. As he approached the double doors under the green awning, a thick white man with a goatee waved him up to the front of the line.

"Evan Grayson?" When Grayson nodded, the man pointed at himself. "Rocky. Reece said you were coming. You're his boyfriend, right?"

"Actually, I'm his—his—Reece is here already?"

"Got here maybe an hour ago." Rocky spoke with the comfort of a man who clearly no idea what kind of empath was now in his club. "How's Diesel? Never the same without him, but it sounds like he caught a hell of a flu in Vancouver. He said you were letting him crash at your place in BC."

"He can stay long as he wants," Grayson said. "Where did Reece go?"

"He mentioned he was going to find Ben." Rocky was sizing Grayson up with a professional sort of air. "You're not the jealous type, are you?"

"The what?"

"My man, you're the size of Godzilla," Rocky said patiently. "I gotta know if I'm going to be breaking up your fights."

"My . . . fights?"

"I get it," Rocky said. "Pretty dude like you—you're used to being the one people want."

"Well—"

"But in here, they got a specific taste. And no offense, but that taste ain't you." Rocky said it real kind, like Grayson's ego needed to be let down gently. "This crowd comes for the empaths, and they will be all over Reece."

Oh. Grayson cleared his throat. "He's, um—kind of a handful, actually. These days especially."

"No, see, that's not going to turn anyone here *off.*" Rocky patted his shoulder sympathetically. Grayson was beginning to understand why he worked at an empathy-themed club. "Look, I get it: Every asshole in here wants to take Ben home. Do I love that? Of course not. But I deal, right? I process my feelings like a grown-up. So you gotta deal too, especially when we're short a bouncer without Diesel. If someone hits on Reece, I need to know that my new friend Godzilla won't start swinging."

"I do try to avoid violence in front of empaths," Grayson said.

"So you're not going to hit anyone tonight?"

Grayson opened his mouth, then hesitated. "I probably shouldn't make that promise."

Rocky sighed. "Then you better watch your man."

"I'm gonna watch him *real* close," Grayson promised.

Rocky let him inside, and Grayson climbed the stairs up to the second floor. The music was loud and the crowd thick: A lot of folks *had* shown up after the Macys' deaths. Even folks who didn't know about corrupted empaths couldn't be missing the sheer number of empathy-related murders that kept happening in Seattle.

He scanned the crowd, checking the dance floor and every table for any sign of Reece. Fake empaths in gloves were all over the place, all of them about Reece's height and build and dressed in costumes of various kinds. Reece could be in disguise, blend in perfectly and have a whole crowd of potential thralls; he'd definitely known what he was doing when he picked this meeting place, and Grayson might've underestimated him yet again.

In his pocket, his phone buzzed. He pulled it out and read the text on-screen.

Reece: Marco

Grayson looked up. At the far end of the club, three bartenders in fake empath gloves were making drinks behind the marble-topped bar: Ben Castillo, his complicated hair partially hidden by a plush hat with moving ears; a short woman with tattoos and a top hat, chatting with two other women; and a third bartender in a domino mask and familiar black bunny ears, looking straight at Grayson.

As Grayson approached, Reece leaned on the bar. "You're supposed to say *Polo*."

"Pardon?"

"You know. When you're seeking someone you can't see, you say *Marco* and they call back *Polo*." Reece rested his chin on one fake-gloved hand, all innocence. "Didn't you ever play that game in the pool?"

Grayson slipped into the empty stool right in front of Reece. "I thought we weren't *playing*." He leaned on the bar too. "After all, you picked a meeting spot where every hapless clubgoer is your hostage."

Reece had already shifted backwards before their arms came anywhere near each other. "I didn't have to meet with you at all."

That was true. Reece could have told Grayson to fuck off with his ask; he looked on the verge of doing it now. Grayson nodded at the bottles stacked on glass shelves behind Reece. "Since when do you bartend?"

"I wanted a bar between us. For obvious reasons. Ben is pretending to be an empath; he was willing to let me pretend too." Reece shrugged lightly. "I mean, I could have *made* him willing. But it hasn't come to that yet."

The mask only covered from his eyebrows to the bridge of his nose. Grayson could just make out his eyes behind the cut-outs. In the dim lighting, they appeared almost glittery black, as they had that one night in the truck, when Reece's empathy had danced free between them.

"It better not come to that ever—" Grayson paused as an out of place but unmistakable scent rose above the other club smells. "Did you use my shampoo?"

Reece scoffed a little too dramatically. "Don't be stupid."

"That's not a no."

"Not everything is about your *hair*—"

"Hey, it's your hot, scary boyfriend!" Ben's cheerful voice broke through their conversation. He grinned at Grayson. "Evan, right? Thanks for helping Cookie."

"Cookie?" Reece repeated.

Ben pointed at one of the fake empath waiters, who was wearing a halo on a headband, white feathered wings and not much else. "He was the one who suddenly went to Australia the night Senator Hathaway died. Your boyfriend had promised me he'd check on him. Turned out the job he'd been offered was fake, but Evan bought him a ticket back, and he came home safe and sound." Ben glanced between them. "Did you guys not talk about that?"

"We're overdue for a lot of conversations, don't you think, sugar?" Grayson said, gaze darting to Reece, who narrowed his eyes.

Ben grinned. "Is Reece getting your drink?"

"Sure am," Reece said, eyes still narrowed. "One Shirley Temple, coming up."

"Ben!" the third bartender called.

Ben gave them a rueful smile and headed back down the bar.

Grayson unzipped his coat, gaze still on Reece, on the club's lights dancing over his profile and the overgrown dark hair disheveled around the base of the bunny ears. His lips had a faint sheen to them, like he'd been drinking a Shirley Temple of his own. Their stolen moments in the truck had ended when their lips met and his touch had knocked Reece out, but the memory lingered; Reece's kiss was one you didn't forget.

A spark of incredibly ill-timed interest went through Grayson. He'd always wanted Reece when he shouldn't, and it apparently didn't matter to his dick that Reece had traded *Care Bear* for *murder rabbit*; his body was in favor of the two of them fucking right there on the bar.

"I want extra cherries in that Shirley Temple," Grayson said to distract himself from that wildly unhelpful thought.

"Dream on." Reece turned back to him, gaze flicking over Grayson's open coat, and visibly twitched. "Why are you wearing that?" he said sharply.

Guess he did recognize the hoodie. "'Cause it's winter in Seattle," Grayson said. "And every time I've gotten clothes recently, they've gone missing. The ones I left in your studio. The ones I left in my truck. Course, my truck's gone missing too."

"Gosh, that's a shame," Reece said, deadpan. "Maybe you should have been more careful with it."

Grayson shrugged. “It’s all right. I found something else to drive.”

“Now you’re *trying* to piss me off.” Reece leaned in. “If I were you, I wouldn’t bait an empath’s temper in a crowded club,” he said with a hint of menace. “Just a tip.”

“That right?” Grayson casually set his hand on the bar, and Reece automatically flinched back to keep distance between them. Grayson cleared his throat meaningfully. “Pretty sure I can handle you and your temper just fine,” he said, pushing away his brain’s immediate and unhelpful ideas of ways he could handle Reece.

Reece’s expression darkened. He tapped the bar. “You wanted to meet. We’ve met. What do you want?”

“I’m leaving town tomorrow.”

It wasn’t really an answer, but it also wasn’t something Grayson had necessarily planned to tell Reece. From the looks of it, Reece hadn’t expected Grayson to be that honest either.

“Okay,” Reece said, drawing it out. “I’ll pencil some extra mayhem in my planner, then.”

“No,” Grayson said firmly. “You won’t.”

“Oh, this should be fun.” Reece rested his chin on his fake-gloved hand again. Care Bear or murder rabbit, he was still way too cute. “Tell me, big bad Dead Man, why should I be good while you’re gone?”

“Because you can give *me* hell,” said Grayson. “Not your sister.”

Reece stiffened. “Leave Jamey out of this,” he said warningly. “She has always been off limits, and she always will be. Maybe you have this obsession with being the Dead Man, but I know Jamey’s mixed up in it too now, and if anything happens to her and I find out—”

He cut himself off, but Grayson didn’t need the details. No question St. James did still matter to Reece, even in his corrupted state.

Then Reece pointed at him. "And what about you?"

Grayson wrinkled his brow in confusion. "Me?"

"Has anything happened to— Never mind." Reece seemed to shake himself. "So is this why you needed to see me?" he said gruffly. "To lecture me about behaving for Jamey?"

I don't know why I'm here. But I couldn't leave town without seeing you. "Did you figure out who's framing you?" Grayson said instead.

"I wouldn't tell you if I had."

"I'm trying to help."

"You're trying to lock me up." Reece's voice was icy. "Don't think for a moment that I've dropped my guard. One wrong twitch from you and I will make this entire club attack. How's that for *giving you hell*—"

"Hey." A brunette in a tie, maybe early thirties, suddenly shoved his way up to the bar. "Hey, cutie." His voice was loud as he put his elbows on the bar top and snapped his fingers at Reece. "I need a beer."

"Oh yeah?" Reece turned toward the brunette. "Well, I think you need to fuck off."

The man drew his head back. "Excuse me?"

"I'm not getting you a fucking beer," Reece said. "You've got your car keys right there in your fist. Only assholes drink and drive." He looked at Grayson. "Not a lie."

"Obviously not," Grayson muttered.

"What the fuck?" the brunette said.

"You can have something without alcohol," Reece told him.

The brunette huffed. "Are you fucking kidding?"

Reece folded his arms, the towel dangling from his hand, and waited.

The brunette frowned. "Fine," he finally said. "Get me a Coke."

"You don't need caffeine this late at night," Reece said.

The brunette threw up his hands. "Ginger ale."

Reece slowly unfolded his arms. He reached under the bar and then set a clear glass full of ice on the bar top. He put the soda dispenser over the glass and filled it, then pushed it toward the man.

The man's gaze flicked to the glass, then back to Reece. "Can I at least have a cherry?"

Reece lifted a maraschino cherry by the stem off the garnish tray and dropped it into the drink. "Yes."

The man's gaze flicked over Reece again. "What about your number?"

"*No*," Grayson said.

The man whirled around, mouth open, and then seemed to clock Grayson's size. "My hero," Reece said sarcastically as the brunette snatched up the ginger ale and disappeared.

"He was hitting on you right in front of your *hot, scary boyfriend*," Grayson said dryly. "*And* he was rude to you."

"And if I'd wanted to, I could make that man pull out his own fingernails and love every second of the pain." Reece folded his arms on the bar. "Stop forgetting that I'm not that helpless weakling anymore," he said, voice lower and gravellier. "I've changed, Evan. And the new me doesn't need a knight in shining armor."

Grayson leaned forward. "Not even a knight to protect you from *me*?"

This time he put his hand on the bar only an inch from Reece's bare arm. Reece jerked back like he'd been stung.

"You talk a big game now," Grayson said. "But when you were that so-called *helpless* pacifist, you weren't scared of me."

Reece's jaw tightened. "You mean I was too stupid and naive to be smart around you."

"You know I've never believed that about you." Grayson

met his eyes. "Don't know why you think talking about yourself like that is gonna fly now."

"No?" Reece said with bite. "If I didn't know better, I'd think you don't like being reminded that I'm a different empath now." His gaze dropped to Grayson's chest. "Did you come here believing you'd find old Reece and give him his hoodie back?"

"You know where I'm staying." Grayson touched the sweatshirt, over his heart. "You want this back, you can come on over and get it."

"I know better than to be anywhere alone with the Dead Man." Reece's gaze had gone to Grayson's shoulder. "And I know I'm right that you wish it was your Care Bear standing here instead of me."

Grayson's hand automatically went his shoulder, where the bullet scar was hidden under the fleece. "The Dead Man doesn't have *wishes*."

"Liar," Reece shot back. "You *wish* you could fuck me."

Grayson stilled.

"Yeah, I can tell," Reece said, a dark boast. "Your body doesn't care about some pesky little morality adjustment; it's still broadcasting that desire to me loud and clear. Like I said: I've changed; you haven't."

He wasn't wrong. This close, Grayson couldn't ignore the scent of his own shampoo layered on Reece's hair, the flush to his cheeks or the flash of familiar dark eyes behind the domino mask. Grayson should be thinking of ways to lock him up, but all his useless brain was suggesting was ways to pin him down. "You haven't changed as much as you think you have."

Reece folded his arms. "What's that supposed to mean?"

Grayson leaned in just a little more. "You can't take your eyes off me either."

Reece's eyes narrowed. And then he was shoving away from the bar and storming off, darting past Ben and the other bartender and heading for the kitchen door.

Grayson jumped over the bar, ignoring Ben's exclaimed "Whoa!" as he chased after Reece into the kitchen. As he burst through the door himself, he could see over everyone's heads that a second door at the back was still swinging. Grayson sprinted toward that one, dodging the kitchen staff making appetizers as he shouldered it open and found himself in a hall.

"You have got to stop underestimating me."

That was all the warning Grayson had before three men his own size, all in black T-shirts and trousers, were on him. Rocky was in front, taking Grayson by surprise with a hard shove that set his back against the wall.

As Grayson's chin came back up, his gaze landed on Reece in the middle of the hall, still in the bunny ears and fake empath gloves but now with his hands curled into fists.

Grayson's gaze darted to Rocky. The man was red with anger, his teeth bared, looking ready to throw a real punch.

"*Rocky*," Grayson said loudly. "Stop."

Rocky paused, his eyes going to Grayson's.

He'd registered his name. This was projection again, not thralling. Reece was angry and dangerous, but he hadn't thralled the bouncers.

One of the other bouncers had seized Grayson's shoulders, holding him to the wall. Grayson could've broken free, but he looked past them to Reece, locking eyes with him. "You done with your tantrum yet?"

Reece took a step forward, pointing at Grayson. "Listen, dick—"

He cut his own words off, his head snapping to the side toward the end of the hall. He watched the door for a moment. Then his head whipped back around, the fury clear on his face.

Oh boy.

"You brought *Stone Solutions*?"

"What?" Grayson said. "Reece, no—"

But Reece had vanished from sight.

The bouncers turned on each other with a roar, even Rocky. Then the door to the kitchen burst open, and three utensil-armed cooks came tumbling out into the hall, just as the hall door opened and a half-dozen armed men that could only be Stone Solutions' undercover response were sprinting their way.

"Son of a bitch," Grayson muttered, and dove into the brawl.

CHAPTER TWENTY

You know I'm always happy to recommend new staff for your security forces, your institutions, or anything else. The job market being what it is, many of them need employment, and I doubt they'll ask many questions. No need to tell me where they'll be working or exactly what roles you're filling. I'll just point soldiers your way and we'll leave things at that.

—Text from Holt Traynor to Charles Stone

Darkness had fallen, turning the evergreen-covered Olympic Mountains into rocky silhouettes. On a clear night, this far from city lights, the stars would have stretched for miles in bright clusters, but clouds were gathering in the night sky, obscuring the view and hinting at more precipitation to come.

Victor Nichols wasn't stargazing anyway. "How far now?" he demanded of the helicopter pilot. "We're descending, but I see nothing."

"The surface lights are hidden from air traffic," the pilot said. "We're not advertising this location."

Nichols steepled his fingers. That was what he liked to hear. "But there *is* power?"

"Generators and satellite communications," the pilot confirmed. "Most of the building is underground, set into the mountainside. There's a laboratory and holding facilities, as well as rooms for the researchers and barracks for the guards." She gestured around them. "And of course, acres and acres of empty forest. Stone Solutions hopes this will make up for the loss of Polaris."

Nichols watched the forest grow closer under the helicopter's light. "I rather think it will," he said.

Reece pulled the truck into the garage at Jason Owens's house, his fingers too tight around the steering wheel.

He'd been in that hall outside McFeely's when he'd felt six new people arrive, their aggression so completely different from the happy feelings of the clubgoers. It had been easy to guess who they were.

He should have expected Grayson to be trying to set a trap.

You drove the truck to McFeely's, the little voice in his head pointed out. *That could have been how they found you.*

It wasn't the truck. It was Grayson selling him out.

He didn't seem like he was expecting Stone Solutions. He said he needed to see you. He told you he's making a trip out of town.

Yeah, well, Grayson was a lying liar who lied. Reece never should have gone to meet him; he was lucky he hadn't ended the night in cuffs.

He was all but stomping as he made his way through Owens's house and into the study. Alex and Cora didn't startle as he entered, which meant they'd felt his anger before he'd even gotten in the room. Great.

Traynor was there too, his gaze fixed on Alex, and Reece really did not need to see Traynor right now.

"You're just in time to hear about today's visit to the Empath Initiative." Cora was curled up on the plush rug in front of the gas fireplace, her back against one of the armchairs. The fire was lit, bathing the end of the room in reddish-orange light.

Reece took a breath through his nose, forcing his voice to be steady. "You went to EI?"

"Mr. Traynor here said he had something I would want, but he needed to stop by his office." Alex was in the other armchair by the fire. "But tell them what happened, Director."

"Someone had already been in my office," Traynor said. "I keep a key taped to the underside of one of the drawers. It was gone. And in its place, someone left new stuff."

Reece frowned. "What stuff?"

Traynor counted things off on his fingers. "An empty envelope in the recycling, postmarked from British Columbia with a recent date. A folder of office floor plans for various EI locations. And several fake receipts."

"What the fuck," Reece said, taking his own seat in the armchair Cora was leaning on.

"The missing key unlocks a safe-deposit box," Traynor said. "That's where I keep the flash drives Victor Nichols sends me. The last one he sent has the research he pretends is about how to reverse corruption."

"*Pretends?*" Reece repeated.

"That's what he told everyone it was, especially Agent Grayson," said Traynor. "But Nichols has never believed there's a way to reverse the corruption. He was only ever looking for ways to make it stronger—and he had some good leads."

Reece's eyes widened. "And that research is in a safe-deposit box?"

"Not anymore," Alex said. "Someone took the key. And guess whose name was in the visitor log for today?"

Traynor leaned down. "Evan Grayson."

Reece frowned. "But that doesn't make any sense," he said. "I mean, yes, Evan might want to get his hands on Nichols's research. But why leave behind maps and receipts?"

"I'm sure Evan had a reason—he always does," Alex said. "He signed the EI log pretty late in the day; I don't think he would've had time to make it to the bank too. So he's probably still got the key." He glanced at Traynor. "I need you to follow Evan tomorrow so we know when he's got that drive."

Reece's stomach lurched.

No! the voice in his head shouted. *No, Traynor can't go anywhere near Evan. It's not safe—*

Reece slammed the metaphorical door on his feelings, too late. Alex and Cora looked at him.

"Traynor's mine now," Alex said. "He's not going to hurt Evan, are you, Director?"

"No, sir," Traynor promised.

"You're just gonna follow him around Seattle," Alex added.

"That's right," Traynor said eagerly.

"Those weren't lies, so you know he believes it," Alex said. "And I'm not even asking him to take that drive back once Evan has it. Just to call us when he's got it."

"Yes, sir," Traynor said fervently.

No. Absolutely not, it's still not safe. What if something happens to set Traynor off the way Eton and Pelham were set off? How can we be certain he can't be triggered to attack—

Reece clenched his jaw, taking more deep breaths. What did it even matter? Grayson had just shown him tonight that he was on EI's side, on Stone Solutions' side, that he would lock Reece up without a second thought.

They needed Traynor to follow him: If Nichols had research on how to enhance the corruption, then the three of them needed it. Not EI. Not Stone Solutions. And definitely not Grayson.

Grayson was the enemy too.

Reece mumbled something about needing a drink—which wasn't a lie, so he could probably add *dehydrated* to his list of shortcomings—and went from the study into the kitchen. The big windows were dark, so he saw not the water of the lake but his own reflection. He looked away from himself, instead pulling out his phone, only to discover Grayson had texted.

Grayson: They weren't with me.

Grayson: I know how it looked, but I didn't bring Stone Solutions and I didn't know they were coming. You probably don't believe me, but it's the truth.

Reece tightened his jaw.

Call him, the voice in his head said. *Warn him about Traynor.*

No, Reece would not be doing that.

You can't let Traynor follow him.

Yes, Reece certainly could.

There was silence in his head for a moment.

Okay, fine, the voice said. *But if Traynor is going to be on Evan's tail tomorrow, then you're going to be on Traynor's. Enjoy waking up at dawn for a stakeout, asshole.*

Reece raised his gaze to the ceiling. "Son of a bitch," he muttered.

CHAPTER TWENTY-ONE

Dear Mr. Davies:

The Department of Transportation for the City of Seattle thanks you for this letter suggesting additional locations for breakers. Your concern that these speed bumps be "large enough they make drivers slow down" but "not so big that they unpleasantly jostle anyone" has been noted.

We will add this to your ongoing file of requests.

—Excerpt from an eight-month-old letter

Between the bruises from the brawl and the questions turning over his mind, it'd taken Grayson a while to fall asleep after McFeely's. He woke to his alarm at dawn and glanced at his phone, but it just confirmed what he'd expected. Reece hadn't responded to his texts. Staring at the messages wasn't gonna change that. He set the phone back down and got up.

He watered the peace lily and then poured some of Reece's cashew milk into a mug and stuck it the microwave, scorching it before adding a packet of instant coffee. He drank it while standing at the kitchen island, gaze on the big windows. Outside, the lightening sky was thick with clouds, and the rain had become a scattering of small wet snowflakes that melted as soon as they touched the windows.

The street four stories below was less full than usual, smarter souls deciding not to chance the snow, perhaps. There were just a handful of cars parked in front of the open coffee shop across the street: two midsize sedans, a black Tahoe and a convertible—top up, of course, but still an optimistic purchase for Seattle.

His gaze went from the window back across the studio, to his phone by the bed. But Reece wasn't gonna be awake this early and likely wasn't gonna text even when he did wake. There was no point in waiting; better to head out now, while the snow was still light and wasn't sticking to the roads.

Grayson got dressed, grabbed the phone and two protein bars, and took the elevator down to the parking garage to squeeze himself into the Smart car. His head brushed the roof as he turned the key and the engine came to life, not with the deep rumble of his truck but with a motorcycle's urgent tenor.

He was tearing open a protein bar and mostly on autopilot as he put it in Reverse and hit the gas. The tiny car flew out of the parking space with a screech, so fast he barely managed to turn the wheel in time to save himself from clipping the Mercedes behind him.

He slammed on the brake, idling in the middle of the garage.

You're supposed to watch that engine, said a little voice in his head. This time it didn't sound like Grayson's own voice. Probably better not to think too hard on whose voice it did sound like.

He looked out the windshield. Outside the garage, the gentle snow was still coming down. Not hard enough to stop the ferries, but he was on his own schedule, and driving the whole way would give him time to think.

Assuming you stay off your phone and drive responsibly and don't send the damn car flying straight off the road into the ocean, said the suspiciously familiar voice in his head.

Grayson pressed the gas again, much more gently this time, and headed out from the garage.

Growing up with Reece had taught Jamey to recognize emotions the way other big sisters might have learned their little brothers' favorite cartoon characters. So when she woke before her alarm, she recognized the tightness in her chest and the queasiness in her stomach all too well.

She was uneasy.

She threw on one of Liam's sweatshirts and slippers and headed to the kitchen on light feet. Gretel was still asleep on the couch, so Jamey kept her movements as quiet as she could as she prepped coffee.

It had just started brewing when her phone started ringing. Jamey quickly silenced it, glancing at the caller ID.

Liam. Thirty minutes earlier than he had been supposed to check in.

Shit.

She stepped back into the bedroom, closing the door and putting the phone to her ear. "Babe, what's going on?" she said softly.

"The empaths aren't here."

She swore softly. "You're sure?"

"Ten empaths all together are not going to be subtle," he said grimly. "Any chance they just all overslept?"

"They're more likely to have shown up early. Empaths hate worrying or inconveniencing others." Jamey blew out a breath. "Maybe they're waiting at the wrong place?"

"I'm heading to the terminal for the Alaska state ferry," he said. "If they're not there, I'll check other docks."

"Okay, but be careful," Jamey said. "I'll do some digging here."

She stared at her phone for a minute after Liam hung up. Then she called Officer Stensby's number.

The line rang and rang in Jamey's ear. "Pick up already, you little shit," she muttered, her eyes narrowed.

Finally, the line clicked on. "Detective St. James," said that lighter, tenor version of Grayson's drawl. "To what do I owe this unexpected—and early—pleasure?"

"You know exactly what."

"I'm afraid I don't." Alex sounded both sleepy and honest. "I've heard what AMI says about us, but respectfully, ma'am, you've got an empath brother. You know we can't actually read minds."

"Where are they?"

There was a pause. "You mean Reece?" Alex finally said, sounding genuinely confused.

"Obviously that's not— Actually, yes, I would very much like to know where the hell my brother is."

In her ear, Alex yawned. "He went out."

"Bullshit," Jamey said. "Reece is never up this early."

"We were surprised too, though in hindsight, we probably shouldn't've been." In the background, she heard his footsteps now. Crossing a hardwood floor, from the sound of it.

"*We*," she repeated meaningfully.

"Yes, *we*," Alex said, more slowly. "As in myself and the lovely Ms. Falcon." He paused. "Who else do you think is here?"

Jamey frowned. Alex could be full of shit, of course, but he sure wasn't acting like someone who'd lured away ten of his fellow empaths the night before.

But if the empaths hadn't gone with Reece, Cora and Alex—

"Reece was with you until this morning, though?" Jamey said as her thoughts began to race. "And Cora is still with you now?"

On the other end of the phone, something opened and closed, a refrigerator by the sound of it. "You do know your voice is bordering on *concerned*?"

Alex was starting to sound more awake. Jamey cleared her throat. "Hazard of being a big sister."

"I see where Reece learned to deflect with sarcasm." He was pouring a glass of something, but underneath the sound of a filling cup was something else. She strained her ears to catch it: a sharp and echoing *caw*, more than one at once, repeating over and over. "While I have you, any chance you're in touch with Gretel Macy?"

Jamey glanced at the closed bedroom door. "Why would that be any of your business?"

"Someone out there is framing us for the murder of her parents. Considering what happened to *my* parents, I'm taking it a bit personal."

That was interesting. Jamey had seen the picture of Alex and Gretel at a hotel restaurant a few weeks ago. Alex had thralled Officer Stensby and that former army major turned airsoft course manager that night, but he'd let Gretel go unharmed. "We could all be working together to solve the murders, you know," Jamey pointed out.

"Which would be mighty fine, right up until you and Evan lock us away with a freak like Dr. Nichols again."

"We don't want—"

"My apologies for hanging up on you, ma'am, but I'm sure you understand my need for discretion."

"Alex—"

He'd already cut the line.

She palmed the phone for a moment. Hardwood floors, a fridge, gulls. Far from conclusive, but maybe they were in a residential house near the water? She filed that thought away to examine more closely later. For the moment, she needed to find ten missing empaths.

She stepped out from the bedroom. On the couch, Gretel's eyes were open. She seemed to be staring out the window, watching the snow.

"I made coffee," Jamey offered.

Gretel's gaze turned her way, eyes deeply bloodshot with purplish circles underneath. "That sounds great," she said, hoarse and quiet.

"Cream and sugar?"

Gretel nodded. Jamey ducked into the kitchen, pouring coffee into two mugs. Taking Gretel Macy to search for missing empaths would be a disaster of epic proportions. Except Jamey also knew what it was like to lose parents, and simply could not leave her by herself.

She stepped back into the living room, handing Gretel one of the mugs over the back of the couch. "I have to make a trip to Bellingham. You up for it?"

But Gretel shook her head. "I wish I could," she said, sounding honest, as she took the mug. "But I have to go see our lawyer today." She swallowed. "Only my lawyer now, I guess."

Jamey bit her lip, then said, "Will you come back afterwards?"

Gretel looked up. "Here?"

"Where there's murder, there are often other crimes," Jamey said. "I don't know yet if that's true for Charles Stone, but I'm certain that if he has any idea you suspect him, you're going to be in danger too. I said I'll help you, and I meant that. I can give you the spare key."

Gretel swallowed again. "Okay," she said with a watery sort of smile. "I'll come back. Thanks, Jamey."

Reece frowned as he followed Traynor's Tahoe around the bend of I-5, heading through Tacoma with no signs of slowing. "Where the fuck is this bank?" he said out loud.

CHAPTER TWENTY-TWO

Name: Dominique Lane (Diesel)

Source of referral: U.S. Marine Corps

Presenting concerns: Depression; grief; hypervigilance; sleep disturbances

Assessment: Patient was exposed to significant trauma overseas and is struggling to adjust to civilian life.

Note: Do not reassign. I'll try to help him, whatever he needs.

—Seattle Veterans Medical Complex patient records, filed by empath therapist Cora Falcon

"Ms. Marist?" Vivian Marist's American assistant, Leah, poked her head around the door of the office. "We have your new schedule for today."

Marist looked up from her email, lips pinching together. "And how many meetings has Senator Braun scheduled for us?"

Leah winced. "Eight."

Marist took a breath through her nose.

"But I do have some other news." Leah looked down at her

phone. “Gretel Macy just responded to your condolences. She said she’ll come by Stone Solutions today.”

“Oh.” Marist blew out a breath. “Good, that’s good,” she said. “I don’t care what Braun has planned—send Gretel straight to me when she gets here.”

“Yes, ma’am.”

“And have someone bring me a second latte.”

“On it.” Leah slipped back out the door.

Marist steepled her fingers. She was sorry for Gretel’s loss; that wasn’t a lie. But Gretel was also now in a position of immense power: the sole heiress of all of Beau Macy’s money, her own *Eyes on Empaths* blog poised to attract more attention than ever, and smart enough to take a leadership role in American Minds Intact, if she wanted.

They needed to talk.

After talking with Reece’s sister, Alex had gone to find Cora. St. James had obviously been looking for missing people when she’d called—people she’d assumed Alex had hidden from her. Pair that with her increased concern when it’d become clear Alex wasn’t behind this disappearance, and it wouldn’t have taken an empath to connect the dots and surmise the missing people were other empaths.

And that whoever might be responsible for their disappearance was potentially more distressing to St. James than the corrupted empaths.

Reece was still out, but Alex and Cora sat together at the table in Jason Owens’s kitchen turned war room, Evan’s laptop open between them and the spreadsheet of empaths and their suspected trigger points on-screen as they began to search.

“So Reece’s sister is missing some empaths.” Alex checked yet another social media site, but Mireya Gomez hadn’t posted in the past two weeks. "I don't like that. And I don't like that I haven't heard from Traynor yet this morning, and he's not answering my calls. How long does it take to get to the bank?"

"I don't think we're supposed to know Reece followed him." Across the table, Cora was also bent over her phone. "But no word from Reece either. And nothing unusual for Chand Gupta."

Alex looked at Evan's laptop to see who was next on the list. "I'll take June Hao."

"That gives me Dawson Jones."

They looked their empaths up in silence. Alex scrolled through June Hao's social media posts, checking the various pictures and captions. June was a Southern California girl who spent a lot of time cleaning up beaches. Her last post had been a week ago about her planned travels to Mexico.

Across the table, Cora suddenly straightened up. "Oh, Dawson. What were you thinking when you posted this?"

She held out the phone to Alex. On-screen was a popular photography-based social site. Dawson Jones, a twentysomething with brown hair and blue eyes, was taking a group selfie at what looked like an airport gate. There were at least five others beaming at the camera with him, some of them making hearts with their hands or peace signs.

Every single one of them wore empath gloves.

Meeting my new friends in Las Vegas! read the caption. *Next stop, Bellingham, Washington!*

The post was time-stamped the evening before.

"Oh my God," Alex said. "The naive little *idiots*."

"They have no idea Stone Solutions tracks their every post online." Cora was shaking her head. "No idea what kind of creeps would be interested that a whole cadre of empaths were congregating in Bellingham."

Their eyes met. "I bet Evan and St. James were trying to move them somewhere safe," Alex said. "But someone out there interfered."

"And we know exactly what kind of *someones* want their hands on empaths." Cora was pulling the laptop close. "I'm sending us both a copy of this spreadsheet for our phones. We want that list of names and then I say we head to Bellingham ourselves. Because someone out there might be messing with these empaths—but that someone isn't counting on *us*."

Grayson stopped for more coffee a little past Bremerton and the signs for the *USS Turner Joy*. The snowflakes were bigger on this side of the sound, and just starting to stick to the ground. His weather app was warning of more snow to come that night; he'd definitely be keeping this to a day trip.

As he stood for a moment, stretching his spine before he folded himself back into the Smart car, his gaze fell on the black Tahoe that was pulling into the gas station across the street. The Tahoe didn't stop at the pumps, but drove around the side of the station, out of sight. Same color and body style as the one that had been parked on the street outside the studio's high-rise.

Grayson watched for another minute, but the Tahoe didn't reappear.

After a long moment, Grayson got back in the car. He pulled back out onto the rural highway, heading off through the evergreens with their light dusting of snow.

After three or so miles, he checked his rearview mirror.

A black Tahoe was behind him, matching his speed.

Gretel hadn't lied to Jamey; she did meet with her family's lawyer. For all of twenty minutes, long enough for Mr. Carrollton to tell her that she'd inherited every last dime, and then, when she'd mentioned the police didn't want to hear her theories, he'd gently suggested that she should let the police do their job, and wasn't it time to put her own projects aside and focus on the real work of AMI, like her dad would have wanted?

She hadn't been able to get out of there fast enough.

Now she sat on a leather couch on the eighteenth floor of Stone Solutions, in a former conference room that had been temporarily transformed into an office suite. The windows framed Mount Rainier, the light snow lending a softness to the view. It was awe-inspiring enough it could have maybe granted her racing thoughts a second of peace.

If she weren't sharing the office with Stone Solutions' media director.

"—my condolences about your father: He was a great man, and of course everyone's so curious who's going to fill his shoes," Anthony, the director, went on, apparently oblivious to Gretel's grinding teeth. "Your blog has always been one of AMI's best publications, and naturally this sad event will mean your readership will only increase. It's really going to be all eyes on *you* now, and if you were to, say, write an article that was, say, endorsing a particular senator, well, I'm sure everyone would be reading. We're backing Senator Braun to take up Hannah Hathaway's anti-empathy mantle now, you know, and it just feels like you're uniquely positioned to use this tragedy to shine a light in dark places—perhaps it's even what your father would have wanted—"

Gretel's fingers tightened on her coffee cup.

"Anthony." That was Vivian Marist's voice, breaking in and finally stopping him. Marist was stepping around the couch, closer to Gretel's side. "Have someone get Ms. Macy another coffee, won't you?" Her voice was friendly but with a note of steel.

Gretel's coffee cup was still mostly full. But Anthony was already scrambling up to his feet. "Yes, of course."

The office door opened and then shut somewhere behind Gretel as Marist took a seat at her side on the leather sofa, the embodiment of feminine corporate chic from her pumps to her smooth French twist to the softest hint of perfume. "How are you holding up?" she asked, her voice much kinder.

Gretel set her coffee cup on the coffee table. "I'm not," she said flatly, too tired to mask and find something more socially acceptable to say.

Marist gave her a sad smile. "I'm sorry. I considered both of your parents my friends. It's a great loss."

She sounded sincere enough, but it didn't help Gretel get answers. "The police won't let me see my parents," she said, watching Marist. "I wish someone would tell me more about what happened to them."

"Murder is such a terrible, shocking crime," Marist said, which was true and also completely evasive. "And I'm sure you must be going mad with all the bureaucracy around the investigation. You've obviously got a sharp mind—it's evident in all your writing."

Marist picked up the coffee cup and pressed it back into Gretel's hands. "I read your blog, you know," she added.

What a neat little trick, turning the topic right back to Gretel. "I talked to our family lawyer today," Gretel said. "Mr. Carrollton was sympathetic, of course, but he said I should just listen to the police. What a strange answer from a lawyer to their client, don't you think?"

"I'm afraid I've never known much about criminal law," Marist said.

"I think you probably know Carrollton, though," Gretel said. "He used to be Stone Solutions' general counsel."

"It's such a small world around the empaths," Marist said with a rueful smile. "As you well know, of course: *Eyes on Empaths* has always been a key player."

It should have made Gretel proud to hear Marist praise the blog she'd worked so hard to build, to be included in the elite circle with AMI and Stone Solutions. But it felt hollow compared to Jamey's sympathetic hugs and warm mugs of tea, her concern that Gretel have a safe place to stay and her promises to help.

"Have you thought about your own future role with AMI?" Marist asked. "All your members are looking for guidance now. They know you and trust you. And of course, AMI and Stone Solutions have always had such a close relationship."

Gretel was pretty sure close relationships weren't supposed to end in *murder.* She set her mug back down. "So are you the official CEO now?"

Marist shook her head. "I'm simply holding down the fort for Cedrick," she said, and if she had ambitions beyond that, she hid it perfectly.

"But the board of directors could make you CEO, right?" Gretel said. "Except, of course, Charles Stone just came out of retirement."

"Where did you hear that?" Marist said with a tiny bit more of an edge.

"I like to stay informed," Gretel said politely, because Marist wasn't the only one who could give bullshit nonanswers. "Is he going to be running Stone Solutions?"

Marist delicately shook her head. "Charles has always preferred the freedom to move behind the scenes. He was the first director of the Empath Initiative, after all, but quickly passed that to Holt Traynor."

"He kept those connections close, though, didn't he?" Gretel said. "Wasn't it Charles who secured some of the military funding that goes to Stone Solutions? How did he ever move from defense contracting into the empathy business?"

Marist cleared her throat. "They're really not as different as everyone assumes."

"Except that empaths are harmless," Gretel said.

Marist's expression seemed to stay extra still. "That's what they tell everyone."

"I've seen that it's the truth," Gretel said. "I was here at an AMI meeting the night an empath broke in."

"Reece Davies, you mean?" Marist said. "Yes, he's been rather a problem for Stone Solutions for some time now."

"But your guards roughed him up," Gretel said. "And his pacifism runs so deep that he didn't even defend himself."

"The empaths are more complicated than the public has been led to believe," Marist said more softly. "I'm not at liberty to say more than that. Just know your sympathy for the empaths, and Reece Davies in particular, is misplaced, and our funding is more necessary than most could even imagine."

Gretel stared at her. What exactly was she implying—

The door opened. "Vivian, I'm sorry to bother you," Anthony said, peeking his head in. "I've got the coffee, but the senator is asking for you. He's doing another interview from conference room C in fifteen minutes, and he'd love for you to join him."

Marist's lips pursed ever so slightly. Then she glanced at Gretel.

Gretel faked a smile. "I need to be heading out anyway."

"Anthony can see you out. But know you always have Stone Solutions to turn to." Marist reached into her purse and then withdrew a business card. "My personal number. Call anytime." She stood up, stilettos clicking on the floor as she made her way out the door Anthony was still holding.

How very different this leather couch in this high-rise office was from the ancient couch in Jamey's little house. Gretel had been awake that morning, on the couch, and heard Jamey's quiet voice in the bedroom on one side of a phone call.

Actually, yes, I would very much like to know where the hell my brother is, Jamey had said.

Which didn't make any damn sense. How could Jamey not know where Reece was? From what Gretel understood of Reece, and empaths generally, they didn't like to make anyone worry about them. Why would Reece disappear and not tell his only family where he was?

She pulled her phone out, her gaze lingering on her texts, and a message that had come in the day before.

Alex: I'm sorry about your parents

It was the first message the two of them had exchanged since he'd sent the inexplicable picture of Officer Stensby and an airsoft course manager outside Cedrick Stone's office on the twenty-second floor of this very building. A fire had been set at Stone Solutions that same night. Was that why she was now in a temporary office on the eighteenth floor?

She could have sworn Alex had been genuinely interested in *Eyes on Empaths*, had wanted to hear all of her theories and thoughts. What would he say now if he knew where she was and who she suspected was behind her parents' murders?

Her gaze stole to the closed door along the wall, the one that led into Marist's temporary office.

Behind her, Anthony was approaching with a fresh coffee. "Here you are." Gretel was already holding her cup, so he set it awkwardly on the table. "Is there anything else I can help with before you go?" Anthony offered. "Senator Braun was just saying—"

"Actually," Gretel interrupted, a glimmer of an idea waking up inside her, "I really do need to get a blog post up. Maybe something about how hard Senator Braun is working in the wake of my dad's death."

She wouldn't write that in a million years, but sure enough, Anthony's eyes lit up. "Oh, that would hit very well," he said eagerly. "I could get you a visitor's office—"

"Maybe I could work in here?" Gretel said innocently.

Anthony hesitated. "In here?"

It was a long shot, thinking he'd let her stay in Marist's suite unsupervised, but she had to try. "I won't be long," she promised, holding the phone up. "Just a quick post from my cell. But I'd like to get it up as soon as possible: as you said, there are a lot of eyes on me right now."

"Well, I'd like to say yes, but this suite is really supposed to be private—" He cut himself off, pausing. "Actually, on second thought, I think we can make an exception for you. After all, you don't do anything except write blog posts, do you? You wouldn't need Vivian's computer, because AMI handles all the technical stuff?"

Gretel forced a bland smile on her lips. "Everyone knows I'm just a figurehead. I write and post from my phone; I can barely work a computer mouse."

"Great!" Anthony got to his feet. "I have to join Vivian and the new senator for their interviews." He added conspiratorially, "You'll have lots of peace and quiet to write your article about Senator Braun; it's just going to be empty in here all day."

"Sounds perfect," Gretel said, her gaze straying back to the door to the office.

CHAPTER TWENTY-THREE

On this episode of Heartfelt High, *the school's only empath struggles when the girl she's crushing on unexpectedly becomes captain of the field hockey team. Can an empath find a way to talk to her crush when just the sight of field hockey sticks sends her into a panic?*

—Advertisement for an early 2000s TV show

There was no trace of the pacifist empaths at Archipelago Air's Bellingham terminal. No trace of them at the Alaska state ferry terminal or the other piers. Jamey and Liam had gone to the hotel where they had booked rooms, and exactly none of the empaths had even checked in.

They stood on the curb outside of the hotel together, where the light snow was starting to stick at the sidewalk's edge. "Son of a bitch," Jamey said, aware she sounded very much like Reece. "Who took our empaths?"

Liam shrugged helplessly. "What now?"

"I think you should go get Aisha and Diesel," Jamey said. "The safe house might be compromised."

"I can fly up," Liam said. "You coming?"

Jamey shook her head. "I need to head back to Seattle for Gretel. I'm worried about her, especially if Charles Stone gets wind that Gretel figured out he called her dad and set up that meeting at AMI."

They kissed, holding each other tightly. "Meet me at home, okay? And be safe," Jamey said. "I'll see you soon."

When Grayson started nearing Port Angeles, he began watching the turnoffs. After a few more miles, he took an unpaved road off the highway that quickly turned narrow and tree-lined. He followed it south for a couple of miles, then pulled over into the narrow shoulder and parked.

He glanced at his phone as he climbed out of the Smart car. No signal. Perfect.

Grayson leaned against the car, snowflakes dusting his shoulders and coat as he waited. And sure enough, just a couple of minutes later, the black Tahoe came barreling down the same road.

Grayson stepped out straight into its path. The Tahoe slammed on the brakes, and Grayson caught sight of the driver.

"Director Traynor?"

Traynor was alive. But what the hell was he doing following Grayson? He strode over to the Tahoe and knocked on the glass. "Where have you been?" Grayson asked.

Traynor had his phone out and seemed to be typing very quickly. Not that it was gonna do him any good when he wasn't gonna be able to contact anyone. Grayson had chosen a spot with no signal for a reason.

Grayson rapped on the glass again. "We've been looking for you."

Traynor didn't lower the window. He didn't even look at Grayson. The close-cropped brown hair and broad build were familiar, even if Grayson had never seen the ex-general with a full beard before, but even through the glass, there was something unfamiliar about Traynor's movements, something almost robotic.

Grayson's senses went on higher alert, his muscles tensing. "Where have you been?" he asked again more slowly.

Yet again, Traynor ignored him. And then he wiped at his face.

Grayson peered through the tinted window, and caught a glimpse of streaks of red beneath Traynor's eyes.

Oh boy.

No one could say exactly how long empath thralls lasted, but the general theory was the more stress you put one under, the faster they burned out. Traynor had to be pretty stressed to find himself suddenly stranded with Grayson. Add in that they were a long way from Seattle now, far from whichever empath had thralled him, and the extra hormones forced into Traynor were likely running way too high.

Grayson considered him for a long moment. Then he said, enunciating each word, "Reece Davies makes terrible decisions."

Traynor didn't look up.

"Cora Falcon is hell-bent on vengeance," Grayson tried, still watching Traynor closely.

Traynor wiped at his eye, his gaze still on the phone.

Grayson cleared his throat. "Alex Grayson—"

"Shut up shut up *shut up*!"

The Tahoe's door flew open so hard and fast it came off its hinges. Grayson barely managed to dodge the door as Traynor burst out of the vehicle, arms outstretched, hands coming straight for Grayson's throat.

Traynor hit him like a freight train. They slammed down to the ground together, Traynor on top, Grayson's skull connecting with the dirt. He ignored the pain, trying to shove

Traynor off. But he was Grayson's own height, with a heavier build, and far stronger than he should have been from the empathy hijacking his systems.

They fought for several moments, Traynor's face twisting into a rictus smile as his hands came again for Grayson's throat. Grayson twisted, bringing his leg up to smash his boot into Traynor's side with enough force to finally topple him off.

As Traynor hit the ground, Grayson rolled to the side and grabbed the Tahoe door. Before Traynor could stand, Grayson smashed it down like a shield, holding it in place with his hands and knee and pinning Traynor under the metal.

Traynor bared his teeth.

"So Alex thralled you." Grayson didn't know when that had happened, but Traynor wasn't going to make it much longer. "Where is he now?"

"Leave Alex alone," Traynor said, a rage-infused growl.

"Where is Cora Falcon?" Grayson tried. "Or Reece Davies?"

Traynor's eyes were bleeding freely now, red tear tracks on his muddy face. "Reece is angry."

"Angry? Why?" Traynor pushed up against the car door with a renewed burst. Grayson slammed his knee into the metal, shoving him back down. "Why is Reece angry?"

"Because I'm following you."

"And?" Grayson said, confused. "Why would Reece be angry about that?"

"Because we were going to kill you."

"Alex sent you to kill me?"

"*No,*" Traynor snapped. "Alex said *don't hurt. Just follow.*"

None of this was making any sense. "But you just said Reece was angry because you were going to kill me."

"Not today," Traynor hissed. *"Before."*

Traynor shoved up again. There was more blood on his face now, from his eyes and nose both, his unnatural strength fueled by the empathy destroying him from the inside out. Grayson wasn't going to be able to keep him under the Tahoe door much longer. "When before?" Grayson said.

"In Vancouver."

Vancouver? Grayson stared at Traynor. "You were going to kill me . . . in Vancouver?"

"Yes," Traynor said. "You lied. About Alex. You had to die."

Go to the location Vivian Marist sent you, Reece had told him that night at the dock.

Marist? Grayson had replied. *Surprised to hear you pick Stone Solutions over the Empath Initiative. I was thinking if I had to pick, I'd meet Director Traynor.*

No, Reece had said. *Go to Marist.*

That night in Vancouver, Reece had sent Grayson to Marist's location to get him out of the way and clear the path for the empaths to ambush Traynor. It had worked and they'd taken Traynor with them, somehow keeping him alive and making him their thrall.

At least, that's what Grayson had assumed.

"You were going to kill me that night in Vancouver," Grayson said, half to himself. "But I never showed up."

"It was Reece in your truck," Traynor said. "He knew."

"Reece *knew*?"

No. Traynor had to be wrong, because that was impossible. How the hell could Reece have possibly known that Traynor planned to kill him—

But there was one way, wasn't there?

Reece had damn powerful empathy. He'd been suspicious already, had suspected that Grayson had pissed off Stone Solutions and the Empath Initiative by taking the empaths' side. Reece had told Grayson as much, had been worried they weren't going to tolerate that from Grayson forever, but Grayson had assumed he was untouchable.

Your arrogance is your biggest weakness, Evan.

The pacifist version of Reece in the truck with Grayson that night hadn't had a single shred of self-defense. If Reece had believed someone else was in danger, he would have tried to save them, no matter the potential cost to himself.

And the best chance he would've had to figure out where the danger might be coming from was using the corrupted empath's power of insight.

Reece had been on the edge between pacifism and corruption for months. If he had believed there was danger to Grayson and had reached for the power of insight on purpose, that might've been the final straw to push him fully into corruption.

Thoughts and memories were rising in Grayson's mind, insistent and strong. Grayson shook his head, clearing all of it away. "You said, 'We were going to kill you.' Who's *we*?"

Traynor only pushed at the car door, growling inhumanly.

"Who were you working with to kill me?" Grayson tried again.

But Traynor didn't speak. Now blood was running freely from his nose as well as his eyes. He wasn't coming back. Not from this.

Grayson stepped back, simultaneously drawing his gun in a rapid motion. Traynor roared and pushed up at the car door. Grayson fired a single bullet, right in the center of his forehead.

Traynor slumped to the ground, instantly dead. A more merciful death, maybe, than letting the corruption eat away at him for a couple more hours until it inevitably killed him.

Grayson's chest felt tighter than normal, his heart beating a little too fast. But then, he was sweaty from the fight, still breathing hard from the physical exertion.

He got back in the Smart car, starting the engine.

Reece might have sacrificed his pacifism for the chance to save Grayson's life. Knowing that was exactly the kind of thing that might've given someone else feelings.

So it was a good thing Grayson didn't have any. However it had happened, Reece was corrupted now, and innocent people couldn't afford for the Dead Man to forget that.

But if Reece could choose corruption to save you, maybe there is *a chance it could be reversed. For Reece—for Alex—for all of the empaths—*

Grayson ignored the voice, pulling the Smart car back onto the road. St. James could hope the empaths could be saved; he'd remember that they needed to be stopped. He'd get Nichols's research for her so she could keep having hope, and the Dead Man would stay the empaths' enemy.

CHAPTER TWENTY-FOUR

Remember our conversation about whether empaths could potentially be acclimated to violence if we started exposure young enough?

Get on the next plane to Seattle.

You're not going to believe this.

—Thirty-eight-year-old note buried in a filing cabinet at the Empath Initiative

Alex leaned on the rail on the Bellingham Boardwalk, gaze not on the water but on his phone. Gretel had responded to his condolences about her parents.

Gretel: What would you say if I told you I think my parents' murder was a setup?

His eyebrows went up. How much did she know? Who did she suspect? The waves rolled in quietly as he typed a message back.

Alex: I'd say you're probably right. Your parents were pretty powerful people.

Another pair of texts came in a moment later.

Gretel: Not as much power as the person who had them murdered.

Gretel: Nobody is going to believe me about this. I'm never going to get to justice.

Had she even been told anything about her parents? Was she ever going to be allowed to see her parents' bodies—to bury them? Or was she just going to be kept in the dark for the rest of her life, never getting answers or closures?

And suddenly he was typing again, too honestly.

Alex: One of the most powerful men you can think of had my parents murdered too. I'm still working on "justice."

Cora's steps echoed on the boardwalk as she came to join him at the railing. "I found a park staffer," she said. "But she said she hasn't seen any boats on the water today with the weather."

"So where the hell did a group of pacifist empaths go by land?" Alex said, pocketing his phone.

Cora closed her eyes. A minute went by. Then she swallowed. "Stone Solutions has access to that abandoned pulp mill by Everett. Plenty of space, right on the water with enough land that no one hears anything. Even screaming."

Rage flared in Alex, the reminder of what Cora and her fiancé, John, had been put through in November. Stopping Nichols, stopping Stone—it wasn't just about the chaos. It was vengeance, for all the people they'd hurt—John, Gretel's parents, his parents, Evan.

He reached for her hand. Their fingers intertwined, and emotion flowed between them for a moment, no words needed.

Finally she seemed to shake herself. "So are we gonna look for some empaths?"

He nodded. "Let's go."

As soon as Anthony left, Gretel wasted no time crossing the swanky sitting area and opening the unlocked door to Vivian Marist's office. She stepped inside, taking in the oversized mahogany desk with its expensive ergonomic chair and the personal printer in the corner. The wall held framed art of mountains hung beside an oversized flat-screen monitor, and a few of Marist's things were scattered around the office, including her coat and scarf hanging in the corner.

The desk held a monitor, a mousepad and a laptop in the dock. Gretel took a seat at the desk and booted up the laptop. It was password-protected, but in the corner was the option to log in as Guest. She clicked on that, and the screen opened to an internal homepage.

She didn't actually expect to find proof Charles Stone was a murderer on the Stone Solutions intranet. But on that call with Charles, her dad had mentioned that shareholders were concerned about a suspicious filing from October.

Where there's murder, there are often other crimes, Jamey had said that morning.

Gretel had already glanced over the 8-K in question herself. It seemed like nothing more than the required notice to Stone Solutions shareholders regarding the acquisition of three small companies that made materials used in the empath gloves. Building a vertical supply chain sounded like profit as usual to her, not something to raise suspicion, but she was printing all of it to go through with Jamey, just in case.

As she waited for the exhibits and attachments to print, her gaze fell on the monitor on the wall. Could this be some kind of stock ticker? Or something else tracking the financial information she was looking for?

Gretel stood up and stepped toward it. She ran a hand along the bottom edge of the monitor until she found the power button. She pressed it, and the screen burst into life.

It was a map of North America, speckled with blue dots. There were no controls visible, so she touched the screen like she would her phone, and the map shifted slightly. She made a flicking motion with her fingers, zooming in more closely on a cluster in Chicago, watching as three of the blue dots slowly moved together along Shoreline Drive heading north. She touched one of the dots, and a profile popped up with a picture and biographical details for a thirtysomething empath nurse.

"Oh my God," Gretel said out loud as her stomach turned over. She clicked on a second blue dot, then the third, and then a fourth in Madison and a fifth in Minneapolis. Each one pulled up a profile for an empath.

Stone Solutions was tracking all of them.

Two days ago, she might have believed anything Stone Solutions had done was for the greater good. But then, two days ago, she hadn't been convinced the CEO's father was a stone-cold murderer.

Her phone chimed. She kept one eye on the door and pulled out her phone to see a new text from Alex.

Alex: One of the most powerful men you can think of had my parents murdered too. I'm still working on "justice."

She stilled, gaze flicking between the door and the monitor and her phone.

Alex's parents had been murdered too? But he'd said he was from Texas. What powerful man that she might think of would have reach all the way into Texas?

Charles and Cedrick Stone, her mind supplied. *You're looking right now at how their control stretches across every inch of the country.*

Her gaze went back to the screen. She zoomed out, and then zoomed back in on northwest Washington. Her brow furrowed. There were no blue dots in Washington.

"Where are Cora and Reece?" she said out loud as she zoomed back out, scanning the West Coast for dots. Then, on one side of the map, her gaze fell on three red dots clustered in the ocean. She clicked on one of them and pulled up a picture of a familiar empath.

Reece Davies, location unknown, said the caption.

Gretel stared at Reece's picture, Marist's words coming back to her.

The empaths are more complicated than the public has been led to believe. I'm not at liberty to say more than that. Just know your sympathy for the empaths, and Reece Davies in particular, is misplaced, and our funding is more necessary than most could even imagine.

Gretel clicked on the second red dot and found herself looking at a picture of Cora.

Cora Falcon, location unknown.

Gretel furrowed her brow. She looked back at the map and pressed on the third red dot. And suddenly she was staring at a younger version of the man she'd had brunch with, who'd texted to say he was sorry about her parents.

Alex Grayson, said the caption. *Location unknown.*

Reece scrolled through search results on his phone as he waited for the gas pump—because maybe Grayson could drive Reece's Smart car for ages on a single tank, but Reece had to fill up—and frowned. The only connection to EI that was turning up in the area was the old unfinished facility outside Port A. Why the hell would Evan be heading *there*?

The pump finally stopped, and Reece got back on the road as quickly as he could.

But the minutes ticked by with no sign of Traynor's Tahoe.

"Where the fuck are you?" he muttered as he finally pulled onto the shoulder and idled the truck. The wipers swished away the falling snow as he opened his GPS. It only took a moment to pull up the tracker they'd put on Traynor's Tahoe: He was actually *behind* Reece, a little ways down some tiny side road that didn't even have a name.

"What. The. Hell." Reece put the truck back in gear. He had the advantage of a vehicle capable of handling a snowy road, so he cut straight across the two lanes and the median to head back east. A few minutes later, he made a right turn at a gas station, heading south on a road that turned empty almost instantly.

Reece didn't like this at all.

A couple of miles down the road, he caught sight of a black Tahoe on the shoulder, looking abandoned at the base of green pine trees.

"Son of a bitch." Reece slammed on the brakes, pulling over onto the opposite shoulder. He hopped down from the truck and approached the vehicle.

The snow was sticking to the ground now, beginning to pile, but not quite high enough yet to hide the evidence of a recent struggle: mud churned up, footprints everywhere, the Tahoe's driver's door smashed on the ground.

Red streaks all over the snow.

Reece crouched down by a particularly bloody patch of snow next to the Tahoe's smashed door, cold snowflakes dotting the back of his neck. There was no sign of Traynor himself. Was this his blood?

Traynor was following Evan, the little voice in Reece's head pointed out.

His fingers curled into a fist. If one single drop of this blood was Grayson's—

He shot to his feet and followed the red trail into the tree line. Then he stilled.

At the base of a pine lay Holt Traynor, eyes open and glassy, blood smeared across his face from his eyes, his nose and the single bullet wound in the center of his forehead.

Reece felt himself tense.

The bullet would have torn through skin, burning flesh and bone in its wake—

He brushed angrily at his own forehead before an echo could bloom on his skin. He wasn't that goddamn pacifist anymore, and he would not feel grief or phantom pain over fucking Traynor.

He forced himself to stare at the corpse, to try to piece the scene together. Had Traynor been too far from Alex, burning out, bleeding from the eyes, maybe losing all control? And someone else had been here with Traynor, someone armed and with good enough aim to take him out with one bullet, giving Traynor a more merciful death than the inevitable thrall burnout?

Reece could take a pretty good guess who'd fired the shot.

He backtracked to the Tahoe and then headed several paces down the road, already suspecting what he'd find. And sure enough, in the mud beyond the Tahoe was a different set of tire tracks; these were small and narrow, the perfect size to have been left by a Smart car.

He went back to the truck, starting the engine right up and doing a tight U-turn to head back to the highway, this time with more speed.

If this was Grayson's work—as it almost certainly was—he

would have made arrangements for the body's removal, which meant Reece needed to be out of there immediately.

He didn't know for sure where Grayson was going, but they weren't too far from the abandoned EI facility now. Reece was going to trust his gut. He punched the gas, and the engine opened up full throttle, the high-pitched whine of the turbos echoing around empty trees as he sped back north.

CHAPTER TWENTY-FIVE

. . . the Dead Man kept Reece the empath pinned to the hood of the Smart car. "I know just about everything there is to know about empaths," said the bigger man. "Except this: Is it true you can feel what people are feeling all the time . . . even in bed?"

Reece squirmed on the car hood. "Why?" He smirked. "Would you let me go if I said yes?"

The Dead Man tightened his grip. He was supposed to be an empath hunter, but he wanted to hunt Reece right into the nearest bedroom.

(continued in the next comment)

—Excerpt from *Hunting for Love*, an empath/empath hunter fan fiction

Between the snow, the icy road and the Hayabusa engine, Grayson had had to drive like a snail. Finally, though, he made it to the closed Empath Initiative facility outside the Port Angeles city limits, where it stood alone on the several tree-covered acres originally planned for expansive research facilities.

Of course, after EI had decided it'd be easier to funnel tax-payer money into a private institution than jump through all the government hoops to keep their own research aboveboard, Stone Solutions had taken over research and development, moving all operations to Seattle and shuttering this facility. It felt as unused as it was, the lights off and graffiti on one wall—not the good kind, with bright colors and art, but some smeared black spray paint spelling out four words.

We don't want empathy!

The painter probably hadn't even realized the irony.

The old parking lot was blanketed in a thin sheet of undisturbed snow. Grayson inched the Smart car into the lot, pulling into a spot at the edge, under pine branches. The snow was still coming down, and harder now; he'd need to move fast, because it wouldn't take much for him to come back to the little Smart car buried in snow.

He climbed out from the car and ducked under the edge of the tree line, following it along the parking lot, although stray flakes of snow still landed on his hat and shoulders between the branches. He skipped the front of the building, heading for the entrances at the back, where he found a door already loose on its hinges, so that Grayson was able to nudge it open and slip inside.

It opened to a small foyer with a linoleum hall heading toward the building's core. There was no furniture to be seen and the electricity had been turned off, or maybe never connected, making the interior cold and dim, lit by only the light that made it through the windows with their years of grimy buildup.

The abandoned feeling was even stronger inside. But as Grayson started forward to the hall, he heard the softest sound above his head.

Not a mouse or other rodent visitor.

Footsteps. One floor up.

Grayson pulled out his gun. Keeping his own footfalls silent, he traversed the hall until he came to a large staircase heading up and out of view. After one flight, a large landing opened to the second floor, the stairs continuing up to the third and fourth floors above.

Following his memory of the floor plan, Grayson stepped out onto the carpets of the second floor. Similar to EI's Seattle office, the center of the floor was a mazelike run of basic cubicles with half-height walls, and the perimeter was lined with office doors, all of them closed.

Except one, at the very end of the hall.

Eyes sharp and gun at the ready, Grayson crept down the hall, to the door with its plaque reading *Director.* It was cracked open just a few inches.

As silently as he could, Grayson inched closer. He raised the gun and then, in one smooth motion, shouldered open the door and spun into the room.

The office was empty.

Grayson's gaze darted around the space, ears pricked for any more sounds. But it wasn't his eyes or ears that picked something up. It was his nose.

Because as Grayson inhaled, he caught a faint scent he'd noticed at McFeely's: his own shampoo.

The empty EI building was silent around Grayson, like it was holding its breath. As quietly as he could, he pulled out his phone.

Grayson: Marco

He sent the text and waited.

A few seconds ticked by.

Then, somewhere on the third floor over his head, he heard the unmistakable chime—the sound of an empath who'd forgotten to silence his phone.

Grayson was off the mark like a sprinter. Above his head, footsteps were racing down the third-floor hall. Grayson tracked them, following as the footfalls on the ceiling sped back to the stairs. He reached the stairs first, tucking himself out of sight behind the wall.

Just as the footsteps hit the second floor, he spun back out onto the landing, putting himself right into the intruder's path, gun aimed straight at them.

"Freeze."

Reece did.

Silence fell around them, broken only by Reece's panting breaths. There was a flush on his cheeks, a light sheen of sweat to his skin. "Polo," he finally said through clenched teeth.

Here they were again, the Dead Man versus a corrupted empath.

He might be corrupted because he sacrificed his pacifism for a chance to save your life, said a voice in Grayson's head. *Because he chose you over himself, just like he did before—*

Grayson couldn't afford those thoughts, not right now. "You didn't answer my texts."

"Yes, and I realize that's probably a new experience for someone as hot as you." Reece was still breathing hard from his run. At his sides, his bare hands were balled into fists. "But gunpoint is a little extreme, don't you think?"

"Actually, I think gunpoint is right where we're at these days." Grayson didn't lower the Magnum. "What are you doing here?"

"Aren't you going to tell me to put my hands up before you start the interrogation?"

"Why would I? You're not carrying a weapon; you *are* the weapon. It just doesn't work on me," Grayson said. "And I asked why you're here."

"Scoping out the real estate," Reece said. "Your brother wants a new evil lair."

"You're gonna sass me *now*? Right now, when I have you isolated and at gunpoint?"

"I think we'll have to cross this location off the list, though," Reece said. "Where would we put our moat of emotionally enslaved sharks—"

"Did you come here for Victor Nichols's research?"

Reece's eyebrows went up. "Why would it be here, and not tucked away in—oh, say, a safe-deposit box back in Seattle?"

They eyed each other for a long moment.

That had been a very specific thing to say.

"You know something you ought to tell me?" Grayson said.

"Aw, baby," Reece said with cloying sweetness. "You really got to accept that I'm never gonna tell you shit."

Silence fell again around them, and really, what had Grayson thought was gonna happen? That Reece would confess he'd used insight to save Grayson's life? That Reece would say *let's work together, Evan*?

Maybe the old Reece had saved Grayson's life, but that Reece was gone, and this new Reece didn't care if Grayson lived or died. It didn't matter *how* Reece had become corrupted; what mattered was that he *was* corrupted, and the Dead Man needed to take him somewhere that he couldn't hurt anyone else. Needed to knock Reece out. Nice and easy. Right now.

"If you like," Grayson heard himself say instead. "But the way I see it, it's pretty simple: Either you answer my questions, or I search you, and we both know what's gonna happen if I put my hands on you. Seems like you might prefer to stay conscious, but what do I know?"

Reece's eyes narrowed. "We've touched plenty of times already. Every time I've gotten more immune to it. So you don't even know if your touch will still knock me out."

"Want to find out?"

Reece's jaw tightened. But he didn't answer.

Grayson's gaze darted over Reece's body, the close-fitting hoodie and jeans. Plenty of pockets to hide a small item, though Grayson probably shouldn't think too hard about what else was under Reece's clothes. Something a lot more fun than a flash drive, at any rate.

He gestured with the gun. "*Now* I need you to put your hands up."

"Why?" Reece said suspiciously.

"Because I said so. And either you follow directions or you take a little nap and wake up behind bars. Up to you, sugar."

Reece rolled his eyes but stuck his hands in the air.

"Take three steps backward," Grayson said. "So your back is against the wall. And keep those hands up."

With obvious reluctance, Reece obeyed, never taking his eyes off Grayson.

Grayson transferred the gun to his left hand, lowering it but keeping it at his side. He stepped within arm's reach of Reece, close enough he could scent the shampoo again. Close enough he could feel the warmth Reece always radiated.

Reece raised his chin. Grayson was more than a head taller, dwarfing him this close, so that Reece fit like a puzzle piece into the small space between Grayson's body and the wall. "I'm trying not to touch you, but you decided not to wear gloves. Which means if our hands brush, it's bare skin." Grayson had lowered his voice without planning to. "So unless you're itching to pass out on this floor, keep those hands nice and high and out of the way for me."

Reece exhaled, and Grayson felt the air skate over his collarbone. He was hyperaware of Reece's lips, his own lips suddenly tingling with the memory of just how good their one stolen kiss had been. He'd be lying if he pretended part of him wasn't aching to lift Reece right up against the wall and steal another.

But the more they touched, the more they risked Reece becoming immune to his knockout ability. Grayson slipped his hand in the hoodie's left pocket, finding nothing. "Don't tell me I'm gonna have to go into your jeans," he said as he checked the second pocket and found it empty too.

"Not like it's your first time." Was it Grayson's imagination, or had Reece's voice also gone lower and more strained?

Grayson rested his hand on the wall, just to the side of Reece's hands, as he eyed the jeans in question. "You couldn't've worn them looser?"

"I thought you liked *tight fits.*" Oh, Reece's voice was definitely lower, and he was still breathing too hard. His hands remained up against the wall, on either side of his head, his fingers occasionally flexing, like all that empathy at his literal fingertips was being held back from reaching for Grayson.

Grayson tried to push all those thoughts out of his head, but it was so much harder to ignore how much his body still wanted Reece when he had him *right fucking here.* "Front or back?"

"That seems like a very forward question."

"Pockets," Grayson drawled, even though Reece had known damn well what he was asking. He hooked his finger through the belt loop on Reece's hip and tugged. "Unless you're really counting on a layer of denim to protect you from my touch?"

"It will," Reece said. "And guess what? That's not a lie."

"Just means *you* believe it."

"Mmm, maybe. But if you'll cast your memory back to our little interlude in the truck, you'll remember we locked lips for a few seconds before I passed out."

"I'm not exactly gonna forget," Grayson said, his whisper low and gravelly. "But what's that got to do with your jeans?"

Reece took a breath through his nose. His cheeks had a flush that seemed out of place in the freezing, unheated air of the old EI facility. "Do the math, Evan. If we can kiss, I don't think you can knock me out through denim. In fact, I bet the next time we touch, I'll last even longer. So to speak."

Grayson slid his hand around Reece's hip to run it over his back pocket, feeling for the outline of a flash drive. Reece inhaled sharply, his head falling back against the wall and exposing his throat.

"You go right ahead and test that theory," Grayson said, letting his palm come to rest over Reece's back pocket. "Put your hand on me and see what happens."

Reece's throat moved as he swallowed. "As if you're not being *handsy* enough for both of us. Is this how polite Southern boys behave?"

His sarcasm was belied by the breaths that hadn't slowed, but then, Grayson was breathing more shallowly himself. Every nerve felt hyperaware of Reece, scent and sight and sound overwhelming his own good sense.

His hand was still on that back pocket, right on Reece's ass. Grayson flexed his arm, using his grip to nudge Reece just that tiny bit closer. "You could just give me Nichols's research."

"What makes you think I have it?"

Grayson squeezed his ass pointedly. "If you *don't* have it, you could just tell me instead of making me grope you to find out."

"We're not on the same side, asshole. I'm not here to draw you maps." Except Reece was pressing *into* his touch, not away from it, a small arch of his back, stretching up just one more inch. "Why did you leave those office maps in Traynor's office anyway?"

"What are you talking about?"

"You *know* what I'm talking about."

Reece wasn't making a lick of sense—or maybe finally having his hand on Reece, even through jeans, had wreaked havoc on Grayson's ability to form thoughts.

Reece's cheeks were even more flushed now, and against

the wall, his fingers flexed again. "Do I really have to keep my hands up and off you?"

"Yeah. You do," Grayson said. "'Cause you're the one who didn't want to talk."

He slid his hand into Reece's back pocket, drawing another sharp inhale. Reece's gaze fell to his lips, his tongue darting out to wet his own lips. "Why should I talk when we could kiss?"

Another pulse of desire went through Grayson. He tried to ignore it. "You do remember what happened last time you tried that?"

Reece shrugged lightly, a small movement with his hands still up by his head. "I bet if we kiss for only a second, it won't knock me out."

That was probably true. And also a damn trap.

"Nice try," Grayson said, "but I'm not falling for that."

"Falling for what?" Reece said, too innocent.

"You know what." It'd be so easy for Grayson to pull him right into his arms and kiss him. And Reece was right; if they kept it short enough, he should stay conscious. But giving in to the pull was out of the question.

"We're not gonna keep building your immunity to me. I'm not gonna let you get any more used to my touch than you already are." Grayson's body made a liar of him as he bent his head another inch. "We're not kissing. Not a chance."

"You sure?" Reece's voice was barely louder than his breaths. "Because you look like a man about to make a bad decision."

"You make me want to," Grayson heard himself whisper.

He might have been leaning down, or maybe Reece was stretching up on his toes, when Reece suddenly yanked back. "Who the fuck is that?"

"Who?" Grayson started to ask. But then he heard it: an engine—no, *several* engines, pulling into the building's parking lot.

"You brought Stone Solutions with you again?" Reece's tone was accusing, maybe even hurt.

"*No,*" Grayson said, pulling his hand off Reece. "I came alone last night; I came alone today. I always work alone; it's safer."

"Don't lie to me, Evan—"

"Reece, I swear," Grayson said. "I didn't bring anyone. I didn't even know you were here."

Reece took a hard breath. "Fine." His pupils had dilated, making his eyes glittery black, as his empathy went on high alert, picking up the emotions around them. "But at least two dozen people just arrived. And they are ready for a fight."

Grayson stepped back, straining his ears.

"—that's the Smart car, he must be here somewhere—we have nothing to fear, we're ready for him this time—"

He knew that voice.

Grayson grabbed Reece by the hoodie sleeve. "This way," he said, as he yanked him out of the stairwell.

Reece stumbled on his shorter legs as Grayson tugged him down the hall. "Where are we going?"

"You have to get out of here." Grayson pulled Reece into the closest office. "Right *now.*"

He jammed the Magnum into its holster. He could hear the footsteps spreading out through the parking lot as he stretched up to the ceiling.

"I can handle twenty people," Reece started as Grayson popped a ceiling tile loose.

"I still got bruises from the last time you handled people." Grayson pointed to the hole he'd just made in the ceiling. "There are industrial-sized air vents above us that feed this office and the building. They can handle your average-sized maintenance man and can definitely handle an empath. Follow them to the end of the building, and you can get into the fire stairs from there." He held out his pocket-sized flashlight. "Be careful and don't get caught."

Reece took the flashlight delicately so their fingers didn't brush. "And you'll climb up behind me?"

Grayson shook his head. "I'm too heavy for the vents. But it doesn't matter if this group finds me. I got every right to be here." He held out his hands, cupped together to make a footrest. "Just like old times, right?"

In the distance, he could hear the voices.

"—spread out and search the building—"

They were getting closer, maybe in the lobby already.

"Come *on*," Grayson said. "Do you want to be a lab rat? You gotta move, Reece. I'll buy you time."

Reece swallowed. He set his foot into Grayson's hands, gripping his shoulders, just like they'd done a short time and a lifetime ago. "But *why*?" He sounded so lost as he looked into Grayson's eyes, his oversized pupils like twin night skies. "Why are you helping me escape?"

Because I hear Victor Nichols downstairs. And I can't let him have you.

And Grayson couldn't stop himself: He darted in and brushed their lips together. It lasted less than a heartbeat, but he heard Reece's breath catch, and the spark their split-second kiss lit across Grayson's skin should've powered the whole building.

"I got my reasons," Grayson whispered.

And before Reece could speak, Grayson boosted him up. Reece grabbed the ceiling and levered himself inside, disappearing into the vent. Grayson snatched up the ceiling tile from the floor as Reece looked down from the opening.

"*Go*," Grayson urged him in a whisper. "Care Bear, please."

Reece seemed about to say something. But then he swallowed down whatever it was and disappeared. Grayson fit the ceiling tile back in place as quickly as he could, hiding all evidence of

Reece. Then he strolled out of the office, pulling the door closed behind him just seconds before a half-dozen armed soldiers in balaclavas and fatigues burst from the stairs.

"Can I help you?" Grayson said, flat as he said everything.

But the soldiers kept coming, pouring out of the stairwell without stopping. Safeties were being disengaged, weapons clicking in three hundred sixty degrees as they formed a tight circle around Grayson.

"Agent Grayson." That was Victor Nichols's voice. The circle around Grayson parted just enough to let Nichols's familiar figure through. He stood with his forces ringing them and met Grayson's eyes. "I've been waiting for you."

—that's the Smart car, he must be here somewhere—we have nothing to fear, we're ready for him this time—

The realization hit too late.

Nichols had never known Reece was here.

"Take him down," Nichols said calmly.

And then the soldiers were on him.

CHAPTER TWENTY-SIX

Formidable though he may be, the Dead Man has a fatal weakness as surely as Achilles: he will always choose to act as a guardian of the empaths, even when it poses a risk to himself. A stupid and worthless flaw. The empaths only fear him. They'll never reciprocate his protectiveness.

—One-year-old text from Victor Nichols to [REDACTED]

Sean Lennox, head of Charles Stone's personal security, looked over the message he'd just received with a flash of irritation.

Snow increasing. Communications limited.

"Get it the fuck together," Lennox snapped at his phone. The snow was still mild enough on the east side of the sound. He ducked under the roof of one of the structures that made up the former pulp mill north of Everett and put his phone to his ear as he made his scheduled call.

"Ah, Sean, right on time," Charles Stone said, as he answered. "I always do appreciate your punctuality."

"Yes, sir," Lennox said. "We're ready to transport the empaths to the Olympia facility, but that team is pushing back."

"The snow is picking up in the mountains," Charles said. "I'm choosing to see it as an excuse for a slight change in the plans."

Lennox raised his eyebrows. "I was under the impression Dr. Nichols wanted to keep a tight schedule," he said delicately.

"Well, yes," Charles admitted. "But you see, I take pride in correctly predicting the tides of public opinion, and I feel that Seattle may still need a little more nudging in the right direction."

Lennox was pretty sure *the right direction* was just another way to say *supporting the big anti-empathy senate bill*, but he liked his paycheck enough to keep his mouth shut.

"I'm afraid Victor will need to wait one more day for the rest of his guests," Charles went on. "He'll understand that the weather simply doesn't permit us to deliver them yet anyway." He cleared his throat. "We will be moving them to a different location, however. Prepare the vehicles."

"Yes, sir," Lennox said. Whatever the boss man wanted.

Grayson had been right: Reece had found the maintenance vents comfortably big enough to fit him. He crawled the length of the old EI building on hands and knees, then kicked off the metal cover at the end and ducked out onto a landing in the fire stairs. He used Grayson's flashlight to make his way down the stairs to the ground floor and the exit, his empathy on high alert for any sense of others' emotions moving in his direction.

But as he stepped outside, he was still alone. Twilight was falling, giving him cover as he darted across the parking lot and into the trees, the jumble of emotions in the facility behind him fading with distance as he hurried back to the truck he'd carefully parked offroad, where it wouldn't be seen.

He levered himself up into the truck and slammed the door, then blew out a breath.

That had been easy.

He went to start the engine, then paused.

That had been *too* easy.

He sat back against the driver's seat, gaze going out the windshield to the darkening trees. More than two dozen people arriving together, all of them itching for a fight, and yet none of them had chased him? None of them were following, none searching the grounds?

No. There was a much more likely explanation.

Reece had never been the target.

He put a hand over his mouth, where his lips still tingled from their brush with Grayson's.

You have to get out of here, Grayson had said.

Whatever Grayson had heard, he'd thought it meant danger to Reece. Reece had assumed that meant the newcomers were from Stone Solutions.

But if Reece hadn't been the target, then maybe it wasn't Stone Solutions that had arrived. But then who had Grayson heard—

Do you want to be a lab rat?

Reece's eyes widened.

Not Stone Solutions.

Polaris.

And if *Reece* hadn't been their target—

You know something you ought to tell me? Grayson had asked.

Aw, baby, Reece had said. *You really got to accept that I'm never gonna tell you shit.*

Son of a bitch.

Reece was scrambling back down from the truck before he'd realized he was moving.

What are you doing? some part of him screamed. *You know what Nichols is capable of. You have to get out of here.*

Reece was already back in the tree line, gaze on the parking lot as he scurried along the edge. He could feel the people again, little suns of emotion up ahead.

Grayson hadn't known what Reece was talking about when he mentioned the maps in Traynor's office. If Polaris hadn't come for Reece, if Grayson had been the target all along, then maybe someone else had put them there, to lure him to Port Angeles.

And Grayson had had no idea he was in danger because Reece had refused to talk to him.

Reece moved across the slippery wet snow, closer to the building.

Evan *is a big boy,* said the voice. *He can take care of himself. He tells you that all the time.*

Not this time. He was outnumbered and had walked right into a trap.

He doesn't feel fear.

No.

But he could feel pain.

Reece skidded to a stop in the mud at the tree line's edge. Up ahead in the EI parking lot were three black SUVs and one unmarked van. The doors of the van were open, and two burly soldiers were stuffing a limp body into the back.

"*Evan,*" Reece said, the name coming out in an exhaled rush, like he'd been gut-punched.

But before he could take even one more step, the soldiers had jumped into the van, slamming the doors.

And then the vehicles were on the move, taking Grayson with them.

The driveway was empty when Jamey returned to her house, the patchy layer of snow undisturbed by tire tracks. She had just pulled out her phone to call Gretel when she heard a car coming down her street. A moment later, the white BMW coupe was pulling in next to her.

Relief washed through Jamey as she got out of Liam's Corolla. Gretel was getting out of her car as well. "Long time at the lawyer's?" Jamey asked as she made her way toward Gretel.

"Well," Gretel said cagily, "I had to make another stop too."

Wet snowflakes fell on Jamey's hair as she peered inside the car and saw several accordion folders stacked on the passenger seat. "What's all this?"

"Research." Gretel added ruefully, "You probably didn't know what you were getting into when you agreed to help an obsessive neurodivergent blogger."

Jamey snorted. "I said I'd help. I meant it. Are you hungry—"

"I picked up dinner too." Gretel was folding the driver's seat forward and reaching into the back seat, lifting a stack of Styrofoam containers in a plastic bag that smelled amazing. "You like tikka masala?"

Inside the house, Jamey set the stack of folders on the dining table. "Liam is on his way here," she said. "He's bringing a couple more friends, people I trust. They'll want to help too."

Gretel was by the couch, opening her bag, but at that she looked up and over at Jamey. "Your friends would help me too?"

"Of course." Jamey tapped the folders. "You said there might be something fishy about one of these filings, an 8-K?"

"That's what I heard my dad imply on his call." Gretel pulled a laptop out of her bag. "This was his," she said as she crossed to the table and set it down next to the containers and folders. "My dad also mentioned he had talked to another shareholder that I know. We can look through his emails."

Jamey raised her eyebrows. "Do the cops know you have your dad's laptop?"

"Nope." Gretel smiled without humor. "You'd think it'd be obvious that I might have borrowed it, but everyone in Seattle thinks I'm a useless figurehead while an AMI team does all the actual work on my blog. Well." She cleared her throat. "Almost everyone, I should say. Reece knew the truth."

Jamey swallowed. "Yeah," she said. "A lot of people underestimate him too."

"I bet," Gretel said lightly. "Is Liam bringing Reece over tonight?"

"Um . . . no," Jamey said awkwardly. "But—"

"Because you've never actually mentioned where Reece is."

Jamey hid her wince. "He's . . . traveling. Out of town."

"Is he." Gretel folded her arms. "Speaking of empaths, how about Cora Falcon? I haven't seen her lately either."

"Oh." Jamey cleared her throat. "I, um. I'm not sure. Maybe the hospital knows?"

"Right," Gretel said, drawing the word out. "And by chance do you know an empath named Alex Grayson?"

Shit. They stood there for a moment, on either side of Jamey's cozy dining table, their gazes locked. "Why do you ask?" Jamey finally said.

"I've been noticing things lately, things that don't add up around the empaths. Then today Vivian Marist made some comments that seemed . . . odd," Gretel said. "Is there something more to know about Reece and the empaths, Jamey?"

Jamey bit her lip.

The silence fell again.

Eventually, Gretel sighed. "All right, I do get it," she said, sounding more resigned and rueful than angry. "*Eyes on Empaths* hasn't exactly been a beacon of positivity in your life. If it was my brother, I wouldn't tell me anything either."

Outside, another car was pulling into the driveway. Jamey nodded toward the door. "That will be Liam and our friends."

Gretel looked out the window, then back at Jamey in confusion, the overhead light catching the circles under her eyes. "One of your friends is the hot McFeely's bouncer?"

Outside of Everett, in the woods on the same property as the abandoned pulp mill, Alex crouched next to Cora behind the tree line, watching the guards opening the back doors of a windowless van.

"There," he said quietly.

A large man, armed with an equally large gun, was trying to direct empaths toward the van. One of the empaths, probably half the man's size, was shaking her head rapidly and pointing at the gun in fear.

As Alex watched, the man backhanded the empath, sending her staggering into the others, who instantly crowded around her like worried ducklings.

Anger flooded him, in tandem with Cora's hissed breath. "I'm going to make that man break his own teeth," Alex said under his breath.

"I want my shot at him first," Cora said through a clenched jaw. "But what's happening here? Where are they taking this many empaths?"

The guards seemed to have gotten tired of waiting. They were grabbing the empaths, who were utterly without defense, limp and unresisting as the guards forced them into the van.

Alex and Cora exchanged a look. "Thrall or investigate?" Alex whispered.

"Investigate," Cora said decisively. "This isn't the head of the snake, but maybe they'll lead us there. Come on; I have an idea."

She ducked out from behind the trees. "Hi, guards!" Cora called brightly as Alex scrambled after her.

All of the guards turned as one to stare at them. "Where the fuck did you come from?" said the big guard with the gun.

"Oh, we got loose last night," Cora said, still bright. "We were going to run away, but then we realized that your boss might get mad at you, so obviously we had to come back."

"What she said." Alex matched her tone with a sugary-sweet one of his own. "We sure don't want you to get in trouble," he added, all big eyes and innocence and of course, lies. "We wouldn't ever be able to stand someone else getting hurt."

"Empaths. Jesus Christ," one of the guards muttered.

The biggest one gestured with his gun. "Get the fuck over here," he snapped. "And get in the fucking van with the others."

"Yes, sir," Alex and Cora said together, and climbed inside.

CHAPTER TWENTY-SEVEN

Whether Hades's guardian was a monster or a protector depends on your point of view. Either way, don't start a fight with the darkness unless you're ready for Cerberus.

—A.G., untitled blog

Private Dane had done a lot of sketchy assignments in his life, but guarding some weird-ass secret laboratory two thirds of the way up a mountain, on countless private forested acres hours away from the nearest town, had to top the list.

"I'm freezing my nuts off." Croft, Dane's squad mate, wasn't hiding his annoyance as they continued their patrol around the perimeter of the building, which looked short and squat from the outside, its low profile set into the mountainside with most of the floors underground. "Snow's fucking burying us now."

Dane grunted. They weren't supposed to talk on the watch.

Croft wasn't wrong, though. The morning had started with a dusting of snow that had picked up strength with the falling night, piling on the ground and weighing down the tree branches. Now, the darkness around them had an eerie white cast to it, with thick clouds overhead and ceaseless snow blurring the view like static on an old television.

"Stupid to make us come out," Croft went on. "What are we even watching for?"

"That guy we took down," Dane said, against his better judgment.

"What, Agent Grayson?" Croft scoffed. "Did you see how deep into this hellhole they took him? He's not getting out of that lab."

"He ain't normal."

"No shit he ain't normal," said Croft. "He's the one they call the Dead Man."

Dane knew that—they'd gotten the same fucking briefing on the target. "Yeah, and he's the only Dead Man in the fucking world. Someone might want him back."

"You see this fucking snow? And this fucking mountain?" Croft gestured to the sky and then the steep mountainside, the snow dense enough to block the view of the chain link and barbed wire fence below. "There are no plows because there's no fucking roads here. No fucking towns. Even if someone managed to find us—big fucking if—you'd have to be a world-class driver with an all-terrain vehicle to make it up the mountain. No one is coming for the Dead Man."

They fell silent. Gusts of snow blew across their path as the wind howled between them, deep and powerful and rumbling like a supercharged V-8.

Dane paused. "Did you hear something?"

The table beneath him was cold against his bare back. Grayson registered it distantly, the way he would have registered the clouds in the sky—or the way he registered the bite of metal on his wrists and ankles. The air was cold too; there was the low, persistent hum of a generator somewhere, but whatever power it provided sure wasn't being used for heat. In his nose were the scents of strong antiseptics and an unpleasant earthy smell of damp underground.

He opened his eyes to overly bright fluorescent lights on a low ceiling and stark white walls. Whatever table he was on seemed to be in the middle of a good-sized room. The wall to his right had windows in the top half, the better to observe him with, maybe. On the wall to his left was a metal cabinet and a desk, only the back of a monitor visible, and above his head was the telltale red dot of a camera. Everything had a hazy sort of quality, which he was gonna blame on whatever was coming through the IV hooked into his left arm, and he was cold because they'd taken everything except his boxer briefs.

Whatever was coming, it wasn't gonna be a good time.

He flexed experimentally, not surprised when the metal on his wrists and ankles refused to budge. He hadn't been captured by amateurs. They knew how strong he was.

Grayson looked up at the camera. "Can I have my clothes back, please?" he said dryly.

A moment later, a door in the wall at his feet swung open. In walked Victor Nichols, in a lab coat and carrying a tablet, his pale blue eyes eager behind the glasses. "Agent Grayson. You woke earlier than expected."

More people in lab coats were following Nichols into the room, four of them. They were spreading across the room like efficient robots, never meeting Grayson's gaze.

His eyes went back to Nichols, whose edges seemed blurred in the too-bright lights. "How about you put me back to sleep?" Grayson said. "And I wake up in a bed, in a room that isn't forty below?"

"Your sense of humor is lacking." Nichols was typing into the tablet. "But given your circumstances, I suppose it is remarkable that you kept it all."

One of the scientists had stepped up to the desk on his left and seemed to be booting up the computer. Grayson watched as Nichols strode over to the desk and set the tablet carelessly on the surface. "What are we doing here, Doctor?"

"Tests. Obviously," Nichols said, like Grayson was stupid, as he made his way from the desk to the metal cabinet, which was being unlocked by a second scientist.

"What kind of *tests* require me to be chained to a table?"

"Did your brother destroy your imagination along with your feelings?" Nichols snapped.

The metal cabinet door swung open, blocking what little view Grayson had from the table. A moment later he heard wheels behind him, rolling along the smooth floor.

Nichols was suddenly leaning over him. "We're going to spend significant time together over the next few months, so I want to make something clear: You are not unique."

Grayson pushed the word *months* out of his mind. "What're you talking about?"

"You are not the precious snowflake so many in our field believe," Nichols said with a nasty sort of smile. "You are simply an experiment. And experiments can be duplicated."

Grayson squinted against lights beyond Nichols, too-bright and oddly haloed through the drugs. "You think you can make more Dead Men?"

"I *will* make more Dead Men," Nichols said. "In this lab I'll have all of the materials I need."

"Materials." Grayson pulled uselessly against the restraints. "What's that code for? Empaths?"

"Observe," Nichols said, turning his head to talk over his shoulder at the lab coat–clad figure behind the desk. "Merely the implication of empaths in danger triggers a protective reaction. This is exactly the flaw we cannot tolerate in our new subjects. Make a note of this moment."

Grayson flexed again, even though it was pointless. "Who're your new Dead Men going to be? You gonna have more soldiers kidnapped, like the ones you took to Polaris?"

"No need this time," Nichols said distractedly. "This lab has been staffed with a larger-than-average security force of trained military personnel. I'm authorized to make any of them my test subjects at will."

"Do they know that?" Grayson said. "For that matter, does Stone Solutions know you've got me here and what you're planning?"

"You mean Vivian?" Nichols scoffed. "As if she'd ever have the stomach for it. But rest assured, I am backed by those with the *real* power." He moved the tray closer, the wheels squeaking along the floor. "I'd hardly expect you to grasp the importance of my work, but we do not require your approval, and your cooperation can be forced. I have my soldiers and I will have my empaths, and I cannot wait to see all we can accomplish now that we no longer have to kowtow to your infantile demands about their treatment."

Nichols leaned over Grayson again, his pale eyes very large behind the glasses. "You know, I had actually thought it was safest to dispose of you completely. I even had Holt on my side," he said. "But I can admit that this is better: Now I can harvest everything of use from you until we can recreate the experiment. And *then* you can die."

Grayson could just barely see the edge of the tray at the bedside: a selection of syringes and surgical instruments, their shapes fogged along the edges, just like the room's people.

Nichols was now giving his bare arms and chest a cursory glance. "I can see the evidence of your empathy-induced enhancements, particularly the accelerated healing. You have very few scars, especially given your history." He leaned closer. "Though there is this one here. I assume this is from the incident in November?"

He was pointing to Grayson's shoulder, to the round bullet scar.

You got this scar protecting me from corruption, Reece had whispered the night in the truck in Vancouver. *You took a bullet for me.*

You believed saving my life was worth more than your freedom, Grayson had answered. *A bullet was more than worth a chance to save your heart.*

Grayson hadn't saved Reece from corruption after all.

But that bullet had still been worth it, and he should've told Reece that when he'd had the chance.

Nichols seemed to realize Grayson wasn't going to answer. He huffed. "Silence is pointless. I have your medical records." He reached for the tray again, and as he straightened, he was holding a syringe and a small vial. "We're going to start with some chemical testing. I have theories, of course, but I need to confirm—"

The door at Grayson's feet opened. Nichols turned sharply toward the sound, his eyes widening with shock for a split-second before they immediately narrowed. Grayson craned his neck as much as he could to see.

Standing in the doorway was Reece.

He was completely alone, in the same hoodie and jeans from the EI facility, looking particularly short and slight in the frame of the door.

"Reece." Grayson's voice was hoarser than he'd expected, not much more than a quiet croak. "Get out of here."

Behind Grayson and around the room, scientists were springing into action. Grayson could hear them on the phone, the words *security* and *get to the main lab immediately*. Could hear an insistent alarm start up on the floor above.

"Mr. Davies," Nichols said, his lip curling. "How are you here?"

Reece still stood motionless in the doorway. His eyes were

on Grayson, flicking from the IV to his bare chest to his cuffed wrists. "Front door was open."

Reece's sarcasm was gonna get him killed. "*Reece*," Grayson said again, more insistent and even more hoarse. "This is Victor Nichols. You have to run—"

"Mr. Davies," Nichols said again, talking over Grayson. "Your attitude has no place here, and you are about to regret breaking into my facility."

Reece finally raised his gaze from Grayson to Nichols. "That's not a lie," he said, with the calm of a first distant roll of thunder. "So I guess you actually believe that."

"I assure you," Nichols started, "our security is uniquely ready to handle—"

"What were you going to do to Evan, Dr. Nichols?"

Reece's question hadn't been loud, but there was an edge of ice to it that somehow dropped the temperature in the room even lower. The alarm on the floor above was suddenly louder in the moment of silence that followed.

"Why isn't security here?" one of the scientists whispered.

Grayson pulled against his restraints. "*Reece*—"

"Shh," Reece said, putting a finger to his lips, his gaze still fixed on Nichols. "Not now, baby. It's my turn to handle things."

Nichols made a choked noise of surprise. "You've been having a romantic liaison with a corrupted empath?" he hissed at Grayson.

Grayson opened his mouth.

"The bigger problem is that you kidnapped a corrupted empath's *romantic liaison*," Reece said, speaking first. "And *I found him in chains*."

The words echoed around the room, the thunder no longer a distant threat but directly overhead as Reece's empathically fueled anger vibrated underneath his words.

Then Reece took a step into the lab. "I asked you what you were planning for Evan, Dr. Nichols."

"Where is security?" Nichols hissed at his scientists, who were already backing up.

Reece took another step forward. "Those are some pretty nasty-looking tools on that tray."

"We need *security*—"

"Were you going to use any of that on him?"

The syringe and vial clattered to the floor as Nichols snatched up a scalpel from the tray. "Stay back," he demanded, brandishing it at Reece. "Security is on their way, and they're ready for you—"

"You mean these guys?"

As Reece gestured around him, more people were already flowing into the room. Three, now seven, now ten, some in lab coats and some in fatigues, all of them wearing identical expressions of menace trained on Nichols.

"My first thralls," Reece said as the newcomers advanced, parting around him like a river around a rock and fanning out to flank him. "Go big or go home, as they say."

He shrugged. "I can admit I've made a bad decision or two in my day. But I'm making only good decisions tonight."

Nichols's eyes widened. And then he was lunging not for Reece but for Grayson on the table, scalpel brandished like a sword.

Reece's thralls were faster. Screams erupted as four of them surged at Nichols, wrestling him back before the scalpel made contact and dragging him away from Grayson. As the screams rose in pitch, Grayson heard Reece over the din.

"Get Evan free and maul the rest of them. Bring Nichols to me."

The roars of the thralls joined the unceasing upstairs alarm and fresh screams. Grayson yanked uselessly against his cuffs. "Reece—"

In the edge of his vision, he caught Reece and Nichols. Reece's hand was on Nichols's face as his expression transformed from terror to wide-eyed devotion, and then thralled soldiers and scientists were blocking Grayson's view.

"Here's what you're going to do for me," he heard Reece say somewhere in the chaos as the thralls spread out around the exam table. "You're going to take that tray of yours into the next room and lock yourself in. And then anything you've ever done to another empath, or their siblings, and *especially* anything you were planning to do to Evan, you're going to do to yourself instead. Sound fair?"

Jesus. "Reece," Grayson tried as a new thrall popped up on his right, key in hand. *"Reece—"*

Nichols voice came with an unrecognizable bright eagerness. "Yes, sir, Mr. Davies."

On Grayson's left, beyond the thralls, a body hit the metal cabinet with a dull clang. Then, under the clamor around him, he caught that same sound of wheels on smooth flooring as Nichols grabbed the edge of the tray, pushing it like a shopping cart and practically skipping with glee out the still-open door at Grayson's feet.

A petite woman in a blood-splattered white lab coat was now unlocking the cuff on Grayson's wrist. Reece appeared next to her. "Get him free," he said to the woman. "And make sure he gets out safe."

Reece began to turn.

"Wait," Grayson said as his right wrist came free and the petite woman passed the key to a thrall on his left side. "Don't go."

"You don't want me here," Reece said, not turning around or looking back at him. "You always knew it was only a matter of time before I became a monster. That time has thoroughly arrived."

There was a wet squishy sound somewhere behind Grayson, and a new scream. The cuff on his left wrist came loose. He sat up, pulling the IV line out of his arm. "I'm coming with you."

"Evan, no," Reece snapped. "You don't want—"

"I *do* want," Grayson said. "You think you can rescue me out of a nightmare and then I'm gonna let you *leave*?"

"You can find your way out, I promise. Just follow the trail of breadcrumbs I left in my wake," Reece said bitingly. "And by *breadcrumbs*, I mean *bodies*."

The cuffs on Grayson's ankles popped free. "I'm coming with you," Grayson said again. "Wherever you go now. We're staying together."

Reece stood for a moment with his back to Grayson, hands balled into fists. "Son of a bitch," he finally muttered. He then turned around. "Okay. Together. But *I'm* handling things."

Grayson slid off the table and onto his feet. "I can handle myself—" He swayed, blinking hard against the black dots threatening his vision, aware of the goose bumps all over his skin. "Never mind. That's a damn lie. This is your show. Just find me some clothes."

From an underground level, they stumbled up the stairs together. Reece should have fucking glowed, the way his empathy was crackling like lightning along his skin.

He could feel fear and fury throughout the facility like dots on a radar. "Ten people on this floor, maybe twenty more still up top."

Grayson was obviously still woozy, clinging to the railing for support as his bare feet climbed stair after stair. It was enough to make Reece want to head back down and make Nichols suffer more.

But getting Grayson warm, and the absolute hell out of here, was more important. "He needs clothes," Reece snapped at one of the thralls. "And we need an exit."

"Barracks," one of the men in fatigues said eagerly. He was one of the first pair Reece had thralled, after he'd driven the truck through the fence and two men had come running to investigate. "Follow me and Croft."

They pushed open the door at the landing.

"Freeze—" a voice started.

One of the thralls in a lab coat threw himself ahead of Reece, snarling like a rabid dog. He smacked into the security guard in the hall, and the two of them went crashing to the ground.

"This way!" Croft led them away from the fight, down a hall and through another door into a large room lined with bunk beds every few feet on either side.

"Finally, some heat," Grayson muttered.

Two of the thralls in fatigues scurried off to a cabinet on the wall. Reece followed Croft down to the end of the room, to a small foyer with a door. "This is how you can get out," Croft said.

"What's the security situation?" Reece asked another man in fatigues.

"They'll have unleashed the dogs by now." The man cracked the door, and the wind howled past. "But if you cut straight across this field, you can get back to your truck. Snow's still coming down, though; we got ATVs and snowmobiles, but they're on the other side of the lab—"

A swirl of snowflakes came in through the open door. "No time to get them," Reece said. "Every alarm here is going off. Someone is going to be responding to this mess. We'll get the truck."

"Can you drive in this?" Grayson asked, catching up. There

was still a slight slur in his hoarse voice as he tugged a long-sleeved thermal over his head, at least a size too small and not quite reaching the top of the camouflage pants he was now wearing, like a crop top.

Reece waved the question away. "All of you," he snapped, raising his voice.

His thralls came running over eagerly.

"We're escaping, and I need you to buy us time, understand?" Reece said to them. "Fuck this place up. And then burn it down."

The thralls cheered. "Weapons locker is this way!" one of them shouted.

"Damn, Reece," he heard Grayson mutter as the thralls scattered.

It took only a moment for Grayson to pull on the army boots and coat. And then they were plunging out into the snowstorm, the wind making Reece's eyes water as ice-cold droplets stung his face.

"You didn't answer my question about whether you can drive in this," Grayson shouted over the wind.

"Because nobody should drive in this weather," Reece shouted back.

Behind them, the alarms were still blaring. A few steps forward and the flat area in front of the lab became an abrupt incline that disappeared into darkness, forcing them to temper their speed to the steep ground as they fought their way through the snow.

"I think I smell smoke," Grayson said as they stumbled downhill. "And I definitely hear dogs."

"And I can't fucking thrall dogs." Reece spotted an opening between the dark outlines of two trees. "Let's try this path."

"Reece, wait!"

But just as Reece had stepped forward, the snow gave way

under his feet and he was falling, stomach plummeting as he went tumbling several feet down the mountainside.

He landed in a snowbank, and the shock of cold against his face was like a physical slap. Why hadn't *he* grabbed a coat from the barracks—

The snow was suddenly brushed away at his side. "Are you all right?"

"I'm okay." Reece distantly registered the lie. "Just fucking cold."

"At least you missed the trees." There was an insistent tug on his sweatshirt sleeve. "I got you," said Grayson, his grip strong enough to help Reece up. "Come on."

Moments later, they were back on their feet, fighting their way through the snow but having to temper their walks to the steep ground.

Up ahead through the trees, Reece could just make out a shiny black mass. "There she is!"

"Hallelujah." Grayson followed him forward, still without his usual grace.

They got into the truck just as a loud boom echoed around the mountainside. Reece looked back at the lab just in time to see flames erupt from a set of ground-floor windows, leaping red and orange illuminating the snow.

"Someone's playing with chemicals," he observed as he turned the key. The truck came to life with a beautiful roar. "I love this thing," Reece admitted, shivering hard enough to make his hand shaky as he went for the seat belt. "You're never getting her back. Put your damn seat belt on."

"Reece—"

"This is going to be a bitch of a drive, and I promise nothing," Reece said. "Seat belt. On."

As slow as he could, he pulled the truck out into the snow and began to inch down the mountainside.

Grayson was going for the heat and seat warmers. "Where are we?"

"Olympic Mountains. Really fucking far from anything." Reece swore again as the tires slipped and the truck slid several feet down the mountainside. "Evan, trying to drive might be a bad decision."

"Of course it is." Grayson's teeth were chattering. "But staying in that lab to await the cavalry would've been worse."

The truck slid again, then got its grip. Reece tightened his hands on the steering wheel as he swerved around a cluster of trees.

"How damp are your clothes?" Grayson asked.

"I'm soaked, but it doesn't matter," Reece said. "The heat's on—"

A sudden crack split the air. A moment later, a giant branch smashed the windshield, and the truck spiraled out of his control, sliding straight for another grouping of trees.

Reece had a split second to react: Continue the slide right and smash the passenger side; turn the wheel and collide on the driver's side.

But he knew in his bones that when it came to Evan, there was only one decision he was ever going to make.

He yanked the wheel to spin Grayson safely out of reach just as the truck impacted hard enough to rattle his teeth. There was a loud crunch and a burst of white.

And then everything was black.

CHAPTER TWENTY-EIGHT

...I'm willing to admit that I don't have the first clue how Alex Grayson turned Evan Grayson into the Dead Man, but it hardly matters. We might not know how it was achieved, but we know he can no longer be swayed by emotion. We can be certain that in any situation, Agent Grayson will always follow the most logical path.

—Confidential communication between the Empath Initiative and Stone Solutions

Jamey's house was bustling that night. Liam and Gretel were sharing the kitchen table, bent over Beau Macy's laptop. Aisha and Diesel were in the living room, Gretel's printouts from Stone Solutions spread out over the coffee table.

Jamey herself was pacing the hall. She'd had no word from Grayson since he'd left that morning for Port Angeles, and her last text to him still sat on her phone unanswered. She looked at her other unanswered calls and texts, to Reece, to Cora, to Alex.

She didn't like this at all.

Gretel had heard her dad imply there was something suspicious about an 8-K Stone Solutions had filed in October, which detailed the acquisition of three small manufacturing companies that made materials for the gloves.

And just a couple of days ago, the empaths had interfered with a delivery of heavy metals destined for the empath gloves, sending the ship off to a wind farm in California instead.

Could there be some kind of connection, maybe the shipment coming from one of the new acquisitions? The empaths had gone into the delivery room during their break-in at Stone Solutions, but the head of security, Wayne Smith, had said there was nothing in there. So where had the empaths learned about the shipment?

If only she could get one of them to pick up, for this and so many other reasons.

Or if only she could find them.

She sat down on the shoe bench by her front door and put her head in her hands. Her mind replayed the sounds she'd heard in the background during her call with Alex that day: hardwood floors, a refrigerator, gulls.

The picture of a residential house near the water rose in her mind again, something upscale with those floors and the waterside location. She turned the image over in her mind. She'd never met an empath who cared about luxury; would corrupted empaths really be any different?

"Think, Jamey," she whispered to herself. "Don't think like your average Joe; think like an empath. If they don't care about luxury, why would Alex, Reece and Cora hide in a high-end house?"

Because they think it's the last place anyone will look for them.

She ran a hand over her hair. But why? Why would an upscale residential home by the water be the last place anyone would look for empaths? Hell, how did they even know about a place like that unless it was—

She shot to her feet. "Jason fucking Owens's house."

Aisha looked up from that couch. "What was that, Jamey?"

But Jamey was already moving. "Liam, I'm taking your car," she called over her shoulder, just catching the noise of assent as she grabbed the keys on her way out the door.

One moment, Grayson and Reece had been careening down the mountainside through the staticky snow, the wind loud enough to hear over the engine, the red-orange glow of the laboratory fire long gone behind them.

Then a branch had shattered the windshield, the truck had started slipping, and Reece had suddenly yanked the steering wheel.

There had been a crunch so loud it hurt Grayson's ears, the impact rattling the entire cab. The air bags had gone off, knocking Grayson's head against the back of the seat, and whatever cocktail of drugs was still in his system finally overwhelmed him and the world went dark.

When he opened his eyes, the truck was cold as ice, and snow had built up in a layer on the windshield.

"Reece?" He shoved the airbag aside. *"Reece."*

He sat up, looking over to where Reece was slumped in the driver's seat.

Not moving.

Grayson's mind was rapidly piecing everything together, the branch, Reece suddenly turning the truck, the impact—

The impact that had hit on the *driver's* side. Reece's own side, protecting Grayson from the worst of the collision.

"Reece," Grayson said again, uselessly. Why had he turned the truck? Grayson was so much bigger, so much stronger—he could've taken the hit. And now Reece was out cold—maybe worse—

Well, no reason to worry about his knockout touch *now.* His arm shot out over the console to find Reece's neck, his fingers resting against his jugular.

A pulse.

Alive.

Grayson twisted, unbuckling his seat belt so he could move freely. Subfreezing temperatures, unceasing snow, and Reece unconscious: He had to get the truck running to get them out of the storm, or at least get some heat.

But the situation was pretty grim. Grayson reached around Reece to try the truck's key first, but not a single light came on, and the engine wouldn't turn over. He rummaged over the airbag and in the glove box, because Reece had to have a flashlight somewhere, but all he came up with was the bear hat and the headband with bunny ears Reece had worn at McFeely's.

The clouds blocked any moonlight as Grayson opened the passenger door and stepped out into the snow, which was deep enough to reach his thighs. He pushed through it on shaky legs to the front of the truck to investigate, feeling carefully around with his half-frozen fingers. Seemed like the collision had impacted on the driver's-side corner, and Reece's quick maneuvering had probably saved their lives, but whether the engine had taken damage and what kind wasn't gonna be clear without light.

All right. Truck wasn't gonna start. Snow wasn't gonna stop. Grayson could carry Reece, but carry him where? Grayson had been unconscious for the trip that had hauled him here from Port A and had no idea how long or far they'd traveled.

Olympic Mountains, Reece had said when Grayson had asked where they were. *Really fucking far from anything.*

Reece knew where they were, but Grayson was gonna need him to wake up to tell him.

Grayson carefully made his way around the tree through the snow and got the driver's door open. He reached for the unmoving silhouette outlined in the driver's seat, his hand touching Reece's cheek. Not a scarily powerful corrupted paranormal in that moment, just an unconscious, injured empath whose body temperature was probably dangerously low.

You got to check him for injuries, his mind pointed out. *That's gonna mean touching him. A lot.*

Grayson blew out a breath. So he'd have his hands on Reece. It would be fine. The Dead Man was a professional.

Keeping his touch light and gentle, he ran his hands over Reece, assessing and searching. There was a bump on his head, and his neck was probably gonna hurt, but nothing felt broken or alarmingly swollen. His cold, wet clothes, however, confirmed what Grayson had earlier suspected: The tumble Reece had taken into the snowdrift had soaked him through. How long had they both been unconscious, with Reece freezing in wet clothes?

Snow was coming into the truck through his open door. He shouldn't move Reece in case of injuries, but it was looking like they were gonna have to hunker down in the truck through the storm with no heat, waiting for morning or Reece to wake up. Even empath blood wasn't gonna save Reece from possible frostbite.

Grayson's hand came to rest on Reece's cheek again in the dark. "I'm not too proud to admit it should be you awake right now, not me," he said a little helplessly to Reece. "You might know how to get the truck running or where we should go. I might've called you Bad Decision Bear, but—"

Memories abruptly came crashing back. Grayson had bought Reece the bear hat in Vancouver, but Reece had bought him something that night too: a big-and-tall sleeping bag, so that Grayson would have a warm place to sleep when he caught a nap in his truck. It had been in the back seat when Reece had stolen the truck from him. Was there a chance it was still there, something to keep Reece warm until he woke up?

Grayson got out of the truck and opened the back door. The only light came from the glow of the snow, but he got the seats up, and when he stuck his hand into the dark storage compartment under the seats, it landed on the sleeping bag. He pulled it out and put the seats back in place, then unzipped the sleeping bag and laid it out on the back seat. He was already shivering himself, but he'd deal with that after he got Reece settled.

Grayson would have to get him out of the wet clothes first, though. In other words, get him out of *all* his clothes and manhandle him into the sleeping bag.

Grayson took a breath through his nose.

Professional. Yes he was.

It wasn't easy to strip off the wet clothes, especially when Grayson needed to move achingly slow and careful, trying to jostle Reece as little as possible. He spread the clothes out on the passenger seat best he could; pointless, because they weren't gonna dry in these temperatures, but it didn't hurt to try. Then he carefully lifted Reece out of the driver's seat.

It took a lot more awkward maneuvering, but he finally got Reece onto the back seat on top of the unzipped sleeping bag, and all the truck doors securely closed around them. Grayson was shivering harder, and more concerning, Reece's skin was icy cold under Grayson's already cold hands. He knew more about surviving heat stroke than frostbite, but getting Reece warm as fast as possible was probably the most important thing right now.

There was, of course, something Grayson could do to warm Reece more quickly.

He could get in the sleeping bag with him.

Your clothes are wet from snow too, a little voice in his head pointed out. *You have to take them off. If you're in there, with all that skin-to-skin contact, one of two things is gonna happen: Reece is going to stay unconscious until you stop touching him—or he's gonna get used to your touch and wake up.*

And if that happens, you'll never get that power back. You'll never have that defense against him ever again.

Grayson touched his fingers to Reece's lips, feeling the cold blue, even if he couldn't see it in the dark.

Reece's life was in danger. So he could risk losing his last Dead Man defense against corrupted Reece. Or he could risk losing every version of Reece—forever.

Grayson reached for his own shirt hem, and a moment later, he'd shed his damp fatigues. He crawled onto the back seat, balancing on one arm as he slid the other arm beneath Reece. As carefully as he could, he pulled Reece up and over, rolling them both so that Grayson was the one on his back on the sleeping bag that was open on the truck's back seat, now with Reece sprawled directly on top of him. He shifted Reece so that his head was set on Grayson's chest, and then reached for the sleeping bag's edge, pulling it over them.

It took a few trics, especially with his own cold, unsteady fingers, but Grayson managed to get the zipper aligned. "I'm real glad right now that you insisted on getting the big-and-tall size," Grayson informed Reece as he pulled the zipper all the way up.

The back of the sleeping bag came up around his own head like a hood, and he made sure the front of it had Reece fully covered, all the way over the top of his head. It was a tight fit—and no, Grayson would not think about tight fits right now, not with Reece *right on top of him*—and their skin was cold together. But Reece, in his concern for Grayson, had picked a thick, warm sleeping bag designed for freezing temperatures; if anything could warm them up, this would.

Grayson wrapped his arms around Reece—trying to warm him up, that's what he was doing, that's what this was, and where the hell else was he supposed to put his arms anyway?—and pulled him up just a little higher, tucked up under his chin.

What if Reece wakes up like this? said the little voice in his head. *Immune to your Dead Man touch?*

Well. Grayson would just cross that bridge if they came to it.

At least it would mean they were both alive.

Outside the truck, the wind was still howling, rushing through the trees like an eighteen-wheeler blowing past on the highway. Inside the truck, Grayson couldn't even see the front seats anymore. The snow had coated the windows, so that everywhere he looked was either black or faintly white. But he could feel Reece on top of him, the rise and fall of breath, the soft, cold skin under his hands, the hair tickling Grayson's collarbone.

He heard his own quiet voice in the truck cab. "Probably good I don't have feelings. 'Cause if I did, I bet I'd be having a lot of them right now."

Why was he talking? Reece couldn't hear him. But words were falling from his lips all the same. "And I haven't said thanks. For coming for me—for *saving* me. I owe you, Care Bear."

I'm not your Care Bear anymore, Reece had said.

Grayson tightened his arms.

"The hell you're not," he whispered into the silent truck.

CHAPTER TWENTY-NINE

. . . and while some have called our research "sensationalized," a survey of diverse mythology suggests sexual demons were believed to prey on mortals, drawing their own energy from their partners' pleasure. In this paper we will argue that through their emotional absorption, empaths possess this same quality . . .

—Excerpt from *Empaths: The Modern-Day Incubus*, a privately funded study

Lumen Field was eerily silent after midnight, with a ghostlike quality to the endless rows of seats. Sean Lennox and his team were in a press box rented for the day, a security camera broadcasting to a large monitor and several empty pizza boxes and energy drink cans scattered about the room.

Lennox himself had been watching the camera for several minutes, but the empaths weren't doing anything. Just huddled together in the Stone Solutions luxury box on another level, hugging and comforting each other.

He counted their bent heads again. Definitely twelve. Hadn't they only grabbed ten in Bellingham?

The door to the press box opened, and Charles Stone

stepped inside. “Well done, Sean,” he said to Lennox. “I trust everything is in order?”

“Absolutely. No issues at all transporting the empaths here.” He wasn’t gonna fucking say anything about the numbers. More empaths could only be a good thing.

“Excellent,” Charles said. “And are we ready to broadcast to the empaths?”

Lennox nodded. A moment later, Charles was seated at the table in front of a laptop. “Go ahead and put me through.”

Lennox clicked through, and a moment later, the empaths were all looking up and over at the television in the suite.

Charles leaned forward. “Hello, empaths. I trust you’re comfortable enough, although perhaps wondering why you’ve been locked into our corporate box at Lumen Field?”

The empaths exchanged confused looks, some of them nodding.

Charles steepled his fingers. “Tomorrow, our home team will be playing one of their rival teams. We expect a very full stadium, but in that stadium, we unfortunately also expect some violent and dangerous elements to appear.”

The empaths collectively gasped. Several covered their mouths in horror. Lennox rolled his eyes. Fucking little drama queens.

“It is essential that you remain in that box and make no attempts to communicate with the press or anyone else, or quite a lot of people may be hurt,” Charles said. “Or worse.”

There was outpouring of protests from the empaths, cries about the danger to the stadium. “Why is this happening?” one of the empaths demanded.

But Charles had already ended the call, the screen in front of him going black. “I’m handling the transportation, but I want every man we have watching this stadium tomorrow,” he said to Lennox. "Because when the crowd needs a scapegoat—as they always do—they will learn that empaths were present at the game. And they'll be there to take the blame."

Lennox nodded. "Yes, sir."

"And make sure the empaths don't actually see any violence," Charles added.

Lennox wrinkled his nose. "Why?"

"The threat of violence is a very useful and powerful tool for manipulating empaths," said Charles. "Exposing empaths to actual violence, however—well. You had best be prepared for the consequences."

He looked at his phone and frowned. "Why the hell haven't I heard from Victor?"

Fury as he sees Evan in chains on that table—

Vengeance as he sets the thralls loose on the lab—

Fear as they slide down the mountainside, because even the best drivers can't win against Mother Nature—

Certainty as he knows he has to protect his passenger—

Emotions and thoughts came to Reece as if from a distance. His eyelids didn't seem to want to open, but there was velvet softness under his cheek, smooth fabric against his shoulder, comforting weight on his back. A soft and steady pulse under his ear, like the rhythm of a heartbeat.

Evan, his mind nudged.

Reece's empathy was reaching out before his thoughts could take form, searching, wanting—

And then everything was black.

Jason Owens's mansion was at the end of a residential street on Mercer Island. Jamey remembered the location from the day she'd been called to his murder scene. Tonight, a light snow blanketed everything, more flakes still falling on her windshield as she pulled her car along the curb and peered at what she could see of the house ahead, the four-car garage, the driveway.

It seemed empty, but then, if the empaths were here, they wouldn't exactly be advertising it. And if the empaths *were* here, they were going to pick up on her emotions. There was no point in trying to hide.

She got out of the car and made her way toward the house under the dusting of tiny snowflakes. The neighboring homes had their lights dimmed too, the residents probably enjoying their winters somewhere tropical, and the night was quiet other than her footsteps on the pavement.

She headed for the front door and knocked. She waited, ears pricked for any sound, but all was silent. After a long moment, she tried the knob and found it unlocked. But then, empaths who could feel others approaching didn't exactly need to lock the door.

She stepped into the house. It was eerily still, in a way that raised the hairs on her neck. She left the lights off, moving through the rooms based on her memories of her one previous visit. She paused in the study, where the faint scent of ash lingered in the fireplace; someone had lit the fire within the last couple of days.

Eventually she found the kitchen, which was a little lighter from the glow coming off the snow outside the large windows. Her eyebrows went up as she made out the faint shapes on the kitchen table: the silhouette of a laptop, the pale glow of papers.

Keeping her steps silent, she approached the table. "Here we go," she said under her breath as she pulled a flash drive out of the side of the laptop. She used her phone flashlight to illuminate the papers, fanning them out.

Deliveries to Stone Solutions, one of them was titled in handwriting. Below it, Jamey could see more handwritten notes from the past couple weeks. Someone had circled a company called Metallic Tailors and added three question marks.

Jamey folded up all of the papers and pocketed them along with the flash drive. She had just closed the laptop, ready to take it, when the faint sound of footsteps came from down the hall.

Jamey straightened, drawing her gun. "Who's there?"

The footsteps continued without hesitation, coming closer.

She moved into the kitchen, behind the island, as the footsteps reached the doorway, and then abruptly she was staring into the blood-streaked eyes and menacing expression of a clearly thralled Officer Kosler.

Well, shit.

Kosler roared as Jamey lunged forward and got ready to kick some thrall ass.

Wake up.

Come on.

Wake UP.

Reece's thoughts broke through the darkness again, a little louder, a little clearer. The distant rhythms were still there, a heartbeat, the rise and fall of breath. And the sensation of that soft skin, of muscle, of warmth beneath him.

He was warmer now too, his core temperature rising, the presence of another person making his empathy perk up. There was still a gentle weight on his back, pleasant and secure.

Arms, his mind supplied. *Evan's arms are around you.*

Wake the fuck up and make sure he's okay.

Reece twitched.

Grayson's arms? Around *him*? Where were they? The truck still? Why was it so dark?

Reece tried to open his eyes.

But his empathy was faster, on fire at the thought of touching Grayson, reaching for him, desperately wanting—

And then everything was black.

Alex huddled behind one of the couches in the Stone Solutions' luxury box, Cora at his side. The other ten empaths were in a tight knot in the center of the room, some of them sniffling.

"I don't understand why Stone Solutions would do this." On the couch on the other side of Alex, Mireya Gomez was curled in a tight ball, her head in her hands and her face stained with tears. Dawson Jones was next to her, also looking crushed. "Why would they want to hurt anyone?"

Alex exchanged a covert glance with Cora. They'd kept their heads down during Charles Stone's broadcast, but if Charles spent any time watching the camera, they'd be recognized.

They had to act.

"We still have our phones, and the spreadsheet of all these empaths from the flash drive," Alex said under his breath. "The one with their trigger points."

"We do," Cora acknowledged. "What are you thinking?"

"Can you cut the camera?"

She nodded. Their captors hadn't bothered to do anything complicated; they'd set up a webcam in the middle of the room and warned the empaths that if they cut the feed, they'd be forced to watch each other bleed.

The pacifists had been whimpering putty after that. Alex and Cora had added another tally to their list of reasons their captors were going to regret this night.

Keeping behind the furniture, Cora snuck across the room on hands and knees, and pulled the plug on the webcam.

As the red dot faded from view, Alex stood up and cleared his throat. "Hey, y'all," he said, finding a sympathetic tone. "How are we doing?"

Dawson and Mireya exchanged a look with each other and the others. "Not very good." Mireya sniffed. "You're one of the two who joined us at the pulp mill, right?"

"Yeah. Yeah, I am." Alex palmed his phone. "I know this is bad. But I'm afraid things might get a lot worse."

Dawson furrowed his brow. "What do you mean?"

Alex held up his phone. "I have a copy of a spreadsheet created by Stone Solutions," he said quietly. "It has all of our names, and the names of our loved ones—and a plan for how to kill our loved ones in the most horrible way possible."

The room went instantly, deathly silent.

Alex glanced at Cora. Her eyes were haunted, the way they always were when the loss of her fiancé hurt fresh.

"Cora and I have a story to tell you about Stone Solutions, and the people we loved most in the world," Alex said. "It's not a very nice story. But maybe if you hear the story, you can decide to protect the ones *you* love before the same thing happens to them."

Wake up.

Come on.

Evan needs you.

Reece's fingers twitched. That was the velvety warmth of skin and muscle under his hand, under his cheek and his body, with no clothes blocking the way. Grayson underneath him, heartbeat in his ear, his breaths gently rising and falling under Reece's head. His arms were a soft weight on Reece's back, their legs tangled together with one of his feet tucked under Grayson's calf.

The voice in his head rose again, even more insistent.

Stay awake—

But before he could stop himself, Reece had spread his hand so that his whole palm and fingers rested flat on Grayson's chest, as much contact as he could get. His empathy was already leaping from his control again, seeking, reaching.

And everything was—

Gray?

Reece's eyes popped open. But he was seeing nothing but black with his eyes, nothing but gray with his empathy. Reece's hand scrabbled against Grayson's chest, like he could cling to the physical sensation of warmth under his palm and fingers as he spun through a night fog, gray over black, unconsciousness looming like a tidal wave—

"Reece?"

The voice was just a whisper, a quiet rumbling under his ear. But it was the anchor he needed to drive away the threatening wave of unconsciousness, so that the body under him became solid and real, so that the thick gray fog of missing emotions receded to a light mist.

He turned his face and let his lips brush the bare skin of Grayson's chest.

Arms tightened around him. "Reece?" His name again, muffled and distant, a vibration under him. "You awake?"

Reece let his lips brush Grayson's skin again, right over his heart. "Maybe."

Grayson exhaled, the gentle movement shifting Reece with it. *"Maybe?"*

"This could be a really good dream." Grayson's skin was so warm under his lips. "Goddamn, are we really touching?"

"Sure, sure, that's definitely the thing to focus on." Grayson's dry sarcasm hitched as Reece began kissing a trail up his skin. "After all, why would you want me to explain where you are—"

"Doesn't matter."

"—or tell you what happened—"

"Didn't ask."

"—or let you know if you're in danger—"

"Don't care." Reece kissed his collarbone. "Fuck. We can *touch*."

He felt Grayson's breath hitch again under him. He moved his lips to the hollow of Grayson's throat as his hands traced Grayson's chest, his ribs, anything they could reach, until he tried to push up and met a wall of restraining fabric. "Wait. Are we in the *sleeping bag*?"

"I could tell you if you'd stop *distracting me*—"

Reece pushed his head out from beneath the sleeping bag's edge, emerging under Grayson's chin into air that was shockingly cold. The darkness was still encompassing, but he could just make out Grayson's outline in the sleeping bag under him, their small space lit by patches of pale glow in the shapes of squares and rectangles. The truck's windows now covered in snow.

Grayson's hands ran up his back, and Reece was arching into the touch before he'd known he was going to move. "You were like ice before," Grayson said, fingers and palms splaying on Reece's upper back. "You feel warmer now."

Reece squirmed under his hands, managing to pull himself another few inches forward. "Bet we can get warmer still."

And he lifted his head, stretching up in the dark, lips finding the top of Grayson's throat, then his scratchy jaw, then—

"Fucking *finally*," he muttered as his mouth aligned with Grayson's.

Grayson made a sound that cut straight to Reece's chest. The last of the fog abruptly cleared, or maybe that was the entire world disappearing as suddenly they were kissing, really kissing.

"*Fuck*," he heard Grayson mutter, more of an exhale than an actual word. The hands on Reece's back tightened, then slid back to his waist. A moment later, Grayson hitched Reece up like he weighed nothing, so their mouths were better aligned as he slipped his tongue between Reece's lips.

Reece fought the sleeping bag still tight around his shoulders, not breaking the kiss as he shifted until he was fully on top of Grayson. One of his hands found its way into the upper part of the sleeping bag, lingering along Grayson's stubbled jaw before sliding up.

"So you do let people touch your hair," Reece whispered against his mouth as he twined soft strands between his fingers.

"Some people." Grayson's hands were sliding lower on his back, sending sparks over Reece's rapidly heating skin. "You still a hypothermia risk?"

"Definitely," Reece said without breaking the kiss, hearing the lie in his words. "You better not let me go."

"That was a serious question."

"That was a serious order." Reece felt Grayson's hands slide another inch lower on his back, and realization set in. He broke the kiss, pulling back just an inch. "Am I *naked* in this sleeping bag?"

"I've been trying to tell you what happened. We're stranded in the—" Grayson's words became a soft groan deep in his throat as Reece shifted his thigh, exploring "—stranded in the truck somewhere in the forest. It was storming and—"

"And the snowflakes stole my clothes?" The endless expanse of Grayson's skin was making him dizzy. "Doesn't feel like you've got much on either."

"I did keep my boxer briefs—"

"I can tell." Reece moved his thigh again, adding some purposeful pressure against the hardening length under him, and Grayson groaned again. "Trying to be a gentleman? Because that's cute, but really, I am all for you handling me as *un*-gentlemanly as possible."

"Did you already forget your little tumble in the snow?" Grayson's hands were still distractingly low on his back, especially now that Reece had clocked there were no barriers between him and those hands. "Your clothes were soaked through. I found you cold as ice when I woke up. So what I was trying to do was keep you from dying of hypothermia—"

"Back up one fucking minute." Reece paused his movements. "You passed out too?"

"We're talking about *you*—"

"Are you hurt?"

"—and *your* safety. Besides, I heal fast—"

"Not what I asked," Reece said warningly. The glow of the snowy windows seemed slightly lighter than earlier, enough to see some of Grayson's face, the high cheekbones, the outline of his brow and nose. "Answer my question."

One of Grayson's hands slid down to his ass, making Reece draw a sharp breath as sensation rocked through him. "Who're you trying to boss around?"

Reece slid his hand around through the sleeping bag, brushing the slight ridge of the round bullet scar on Grayson's shoulder. "I don't like you getting hurt," he said softly, dangerously, as he brought his thumb to rest on the delicate skin of Grayson's lower lip. "I think I made that pretty clear tonight, but I'm happy to clear it up to the rest of Seattle if I have to."

Grayson seemed to still, letting Reece trace his lip. "I got a couple bruises but nothing broken," he finally said, sounding honest. "My body doesn't appreciate being drugged, but it's almost burned off." He kissed Reece's thumb. "That's all."

"Good." Reece slid his hand to Grayson's jaw, holding him in place as he brought their mouths together again, deep and firm. Grayson's hand was still on his ass, his cock stiffening against Reece's hip. "Make sure you know who you're kissing," he whispered against Grayson's lips. "I am still not the helpless pacifist you took that bullet for. I'm the monster you're protecting everyone else from. That's not a lie, Evan; I believe it."

"That right?" Grayson tightened his hold, so that Reece's own hardening dick slid against the firm planes of Grayson's stomach where it was trapped between their bodies. Pleasure ricocheted through him again, and a groan escaped him. "Why'd you turn the truck?"

Grayson moved him again, sending another bolt of pleasure through Reece, strong enough to make his kiss falter. "Evan—"

"I know you did. You could've let my side slam that tree, but you took the blow yourself."

Reece groaned again into his mouth. "Shut up."

"Why'd you come for me at all? Risk your own safety and freedom to pull me out of that lab?"

"I would *never* have left you with Nichols—"

"You traded your pacifism for my life."

Reece stiffened. He broke the kiss, pulling back. "Who told you that?" he said sharply.

"Traynor," Grayson said. "I was too arrogant to see the danger I was in, so you took care of it for me." Reece could just make out the shape of those unreadable eyes. "And maybe I can't feel grateful, or guilty, or anything else, but a monster wouldn't've done all that you did."

Reece tightened his jaw. "It doesn't matter how corruption happened. I am what I am now."

"Maybe," said Grayson. "But I should've told you before, so I'll tell you now: Any version of you is still worth that bullet."

That stirred something in Reece's chest, an emotion he absolutely was not going to look at more closely. "That's just proof you're also making questionable decisions," he said gruffly, shifting so his hip brushed Grayson's cock, drawing a sharp breath. "Like getting in this sleeping bag with me and letting me get used to your touch."

He ground down against Grayson again, watching a flutter of lashes, drinking in the hitch in his breath. "Your knockout ability was the last Dead Man power you had against me. And you gave it up."

Grayson's whisper came, hoarse and strained. "Was I supposed to let you die?"

And then Reece was kissing him again. There were no emotions to sense, but he could feel the shifts of muscles, hear the soft sounds that escaped, could let Grayson's body give the signals to guide his hands and mouth. He shoved one of his arms back into the sleeping bag, fingers gliding over the warm, bare skin of Grayson's stomach. "Jesus, no gloves. Nothing between us." He sounded hoarse to his own ears. He tried to slide his hand lower, making a noise of frustration when he couldn't reach any further. "I need room to move; let's get out of this sleeping bag."

"The hell we will," Grayson said. "It's literally freezing. You were on the verge of hypothermia."

"*Was*, past tense," said Reece. "And counterpoint: I really want you to fuck me."

Grayson's breath hitched again. And suddenly he was twisting, not the awkward way Reece had tried to maneuver in the sleeping bag's confines, but graceful and strong as he rolled them together onto their sides, Reece on the edge of the truck's back seat but held by the curve of the sleeping bag with no risk of falling.

Grayson kissed him again, and it was Reece's turn for a broken groan as he was pulled in closer by the hand still on his ass. "That your preference?"

"Oh, I'm *very* flexible. Don't you remember me accidentally spilling that detail to the press?" Reece said into the kiss. "But I can't get all our talk about *tight fits* out of my head."

"I'm not gonna let you get frostbite just so I can get you on my dick."

"I'm not going to get *frostbite*," Reece said. "I'm back up to normal temperature now—"

"Believe me, I'm well aware you got all your empath body heat back. Been a long time since anything felt as good as you." Grayson sounded very honest, his hands exploring Reece as they kissed, leaving fireworks everywhere they touched. "We finally got you warm, so I'm gonna keep you right here in this sleeping bag."

"But if your body can warm me this much, think what your dick could do."

Grayson snorted. "Even if I was willing to let you freeze—which I'm *not*—we don't have anything like lube in this truck. We keep talking *tight fits* because I'm twice your size, sugar; you really gonna take me without it?"

"Oh my God, you're so *vain*." Reece broke the kiss, squirming down into the sleeping bag until he could slide his hand under the elastic waistband of the boxer briefs. "Your dick isn't as huge as you're convinced it—" His words twisted into telltale discordance as his hand found Grayson's cock.

"Did you just hear yourself lie . . . about my dick?"

"Shut up."

"More inches of *vanity* than you expected?"

"Why are you still talking?"

"How is this a surprise?" Grayson said. "You've had your hands on me before."

"Yeah, but through empath gloves." Reece curled his palm around Grayson's dick. "There's a lot more to feel without heavy metals in the way."

"Like what?"

"Like whether or not my fucking fingers can or can't touch and look, I'm not feeding your ego!" Their new position on the seat did at least give Reece a tiny bit more room, letting him run his hand along that thick dick while still able to feel

Grayson's stuttering breaths against him, the arms that didn't seem to want to let him go. "But damn. Now I really want you to fuck me."

"That's your empath lack of self-preservation talking. And I'll be the one to feed *your* ego." Grayson's voice broke. "You're way too good at this."

Reece's lips grudgingly turned up. He tightened his hand, savoring every sound and shift his strokes drew from Grayson. He was seeing more than ever, not because of dawn's arrival, not yet, but because his empathy was dilating his pupils, letting in even the faintest glow of moonlight on snow.

Now that they could touch, the ideas were endless, and Reece wanted to feel Grayson get off in every possible way and position. With his free hand, he fumbled for the sleeping bag's zipper, finding a pull tab on the inside and tugging. "If we aren't going to fuck, we're going to compromise."

"What's that mean?"

"What do you think?" With a few inches unzipped, the fabric had enough give that Reece could slip farther down, completely into the sleeping bag. His lips found Grayson's ribs, then his stomach, pressing lingering kisses lower and lower.

Grayson swore, his breath coming in sharp pants now. "I think your kiss should be illegal."

"This isn't kissing, this is claiming." Reece ran his tongue over his hip bone. "No more soldiers or scientists. You're mine now."

He didn't let him answer before taking his cock into his mouth, so that the attempt at words was stolen by the groan from deep in Grayson's chest. Reece drank in the vibration, not a feeling but a sensation he could ride like one. His empathy was beyond his control, trying to find something to read, a way to escape into another person and let their feelings subsume his own. But where trying to read Grayson before had been smashing headfirst into black asphalt, now it was dancing along the edge of a quicksilver pool, unable to dive in but able to let the shimmering mercury carry him away all the same.

The angle was awkward, and yeah, this was a tight fit of its own, but Reece worked him deeper into his mouth anyway, losing himself in the pleasure signals of Grayson's body, the flex of muscle, the hitch of breath. He ran his tongue up the hard length and let Grayson's answering groan soothe the jagged anger inside him that still wanted revenge, even now. Here, in this truck, Grayson was his, and no one could reach him without going through Reece first.

Grayson's hands ran over his hair, his upper back. "Come up here," he said hoarsely. "I'm too big to maneuver in this damn thing; I can't reach you."

Reece wrapped his hand around the base of Grayson's cock and didn't budge.

Hands tugged at his shoulders. *"Reece."*

Grayson could try all he wanted to be chivalrous and reciprocate. Too bad; wasn't happening. Reece wasn't fucking moving. They could bury him in this truck on this mountain, with *death by Evan Grayson's cock* on his gravestone.

He took Grayson in another inch, and victory rushed him as he heard Grayson's groan of surrender, felt him finally cede control completely. Reece fought the sleeping bag so he could twist a little more, get a slightly better angle, use his hand on the inches that didn't fit in his mouth, following Grayson's every noise and twitch like a map. His own excitement was rising, because corruption hadn't changed this, hadn't lessened the heady thrill of causing someone else's pleasure. And knowing that it wasn't just anyone, but Grayson who was losing it under his hands and mouth, well. Reece wasn't going to last a second longer than Grayson himself.

When Grayson started tensing, Reece felt the mirroring

tenseness in his own body. The hands in Reece's hair tightened, just slightly, because even this far gone, Grayson was being careful not to hurt him, and through the muffled sleeping back he thought he heard, or maybe felt, Grayson stutter his name.

And then all of Reece's coherent thoughts were gone, swallowed by the tide of pleasure that overtook him, and the feel of Grayson against him, and the bone-deep certainty that whatever happened next, Evan was his and no one could ever take his touch away again.

CHAPTER THIRTY

I hate to be the bearer of bad news, but Stone Solutions has "requested" that we kill your feature piece, "The Empathy Industrial Complex or: How the American War Machine Learned to Leverage Fear and Feelings for Profit," and leadership has agreed.

It sure is interesting what kind of stories get censored when the people who own the corporations also own the media.

—Internal note at the *Emerald Tribune*

The night's storm had left Seattle blanketed in a thin layer of snow that had quickly turned ice-edged and slushy. Kickoff wasn't until noon, but as the wet, gray morning stretched over downtown, the early crew was already trickling into Lumen Field: sports analysts settling into the press box, vendors starting up their kitchens, ushers prepping for the fans' arrival, local news reporting live from the field's bright green Astroturf coated with its patchy layer of white.

Lennox stood in the aisle of the club seats at center field, looking over with narrowed eyes at the floor-to-ceiling glass that enclosed the Stone Solutions' luxury box.

Guarding a dozen empaths was about the most unnecessary thing Lennox had ever done for Charles Stone. After their call with Charles, the empaths had been huddled in weepy circles, and Lennox had been so bored he'd dozed off.

When he'd woken, however, the camera in the suite had been dark.

Now he craned his neck, trying to catch a glimpse of the empaths through the box's glass walls, but they must have been huddled too deeply in the suite to be seen. Charles had been right about that too, then; they weren't trying to draw attention from reporters or anyone else, just meekly hiding in the box as instructed under threat of violence to the others.

Stupidly easy to manipulate or not, Lennox still needed eyes on them. He'd been planning to try to catch the players warming up, and now he'd have to deal with the annoying little fucks first.

His eyes were still narrowed as he climbed the stairs from the club to the suite level, and then strode with quick, irritated steps down the hall to the Stone Solutions' box, unlocking the door and ducking inside.

Sure enough, the empaths were huddled together around the coffee table, some of them on the couch and chairs, some on the rug, a couple of them in each other's laps. Beyond them, the glass surrounding the dual rows of recliners framed a slice of downtown's skyscrapers and the snow-spotted green field below.

The empaths hadn't looked up when he stepped inside, involved in their own whispered discussion. Lennox yanked the door shut behind him with a loud bang. "Hey!"

The empaths still didn't look up. They didn't even twitch.

"Hey," Lennox said again. "Fix the camera."

Not a single head even turned his way. Lennox rapped his knuckles on the wall, harsh and loud. "I'm talking to you," he snapped. "The camera is down. And you will be so fucking sorry if I have to come over there and fix it myself."

No response again. He might as well have been invisible.

Lennox cracked his knuckles pointedly. Looked like he was going to get a target for his irritation, at least. And empaths were the easiest targets he'd ever faced: a couple of slaps to one of them and the rest would be begging him to stop and rushing to do what he wanted.

"If that's how you want it," he said, fists curling automatically. "I don't actually like hitting you little freaks, you know."

All of the empaths looked up and over at him as one.

The hairs on the back of his neck rose.

"That was a lie," one of the empaths said, in a whisper that filled the suite.

"What?" Lennox started to say.

But the empaths were on him.

The chime of her phone woke Gretel from a restless sleep. She stared for a moment at the living room ceiling above Jamey's couch, her thoughts immediately taking off like a sprinter, as if she hadn't slept at all.

She reached for her phone. Her dad's friend from the Stone Solutions board of directors, Roger Spade, had responded to her email.

To: gretel@eyesonempaths.com

From: r.spade@seattlemail.com

It's good to hear from you, Gretel. Yes, I told your father I thought the October 8-K was suspicious. Cedrick had discussed the acquisition of two small suppliers to me in July, but the 8-K listed three. When I asked which company had been added and why, no one would give me an answer.

I'd be happy to speak with you further. I'm so sorry for your loss.

She pushed the blankets off and got to her feet as silently as she could. The rest of the house felt still as a church, with everyone else asleep after their late night. Jamey in particular had been out late, disappearing in Liam's car and then returning a couple of hours later, looking disheveled with suspicious red stains on her clothes but promising she'd found some more documents that might help.

Gretel crossed the wood floor noiselessly, throat tightening as her eyes fell on the dining table, still covered with their work from the night before: her dad's laptop opened in front of two chairs where Liam and Aisha had been searching for clues; the nearby pile of financial data and files from Stone Solutions that Diesel had made sure to neatly organize and stack; the handwritten delivery list that Jamey had appeared with the night before.

Gretel reached the table and carefully tugged the handwritten delivery list closer, gaze on the words *Metallic Tailors*, circled with its question marks.

"Where there's murder, there are other crimes," she echoed under her breath. "You really think an obsessive weirdo like me doesn't know all about shell companies?"

Jamey had likely disagreed with every word Gretel had ever written on *Eyes on Empaths*. But when the worst had happened, Jamey and her friends had been there for Gretel, made sure she had company and a warm place to sleep, given their best efforts to solve her parents' murders.

She scratched out a note on a spare piece of paper, then carefully closed her dad's laptop and tucked it under her arm. She grabbed up the records, and two minutes later, she'd packed her few items away and was slipping out Jamey's front door.

As she took her seat in her car, she pulled Vivian Marist's business card from her purse. *My personal number,* Marist had said. *Call anytime.*

"Don't mind if I do," Gretel muttered, dialing the number as she pulled out of Jamey's driveway and into the street.

Dawn had finally arrived, setting the truck's snow-covered windows and windshield aglow with a silvery sheen. Grayson knew damn well that they couldn't stay in the forest forever; they needed to get up, try to get the truck running, and get the hell back to civilization. And they would.

As soon as he managed to let go of Reece.

"We *can't*," Grayson said against Reece's mouth as their lips locked on to each other yet again. "We got to get out of here."

"But what if I'm still a hypothermia risk?" Reece was fully on top of him, his smaller, slighter body a heavenly weight on Grayson as he lay on his back flat against the seat. "Shouldn't you just stay right here and keep me warm?"

Grayson groaned, even as he was unable to resist running his hands over that soft skin. "I don't think we got far enough from the lab to relax. There's gonna be a response team."

"There sure is." Reece arched into Grayson's touch even as he shifted to kiss the sensitive skin of his throat. "But I'll handle them."

"You can't *thrall* folks just so we can keep fooling around."

"I really can."

Grayson tightened his arms around him. "Mr. Davies."

"You really think the formal name treatment is going to turn me *off*?" Reece lifted his head, and then pressed one long, lingering kiss to Grayson's lips. "Fine," he whispered, like he hadn't just left Grayson dazed and dizzy. "Let's see if we can fix the truck."

It took a few more minutes, but finally they emerged from the sleeping bag. As Grayson had suspected, their clothes were still damp, despite being spread out on the dash in an attempt to dry them. But it turned out that under the truck's back seat, Reece had kept not only the sleeping bag they'd bought on their trip to Vancouver but also Grayson's backpack from that same trip, which still held enough of his purchases that they managed to get a full set of dry clothes each.

Grayson had always kept basic safety equipment on hand, but in the few days Reece had the truck, he'd also acquired an emergency battery charger and a specialized diagnostic code reader. Grayson scraped the windshield and windows as Reece examined the damage.

"Flat tire first," he finally said. "Then we'll try and get the engine running."

Grayson had changed a flat more than once but never on a steep and snowy mountainside, so he shut his mouth and followed all of Reece's directions as they jacked up the truck and changed out the punctured tire for the spare under the bed.

Wheel in place, Reece popped the hood. "I think this tough girl mostly took cosmetic damage," he said, sounding pleased as he scanned the engine. "With any luck, we're dealing with a drained battery from the lights running while we were unconscious." He raised his head. "Can you get behind the wheel?"

"Really?"

Reece gave him an amused look over the engine. "So you can start her up when I tell you. And then you can move right back into the passenger seat where you belong."

"The hell I will," Grayson muttered under his breath, squeezing himself into the driver's seat with difficulty, set as it was for Reece's much shorter frame with no power to move it back.

After one false attempt, the V-8 finally kicked in with a deep rumble that shook the trees.

"*Yes*," Grayson heard Reece crow. He dropped the hood into place, looking over it to Grayson. "She's going to need a body shop for those dents, but she'll get us back to Seattle."

Grayson was already moving the electric seat backwards as Reece headed to his open driver's door. "So we ready to go?"

Reece put a foot on the truck's step, stepping up so their eyes were level, deceptively cute and harmless-appearing in a recycled-fleece pullover big enough to fit Grayson. "As soon as you get out of my seat."

The driver's seat stopped, having reached as far as it could go. Grayson stretched out his legs and nodded at the passenger seat. "Shotgun's free."

"It's cute you think you're driving." Reece dropped into his lap, and oh, their size difference opened up even more fun possibilities out of the sleeping bag.

This was going to be a problem.

"It's *my* truck," Grayson said, trying futilely not to get distracted by their closeness, especially as Reece's arms snaked around his shoulders. "Of course I'm driving—"

"You don't even know where we are." Their faces were close enough he could feel Reece's breath on his lips. "We still have to make it the rest of the way down the mountain. Off-roading through snow until we find some real roads—with half the roads closed for the weather, I should note. And we have to do it all on the spare tire."

Grayson's tongue darted out and wet his lips. "It really shouldn't be hot when you bust my ass about cars."

"What was it you said to me once? There's no accounting for taste?" Reece's gaze had gone to Grayson's mouth. "Look at us. *Touching*," he said softly, gliding his fingers along the back of Grayson's neck and sending shivers over his skin. "It's a fucking tragedy we have to get going."

"You're the one who got in my lap," Grayson said, even as his hands slipped around Reece's waist to the small of his back. "And somehow you still keep getting closer and closer."

"Not my fault it's such a tight fit between you and the steering wheel."

Grayson slipped his hands lower, pulling Reece even closer. "You do not get to talk about *tight fits* when you're literally sitting on my dick."

Reece groaned. "We're never getting out of here if you keep giving me ideas," he said, and leaned in for a kiss, soft lips and skilled tongue, way too good.

Too soon, Reece pulled back, and their eyes met, those black pupils normal-sized at the moment, ringed by bands of deep autumn-brown. Thick, dark hair lay in tousled waves on his forehead, and there was a flush to Reece's cheeks and lips, maybe from the cold, maybe from the kiss.

"Your eyes seem different." Reece was studying him. "Are all the drugs out of your system?"

Grayson would've said yes, but in fairness, he *was* feeling a little hazy. "Probably?"

Reece's eyes narrowed. "I should have had Nichols boil himself alive," he said lightly.

Because Reece was a corrupted empath. No longer a violence-averse pacifist squeamish about others' pain, but a paranormal killer with his own streak of sadism.

The exact kind of empath the Dead Man should take to Stone Solutions.

"We better get on the road." Reece still seemed to be intently examining his face. "As you said, there has to be a response team on its way, and we need to get you out of here before they arrive."

And for a moment, Grayson forgot about corruption, forgot about the Dead Man and thralls and Stone Solutions. All he could see was the empath he could have lost to frostbite because Reece had braved a mountain storm and an army of guards to rescue him. The same empath who'd once been willing to trade his own freedom for Grayson's life, who'd made an unthinkable sacrifice to make sure Grayson was safe.

Who was still looking out for him even now.

And suddenly Grayson was the one to kiss him, raw and with no finesse, his body taking control like it was trying to say something his heart was no longer capable of feeling.

Reece made a soft noise, surprise and pleasure, fingers tightening where they intertwined in Grayson's hair. And in that kiss, something moved in his chest, like a curtain lifted by the breeze—

Grayson yanked backwards, out of the kiss. He stared at Reece for a moment, his heart pounding.

Reece was looking into his eyes, brows furrowed. "Are you all right?"

Grayson took a breath through his nose. *Was* he all right?

But yes, of course he was. His body had been under significant stress and his equilibrium was still a mess; was arrhythmia really that surprising? Whatever that moment had been had passed anyway, like a candle snuffed out by the wind.

"I'm fine," he said. "Or I will be, eventually."

"Hmm." Reece brushed fingers up Grayson's neck, ruffling the short hairs on the back of his head. "You know you don't actually have to go back to Seattle and Stone Solutions, don't you? I could take you to your own safe house, or anywhere you wanted. You don't have to be an empath hunter; you could just be Evan Grayson again."

Grayson met his eyes. "We both know that's not true," he

said quietly. "I'll always be the Dead Man. And I can't ever care about that one way or the other."

Reece opened his mouth, like he was going to say something. But then he leaned in instead, and brought their lips together.

Grayson's eyes closed, but almost immediately Reece was pulling back again. "We have to go," he said, shifting off Grayson's lap, to the step. "And Dead Man or not, I'm the one who knows where we are, where we need to go now, and wasn't drugged with who knows what last night. *I'm* driving."

Even Grayson had to admit that Reece was the better choice in this situation. He maneuvered out of the driver's seat and went around to the passenger side of the truck.

As he put his hand on the handle of the passenger door, his gaze swept out past the trees. Now that the sun was out, he could take in the miles around them, his vision filled with snow-dusted evergreens and blue mountains with tops lost to the white clouds that stretched across the mercury sky.

He hesitated for a moment, his hand on the door handle, his eyes on the view.

Then he opened the truck door and climbed in without further thought.

Charles Stone was in his preferred recliner in the back of the Maybach, frowning at his text messages, when his phone began to ring. The caller ID identified Emily Lowe, Stone Solutions' director of response operations.

On the other side of the privacy glass, the driver, Mr. Huang, was drumming fingers on the steering wheel as they waited for a red light to change. Charles answered his call. "Emily," he said pleasantly into his earpiece. "I was just about to call for an update."

"You're not going to like the one I'm about to deliver."

Stone's frown deepened. "What's happened?"

"Park rangers reported smoke near the Olympia National Forest. The call escalated up through local law enforcement, and we intercepted it," Lowe said shortly. "It's the new Olympia facility, sir. The building is in shambles, and several of the facility staff are dead, including Dr. Nichols."

Charles sat forward in his seat. "Victor's *dead*?"

"Oh yes," Lowe said with feeling. "Very, *very* dead."

"But how?"

"The security cameras were cut," she said. "But just before they went out, Reece Davies was captured walking in through the front doors."

"Ah. Of course." Charles's jaw tightened ever so slightly. "Mr. Davies does seem to have a knack for disrupting my plans."

The car began moving again. Charles sat back in his seat, steepling his fingers. "There were no empaths at the facility yet. It is possible Mr. Davies was acting preemptively with his destruction, but that requires intelligence and foresight that I simply don't attribute to empaths. Out of curiosity, was the Dead Man's body among the victims discovered?"

"No, sir," said Lowe. "We're not sure exactly what happened, but Agent Grayson appears to have escaped Mr. Davies's rampage."

"Isn't that interesting," Charles said slowly.

The car was picking up speed now, making its way toward downtown. "The situation at the Olympia facility is being handled," Lowe went on. "I assume you would like any thralls with a pulse to join the others?"

The Maybach passed a shuttle bus, every seat full. "Yes, thank you," said Charles. "I think Mr. Davies may have unintentionally shown his hand."

"Sir?"

A dark hint of a smile curled on Charles's lips. "Just adjusting course ever so slightly. I can't always control the sea, despite my efforts, but a good captain can weather any storm to port." He cleared his throat. "I'll need to amend your instructions at Lumen Field, but first I would appreciate a status update on those others."

"Ambulances two through four are on their way to the stadium," she said. "All thralls recovered over the past weeks are on board. Their IV drips have just been altered to the same formula given to Dr. Whitman before her rampage at AMI. We'll inject that formula into the surviving Olympia thralls as well, and all will be ready for release on arrival, sir. Forgive my language, but it's going to get fucking ugly."

"Excellent," Charles said, with a slight edge. "And ambulance one?"

"It has acquired its patient from the airfield." She cleared her throat. "He's being transported with the utmost care and will be waiting for you when you arrive."

The pieces were moving into place. They would need a new facility for the corrupted empaths now, and a replacement for Nichols, but Charles would have even more money and resources at his disposal after today. He would find both.

He'd find somewhere very special, just for Davies.

"Thank you, Emily. Your service won't be forgotten." Charles went to hang up, then paused. "Any chance you've heard from Lennox?"

Alex surveyed the ten newly corrupted empaths sprawled throughout Stone Solutions' luxury suite with an almost parental pride.

Stone Solutions should have known better than to develop that sick little spreadsheet with its twisted plans for these empaths' most treasured people. And tonight had confirmed that Reece wasn't a fluke, providing a nice little data point that

Stone Solutions' sick scientists would never, ever get their hands on: that even the gentlest of empaths could find their dark side when they were motivated by protecting their loved ones.

Sweet, sappy Dawson had even made Charles Stone's lackey, Lennox, his first thrall.

Alex stepped up to the glass, watching the crowd gather in the stadium stands below. "All right," he said, rubbing his hands together. "Door is unlocked now, and the crowd is trickling in. We should be able to lose ourselves in them pretty quick and find the best exit—"

"Why would we want to do that?"

Alex turned at the sound of Mireya Gomez's voice. She was watching him, her head tilted, and her eyes had a dark gleam that hadn't been there a few hours ago.

"We don't want to stay in a stadium of people—" Cora started.

"Except we do," said one of the empaths. "We want to stay. And we want to see this place burn."

The other empaths cheered.

Oh. Shit. "*Wait*," Alex said, holding up a hand. "We're way outnumbered. If we storm this stadium, we're going to get caught."

"We're dealing with Charles Stone," Cora said. "He's going to have a plan—"

"*I* have a plan," Dawson said. "We fuck this place up."

"Yes!" That shout came from Dawson's new thrall, Lennox, as he grabbed the Stone Solutions sign off the wall and swung it into the glass bar. A few thousand dollars' worth of high-end liquor shattered on impact, filling the kitchen with broken glass. "Fuck it up!"

"Oh no," Alex said. *"Wait—"*

But the empaths were already pouring out the suite door.

CHAPTER THIRTY-ONE

On the next episode of Love Versus Logic, *an empath and an undercover operative must choose between their destinies and their passionate romance. Can they find a way to be together? Or will they have to leave each other behind yet again?*

—Advertisement for a long-running soap opera

For most of his life, Reece had been drawn to the bustle of the city, the buzz of emotions from the countless people surrounding him. But he'd spent plenty of time in Washington's parks tagging along with nature-adoring Jamey, because her happiness when hiking or camping had more than made up for the sweat and mosquitoes.

With his dead phone charging, he drew on those memories and the truck's navigation pane to find his way east through the mountains, away from the hidden laboratory until he picked up narrow, snow-buried roads meant for trailheads and campgrounds. Eventually he connected with a bigger road that led to 101 and from there wound his way over to Bremerton.

Grayson furrowed his brow as they passed through the city center. "Are we heading to a ferry terminal?"

"I want nothing to do with I-5 after snow." Reece brought the truck around the curve of the road and headed for the water. "This will take us straight downtown."

"But—"

"And there's food on the ferry. And coffee."

"Oh." Grayson settled against the seat. "Next time, lead with that."

Despite the weather, the terminal was bustling with a good crowd of morning commuters on their way to Seattle, and Reece had to pull the truck into a short line to buy tickets.

"And now I get to have a crisis of manners," Grayson muttered as Reece finally rolled up to the ticketing booth. "I oughta pay for the ticket and buy you breakfast, but you stole this truck from me, and I don't have a wallet."

"The mighty empath hunter, forced to rely on an empath." Reece held up a credit card. "Oh, how the tables have turned."

He lowered the truck window, then had to lean way out the window to reach the woman in the booth. She took the card and promptly shut her own booth window.

Grayson raised an eyebrow. "I know that card's not yours, sugar."

"That's sugar *daddy* to you. And don't insult my manners."

"Your manners are fooling around in the back seat, then buying your date ferry coffee with a stolen credit card?"

"Hey now," Reece said. "I'm going to buy you food too."

Grayson leaned forward, looking around Reece at the woman who was swiping the credit card. "Do I want to know whose name is actually on that card?"

"Traynor's."

"You're charging our ferry ride to *Director Traynor*? I *shot* him."

"Yeah, but he tried to kill you first," Reece said. *"Twice."*

Grayson pursed his lips but sat back in the seat again.

A moment later, the booth's window opened. Reece collected the card and drove forward, following the staff's directions into a long row of vehicles as they were loaded onto the ferry's car deck.

From there, they took the stairs up to the passenger deck and found the galley. As the ferry got underway, they bought a collection of bakery items, protein bars and drinks, taking it all to one of the small booths.

While they worked their way through breakfast, Grayson was looking out the ferry windows. "I don't remember the last time I was on a ferry. How long's the crossing?"

"Barely an hour." Reece tilted his head, watching Grayson watch the ocean. Grayson had mentioned once that he used to love camping. Did he even know that his eyes always seemed drawn to the view?

There were words that needed to be said between them, a *what the fuck happens now* conversation. But Reece didn't say them, because his own gaze kept darting from Grayson to the other passengers.

It was so easy to thrall security in that laboratory, the voice in his head pointed out.

It had been. And it had felt *good* to finally let loose. But Reece didn't need more thralls right now.

This ferry can hold two thousand people, and it's more than half full. You could take your pick for your thralls on board.

Reece's gaze wandered to a man in a suit, barking into his phone loud enough that everyone could hear his conversation as he carried his coffee toward the lounge. Reece's skin prickled, the black lighting crawling over him like electric centipedes.

That guy's probably an asshole. You could start with him. Find a couple more.

Reece forced his eyes back to Grayson. He was still the Dead Man, and while he might accept that Reece had done what he'd had to do for a rescue, he'd probably be a lot less willing to let Reece walk off the Bremerton ferry with a new army of emotional slaves.

Evan's touch doesn't knock you out now.

He can't stop you anymore.

Reece cleared his throat. "You want to go up to the top deck?"

"Outside?" Grayson glanced back at him. "It just *snowed*."

"I could use the fresh air," Reece said, and it wasn't a lie, which probably said a lot about how much he needed to get some distance from people, or maybe how much time he spent skulking indoors.

"Suit yourself," Grayson muttered as they got to their feet.

The air at the top of the ferry was icy cold, but the view was unbeatable, and they were the only ones out on the deck. Reece watched as Grayson's gaze went to the waves of the sound, the distant green hills, the endless gray sky, and finally settled on the distant Seattle skyline where it waited on the horizon. After a moment, Grayson leaned on the railing, gaze still on Seattle. "So what's our plan when we dock at the pier?"

Reece shrugged lightly, like he hadn't been ruminating on that same question. "We'll be right downtown. I could take the truck, and you can walk off the ferry."

"*Or*," said Grayson, "you could give me back my truck, and I can drop you off somewhere."

Reece side-eyed him. "And is that *somewhere* a corrupted empath prison?"

"I might settle for your secret empath lair."

Reece scoffed. "Nice try. But if I were giving up the location of my secret empath lair, it'd be to take *you* prisoner. And I'd have the courtesy not to throw you in some dungeon; I'd just keep you chained naked to a bed."

"I'm sure Alex would be thrilled with that," Grayson said dryly.

That drew a huff from Reece, edged with something that was almost a laugh. He leaned on the rail next to Grayson, close enough that their arms pressed together. It was better up here. He could block out all sensations from other passengers, the crisp fresh air and the quiet settling the corruption enough he could ignore its hunger.

"We could go back to the studio apartment," Reece said. "And I could try to fuck you over to the dark side."

"I should not be tempted by that," Grayson muttered. "Maybe I should try to fuck the bad out of *you*."

Reece shivered as a frisson of desire went through him. "You're more than welcome to try," he said meaningfully. "And if at first you don't succeed, you can try and try again."

Grayson snorted. He pressed his shoulder and arm more firmly against Reece and then didn't pull away. "You cold?" Reece asked.

"Yeah," Grayson said. "But you're warm."

They stood together at the rail, watching as Seattle came closer, sprawled out in front of them and getting bigger with every passing minute.

Eventually Grayson nudged him. "I wouldn't put you in a dungeon."

Reece glanced up at him. "No?"

"No." Grayson was still watching Seattle. "I mean, I don't know what I'm gonna do with you. But then, I've never known what to do with you, so why should that change now?"

The corner of Reece's mouth turned up, but then the trace of a smile slipped off his face. "Nothing else has changed either. We're still enemies."

Grayson turned his head toward him. "No chance of that changing?"

The black lightning sent warning sparks across Reece. "You're the one who's always believed corruption is permanent," Reece pointed out. "And even if there somehow had been a trace of my pacifism left, I'm pretty sure it's gone after my stunt in that laboratory."

"You were saving *me*—"

"Next time I might not be," Reece warned. "Corruption isn't just a bad mood, Evan, and it's got its hands on my throat—" He broke it off with an angry shake of his head. "I'm dangerous to you and everyone else in Seattle. I don't believe that's going to change—and I don't believe you're going to give up being the Dead Man."

Grayson's gaze darted to Seattle, then back to Reece. "No," he admitted. "I'm not."

Reece wrapped his hands around the railing, feeling the cold under his bare palms. "You're an empath hunter. I'm a corrupted empath. And we're going to have to say goodbye, just like we always do."

Grayson nodded slowly. They fell quiet again, the space between them filled with the rumble of the ferry's engine. The air was wet, the cold droplets occasionally dotting Reece's face.

Grayson finally spoke. "Keep the truck for now. I'll walk off the ferry."

"I get the truck?" Reece frowned. "You heard me say I'm still corrupted, right? You're not getting me mixed up with your Care Bear again?"

"It's not a mix-up." Grayson folded his arms on the rail. "You keep telling me you're not the same empath, but I don't see your dark side and your light side as separate. You're *Reece*. All of you." He turned his head toward Reece. "And I might have a bullet scar, but you gave up more than that for me. Maybe you're dangerous as hell now, but you're never ever gonna hurt *me*."

Reece tightened his hands on the railing.

Grayson shrugged. "So maybe we just need to tweak the name. Do you think Danger Bear has kind of a ring to it?"

Reece huffed again, and this time it sounded even more like a laugh. "Evan."

"Beware Bear."

"Evan."

And Grayson leaned down just as Reece stretched up on his toes, and they were kissing at the ferry railing in the shadow of Seattle, the skyline and their inevitable goodbye looming ahead of them.

Too soon, there was a chime that echoed through the ferry. "We will soon be arriving at Colman Dock, Pier 52. Drivers, please make your way to your vehicles."

Grayson pulled back just a bit. "Guess you should head to the truck," he said, his words ghosting over Reece's lips.

Reece exhaled. "Guess I should."

He stepped back, eyes on the tall figure at the railing. He wasn't going to name the feeling flooding his chest, but it was fair to say he'd burn the fucking world to keep Grayson safe.

Literally.

And that was exactly why they had to part.

Reece turned away and found the stairs. He hurried down them, heading for the car deck.

But as he stepped into the lounge area to cut through it, he abruptly stopped short. He could practically taste the anxiety, unease and irritation coming off the other passengers. His gaze darted around the full lounge in confusion.

The intercom chimed again, and this time, a new voice came on. "This is your porter. We've gotten reports of a disturbance near downtown. There will be a delay as we ask everyone to remain on board the ferry until we're advised that it's safe for passengers to disembark."

Safe?

Around him, the passengers burst into nervous chatter. Reece needed to know what was happening—needed his phone. He took off at a run, darting down the stairs to the car deck. Beyond the open front of the ferry, downtown loomed bigger than ever. They'd be docking at the pier in minutes.

He yanked open the truck's door and grabbed his phone, booting it up. "Son of a bitch," he said out loud as his text messages exploded. He quickly scanned the most recent text from Alex.

Alex: Charles Stone has trapped 10 empaths in a suite at Lumen Field. He doesn't know Cora and I are with them.

Alex: We're going to make sure he's sorry

Reece jabbed the icon for his internet browser.

BREAKING NEWS: CHAOS AT LUMEN FIELD

Reece swore again. He had to join Alex and Cora at Lumen Field.

And he obviously couldn't bring the Dead Man.

The front of the ferry was pulling up to the dock, the car ramp lowering into place. They'd be held here until it was safe to disembark, but Grayson wasn't exactly going to wait around. Their pier was only a fifteen-minute walk from Lumen Field.

Reece looked around the car deck, then up to the high ceiling above him. He took a deep breath, reaching for the tumult of feelings inside him.

Those hundreds of people he hadn't thralled were still on the ferry. Maybe Reece couldn't stop Grayson from running for the stadium.

But he could sure as hell slow him down.

★

I think one of these companies, Metallic Tailors, doesn't exist.

My dad had friends on the BOD that I think will help me dig for details, but Charles Stone has a lot of power, and I don't want you or your friends caught in the fallout.

Thanks for being there for me. It means more than you know.

Jamey stared at Gretel's note, left on the now-empty dining table. The couch was likewise empty, her things gone along with her BMW.

"You've got to be kidding," she said out loud, as if Gretel could hear her.

After taking on Kosler the night before, Jamey had knocked him out. Then, with still no word from Grayson and no idea what to do, she'd packed up everything on the kitchen table and taken Kosler to the Stone Solutions hospital in Kirkland. She'd come home and fallen into a deep enough sleep that she hadn't heard Gretel sneak out.

She could grudgingly admire Gretel for trying to protect them by leaving, but Jamey was certain she could speak for the whole house in saying they had no intention of abandoning her to Charles Stone and his twisted empire.

Jamey was going to call her and straighten this out right now. But as she snatched up her phone, it began to ring. Jamey took in the caller ID, eyebrows going up. After a moment, she answered. "Lieutenant Parson?"

She hadn't talked to Parson since the day Stensby's police cruiser had been found smashed up by Lake Sammamish.

"The force still has standing instructions to inform you

when an incident could be empathy-related." Parson couldn't have been particularly happy about that, but he was a man who did what he was ordered. "There's a situation at Lumen Field."

Liam was tumbling of the bedroom, his wide eyes locked on his own phone. *"Jamey."*

"Okay," Jamey said slowly into the phone. "What does *situation* mean?"

"It means there's a stampeding crowd of panicked football fans fleeing the stadium," Parson said just as Liam held up his phone a few inches from Jamey's face. "And we're hearing reports of assault inside the stands."

CHAOS ERUPTING AT LUMEN FIELD, the headlines screamed, with a time stamp of six minutes prior.

Oh shit. "Why do you think empaths are involved?" Jamey said sharply, her eyes going to Liam's.

"Meet me at the car." Liam was already hurrying past her toward the coat rack. The spare room's door had opened, and Aisha was coming out. Jamey could see Diesel just beyond her, sitting on one of the two camping cots and yanking a fleece over his head.

"Because the rumor is that there are several empaths in the Stone Solutions luxury box," Parson said tightly in her ear. "And the panic is being blamed on them."

"What?" Jamey barked.

"Where's Gretel?" Diesel said as he passed by the dining room.

Jamey shoved the note at him. "Why would empaths be at a football game?" she said sharply to Parson, the worry flaring in her stomach again. "They can't even bear to watch it."

"I'm telling you what we've been told," Parson said, just as sharp.

Aisha joined her, nodding at the phone questioningly. *Parson*, Jamey mouthed, then covered the phone so the lieutenant wouldn't hear her whisper. "I think our missing pacifist empaths might be trapped at Lumen Field," she said to Aisha, whose eyebrows went up.

Diesel's voice came from the front door. "Aisha! St. James!"

Aisha tugged her sleeve. "We're going *now*."

Jamey pressed the phone to her ear as she scrambled toward the front door. "You mentioned assault in the stands," she said to Parson as she jammed her feet into boots. "*That's* not the empaths."

"Not everyone is as certain of that as you," Parson said with an edge. "The violence is escalating, and the stadium is huge; we're having a hard time getting things under control. If you want to go to Lumen Field for your empaths, at least make sure you're armed."

Jesus. Jamey grabbed her coat off the rack. "I'm on my way to Lumen Field," she said, stepping out the front door to her porch. "I promise when I get to the bottom of whatever is happening, the empaths aren't going to be the real villains."

Jamey hung up, zipping her coat as she scrambled down the stairs. As she reached the car, she paused. Liam was in the driver's seat of his Corolla, with Aisha up front and Diesel in the back.

Liam leaned out the window. "Get in, babe. We're going to Lumen Field."

Jamey threw up her hands. "You three are *not* coming with me to a stadium of empaths and chaos!"

"I was a *marine*," Diesel said.

"I'm a doctor who knows more about empaths than *you*," Aisha added.

"And this is *my* car," said Liam. "So come on. Let's go."

Jamey sighed but got in.

"This is your porter. We've gotten reports of a disturbance near downtown. There will be a delay as we ask everyone to remain on board the ferry until we're advised that it's safe for passengers to disembark."

The second announcement on the ferry had Grayson raising an eyebrow. He'd quickly darted down the stairs to the lounge, but Reece was nowhere in sight. He pulled one of the ferry staff aside. "I need to know what's going on," he said quietly, eyes on the tense and anxious passengers.

"You haven't seen the news?" the staff member said in surprise, holding out his phone.

CHAOS ERUPTING AT LUMEN FIELD

Oh boy.

Grayson quickly scanned the article, his eyes picking out key details:

Reports senseless rampaging

Crowd fleeing in terror

Empaths allegedly in Stone Solutions' luxury box

How the hell could there be empaths at a Seahawks game?

And what's Reece gonna do if he thinks other empaths might be in danger? the little voice in his head pointed out.

Grayson had to get to Lumen Field, immediately. "Thank you, ma'am," he said, handing her back the phone. He hurried toward another set of stairs that led to the car deck.

You lost eyes on your corrupted empath on a ferry full of people, the little voice in Grayson's head said, rather unhelpfully. *At the exact same time there's a panic happening at the stadium fifteen minutes away.*

Maybe Reece hadn't discovered the situation yet, and

Grayson could stop him before he dumped more proverbial empathic fuel on the stadium fire.

Sure, sure. You're definitely going to be that lucky. And if there are other empaths involved, Reece is going to be totally good with letting the Dead Man show up. He's definitely not going to try to stop you.

Grayson really needed the little voice in his head to stop sounding so much like a certain sarcastic empath he knew. He reached the stairs, but as he started forward, the crowd around him erupted in screams.

"Why are we trapped here—"

"This is *terrifying*—"

"I'm *so afraid*—"

Grayson was jostled to the side and shoved into the wall as the crowd abruptly swelled around him, stampeding to the stairs like spooked cattle. The staff member Grayson had been speaking with suddenly jumped up on a chair.

"What is happening?" he bellowed, hands clasped to his face, loud enough to hurt Grayson's ears.

Inexplicable and sudden fear setting off every person around him and blocking him in?

Yeah. Reece was making sure he had his work cut out for him getting to Lumen Field.

CHAPTER THIRTY-TWO

. . . there are those who would disagree with me, of course, but frankly it's simply preposterous to think the protective instinct of an empath sibling is reciprocated. The empath is a parasite, nothing more.

—Comment in the manual *Anatomy of a Dead Man*

Liam had been able to drive them downtown, but there'd been roadblocks set up around the stadium, and Jamey was pretty sure some of the hulking enforcers mixed in with the cops were undercover Stone Solutions response.

"They'll let me pass. I'm still with the force," Liam said, starting to roll down his window.

"Let Diesel and me out here," Jamey said, leaning forward to kiss his cheek from the back seat. "You two stay in the car and stay safe."

Liam and Aisha exchanged a look that Jamey was pretty sure meant they had their own ideas, but Diesel was hopping out the other back seat door, and they needed to go. Jamey leaped out of the car, and the two of them ducked past the barrier.

"Hey!" one of the undercover response team members called, but they were already running toward the stadium.

One block over they hit the crowd. Jamey had to fight like a salmon going upstream against the people running from the stadium.

"This is not how I like to watch football," Jamey said as they dodged a group of fans with painted faces.

"Same." Diesel ducked past a pair of men in head-to-toe fleece. "Give me my couch and—oh shit."

But Jamey had seen them too, three women in Seahawks sweatshirts and beanies, struggling to hurry down the sidewalk as they carried five crying kids between them.

"We have to help—" Diesel started.

"You help," she said. "I'll get into the stadium."

She put on a burst of speed, registering Diesel calling his assent behind her as she ran up the sidewalk and found a side door. It was locked, but the hinges were on the outside. She braced a foot on the wall and yanked with all her strength. The door flew open, hanging crazily on its now-broken hinges.

She moved inside, finding her way through the mazelike corridors of the stadium's first floor, following the screams until she emerged at one end of the field and into fresh chaos. The bright green of the Astroturf was covered in melted slush, occasionally streaked by red, and more than one body lay unmoving on the field. There were too many people on the field to count, but her eyes fell on the familiar figure of Officer Stensby, his hands outstretched and heading for a man in a referee uniform.

"No!" She'd figure out how the fucking hell *Stensby* could possibly be here later. She sprinted forward, running into him with her shoulder at full speed. He went flying, smashing into another man and sending them both to the ground.

"Run!" Jamey barked at the ref as she whirled around to find herself face-to-face with Officer Kosler. "*You?*" she said in shock. "You're supposed to be in the hospital—*fuck*."

She ducked as Kosler came at her, then spun and took him down with a hard kick to his knee. He hit the ground and hissed up at her.

He looked *terrible*—even worse than the night before, with blood streaming down a face that was almost unrecognizable, twisted as it was with rage and violence. Jamey took a step back from him. "What the fuck is going on?"

"It's a new kind of party!"

A voice she didn't recognize, high-pitched and almost chirpy, came from her side. Jamey spun to find two empaths standing on the forty-yard line, a young woman with dark brown hair and man around the same age with an unsettling gleam in his blue eyes that could only be corruption. Around the two empaths, a group was gathering, their faces lost to expressions of malicious devotion.

Jamey was pretty sure she recognized them both from pictures and planning, and yeah. She'd found their apparently not-so-pacifist-anymore empaths—and their thralls. "Mireya Gomez? Dawson Jones? What happened to you?"

The empaths ignored her question. "She recognizes us," Mireya said to Dawson as the thralls bared their teeth at Jamey. "We don't want that, do we?"

"No, we don't." Dawson looked at the thralls, then pointed at Jamey. "Take care of her for us."

Jamey stumbled backward. She could fight thralls, but there were eight of them closing in on her, all with murder in their eyes. Behind her, Stensby and Kosler had both gotten to their feet, blocking her exit.

She raised her chin, fingers curling into fists—

"Get away from her."

The familiar voice sliced across the football field, so much empathic power lacing it that Jamey felt it against her skin. The thralls hit the ground, curling into whimpering balls, some of them rocking back and forth, some of them covering their heads.

Jamey looked up in shock. But sure enough, there in the stands was Reece. He was glaring at Dawson and Mireya with an unfamiliar rage. "Get your fucking thralls away from my sister before I make them tear themselves apart."

"Reece?" Jamey said hoarsely.

Dawson and Mireya were backing up rapidly, hands raised in apology. The thralls were crawling after them, dragging themselves along the sideline, still shaking from the cocktail of emotions pouring off Reece, so strong that the hairs on Jamey's arms and neck were raised. Reece himself was almost unrecognizable, his eyes narrowed, his fists clenched, a darkness in his expression that she had never seen on him before. He looked an inch away from making good on his threat.

Then, as Reece's gaze darted back to Jamey and their eyes gazes locked, all that fell away, and all she could see was her brother.

Jamey started forward. "Reece."

But he was turning, sprinting back up the aisle.

Jamey broke into a run. "Wait—"

Reece had reached the top of the aisle, and by the time she'd levered herself over the rail and into the stands, he'd disappeared into the stadium again.

Grayson figured Reece had sent the ferry into a panic hoping to slow him down, but he'd been able to jump from the railing to the pier and from there race onto Alaskan Way. He could make out the top of Lumen Field up ahead, making a beeline for it as he sprinted down the waterfront. A response member recognized him at the barrier and hastily cleared the path.

As Grayson came up on the stadium, he heard his name and turned to see Diesel hurrying his way. "St. James call you?"

Grayson shook his head. "I lost my phone. Reece's phone. It's a long story."

"Where've you been?" Diesel said as they fell into step together.

"Also a long story. You spot any empaths yet?"

Diesel shook his head. "If they're here, they're in the stadium. Come on."

Diesel filled him in on the past twenty-four hours as they darted past the flow of people pouring out from the main doors and headed for a side door that was hanging off its hinges.

"So if you arrived with St. James, Mr. Lee and Dr. Easterby," Grayson said as they reached the door, "then where are . . . ?"

"Evan! Diesel!" Liam was jogging toward them, phone in hand. "I called first responders I know personally," he said, breathing hard. "People are hurt and need medical care, and I don't trust Stone Solutions not to intercept police calls. Have you seen Aisha? She left the car with me. Then I lost her."

"You're not going to keep a doctor away from the injured," Diesel said. "I'll find her."

"Right behind you." Grayson nodded at Liam as Diesel disappeared into the stadium. "You talk to St. James since you got here?"

Liam shook his head. He was paler than usual. "I'm coming with you to find her."

They ducked through the doorway and into the halls in the depths of the stadium, emerging at one end of the football field. Liam froze. "Is that—Stensby? And *Kosler*? How the hell are they here?"

Grayson had seen them too, the bodies unmoving on the end zone. He hurried over and knelt next to Stensby.

"Last I saw him, he was in Stone Solutions' private hospital in Kirkland." Stensby's face was streaked with red. Grayson pressed a hand to his neck, over his jugular, but there was no pulse to feel. "What the hell happened? The corrupted empaths get their hands back on him?"

"Wouldn't have to be the empaths." Liam had pushed up Stensby's sleeve. He pointed to the puncture mark at the wrist. "He'd been on an IV drip. They could have given him the same thing they gave Dr. Whitman when she killed the Macys."

"Another frame job," Grayson mused.

"I wouldn't put that past Stone Solutions," Liam said grimly.

Does Stone Solutions know you've got me here and what you're planning? Grayson had asked Nichols, in that lab.

You mean Vivian? Nichols had scoffed. *As if she'd ever have the stomach for it. But rest assured, I am backed by those with the* real *power.*

Grayson raised his gaze to the stands, tracking up the rows of seats until he found the glass windows of Stone Solutions' luxury box. "No," he said. "I wouldn't either—"

"Ooh, look how big this guy is!" a chirpy voice said, suddenly close.

Grayson looked up to see two empaths heading straight for them, both around his own age, a woman with dark brown hair and a man with big blue eyes.

The second empath rubbed his bare hands together. "He could do some damage." Then he suddenly frowned. "Why am I not getting any emotions from him?"

At his side, Liam stiffened, but Grayson just met their eyes. "There's a reason for that," he said dryly, and watched both empaths hit the end zone, gagging.

"I think all y'all have done enough damage today," he said, getting to his feet. "And it ends now."

Alex cut through a stadium food court, past the trampled remains of beer stands and cotton candy racks, following a new source of emotion so strong it could only be Reece. Cora was at his side, expression grim.

"What pissed Reece off?" she said as they hurried past staircase after staircase leading down to the lower-level seats.

Alex shrugged helplessly. "Take your pick," he said, gesturing around them.

They were getting closer to Reece, who seemed to be seeking them in return. Just before they hit a set of suites, Reece crested a set of concrete stairs from the stands and joined them.

"Where the hell have you been?" Cora demanded as she pulled him into a hug.

"Port Angeles. The Olympic mountains. It's a long story." Reece reached for Alex next. "What the fuck happened here?"

They formed a tight huddle, arms around each other, their conversation half words and half emotions as they filled each other in.

"I'm going to find Charles Stone and make his fate worse than Nichols's," Reece said darkly after Alex told him about the kidnapping and the suite.

Not a lie. Alex could appreciate that, but he was still confused. "So you and Evan spent the night in the truck? During a *snowstorm*? How'd y'all avoid frostbite?"

"Well." Reece licked his lips. "We had, um, a—a blanket—of sorts—anyway, the point is, you two need to get out of here."

"We are not leaving you and the others," Cora said heatedly.

"I guarantee Evan is on his way, if not already here," Reece said. "The others won't know he's the Dead Man, and they won't be prepared for his voice or that knockout touch. He's going to be taking empaths down like dominoes."

"Yeah," said Alex. "Empaths like *you*."

"No, I'll be fine because—never mind," Reece said hurriedly. "Jamey's here too, and all of Stone Solutions' response."

"You've got insight into your detective sister," Cora said. "What is the smartest play we can make here?"

Reece closed his eyes for a long moment, then said, "Scatter and escape. If I can get any of the others out too, I will, but some of us need to stay free today so that we can rescue the ones who get caught. You both need to run."

Not a lie. Alex met Cora's eyes, which mirrored his own turmoil. It hurt like physical pain to think of abandoning the other empaths to capture, but if it was their best chance, then it was their best chance.

"Okay." Cora let out a long breath. "Okay. We'll go. Be safe."

The three of them hugged tightly, and then Reece was gone, running back down the hall toward the suites.

Alex and Cora went the opposite way. Alex kept his eyes peeled for the first exit sign as they backtracked through the food court.

As he started to point to an internal staircase, he felt a spike of dismay from Cora just as he heard her voice. *"Stop!"*

Cora took off at a run, the wrong way, toward the closest stairs down into the stadium stands. Alex tried to catch her sleeve, only to nearly slip on spilled soda. "Cora!"

He chased after her. Down in the stands a few sections over, a woman he vaguely recognized was stumbling backwards through a lower row of seats as two thralls advanced on her. But as she levered herself over the back of a seat and jumped, a thrall grabbed her ankle. She tumbled into the next row with her leg at an unnatural angle.

As the woman's cry of pain reached his ears, anger poured off Cora so strongly Alex felt it against his skin like the wind. The two thralls dropped into balls, cowering between the seats.

Alex finally placed the woman: one of the two people that Cora had wanted to spare at Polaris. "Who is she?"

"A doctor who was used to try to corrupt her empath boyfriend. He didn't make it. She still has scars." Cora met Alex's eyes. "She tried to help me at Polaris. Look at her, Alex. She's not walking out of here on her own. The thralls will be back on her if I leave."

The woman was still crumped in the stands between rows, hands clutching her shin, her face gone very pale. Alex swore quietly. "Evan and St. James are gonna get this place under control—"

"Not soon enough," Cora said. "One of us needs to stay free. You go. Get the hell out of here."

None of her words had been lies. Alex ran a hand over his face. "I'll come for you," he promised. "Wherever they take you, I'll find you and I'll come for you, for *all* of you."

"I know." Cora stretched up and kissed his cheek like a sister. "*Go*," she said again.

She started down the stairs into the stands, toward the other woman. Alex turned and sprinted back up the stairs. He reached the exit he'd seen before and darted into that stairwell.

But as he did, his phone chimed. He yanked it out and glanced at the screen.

Gretel: I don't know if the same man murdered both our parents, but Charles Stone murdered mine. He has all the power and a million escape routes.

Gretel: But I still want justice. And I won't let this go.

He read the rest of her texts, his eyes narrowing, then jammed his phone back in his pocket. He'd make one quick stop before he left, because Charles Stone might have power, but so did Alex.

"Evan!"

Grayson heard his name. Then his eyes found St. James, sprinting toward him through the upper-level club space. Her face was streaked with red. "You all right—"

"It's not mine," she promised, wiping distractedly at the blood. "It's ugly in here." They pivoted in sync, matching each other's quick pace as they headed for the railing. "Where have you been?"

"We're gonna need a lot more time than we have now for that story," Grayson said as they leaned on the railing and scanned the field. "Have you seen Reece in this mess?"

"He saved my life." When Grayson glanced at her, she added, "They're not beyond hope, Evan. We can't give up on him—on any of them."

Grayson's gaze went back to the field. "How many are there?" he said instead of trying to voice his own thoughts.

"Stone Solutions is here with tranqs," St. James said. "I think they've gotten four of the empaths."

"I took down two on the field and four more on the way up here," Grayson said.

"We had ten pacifists," St. James said. "So maybe that's all of them—"

She cut herself off with a gasp, but Grayson had seen it too: Aisha Easterby in the stands, almost at the opposite end zone, running from thralls.

Grayson didn't hesitate; he hurdled himself over the railing and landed in the stands below. He shook off the impact as St. James landed next to him, and the two of them sprinted forward.

Dozens of yards ahead, Aisha had fallen between the seats, the thralls on top of her. Grayson put on a burst of speed, but it wasn't gonna be enough—

Cora Falcon suddenly came racing in ahead of them. The thralls toppled into the stands, curling into balls as Cora reached Aisha, and he and St. James were too late—

But Cora was kneeling at Aisha's side. The women were exchanging words Grayson couldn't hear, and Cora wasn't reaching for Aisha's face or her hands but was pulling her own fleece over her head and handing it to Aisha, pointing at her leg.

"Are you kidding me with this Harley Quinn shit," he heard St. James pant, whatever the hell that meant.

As the two of them came up on Cora and Aisha, it was Aisha who said, "*Wait.*" She held up her hands as Cora watched Grayson and St. James warily. "Wait," Aisha said again. "She's not hurting me."

"You need to talk to your friend here. She's way too trusting," Cora said, her eyes on Grayson and St. James.

But Aisha shook her head. "I'm not your hostage. I know I'm not."

Cora glanced at her, then back at Grayson and St. James. "Her leg is broken," she said to St. James. "She needs a doctor."

"I *am* a doctor," Aisha said.

"You're not setting your own tibia," Cora said dryly, reminding Grayson she'd worked at the veterans' hospital once upon a time.

Two sections over, Diesel and Liam were hurrying their way. "Is Alex here too?" St. James asked Cora.

Cora blinked innocently back at her. "Why would he be?"

"Answering a question with a question," St. James said. "That's exactly how Reece dodges his own lies when he doesn't want me to see him twitch."

"Can we just get this over with?" Cora got to her feet, gaze going to Grayson. "I surrender. It's not a lie this time."

She held out her bare hand.

"*Evan*," Aisha said as Diesel and Liam joined them.

Grayson took Cora's hand. Her long eyelashes fluttered, and she pitched forward. Grayson caught her before she hit the ground. "That's eleven," he said, hoisting the unconscious Cora into a bridal carry. "We're missing Alex and Reece."

Liam had knelt next to Aisha. Diesel held out his arms toward Grayson. "We'll take care of Cora," he said. "You two go find your brothers."

Reece flattened himself to the wall as two uniformed guards sprinted past. He had been trying to let his empathy lead him to other empaths, but he didn't know the feel of them like he knew Alex and Cora, and the sheer amount of emotion ricocheting through the stadium made it difficult to get a reading on anyone.

The feel of the stadium was starting to shift, however, from a dominating sense of panic to the crashing aftermath, which might mean the other empaths weren't in control anymore. Reece ducked into a staircase and climbed. If he could get up to the summit level, he might be able to get a good view of what was happening—

As he stepped onto a landing, however, he came face-to-face with a new set of guards, in new armor: empath glove material from head to toe, blocking Reece's every sense.

He froze.

"This is the one he wants," said one of the guards.

"The one *who* wants—" Reece started.

But he'd already been surrounded.

"Search together or split up?" Grayson asked as he and St. James reached the top of their section.

"I think we have to split up," St. James said grimly. "We

need to find Reece and Alex fast, because if Stone Solutions gets there before us, we may never see them again. I'll go left."

She disappeared as Grayson turned right. St. James wasn't wrong—maybe Alex and Reece had a hell of a body count between them, but someone had helped Nichols kidnap Grayson and had been planning to send more empaths Nichols's way. Maybe Grayson could talk Marist around to better holding conditions for the ten pacifists who'd somehow been caught in this mess, but if Stone Solutions was first to either Alex or Reece, they'd be tranquilized and locked away who the hell knew where before St. James or Grayson could so much as protest. And maybe Grayson couldn't care about that, but St. James sure as hell did.

Grayson ducked into a stairwell and leaned against the landing wall, closing his eyes to think. Alex was going to be reading the stadium's mood like an orchestra conductor; he'd have picked it up the moment things began to shift and empaths started going down. But Alex wouldn't have left just to save himself, wouldn't have abandoned the other empaths to their fate unless he had a damn good reason—

"We need to talk."

Grayson's eyes popped open. His gaze went up the stairs to the familiar figure at the next landing. "That's my line," he said dryly.

Alex calmly took a seat on the top stair. He appeared alone and defenseless, but it was certainly an illusion, the danger lurking just out of sight. "What, I don't get a *hey, little brother, how you doing?*"

Grayson gestured at the door and the stadium beyond. "I got some idea how you are already."

"I suppose so." Alex's gaze was on him. "I can probably guess how you are too."

"I'm fine," Grayson said. "I'm never anything but fine anymore."

Alex's eyes flicked over him. "We have five minutes to talk, maybe only four."

"Or maybe you have thirty seconds before I take you down like all your empath friends," Grayson said. "I do have a real specific job now, you know."

"I'm the one who changed you," Alex said, clearly unimpressed. "I really doubt you'd be able to knock me out."

"Last time I checked, I was still bigger and faster than you—"

"Can you stop being so *dramatic* for the three minutes it will take me to tell you what really happened in this stadium?" Alex steepled his hands together. "Maybe you already know Charles Stone has been framing us. Last night, he had ten empaths kidnapped and locked them in the Stone Solutions suite. This morning, he injected my thralls with some deadly cocktail and turned them loose on the stadium, planning to blame the kidnapped pacifists."

"Okay, but I met several of those empaths," Grayson pointed out. "They weren't pacifists anymore."

"No," Alex agreed. "Stone didn't know Cora and I had joined the others in the suite."

"You turned the other empaths?" When Alex shrugged with fake modesty, Grayson huffed. *"How?"*

"I don't think you or anyone else needs those details." Alex rested his chin on his hands. "Holt Traynor told us that Stone was responsible for what happened to us in that bunker. He might even be the one who orchestrated what happened to Mom and Dad."

Grayson folded his arms. "Is all this your way of trying to convince me that we should work together instead of against each other?"

"Just this once," Alex said. "Because I don't want Charles Stone to get away this time."

Grayson straightened up off the wall. Alex's eyes tracked his every move, and yeah, that relaxed pose was just a front, like a snake sunning itself, harmless-appearing but ready to strike if provoked. "At least one thing that happened in that bunker wasn't Charles Stone's fault."

"Fair enough," Alex said. "Though I wasn't trying to turn you into some secret shadow agent *empath hunter.* That's not even a real thing."

"I made it a real thing."

"Yeah, you did, and if that wasn't bad enough, you had to go work for the very assholes who had us locked in that bunker in the first place?"

"I didn't know who was behind it, did I?" Grayson said. "And even now, I can't feel anger at Stone for what he did."

"But you could help me take him down," Alex said.

"How many lives is that gonna cost?" Grayson said. "Maybe I can help, but maybe I shouldn't. I'm gonna make a logical decision based on protecting innocents and pacifist empaths. That's who I am now. You know that better than anyone else, and you know exactly how permanent the change was when you destroyed my emotions."

"I didn't *destroy* anything," Alex said. "I built a wall. With your full cooperation, I might add."

"Destruction or wall, it's still permanent."

But Alex only rolled his eyes. "I'll tell you exactly what I told Reece: It's permanent *for all intents and purposes.*"

Grayson shook his head. "I don't understand."

"I can't break it; no empath can," said Alex. "The only one who could tear it down is you—but you never, ever will." He leaned forward. "Don't you see? Because to break it, you'd have to *want* to—and you're no longer capable of feeling that emotion."

Memories from that West Texas bunker rose, and Grayson

let them: standing in a cell with Alex, wiping blood off his face, the pain in his body still not a match for the pain in his heart.

Do it, Grayson had said to his brother. *Whatever you need to do to make me stronger, do it. I will get us the fuck out of here, Alex, I swear it.*

I don't want to feel anything anymore anyway.

"You're my brother," Alex said more quietly. "I know I'm not the brother I used to be, but I wanted to get you out of that bunker. And maybe part of me thought giving you relief from the pain almost walked the edge of mercy."

I don't want to feel anything anymore anyway.

Alex would have heard that Grayson was telling the truth.

He shook his head, burying the memories, for now at least. "What do you need me to do about Charles Stone?"

"Find him." Alex jumped up to his feet. "I know that slimy bastard is here, probably just outside the stadium where he's safe, gloating that his plan worked. I'm worried that he might have found Reece."

Grayson stilled.

"Stone will be ready to run, will probably have both his car and his helicopter waiting. Find him and stall him. We'll handle the rest."

"Who's *we*?" Grayson asked.

But Alex was darting back up the stairs. Grayson had a choice: Chase upstairs after Alex and bring him into Stone Solutions with the other empaths, or do what Alex had asked of him and head downstairs to look for Charles Stone.

He didn't hesitate, and a moment later he was running down the stairs, heading for the street level.

CHAPTER THIRTY-THREE

We could have labored for years and never engineered an empathy defense as effective as the Dead Man. A man without a heart, yes, but even more valuably, a man with no wants or desires of his own.

He has become a weapon who can never wish to be anything but a weapon.

—Two-year-old confidential memo from Stone Solutions to the Empath Initiative

Grayson sprinted down staircases and back to the main doors, darting out onto the sidewalk and the street where police cruisers and unmarked SUVs lined the curb. He hurried past them, rounding the corner, and ducked beyond a barrier, into a narrower street that looped around and under the raised expressway between the football and baseball stadiums. Here the street was blocked off, empty save for a grouping of vehicles by the loading door: three black SUVs, a black Maybach, and an unmarked van like the ones used by Stone Solutions' Kirkland hospital. Around the vehicles stood eight or nine men in black gear from head to toe, their firearms in their hands, not their holsters.

As Grayson came up on the group, the backdoor of the Maybach opened.

"Ah, Evan!" Charles Stone stepped from the car. "I was just about to send a team to find you."

But Grayson's ears were picking up another voice from farther away.

"Let me *go.*"

His gaze went toward the parking garage and the street-level door. A moment later, four men emerged, dressed in the same head-to-toe gear as the other Stone Solutions responders, and between them they were frog-marching Reece out of the building and toward the vehicles.

"I think the three of us are long overdue for a conversation, don't you?" Charles said, his tone conversational but with an unmistakable hint of menace underneath.

Grayson's gaze stayed on Reece. He was a head shorter and at least a hundred pounds lighter than any of the men dragging him down the sidewalk, still wearing the oversized fleece pullover from the truck, his face flushed with anger and his sweaty hair sticking to his forehead.

"What I think," Grayson said, eyes still on Reece, "is that your men should get their hands off Mr. Davies."

Reece looked up at that moment, his gaze going to Grayson. Several emotions flashed over his face, too fast for Grayson to parse through. "Well, isn't this cozy," he bit out through gritted teeth as the men yanked him forward. "Stone Solutions and the Dead Man, the dream team, waiting for me together."

Grayson opened his mouth, but Charles spoke first. "Oh, please," he said derisively. "Evan is a liar and our enemy. He's been on the empaths' team since the start. You know that better than most, Mr. Davies." He gestured around them as more men closed ranks. "And you can stop your useless efforts to project emotions on this group. My men wear the same material we make our gloves from. It's extremely expensive to create these suits, but worth it. And as for me . . ."

His eyes fixed on Reece. "I have been dealing with your kind since long before your birth. The only thing your projected anger will achieve is making me more irritated with *you*. I know you can hear the truth in my voice."

Reece's expression darkened even further. The man holding his arms behind his back was as big as Grayson, and his grip was hard. "Have your man let go of him, Mr. Stone," Grayson said evenly.

"I don't think we will, Evan," Charles said. "I told you: The three of us have business together. And I'd hate for Mr. Davies to be holding out hope that his sister will come for him: Ms. St. James is currently looking for you on the other side of the stadium. I've requested Vivian call and try to convince her to support your imprisonment. Useless, of course, as an empath sibling would never agree to such a thing, but it will keep them both distracted."

Reece's expression grew even more dangerous. Grayson did another head count: thirteen armed men, possibly more in the vehicles, and guns very close to Reece.

Stone will be ready to run, will probably have both his car and his helicopter waiting, Alex had said. *Find him and stall him. We're taking care of the rest.*

Grayson was gonna have to put his trust in Alex. "You still haven't said what we're doing here," he said to Charles.

"It will be easier if I show you." Charles made a beckoning motion with his finger and began to walk toward the unmarked van.

Grayson met Reece's eyes, the big black pupils glittery with anger now. "That means move it," said the man holding Reece, shoving him toward the waiting van.

"Hey." Grayson's voice wasn't loud, but it cut through the noise.

The man looked over, his face hidden by a balaclava-style mask, his eyes level with Grayson's. "What?"

Grayson nodded pointedly at his death grip on Reece's arms. "You're handling him too rough."

"It's because he's terrified of me," Reece muttered. "Twice my size and armored like a tank, but I'm the scary one."

The balaclava man's hands tightened enough that Reece winced. "If you don't watch your mouth—"

"If you don't watch your grip," Grayson interrupted, "and you leave any bruises on him, I'm gonna pay them back, with interest. Understand?"

The man's eyes narrowed. But his grip loosened ever so slightly as he forced Reece forward, toward the van.

Grayson followed. As they came up on the van, two men opened the back door to reveal what looked like the inside of an ambulance. An array of medical equipment surrounded a bed, and on the bed, lying partially propped up and staring blankly forward, was Cedrick Stone.

Reece's eyes went very wide. His gaze darted between Charles and Cedrick, father and son. "What the fuck is this?" he spat.

Charles made another beckoning motion.

And suddenly, four of the men grabbed for Grayson. But as he raised his arms to fight, Charles moved quickly, and from his coat pocket, drew a gun.

"What this is, Mr. Davies," he said as he pressed the gun against Grayson's temple, "is a hostage situation."

Jamey stood at the overlook at the Summit Level, gaze sweeping across the field and to downtown beyond. Cleanup had started on the field far below. In the stands, she could just make out Aisha on a stretcher, being moved to safety.

Her phone began to ring. She fished it out of her coat pocket to see a number she didn't recognize on-screen. She put it to her ear. "This is Jamey."

"Ms. St. James." The woman on the other end had a very posh and feminine voice. "I don't believe we've had the pleasure of being introduced. My name is Vivian Marist, and I'm—"

"I know who you are," Jamey said testily. "Why are you on my phone and not here at Lumen Field helping clean up the mess?"

"Not that I owe you an explanation, but I'm nearly there," Marist said, her voice with a new testy edge of its own. "I called because Charles Stone has made a request of me, that I try to convince you to agree that your empath brother should be taken into Stone Solutions' custody."

"Oh, really?" Jamey said. "The same Stone Solutions that once threw me in chains on its rooftop and threatened to torture me to see what it would do to Reece?"

Marist made a strangled sound. "I wasn't—"

"Hard pass." Jamey went to hang up.

"Wait! *Please.* I need to speak with you about Gretel Macy."

Jamey immediately put the phone back to her ear. "Is Gretel okay?"

"As far as I know," Marist said. "She called me this morning. You see, I mentioned to you that Charles requested we have a conversation about your brother. But Gretel thought you and I should have a different conversation, about shell companies and diverted funds and why Charles Stone has been pushing so hard to get S.B. 1437 passed and fresh money in our hands. And I'm inclined to agree with her."

She cleared her throat. "Ms. St. James, do you still have anyone you trust on the force?"

Reece stared at the gun against Grayson's temple, a new wave of fury flooding him. "Get away from him—"

Grayson made a noise of surprised pain as one of the soldiers jammed a needle into the side of Grayson's neck and depressed the oversized syringe.

Reece saw red. "What the fuck is that?" he barked at Charles, yanking uselessly against the grip of the gloved soldiers who held him. "How fucking dare you—"

"Calm yourself," Charles snarled, far too loud. "Or else—*no*." He clamped his mouth shut and took a breath through his nose. "Congratulations, Mr. Davies," he said, calm again. "Your ability to project emotion is stronger than even I realized. But ask yourself if it really is your smartest course of action to enrage me while I hold a gun at Evan's head."

Grayson's eyelashes were fluttering, his body going lax in his captors' hold. "What did you just give Evan?" Reece demanded.

"He's simply received a large enough dose of ketamine to keep even an enhanced empath sibling docile. He'll be fine—assuming you cooperate."

Reece could barely hear Charles over the ringing in his ears. "Cooperate with what?"

"A very simple negotiation." Keeping the gun only an inch from Grayson's skin, Charles gestured with his other hand to Cedrick's unconscious body in the back of the ambulance. "You took Cedrick from me. Bring him back, or I take Agent Grayson from you."

Reece sucked in a breath, cold rage and sick understanding rushing through him.

"It's a fascinating data point you've provided us," Charles said. "No matter how deep your corruption goes, there are still people you can't bear to hurt—or to let anyone else hurt. And Evan here is one of yours."

"That's not—"

"Don't bother lying to me, Mr. Davies," said Charles. "I've received the report from Olympia. The building was destroyed from the inside out. An alarming number of bodies were found in the rubble, including Dr. Nichols. We'll be locking the empaths up somewhere even less hospitable now, thanks to you."

"The hell you will," Grayson started, speech slurred, but one of the men elbowed him in the gut, hard.

"Don't touch him," Reece snapped out before he could stop himself.

Charles smiled coldly. "As I said: Useless to pretend. We know Evan's enhancements and limitations intimately and are well-equipped to cause even the Dead Man a world of pain."

"Cedrick experimented on Reece first." Grayson's eyes were half lidded, but he was still fighting to get words out. "None of this would've happened if he'd left empaths alone—"

"Evan, be silent or I'll pull this trigger just to shut you up." Charles gestured impatiently at Cedrick again, his gaze on Reece. "I know when I've found a pressure point. I've dealt with more of your kind than you can imagine. How do you think we discovered empaths can become corrupted in the first place? That was *me*, my research, nearly four decades ago."

Four decades? "We've only had one generation of empaths," Reece said with another pulse of anger. "How old was the empath you experimented on?"

"Ten," Charles said unapologetically. "We thought it'd be better to start young, to see if we could acclimate the pacifists to violence so we could find uses for empaths in the military. Imagine our shock when we discovered so much more."

He pressed the gun into Grayson's temple, metal against skin. "But that's all ancient history. In the here and now, you're going to provide us with another new data point."

Reece ground his teeth. He wanted to tell Charles to go straight to hell, but his gaze was locked on the gun against Grayson's head. "What exactly are you asking me to do?"

"Must I repeat myself?" Charles's gun never wavered. "Bring. Cedrick. Back."

"How do you not understand?" Reece bit out. "What you want is impossible—"

Lie.

Reece's eyes went wide.

Charles cocked the gun. "Make it possible."

"Reece?" Grayson wasn't paying any attention to the gun at his temple, his gaze locked on Reece.

Reece spoke again, this time to himself. "What I did to Cedrick Stone is permanent." *Lie.* "I can never undo it." *Lie.*

How? How could those be lies? Reece couldn't reverse what he'd done to Cedrick: He believed that, believed empaths could never un-thrall their victims—

Part of you believes that, said a little voice in his head, the one he'd thought he had lost forever after the Olympia facility. *The other part of you has always believed you can help.*

Reece stared at Cedrick's catatonic form on the gurney, his breaths starting to come faster. A lifetime ago, in a marina dry dock, he'd told a corrupted Cora he could help her, and it hadn't been a lie. He'd believed he could help.

But he'd still been a pacifist then. Now, the black lightning was leaping along his skin, almost painfully sharp. It didn't want to let go. It wanted revenge, wanted to make Charles and Cedrick Stone pay for everything they'd done. If Reece got his hands on Cedrick right now, he'd kill him, and then Charles would kill Evan.

The corruption in you would kill Cedrick.

But what if there's another path?

Reece's gaze went to Grayson, and the gun still against his temple. Grayson's hazy eyes met his. "Don't listen to them, Reece—"

"Evan, be quiet," Charles snapped. "Stone Solutions is not

protecting you anymore. You are nothing but collateral now, and you'll live longer if you behave accordingly. Do you understand?"

But Grayson was trying to shake his head. "Reece, just *wait.* Don't do anything Stone wants—"

"Shut him up," Charles said to a soldier.

The man smashed a hand over Grayson's mouth, hard enough Reece heard the blow. Fresh anger jolted through him. "You get your fucking hands off Evan—"

"Watch your mouth, you little shit—" Charles cut himself off. He closed his eyes and took a breath through his nose. "No. I won't be influenced." He opened his eyes and gestured at Cedrick. "I'm waiting," he said, calm on the surface but with an undercurrent of anger. "And I won't wait much longer. Undo what you did or Evan pays the price. I know you can hear the truth in my words."

Reece clenched his teeth. Corrupted or pacifist, it didn't matter; there was no part of Reece that wanted to live in a world without Evan.

Your compassion is a strength, Jamey had told him time and time again. Was it true? Was it strong enough to reverse what he'd done to Cedrick—if it was strong enough to return to him in the first place?

"If I can bring Cedrick back," he heard himself say, "I want your word that you won't hurt Evan."

"*Reece*," he heard Grayson try to say.

Reece turned to Charles. "I want to know that no one here will hurt him. I want to hear you say it."

"Give me Cedrick and I will return Evan to you unharmed," Charles said.

Not a lie. "And you'll give us one of your cars and let us leave," Reece said tightly.

"You can have that SUV right there, and we'll let you drive off," Charles said. "Do we have a deal?"

Also not a lie. Reece nodded once.

Charles took one step backwards, gun still aimed at Grayson's head. "Take the empath to Cedrick."

The men holding him began steering him over to the van-turned-ambulance. Reece let them move him without fighting, his gaze trained on the figure of Cedrick Stone on the gurney.

The black lightning was crackling angrily along his skin and the base of his skull, so his whole body was hot and prickling with anger and power.

But corruption had never been alone in him. And from somewhere deep in his chest, something even stronger was rising back up.

And then everything was black.

Grayson tried to force his eyes to stay open, no matter how much the drugs in his system were trying to pull his lids down. There was blood on his lip from the blow, and he swiped his tongue over it, willing the sting and unpleasant taste to wake him up.

"Watch them both," Charles snarled at the uniformed men. "Don't trust either of them or avert your eyes for a moment."

The men were marching Reece toward the van. Did he really think he could fix Cedrick Stone? Un-thrall someone? As far as Grayson knew, it couldn't be done—

Reece suddenly went limp, so that the men holding him stumbled.

"The fuck?" The curse came from one of the men holding Reece, the one Grayson had threatened before, who Reece had said was scared. "Hey! Wake up."

Reece was unmoving in his grip, head lolling and eyes

closed. "Empath!" The man shook Reece, hard. "Wake up and do what you're supposed to do."

Reece didn't respond. He shook Reece again even harder, and when Grayson got free, this guy was getting more than bruises. Grayson tried to open his mouth, but Reece was blinking hard and lifting his head. "What the hell are you doing to me?"

The man huffed with irritation. "You're the one who—"

"There's a curb right in front of us," Reece snapped. "If you get distracted yanking on me, you might trip."

There was a sudden silence.

"What the fuck did he just say?" said one of the men.

"I said this stupid guard could *trip*," Reece repeated. "He's so busy manhandling me he's not paying attention, and could fall off the curb and onto the pavement. You want him to get hurt?"

Grayson stared at Reece. He couldn't have heard that right. He couldn't—

"It can't be," Charles whispered, echoing Grayson's thoughts. "It's impossible."

"And *you*," Reece went on, to another man holding him. "Your grip on my arm is way too tight. If you don't loosen your hold, you could strain a muscle—"

"Stop!" Charles was marching forward, gun still in hand. "*Stop*," he snapped again at a guard. "Don't move. Don't take him any closer to Cedrick." He pointed at another guard. "Let me see his eyes."

One of the soldiers grabbed Reece's chin in a gloved hand and forced his face up. Grayson pulled at the men who held him, his muscles useless and watery as Charles Stone stared at Reece through narrowed eyes.

Whatever Alex had been planning, Grayson was absolutely certain it hadn't included *this*.

"Is this a ruse?" Charles demanded of Reece.

Reece furrowed his brow. "A what?"

Charles turned to the guard with his hand on Reece's jaw. "Is he resisting you? Is he fighting back at all?"

The guard used his hold to jerk Reece's head to the right, then back to the left. "No, sir. He's like a doll."

"I don't believe it," Charles said hoarsely. "This is supposed to be impossible. Someone get this on film—"

"Who are you?" Reece said to Charles, not struggling against the hold on his chin.

"Who am—but of course." Charles clapped his hands together. "Amnesia would have to be an inevitable component of reversion, because how could the pacifist stand to know what was done under corruption—"

Reece's gasp was audible.

"—and the empath would experience a full and instant breakdown—"

"What are you talking about?" Reece's voice had a new note of distress. "Who are you? Why am I here?"

"You're going to fix Cedrick Stone," said the soldier still holding Reece by the chin.

"I'm what?" Reece's eyes went very wide, his gaze going past his captors, to the van-turned-ambulance. "Oh my God—Cedrick Stone—let me go." He leaned in Cedrick's direction.

"Hold him!" Charles snapped.

"No, you have to let me *go*." Reece's voice held not gravelly anger but a note of pleading Grayson hadn't heard in ages. "I have to help Cedrick Stone."

"Hold him *immobile*," Charles barked at a soldier. "Do *not* let him look anywhere but me, understand?" he added as the soldier nodded briskly and held Reece's face steady.

"You don't want me to look?" Reece's eyes were still wide. "Why not? What don't you want me to see?"

Good chance Charles was trying to stop Reece from seeing

Grayson himself, drugged and captured. "*Reece*," Grayson tried to call through the hand on his mouth.

Reece made a choked sound. "Who was that—" He twitched in his captors' grip, and the soldiers tightened their grip, holding him in place.

Charles stepped closer, only inches from Reece. "What is the last thing you remember?" he demanded.

"I—I don't—Vancouver, maybe? A dock, a boat? We can talk about it later. Just let me go, *please*," Reece said, hoarse and begging. "I have to get to Cedrick—"

"Absolutely not." Charles was gesturing at the waiting SUVs with his free hand. "Get him away from Cedrick at once."

"What?" Reece looked like he'd been slapped. "No, no, don't, I'm going to help him—"

"Blindfold him. *Immediately.* And don't let him touch anyone, not a fucking soul." Charles was addressing some of his soldiers. "You two: Take Cedrick back to the hospital, far away from Mr. Davies. And you three, prepare the transport car. Mr. Davies must be brought to a lab at once."

"Wait." Reece was shaking his head rapidly. "We can't go. What about Cedrick—"

"Not now," Charles said impatiently. He gestured at Reece. "You appear to have reverted to a pacifist! That has always been thought impossible. The implications—the potential for us to control your abilities—I can't risk any of that by letting you touch Cedrick. Take him away."

"But—"

"Mr. Stone, sir!" A new soldier was sprinting around the corner over the stadium. "The police are on the next block."

Charles scoffed. "I don't care about the police—"

"They're looking for *you*," said the new soldier. "One of them said something about a warrant for fraud."

Charles stilled. Then he burst into movement. "Clear out,"

he barked, already striding away. "You two with me. The rest of you, keep the empath away from Cedrick and Evan at all costs."

His Maybach was there on the street, but Charles and his two guards were heading for the parking garage—where he might have his helicopter waiting on the top floor. Grayson yanked at his captors again. This was why Alex wanted him stalled—Grayson wasn't gonna fail his brother yet again—

From in front of Charles, behind the loading gate, there came a roar. Then twenty jersey-clad men, Grayson's size and bigger, came pouring out of the loading gate like they were rushing the field for kickoff.

"For Alex!"

One of the defensive linemen launched himself at Charles just as the rest of the team leaped forward with the same battle cry.

Through the din, Grayson caught Reece's noise of distress as the sidewalk erupted into chaos. He kicked out at one of his captors, putting all the force his drugged muscles could muster behind it. Bone snapped, and the man went down. An elbow to the stomach took care of the second guard, and Grayson was free and into the fray.

Up ahead, brakes squealed as the van holding Cedrick Stone gunned it, scraping a Do Not Enter sign as it swung around the bend of the street and sped off. Grayson ducked a punch, staggering forward as he looked for the small, slim figure in a sea of football players and Stone Solutions responders.

He dodged another kick, then finally caught sight of an oversized hoodie and dark hair stumbling into the empty space where Cedrick Stone's van had been. *"Reece."*

One of the Stone Solutions responders was heading straight for Reece, who seemed as lost and unaware of his surroundings as a lemming heading straight for a cliff's edge. Grayson put on a burst of speed, shouldering the man hard enough to send him careening off into a cop, and reached Reece just as he crumpled to hands and knees on the pavement.

"Where did Cedrick Stone go?" The hitched whisper cut through the crowd noise as surely as if Reece had shouted it. "Why are they *fighting*—"

Reece was lifting his head, looking at a linebacker and one of Charles Stone's men locked in combat, and if there was any chance his pacifism was back, this scene was going to overwhelm him quick. Grayson stumbled forward, grabbing Reece off the ground and half tugging, half carrying him toward the empty Maybach up ahead.

Down the street, the first police cruiser had gone right through the barrier, and adding whirling lights and sirens to the chaos was not helping. Grayson managed to duck around the Maybach's trunk just as his drugged knees gave out and sent him tumbling to the pavement behind the car.

Grayson caught Reece just before the impact, twisting to keep him from hitting the ground. Despite the fight around them, Reece was soft and unresisting against him as Grayson leaned against the Maybach's tire for support. Not exactly a fortress, but the closest to shelter they were gonna get.

"Reece," he said again, getting a better hold on him and trying to prop him up. "Can you look at me?"

Reece didn't seem to hear him. His head was down, shaking back and forth in a helpless kind of *no*. "Pain—vengeance—they need help too—"

Grayson ducked his head so he could see Reece's face. Despite the bright gray of the day, Reece's pupils were fully dilated, his empathy in control and his eyes those twin night skies again. Grayson shifted one hand to Reece's wrist, feeling for his pulse. It was hammering under Grayson's fingers unnaturally fast, his blood pressure probably sky-high to match.

"Maybe I can help them all." Words were tumbling from

Reece's lips, though whether he knew what he was saying, Grayson wasn't sure. His breaths were also too quick, hard but shallow puffs. "Why won't they let me try to help Cedrick Stone—"

He listed to the side. Grayson grabbed for him, keeping him up before he could hit the pavement. As far as Grayson knew, no empath had ever come back from corruption. Would Reece's body be able to handle the change?

Wasn't looking real good.

Around them, more cruisers had pulled into the street, cops joining the mess. Grayson tried to shield Reece with his body, pulling him in closer. He reached for one of his hands, aligning their bare palms and intertwining their fingers. "Reece. Look at me."

Reece didn't react, didn't seem to hear Grayson or know he was there. His pupils were still blown, his empathy fully in control.

Grayson squeezed his hand harder, trying to get his attention. "Care Bear, *please*."

Nothing. Grayson might as well have been a ghost—

But then, he was a ghost to Reece's empathy, wasn't he? It didn't matter that they were touching; if Reece was overwhelmed and overtaken by his empathy, he would have no idea that Grayson was even there, because there were no emotions in the Dead Man for that empathy to pick up.

I don't want to feel anything anymore anyway, he'd told Alex in that bunker, and Alex had made it come true, had helped build a wall so strong Grayson had become the Dead Man, completely immune to empathy, as dead inside as a corpse.

I'll tell you exactly what I told Reece: it's permanent for all intents and purposes. I can't break it; no empath can. The only one who could tear it down is you—but you never, ever will.

Don't you see? Because to break it, you'd have to want to—and you're no longer capable of feeling that emotion.

Grayson looked into Reece's lost eyes. There was no one else here they could trust. If Grayson couldn't reach him, what would happen to Reece? Would he stay lost, alone and spiraling, until he was permanently damaged or worse?

Maybe he'd fall back to the corruption.

Or maybe he just wouldn't make it at all.

And we're going to have to say goodbye, Reece had said on the ferry, *just like we always do.*

Grayson's hand tightened on Reece's. This was it, then—there was nothing he could do—

But there is, said a voice in his head, or maybe his heart, one that he barely remembered. *Because walls have two sides. And on the other side of the wall, you* do *want something.*

Grayson leaned down. "You have to come back, Reece," he whispered hoarsely. "Because I want us to be done saying goodbye."

And as he pressed his lips to Reece's, something in his chest gave way like the first crack in a dam.

Reece's eyes went wide. "Evan?" he said against Grayson's lips, his hand tightening where it still held Grayson's. "Oh my God. *Evan.*"

Grayson's heart was starting to pound, a buzzing in his ears growing louder, drowning out the shouts and the sirens. He heard Reece say something more, but the words were lost as Grayson's own heartbeat rose deafeningly loud in his ears. His was the breathing that was too fast now, and his vision was going dark around the edges, like he was in rising water, and his chest was painfully tight—

But suddenly Reece wasn't holding his hands. He was cupping Grayson's face. "I got you." His eyes were so close, big glittery pupils ringed with deep brown. "Okay? I'm here. I got you."

Grayson tried to speak. "Something hurts—"

"That's grief," Reece whispered. "Maybe for the parents you never got to mourn. I'm so sorry. I know it hurts."

Grayson swallowed. It was too much; he couldn't breathe. "What else?" he managed to say.

"Fury. Guilt. Shame. It's all hitting you, and hearts aren't meant to feel two years of buried emotions at once." Reece brought their foreheads together, wrapping his arms around Grayson's neck. "But it's going to be okay, I promise. Because under all that are the good feelings. They survived too. And no matter the feeling, I've got you. I'm here."

Grayson closed his eyes and let Reece pull him into a hug. Around them were shouts, people running, yelling. But they stayed like that, hidden behind the Maybach, arms tight around each other in the empty parking space, as the rain started again.

CHAPTER THIRTY-FOUR

My empath half brother is offering to consult for the police. It's pretty rare to get an empath to do this, but he knows what I do and he wants to help.

I know you're concerned about his pacifism but trust me: He doesn't need to be cold to be tough, and he doesn't need to be cruel to be strong.

—Three-year-old internal memo from
Detective St. James to Lieutenant Parson

A few blocks away from Lumen Field, icy raindrops pelted the sidewalk as a stoplight finally changed from red to green. Across the street, the walk sign lit up, the subtle chirps signaling it was safe to cross. With his hands in his pockets and his shoulders hunched against the falling rain, Alex stepped off the curb into the crosswalk.

And then immediately hopped backwards, back onto the sidewalk, as a white BMW coupe made a sharp right turn. It screeched to a stop directly in front of him, blocking the crosswalk.

As Alex furrowed his eyebrows, the passenger window lowered itself. He bent down and found himself looking directly into Gretel Macy's eyes.

"Hey, Mr. *Grayson*," she said pointedly.

The city rushed around them as they regarded each other, raindrops turning the pavement a slick and darker gray, the crosswalk sign changing from white to red numbers counting down, cars honking as they were forced to swerve around Gretel's Beamer.

Alex's hair was dripping into his eyes, his glasses streaked with droplets that obscured his view. But Gretel's expression was closed off and would have been difficult to read even without the rain. "You know who I am?" he finally said.

"Yes. And I know *what* you are."

Not a lie. "How?"

Gretel leaned forward and turned on her hazard lights. "Vivian Marist dropped some hints about empaths that she thought would turn me fully to Stone Solutions' side."

Another car swerved around Gretel, honking irritably. Alex pulled off his wet glasses. "And did it?" he said as he cleaned them with the hem of his shirt.

"My parents are dead because of Stone Solutions." The hazards clicked like a metronome as raindrops fell in a steady staccato on the Beamer's roof and hood. "Speaking of Stone Solutions, I just saw the breaking news," Gretel said. "Charles Stone was taken into custody for securities fraud. Rumor is he tried to flee to his helicopter on site, but the police were able to catch him before he could escape. Did you have something to do with that?"

Alex shrugged his damp shoulders. "It was a team effort."

Up ahead, a cop car was tearing down the road with its lights on. Alex hunched, sliding his glasses back on as the cruiser blew past them, turning left in the direction of the stadium. "What do you think he did?"

"Funneled money into a shell company to fund who knows what kind of twisted schemes, all the while planning to hide his actions by replacing it with the new money coming in from S.B. 1437," Gretel said. "Stone is going to lawyer up, of course, and he'll probably argue that he deserves whatever funding he steals for his anti-empathy work. But the other shareholders are pretty pissed, so it's going to be a battle of money versus money. I hope they bury him." Her gaze was still on Alex. "I read that there were more empaths at Lumen Field. What happened?"

"Stone Solutions got them." Alex's glasses were already spotting with raindrops again. "They're going to be locked up, and I don't know where." He tried to shrug again, like that didn't tear at him. "Wherever they go, it won't be safe. We're always going to be a target."

"I guess you are." There was real sympathy in Gretel's voice. "But maybe empaths can find empathy in others, too."

At the curb, another car honked twice as it was forced to make the wide turn. Alex rubbed at his dripping hair, scattering droplets. "Maybe the pacifist empaths still can," he said. "But that's not me anymore. Didn't Vivian Marist tell you we're dangerous?"

"She did." Gretel leaned closer. "But Charles Stone murdered my parents, just like you lost yours. You're not the same person you used to be because of it—and I'm not the same person I was before either."

Oh.

There was a new clicking sound as the Beamer's locks disengaged. Gretel nodded at the passenger door, the tiniest smile playing on her lips. "So are you getting in or what?"

Alex huffed, almost a laugh, his mouth also curving in a hint of a real smile for the first time in what felt like years. And then he was ducking out of the rain and into a heated passenger seat as warm as a Texas evening while the BMW pulled away from the curb and onto the road.

The afternoon had darkened and given way to a wet evening around Lumen Field. Reece sat alone on the curb in front of the stadium, gaze fixed on the hands clenched tightly together in his lap. The football players had left, all of them confused at their sudden rampage but none thralled or suffering any lasting harm. Several people in Stone Solutions uniforms were still milling nearby, but so far no one had put cuffs on Reece.

Amnesia, the man he now knew was Charles Stone had said. *Amnesia would have to be an inevitable component of reversion, because how could the pacifist stand to know what was done under corruption? The empath would experience a full and instant breakdown.*

Reece felt pretty damn close to *a full and instant breakdown* now, knowing he'd been corrupted, thinking about what he might have done—

He forced his gaze up from his hands to Grayson, who was maybe thirty feet away and still talking to a very posh-looking blonde woman in a white puffy coat. He could only see Grayson's back from this angle, but just the sight of that familiar figure helped Reece's blood pressure return to something approximating normal.

Except normal blood pressure didn't change the thoughts looping in Reece's head. He'd been corrupted, and maybe he didn't remember anything, but it was a good bet he'd done more than finally watch R-rated movies. Surely he deserved to be locked away wherever Stone Solutions wanted to put him? But if Reece was locked away, who was going to help Grayson navigate an onslaught of two years of buried emotion—

"Reece!"

"Jamey."

And despite his shaky limbs, Reece was on his feet instantly. He'd made it three steps when Jamey appeared from behind the neighboring SUV, sprinting toward him.

"You asshole," she said, and grabbed him in a giant hug.

He hugged her back, his eyes burning. "I'm so sorry—"

"Shut up," she said, and squeezed him tighter. "Evan said

the reversion gave you amnesia—that you don't remember any of it?"

"Nothing since the dock in Vancouver," Reece admitted as they pulled back.

"Good," she said fiercely.

"How is that *good*?" he demanded. "I know I was corrupted. I'm certain I hurt people. Stone Solutions wants to lock me up—"

"No they don't."

Lie. "Jamey," Reece said with a huff. "You know it's pointless to lie to me."

She frowned. "You still hear lies?"

"Yes."

"Then listen to this truth." And then she leaned in, hand on the back of his neck, pulling their foreheads together. "The corrupted version of you saved my life."

Not a lie. Reece blinked. "I did?"

"Yeah, you did, and Evan's life, and a store's worth of AMI shoppers, and that's just what I know about." She ruffled his hair. "I'm not saying you were the good guy in this story. But maybe in the real world, the heroes and villains are never as clear-cut as we're told to believe."

She pulled back again, though not far. "Just believe me when I say Evan and I have strong opinions about what happens to you, and all the other empaths too." Her lips softened into a small smile. "And not just opinions. We both have strong *feelings* about it."

Reece's gaze went to Grayson's back again, where he was still speaking to the blonde woman and gesturing more emphatically than he used to. Reece's fingers twitched at his sides, wanting to reach for him. Grayson had *feelings* now. Reece had barely had a taste, just a glimpse of the most complex and colorful tapestry he'd ever seen, before they'd been forced to part. Every cell craved the chance to dive back in.

But it had to wait, because Grayson was busy, and now Reece got to see Liam, who'd just arrived. "I can't believe how much I missed your sarcasm," Liam said, and hugged Reece as tightly as Jamey had.

Reece hugged him back, throat gone thick again. He'd never had a brother. Maybe someday he'd get to have Liam. "But I bet you didn't miss me running my mouth to the press about my sexual flexibility."

"I'm sure your new boyfriend will be excited to hear all about it," Liam said dryly, which made Reece squawk. Liam turned to Jamey and kissed her hello. "Where's your phone? I promised Diesel we'd call when I found you. He went with Aisha to the hospital."

A few minutes later, Jamey had Diesel on speakerphone. "Aisha's got her cast and is demanding to be released already," he said. "She wants to go with the empaths."

"Go with the empaths *where*?" Jamey said.

"Evan didn't tell you yet?" Diesel said. "He's insisting Stone Solutions hand over their fancy empathy-proof corporate lodge, Orion."

Reece, Jamey and Liam all turned their heads in Grayson's direction, where he was still talking to the blonde woman. "And Stone Solutions is going to agree to that?" Jamey said skeptically.

"With Cedrick Stone still catatonic and Charles Stone arrested, Vivian Marist is fully in charge," Diesel said. "Apparently whatever was done to Evan in the Olympic Mountains has given him some pretty savage leverage."

The blonde woman, Marist, did look a bit pale. Reece frowned. "What happened to Evan?"

"Reece!" Diesel said in surprise. "I didn't know you were there. I heard we've got you back!"

"You're trying to distract me so I don't press for details," Reece accused.

"Yes, but I'm also genuinely happy," Diesel said. "You hanging in there?'

"Are *you*?" Reece asked. "I'm so sorry you got pulled into all of this because you're nice enough to be my friend."

"It's been good for me to be part of this, actually," Diesel said. "My last mission was a bad one, and I came home in a very bad place. It was Cora who helped me through."

Cora, who would be going to this Orion place with all the other empaths. Reece swallowed. "Really?"

"Yeah." Even through the speakerphone, Diesel's voice seemed full of emotion. "Without Cora, I might not have made it, you know what I'm saying? And maybe I won't be able to help her in return, but I can try. I'm going to Orion with Aisha."

"You two can't go without saying goodbye," Jamey said. "Where are you going from the hospital? Your place? Aisha's? We can meet you there."

"You'll probably think we're nuts," Diesel said ruefully, "but we need food and a sanity check. And the best place I know to work through your shit is McFeely's."

Jamey barked out a laugh. "You know what?" she said. "That sounds perfect." She hung up the phone and wrapped her arm around Reece's shoulders. "You too," she said. "I missed your stupid lectures. Come tell me and everyone else not to drink our way through McFeely's bar."

Reece furrowed his brow. "I can leave?"

"We just got you back. We're not giving you up," Jamey said firmly. "If anyone wants to stop you, they'll have to go through me and Liam."

Reece swallowed, throat thick again. "What about Evan?"

"I'll tell him to meet us there," Jamey said. "It's close enough to walk."

Walk. Wait. "Where's my car?" Reece said.

"Um." Jamey cleared her throat. "Port Angeles."

Reece frowned. "What about Evan's truck?"

"Towed off the Bremerton ferry," said Liam.

"But *how*—"

"Stop asking questions." Jamey prodded him in the back. "Move your feet, Reece."

It was still on the early side of night when they arrived at McFeely's, but the club was already crowded and rowdy, people dancing and laughing with giddy relief.

Ben took one look at Reece's face and dragged him to a small, two-person booth at the back. "I don't know what you just went through, but one Shirley Temple, coming up. On me. Unless you wanted to make it yourself?" he added with a grin.

Reece furrowed his brow. "But I'm not a bartender."

"Oh, right! Diesel said you'd had something like a concussion, and your memory might be spotty." Ben held up a hand. "Don't you worry about a thing. I'll get your drink."

Reece's lips curled up at the corner, a helpless sort of smile born of confusion but more so of gratitude. "Okay," he said. "Thanks."

A few minutes later, he sat alone at his booth, sipping the Shirley Temple and letting the sweetness of the cherries bloom over his tongue as his gaze roamed the club. Jamey and Liam were slow-dancing to a fast song, arms locked around each other. Diesel had arrived with Aisha, a kind-faced woman Reece instantly liked. They were now at a table, Aisha's right leg in a cast and propped up on a chair, as short fake empaths fussed over her and hugged the much taller Diesel around his ribs.

A tall presence suddenly loomed over the table. "This seat taken?"

Reece broke into a giant smile at the voice. He looked up, meeting Grayson's eyes. "Sorry, yes," he said, deadpan. "My hot, scary boyfriend is sitting there."

He paused.

A tiny smile curled up the corner of Grayson's lips, shy and rusty. "That wasn't a lie?"

Reece's gaze was entirely fixed on Grayson's mouth. A smile. He smiled now. He was happy. "Not a lie," Reece said, "but I was thinking of you as I said it."

The small, rusty smile got just a little bigger. As Grayson sat down, Reece leaned forward. "How are you holding up?"

Grayson considered the question for a long moment. "It's a lot to take in," he finally admitted. "A lot of . . ." He gestured helplessly at himself. "Feelings. And I've kind of . . . forgotten, you know? How to feel things. What things I'm feeling. And I'm not sure—I don't—well."

Grayson stuck his arm out, resting his hand on the table, palm up.

Reece furrowed his brow, gaze going from the hand to Grayson's eyes. He was looking at Reece, and now those hazel eyes weren't a vault at all. Instead, they were a novel, so many words filling the pages that Reece could have read for days.

Grayson shrugged in a helpless kind of way. "There's no way I'm gonna find words. Maybe we could speak your language instead?"

Reece melted. He took Grayson's hand, eyes fluttering closed at the warmth of his skin, but even more at all the emotions flitting under the surface.

Reece's own feelings were still a mess, too many at once and too extreme, too raw. But Grayson had always understood him better than anyone else. And now here were Grayson's feelings, precious and nearly lost, and Reece let them rush into him, filling him like crystal-clear melted snow clearing away the dust on a riverbed.

They weren't going to recover in an evening. But maybe they could at least be together.

"The studio's not much more than a mile away." Reece intertwined their fingers, unwilling to let go. "We could go home. I could help you with these . . . feelings."

Grayson squeezed his hand, and Reece felt the jolt of their combined desire rush through him.

"In fact," he said, tightening his own hand in return, "we could go *right now*."

With the truck sent to the shop and the Smart car in recovery from Port Angeles, they opted to walk, traversing the Seattle winter streets together back to the studio. Grayson found himself brushing his fingers against Reece's every other block, the way someone tipsy might catch an arm to steady them. Reece understood what he was asking without Grayson having to put it into words, guiding him through both the streets and the return of his heart.

"That's doubt—this intersection's weird but it's okay, I know downtown, we're going the right way—"

"That's overwhelm—and yeah, if I think the sirens are loud, your ears are probably miserable—"

"That's skepticism—which, *really?* I told you this is the right way, I know where I'm going—"

They walked on. High above downtown, Grayson could make out faint stars that made warmth blossom in his chest like the return of old friends. The rain had stopped, but the street was still dotted with puddles that shimmered where they caught the streetlights, and every time they crossed an intersection, a glimpse of the moon was visible, bright and full out over the sound.

"Evan?"

Grayson startled. He looked over at Reece, who was watching him patiently. "You stopped walking," Reece said.

"Oh." Grayson looked back at the sky, the way the moon's glow lit the wispy clouds stretched over the stars, the silvery sheen of its reflection on the water.

Reece's smile was soft. "If I had to guess this one, I'd say you forgot what it feels like to look at the moon."

Had Reece's voice always been this warm, this full of gentle understanding? Grayson hadn't even realized he'd missed the way a voice could resonate in your heart the same way the moon's glow could fill the night sky.

"We can walk down to the water, stargaze, whatever you want," Reece said. "There's no rush."

Grayson reached out and grabbed his hand. "Well," he said wryly as Reece's eyes widened, because there was no way an empath was going to miss the cocktail of emotions buzzing through Grayson. "There's *some* rush."

Reece's smile grew. "Come on," he said, tugging on Grayson's hand. "Let's go."

Finally, they made it to the building and up to the fourth floor of the high-rise. Grayson tried to weather the forgotten sensations of rising anticipation and urgency as he waited for Reece to fumble in his pocket for the key. "I got this, I swear," Reece said, the key unsteady in his hand as he tried to open the door.

"I just watched you twitch because you heard yourself lie, sugar." Grayson took the key right out of Reece's hand, his body lighting up with the brush against warm skin. "Move over."

"Hey." Reece turned around. "*I* am the holder of the keys in this relationship—"

"You're gonna learn to share." Grayson bent, and before

Reece could get another word in, he levered him up and over his shoulder in one easy, graceful lift.

Reece let out a surprised laugh. *"Evan."*

"You were blocking the door."

"But—"

"And you're not gonna give me any empath sass about hurting myself." Grayson wrapped an arm around the back of Reece's thighs to pin him in place as he fit the key into the lock. "You know full well I regularly lift things that weigh more than you."

"Ugh, *fine*." Reece huffed. "But you can't win all our fights by picking me up—son of a bitch."

"That was another lie, wasn't it?"

"Shut up."

Down the hall, a door opened, and a neighbor popped her head out. She saw them, rolled her eyes good-naturedly, and ducked back into her apartment.

Reece half groaned, half laughed. "You're a menace to this building. And that was *not* a lie."

Grayson swung the door open. "You haven't told me to put you down."

"Put me down on the *bed* and I'll forgive all of this."

Grayson stepped inside, kicking the door closed behind them with his foot. He didn't bother with the lights, crossing the space in two strides to tip Reece onto the studio's bed on his back. He crawled over him and bent down so their faces were nearly touching.

For a moment, they were quiet, nothing but the sound of their twin breaths over the distant rumble of cars four stories below. The studio was dark, but downtown itself was lit against the night, and the surrounding high-rises illumined the large uncovered windows with a soft glow.

“I am feeling so many feelings,” Grayson confessed. “I don’t know where one ends and the next begins.”

The city lights danced across Reece’s face as he reached for Grayson, fingers twining in the hair at the back of Grayson’s head. “I got you,” he said, and pulled him down into an achingly gentle kiss.

Grayson let his eyes flutter closed, let himself be kissed, let the skill of Reece’s lips stoke the feelings running through him. Physical desire, which he’d never lost, but so many more feelings with it now, bright and sweet and urgent all at once.

“I can help you with feelings.” Reece slipped his hands under Grayson’s shirt, pushing the fabric up as he slid them over his bare stomach, his oversized pupils glittering with each catch of light. “Or I can make you feel so good that you lose yourself in the way your body feels.”

Grayson’s heart skipped with excitement.

“That would be option two, then?” Reece said slyly, tracing warm hands over Grayson’s skin.

“Fuck.” Grayson dipped his head, kissing Reece’s neck but breathing a little too hard to do it with skill. “You gonna read what I want like an open book?”

“Damn right I am,” Reece said unapologetically, his hands never pausing their exploration. “Going to find every word and every touch that makes these emotions rise.”

Grayson reached for the waistband of Reece’s jeans. “What if I pick option three?” In one move he popped open the button, flicked the zipper down, and bent his head, shoving Reece’s clothes out of the way so he could get his mouth on him.

Reece drew a sharp breath. “Evan.” His hands scrambled for Grayson’s shoulders. “Shit.”

His back arched and his hips lifted, and Grayson used the movement to get more of his cock in his mouth.

"Fuck." Reece sounded desperate and already wrecked. "Fuck, Evan, *wait*—"

Grayson glanced up, and what he could see of Reece's face was as dazed as if he was high. "I just started—"

"You don't *understand*." Reece was panting like they'd already gone three rounds, his fingers twisting Grayson's T-shirt. "Making me feel good makes *you* feel good."

"Well, yeah." Grayson kissed his stomach. Reece groaned loudly. "And?"

"*And?* And the instant you put your mouth on my dick, *it fries my empath brain*." Reece tugged at his shoulders. "Roll over."

"But—"

"*Now*, Evan." Reece tugged on him again. "And get your damn pants off."

Reece's tugs were gentle, because even worked up as he was, an empath was gonna handle someone else with infinite care. And obviously even if he *had* used force, Reece wasn't physically manhandling Grayson anywhere, but he obediently let himself be rolled over and onto his back. "I still don't understand," he said, toeing off his shoes and letting them fall to the floor as Reece kicked off his own sneakers.

"I feel *all of it*, all at once." Reece had already shucked his jeans and was now yanking his hoodie and shirt over his head. "Do you know what it's like feeling your mouth on me while I'm also feeling that *you're* into it?"

"Oh." Grayson sat partway up, getting his own shirt off. "But this can't be the first time—"

"It's different with you." Reece was stretching for the nightstand. "The way you feel about me—it's different. Better. *So much* better, Jesus Christ, I am going to have to work my way up to that."

Grayson felt himself relax. He slid his jeans over his hips. "So it's a good thing?"

"Mind-blowing. Literally." Reece was scrambling for the nightstand. "If I'm going to last more than ten seconds tonight, you're going to have to be more selfish."

A laugh escaped Grayson, and he'd forgotten this pleasure too, forgotten laughter like this existed, born of a moment of joy so deep that your body physically responded.

Reece was crawling over him now, and it was even better like this, no clothes in the way. He kissed Grayson's chest, right over his heart, and then kissed his lips. "How many times did you tell me you were too big for me?"

"Fuck," Grayson muttered, a bolt of want crashing through him. "Not enough times, apparently. It never got through your pretty head."

Reece smiled against his mouth. "It only made me want you more."

"Bad Decisions Bear." Grayson had to reach for him, had to bury his hands in that thick hair, had to pull him more deeply into the kiss.

They kissed until Grayson was dizzy, until the kiss had turned clumsy and messy. Then Reece broke away and sat up. The windows were behind him now, making Reece a silhouette against the city lights as he braced one hand on Grayson's chest and reached back with the other.

A moment later, his hand closed around Grayson's cock, slick and slippery. He swore as Reece stroked him, his head tipping back on the pillows. "I might be closer than I'd realized too," Grayson said, panting.

"Don't worry." Reece flexed his fingers against Grayson's chest meaningfully. "I can tell exactly how close you are. And *exactly* how far I can push. That's why you're going to let me drive, and you're just going to come along for the ride."

Grayson groaned, the sound turning deep and ragged as

Reece kept stroking. "You always got to be the one behind the wheel."

Reece laughed, which somehow didn't disrupt his coordination or slow the hand still on Grayson's dick. "Didn't you ever read that study theorizing that empaths are just modern-day incubi? That paper was the best thing that ever happened to my love life." Then he added, wry and fond, "At least, until some cowboy secret agent turned up and started calling me Care Bear."

That sent a flash of something through Grayson, fiery and sweet and overwhelming. And before he could even try to name that feeling, Reece was shifting on top of him, legs moving to either side of his hips, aligning their bodies in a way that had fresh anticipation and need and desire lighting Grayson up.

He reached for Reece, wrapping hands around his hips to still him. "Be careful with yourself," he said warningly, "and go slow—"

"Don't backseat drive."

And then their bodies were joining together, and Grayson was seeing stars. His hands tightened on Reece as he buried his forehead on Grayson's chest. They stayed like that for a moment, their breaths and maybe even their heartbeats in sync.

Grayson's whisper was thick and dazed. "You feel so good."

"Hell yeah I do." Reece sounded nearly drunk. "I don't know if I've ever felt this good in my whole life."

Grayson slid his hands from his hips around to his back, holding him tighter. "You okay?"

"I want to stay like this forever." Reece hadn't even seemed to comprehend that he'd been asked a question. "Lost in you. Part of you."

He pushed up, hands braced on Grayson's chest again, and the pleasure was overwhelming, the feel of Reece on him.

Reece set a pace that was slow and tight and perfect and quite possibly paranormally engineered to make Grayson lose his mind.

"If you're reading my emotions," Grayson finally said hoarsely. "you gotta know I'm about to throw you over and *drive* you right through this bed."

"There you go again," Reece said raggedly. "Threatening me with a good time."

"Now you're just asking for it."

Grayson wrapped an arm around Reece and flipped them as one, rolling Reece onto his back on the bed with himself between his legs. A breathy *fuck yes* left Reece as he reached for Grayson, sliding hands over his shoulders, his hair, his jaw, like he never wanted to stop touching.

His arm was still under Reece, and he used it to tilt him, shifting them both so he could slide in deeper, at a better angle. "Still good?"

The next snap of his hips drew a full-body shiver from Reece. "Baby," he slurred, "I have never been better. And that's the damn truth."

Grayson broke into a smile. He could just make out Reece's features again, the big eyes now hazy with pleasure, the lower lip caught in his teeth. Looking at him made Grayson's heart stutter and fuck, maybe he should have worked up to this himself, to having sex and happiness at the same time.

Reece's fingers tightened on his shoulders. "You wanted to drive. *Drive.*"

Time lost all meaning, stretching and constricting simultaneously, so that it lasted forever while all too soon Grayson was barreling toward that cliff. Reece was grabbing for his biceps, urging him down into a sloppy and awkward kiss that was barely possible with their height difference and nearly folded Reece in half.

"Do it," he said against Grayson's mouth. "Come on."

Because Reece was going to come with him, *because* of him, because that empathy was drinking in his feelings and Grayson's pleasure was his pleasure—

That tumble of thoughts pushed him over the edge. He fumbled for Reece's hand as he came, hearing the audible gasp as he linked their fingers, and felt Reece's shuddering under him as he fell apart too.

In the afterglow, he rested on top of Reece, their still-joined hands cradled on the pillow next to Reece's head. He wasn't ready to move, but he aligned their palms together, fingers still entwined, and ran his thumb along the side of Reece's hand in a light caress, hoping that empathy could pick up all the affection he couldn't yet put into words. He heard Reece swallow. Then lips brushed his hair. Message received, then.

There was so much still to come, so much still to deal with, so much still to process, for both of them. But for this moment, they were safe here, together. And Grayson's heart—once so shattered he hadn't wanted to feel anymore, so broken he'd chosen the path of the Dead Man—finally had a reason to heal.

"Care Bear?" he heard himself whisper.

"What, baby?"

"Is this feeling what I think it is?"

Reece squeezed his hand. "Yeah," he whispered back. "And I love you too."

EPILOGUE

Three weeks after the panic at Lumen Field, Seattle still has questions: Where did the rampages come from? How did they start? What really happened that day?

We've all heard the rumors that empaths were involved, but savvy readers of the number one empathy advocacy blog in the Pacific Northwest are too smart to fall for that. WE know empaths can't even WATCH football.

And we also know the REAL questions Seattle should be asking: Who is the true mastermind behind a story like this? Why do they want to turn the rest of us against the empaths? Which politicians and corporations have the most to gain from xenophobia?

Read on for a post by Eyes on Empaths' *hottest new guest blogger—I promise no one is ready for him.*

—Gretel Macy, blogging for *Eyes on Empaths*

Reece squinted at Grayson's laptop, which was open on the studio's island kitchen counter, his internet browser launched to a familiar website with its familiar banner sprawling across the top of the page.

Well. Mostly familiar.

"Number one empathy advocacy blog," Reece read out loud. "Huh."

On the other side of the studio, Grayson was pacing back and forth, having a one-sided conversation into the phone against his ear. "Yes. Yes, ma'am, I still think the same thing, that Alex will have gone to ground if he's smart, which he is. You're not gonna find him anytime soon."

At Reece's elbow, his own phone chirped. He pushed up the sleeve of the University of Texas hoodie, which had slipped down to cover his hand again, and lifted the phone from the counter to see a text from Jamey, who was on her way to stay with Liam's family.

Jamey: Just landed in Juneau. Yes, Diesel stayed behind at the new facility with Aisha. Yes, all the empaths are okay. And yes, you still have to stay far away from Orion.

Reece's throat tightened. It wasn't fair. It wasn't fair that he was free and the others were locked away in the Orion facility in BC. It didn't matter that their rooms had mountain views and saunas and cold plunge tubs; gilded prisons were still prisons, and maybe Reece still couldn't remember what all he'd done under corruption's influence, but he was certain he belonged behind bars.

Reece: I deserve the same fate

He sent the text to Jamey. He'd said it to her a thousand times already, but the guilt wouldn't let him go.

Across the studio, Grayson was still on the phone. "No.

No, ma'am, I'm quite sure I don't want to meet with him. I appreciate the update, but respectfully, Senator Braun is still not my problem."

Reece's phone chirped again.

Jamey: I'm going to choose not to be insulted by your ongoing implications that Evan and I are flailing idiots who don't know what we're doing by leaving you in Seattle.

Jamey: But try to remember that we care about the Orion empaths too. We're going to help them. ALL of them. And you'll help us help them—when it's SAFE. Not just for you, for EVERYONE.

"You fighting with your sister again?"

Reece looked up from his phone as Grayson joined him at the counter. "How'd you guess?"

He brushed his finger gently down Reece's forehead. "Your brow's furrowed."

Even that light touch sent sparks over Reece's skin, his empathy automatically picking up the unmistakable warmth of Grayson's affection, like a glimpse of blue sky peeking through the rain clouds of his own mood. "There's no playbook for processing these emotions," he said, throat still too thick as he showed Grayson his phone.

Grayson's eyes flicked over Jamey's texts, then met Reece's eyes. "You deserve to be locked up in Orion."

Lie.

Reece bit his lip.

Grayson set his own phone on the counter. "You heard that lie, right?"

"It doesn't mean it's a real lie. It just means *you* don't believe it—"

"That's true, but my point was that you're still *hearing* lies," Grayson said more softly. "We don't know what that means. We don't know what might happen if you're back in the company of other corrupted empaths, and no one—not me, not your sister, not Dr. Easterby, not even Stone Solutions—wants to risk it."

Reece ran a hand over his face. He could appreciate their logic, but it didn't help the guilt. "Who was that?" he asked to distract himself, nodding at Grayson's phone on the counter.

"Stone Solutions' new CEO, actually, officially approved and instated by the board of directors this week." Grayson folded his arms on the counter. "Ms. Marist and I are gonna have to figure out our new working relationship. She wants the senate bill to pass, but she's not running secret laboratories, so that's one step up from the real low bar set by her predecessors."

Reece bit his thumb. "What's happening with the Stones?"

"Couple of board members are pressing charges against Charles Stone. They're not real swayed by his argument that his ends were justified when his means involved their money."

"And Cedrick?" Reece prodded.

"He's back at Orion. For now." Grayson added a little more softly, "I know being an empath's hard. But you've got to give it time."

There was no sarcasm in his voice, nothing but sweet understanding. Reece sighed.

"I did get good news from Marist," Grayson said. "Stone Solutions is picking up the bill for both our cars."

Reece straightened up. "No more Hayabusa engine ruining my gas mileage?"

"Unfortunately," Grayson said, which made Reece snort. "She didn't understand why I hired Mr. Lane's cousin to fix my old truck instead of buying a brand-new one, but she gave me what I wanted."

Reece broke into a smile. "So are they ready?"

Grayson nodded, then licked his lips.

Reece frowned. "Why are you nervous?"

"I'm not—"

"Big lie right there." Reece narrowed his eyes suspiciously. "What else did you do to my car—"

"*Nothing.* I just—well." Grayson cleared his throat. "Alex is back in hiding. The other empaths are safe for now. And the truck's fixed. I had this thought that—if you were interested—that maybe we could—you know. Hit the road. Together."

Reece blinked.

"Before I met you, I drove so much alone, too dead inside to appreciate all the beauty around me," Grayson said more quietly. "Meanwhile you're still hearing lies, but maybe if we get you somewhere else for a while, away from all the reminders here in Seattle, that'll finally reverse itself too."

"Evan." Reece's heart leaped with want, then crashed. There was no way, simply no way that he could ever let that happen. "We *can't*," he said, swallowing. "You've got your emotions back. If there's any risk the corruption could set back in, then it's not safe for you to be that alone with me—"

"Sugar," Grayson said, patient and gentle. "You don't remember your corruption, but I do. So I know there's no lie in my words when I tell you that no version of you is ever gonna hurt me. I know it like I know my own heartbeat."

Grayson was right: It wasn't a lie, and Reece could read the truth of it in the depths of those open hazel eyes. His throat tightened for a new reason. "I don't know how you can believe that," he said plaintively.

Grayson put his hands on the back of the barstool and turned it so they faced either other, his arms boxing Reece in snugly. "I got my reasons."

The corner of Reece's mouth grudgingly turned up.

Grayson leaned in so their foreheads touched. "I'm safe with you—*all* of you." His fingers brushed the sensitive skin of Reece's neck, making his eyelashes flutter both at the touch and the faith beneath. "Fact is, I'm gonna have a much bigger problem keeping *you* safe."

Not a lie. Reece frowned. "What's that supposed to mean?"

"I'm proposing to take Bad Decisions Bear on a road trip." Grayson's breath tickled his lips as he spoke. "It'll be like having a lemming in my shotgun seat."

"What *lemming*? And what do you mean, *your* shotgun seat—"

"I mean like that time I said *don't wander off* and you did it anyway. Or that other time I said *don't wander off* and you—"

"I'm not going to—son of a bitch," Reece said, groaning as it twisted into a lie.

He gave up on words, closing the distance to bring their lips together. Grayson's hand threaded into his hair, his tongue slipping into his mouth, and his kiss had turned out to be every bit as addictive as Reece had once suspected. He cupped Grayson's jaw and drank in emotions bright as sunshine, the blue skies that had always been behind the gray.

"You really want me to come with you?" he whispered into the kiss.

"Yeah, Care Bear," Grayson whispered back. "I want it so much."

His words were true, and under that warm skin, his feelings told the same story, of desire and joy and affection, so intoxicating Reece could have gotten drunk. Being an empath *was* hard, but being an empath with a partner like Grayson was a special kind of heaven.

Reece tilted his chin up and head back, softening his lips invitingly. And sure enough, he got an answering shift of Grayson's emotions, into something more primal and urgent. "A road trip isn't the only thing you want with me," he said slyly against Grayson's mouth.

Grayson groaned. "You got such an unfair advantage."

"Lucky for you, I would *never* use my empath advantage to convince you we should take the car with better gas mileage—"

"Oh, I know you just heard yourself lie with that—"

"Or to get you to agree that I should do all the driving—"

Reece's world suddenly shifted, drawing a laugh as Grayson lifted him right off the barstool and set him on the high counter.

"Now who's at an advantage?" Reece said, even as his arms went around Grayson's shoulders to pull him in. "Showing off that super strength to win fights?"

"That's what you get for lying to my face." Grayson had fit himself between Reece's legs and was leaning closer. "We're taking the truck, and you'll just have to accept that sometimes I'll be the one behind the wheel."

"In that case." Reece brushed his lips against Grayson's and felt the answering shiver in both of their bodies and hearts. "Remind me you know how to drive."

And then he was back in Grayson's arms, their joined laughter echoing around the studio as they tumbled together down to the bed.

★ ★ ★ ★ ★

AUTHOR'S NOTE

The Sugar & Vice series' alternate universe takes inspiration from the real Seattle and Pacific Northwest, but apart from the setting, all people, corporations, organizations and abilities described herein are intended as entirely fictional.

No generative artificial intelligence was used to create the writing in this book or any other book by Allie Therin.

ACKNOWLEDGMENTS

My deepest gratitude to the amazing people who help make these books possible:

To C, forever and always the best zombie apocalypse partner I could ask for—*pocket sand*—and to my family and friends;

To my author crew, for being there through the wild world of publishing, especially Arianna, for her support (and cookies!) through the journey;

To my readers, who endlessly amaze me with their creativity and enthusiasm, and make me feel like the luckiest person on earth;

To my always amazing editor Mackenzie Walton, whose edits are straight-up magic;

To Stephanie Doig, for taking a chance on Reece and Evan, and for being such a wonderful partner over the years;

To my agent, Laura Zats, for her insights, and to the art, marketing and production teams at Harlequin who help bring our books to life;

And to T, who makes the world a million times brighter just by being in it.